PENGUIN BOOKS

THE SEDUCTION OF MRS PENDLEBURY

Margaret Forster was born in Carlisle in 1938. From the County High School she won an Open Scholarship to Somerville College, Oxford, where she took a degree in history. Her many novels include *Georgy Girl*, *Private Papers*, *Mother Can You Hear Me?*, *Have the Men Had Enough?*, which was shortlisted for the 1989 *Sunday Express* Book of the Year Award, and *Lady's Maid* (1990). All are published by Penguin. She is also the author of a biography of Bonnie Prince Charlie, *The Rash Adventurer* (1973), a highly praised 'autobiography' of Thackeray that was published in 1978, and *Significant Sisters* (1986), which traces the lives and careers of eight pioneering women. Her most recent works of non-fiction are her biography of Elizabeth Barrett Browning, which won the Royal Society of Literature's Award for 1988 under the Heinemann bequest, and a selection of Elizabeth Barrett Browning's poetry. She is now working on the authorized biography of Dame Daphne du Maurier.

Margaret Forster lives in London. She is married to writer and broadcaster Hunter Davies and has three children.

Margaret Forster

The Seduction of
Mrs Pendlebury

Penguin Books

PENGUIN BOOKS

PENGUIN BOOKS

Published by the Penguin Group
Penguin Books Ltd, 27 Wrights Lane, London W8 5TZ, England
Penguin Books USA Inc., 375 Hudson Street, New York, New York 10014, USA
Penguin Books Australia Ltd, Ringwood, Victoria, Australia
Penguin Books Canada Ltd, 2801 John Street, Markham, Ontario, Canada L3R 1B4
Penguin Books (NZ) Ltd, 182–190 Wairau Road, Auckland 10, New Zealand

Penguin Books Ltd, Registered Offices: Harmondsworth, Middlesex, England

First published by Martin Secker & Warburg Ltd 1974
Published in Penguin Books 1978
10 9 8 7 6 5 4 3 2

Printed in England by Clays Ltd, St Ives plc
Set in Intertype Plantin

For my sister Pauline,
to satisfy Nathan and Ben

Chapter One

The white net curtains moved slightly in the breeze coming through the inch or two of open window, opened at such cost, with such tuggings and pullings, never again to be satisfactorily closed. Such was the price she paid, these days, for a bit of fresh air. When the wind snaked through in the winter she'd have to fill the crack up with newspaper where it would rot and discolour and be disgusting to remove in the following spring. Always endless thoughts of season after season, of nights drawing in and out, each chasing the other in continuous movement. Better to be happy, touched by the drifting curtains, cooled by the air, diverted by what she, Rose Pendlebury, could guiltily see.

The guilt was her own invention. Everyone these days was quite happy to live in greenhouses, to flash their all before everyone else and even wave to perfect strangers, flaunting their behaviour. The children were brought up to it, taught to run and jump from one end of these brilliantly lit houses to the other, with never a thought of drawing the curtains on their occasional nakedness. And the adults behaving like people on a stage, sitting down at big tables and eating in full view, then moving away to laugh and shout and be looked at. Rose sighed at such confidence.

But it made a pretty show. Often, at night, she walked along Rawlinson Road, just to admire. Each house was different and yet the same. Everywhere a wild profusion of greenery twisted and climbed up white walls, the dark leaves lit by spots of light or tumbling beneath huge balloons of orange or white, floating bulbous suns that fascinated her. There were acres of gleaming tiles and glowing wood and never a carpet among them. And where did they sit when they were not prancing about? She could not see. Perhaps they walked for ever, like puppets on strings. It

7

was none of her business what they did and she did not care, was only intrigued. They did not bother her, except in the garden. There was no escaping the threat presented there. Once, each garden had its high wall and what went on on either side was a mystery, a matter of small noises. She would never have dreamed of looking out on her neighbours from the top of her house. But they had got round that, built their terraces, raised up their patios, erected their new additions at the back until it was all as public as a railway station and twice as noisy. It was the parties held on these platforms that she found most unbearable. All summer long they were filled with great hordes of shrieking people who did not seem to know what sleep was. Every word, every laugh – and how they laughed! – could be clearly heard. She had no wish to eavesdrop, no wish at all, but knowledge of her neighbours' business was thrust upon her and she resented it.

Her husband, Stanley, said it was all harmless. There were few things in life that Stanley did not classify as harmless. It was his way out of every situation that looked as though it might involve him in some kind of effort. She had suggested he might have a word with their right-hand neighbours, the Stewarts, after they had had parties on the terrace until three in the morning on two successive June Saturdays. She was not asking him to do anything as vulgar as go and shout and complain in an unfriendly and unreasonable manner, but a quiet word, a gentle hint that after midnight they might at least go inside or modulate their voices, would not go amiss. But Stanley did not go. He did not refuse to go – refusing was too definite a step on his part – but he smiled and said 'live and let live' was his motto and that the weather was bound to break soon anyway. So she said no more. Never at any time did she consider talking to the Stewarts herself. If there was one thing she prided herself on, it was keeping herself to herself.

She was aware that her standards were not other people's, particularly in this street she lived in. Twenty-six years ago when they had bought No. 6 Rawlinson Road hardly anybody knew anybody or if they did they were quiet about it. It took her two years to identify who lived in Nos. 4 and 8 on either side, and even longer to recognize who inhabited 17 and 19 opposite.

Gradually, over the years, she had fitted people into the other thirty houses but only with very few did she have any truck. She said good morning to some, but only with the Dalys at No. 8, their adjoining left-hand neighbour, had she ever had any kind of dealings. Mrs Daly had started it. Going out of her front door one day she had been quite alarmed to hear a voice say, 'Cold, isn't it?' and she had looked over the privet and seen a tall, bespectacled lady going into her front door. 'Oh,' she said, 'yes, it is, for the time of year.' That had been the beginning of an endless stream of pleasantries in the same vein. She came to depend on them, and when, after five years, Mrs Daly said, 'Good morning, nice, isn't it? We've the telephone men coming today, so if ever you need to telephone just you come in and use it,' 'Oh,' she had said, 'that's nice, thank you.' She never ever would take such blatant advantage, of course, as she was sure Mrs Daly knew, but it was neighbourly to offer. It pleased her. The invitation remained one of the nicest things that had ever happened to her and she was fierce in her determination to stop Stanley spoiling it. He wanted to go and use the Dalys' phone one winter – it was long before Frank had one installed – when she fell and broke her leg but she told him furiously that the public call-box barely ten yards round the corner had been good enough for the last five years and was good enough now. 'Whatever you think best' had been Stanley's motto for that day but he had taken his time about going. In the event, he had used the Dalys' phone, for, as he related it, he had met Mrs Daly at the gate and she had said, 'Isn't it icy? I'm frightened I'll fall and break a leg,' and he had said, 'That's just what my wife has done. I'm off to telephone for the doctor.' Oh, how Rose Pendlebury had raged at him! But the damage was done. The Dalys' phone was used, if just that once. The next day a blancmange for the invalid had been presented at the front door. 'Did you ask her in?' she had questioned Stanley, terrified of the shame if he hadn't. He had, but she had refused. Relief and pleasure had engulfed her.

Now, the Dalys were dead, and below in the street the new people were moving in. She had, of course, known all about it though there had been no For Sale board – there never were these days, property was so sought after – but still it was a shock. She hadn't thought it would happen quite so soon. It was April and Mrs Daly had only passed on at the beginning of March. Somebody had acted with indecent haste, that was clear, but who she was not sure. The Dalys had no children. It had taken several years of delicate inquiries to establish that they never had had any, but one of the most memorable interchanges of Rose Pendlebury's life had taken place over the low part of the garden wall when Mrs Daly had confessed she had never been blessed and Rose had told her of Ellen's death and Frank's departure. It had been a totally revealing but utterly unemotional scene after which they had both plucked dead heads off flowers for a long time. There were, however, nieces and nephews and a few brothers and sisters so presumably one of, or all of, these had inherited the house and everything in it. Rose only knew one thing: none of them had come near at the end. A crowd had arrived two years ago for Mr Daly's funeral and departed the same day, but since then none had been near. Keen enough to sell the house and get their money, but no thought for who gave it to them. When she stormed about this state of affairs Stanley said you never could tell.

It was no use dwelling on the past. The Dalys had gone. No more nice chats at the front door or over the wall, no longer the comfortable feeling that in the middle of this invasion one's own sort was next door. Those people down there in the street were not her sort. She could tell at a glance that they were the same kind as the others that had moved in during the last few years. It had begun with No. 23. One day a big skip had appeared outside the door and the wreckage had started. The skip was filled and removed, filled and removed, so many times she thought the house must now be a shell. Peering in her clever way through the windows every time she passed she saw that was just what it was. Every wall seemed to have been knocked down, every floor uprooted. Stanley spent hours working out what it must have cost. Ten months it took, and then a family had moved in through the bright yellow front door with its brass knocker and letter-box. They had been followed at regular intervals by other families buying other houses and doing the same kind of thing to them as those at No. 23 to a greater or lesser extent. They all had the same look to them, a look that Rose Pendlebury reacted to very strongly and aggressively.

There were, she noticed, several slightly different features about the new arrivals. She had been, perhaps, a little hasty lumping them with the others, or was it that she had looked harder and closer than she had ever had an opportunity to do before? To begin with, there was no large removal van stacked with pine tables and brass bedsteads. Instead, a Dormobile came four times and discharged a mound of shabby-looking furniture that might have come out of her own house. Oh yes, she told herself, I'm no fool, I know my furniture is shabby and I can see the similarity. Nobody these days had three-piece suites and large wardrobes except her and, apparently, the new people next door. But they were young and looked like the others.

Mrs Pendlebury moved away from the window as the last chair was carried in. Her legs ached with all the standing and her eyes watered. She sat down for a minute on one of the beds and looked around her with dissatisfaction. The room she was in was the spare room. All the rooms were spare rooms, she reflected, except the three they used to eat and sit and sleep in. Six spare rooms, all with beds. Even when they had bought the house it had been obvious the rooms would be spare. Stanley's sister had been scathing. 'I say what I think,' Elsie had said, 'and I think it's silly, plain silly, for folk nearly fifty to buy a big house like this. What will you do with all the rooms? You won't let them. Rose would never take boarders. You have to think of your future. And the garden – the size of it!' Neither Stanley nor Rose had replied. They had waited until Elsie had returned to her plywood bungalow and then they had toured the rooms and breathed easier. They had had their eye on Rawlinson Road all their married life. From their two rooms in Stoke Newington they had visited the lovely squares in Islington on Sunday afternoons and picked out Rawlinson Road as grand but not too grand, quiet but not too quiet and convenient for shops and transport without being on top of them. The canal was near and it was only a short bus ride to Highgate where one could get on the heath or visit Kenwood. Stanley said it was an investment and Rose, who cared nothing for such things, was simply proud. It was lovely to have a house, a whole house, with space inside to wander about and not feel claustrophobic. Elsie had actually tried to suggest it was wrong for them to buy the house as there was just the two of them but Rose was not plagued by any feelings of guilt. They had worked hard for this house, they had paid for it in cash – £1,200 that had taken them twenty-five years to save, twenty-five years of rigid self-denial and discipline. They were entitled to it. What they intended to do with all the rooms was none of Elsie's business.

Frowning into a mirror that she had thought so splendid when she bought it but now saw was vulgar, with its plaster frame of violently pink roses, Mrs Pendlebury touched her hair and pinched her white sagging cheeks. She looked terrible, but there was no one but herself to tell her that she looked terrible and she did not take much notice of herself. Stanley was a hypochondriac, forever trailing off to the doctor with this and that, but she never went. She was sensible, she stayed indoors and went to bed if she had a fever, but she had no intention of taking pills and potions for what she knew were the incurable ills of approaching old age. She never moaned about her back or her legs. The only thing she was prepared to admit she ought possibly to do something about was her eyes. There was something wrong with them and if it was just that after nearly seventy years of perfect sight she at last needed spectacles, then she was prepared to have them. To ignore the real advances of medical science would be perverse. Besides, she missed being able to see everything she wanted to see. Stanley had been going around for years in a haze, unable to see the most essential things like bus numbers, and she had despised him for his dependency on other people. It constantly mortified her to realize how he plagued the life out of perfect strangers over such things.

She went slowly down the stairs and into the back kitchen. The paper was peeling off the pantry wall again. Irritably, she stuck it back on, slapping it against the wall with her hand. It was a damn nuisance. Stanley said he would repaper it 'presently', but he never would. It had to be endured in its messiness like many other things. She slapped it again then stood back to see if it would cling. Slowly, the paper began to curl and droop and she had to turn to the sink to control her rage. Stanley said these little things were sent to try us – but were they so little? This back kitchen had never been right. It was only a lean-to really, a back addition that had never been properly planned. The house was solid but the addition was flimsy, a miserable, poky little hole that she spent more than half her time in. She had nodded her head in approval when she saw all the newcomers making a point of tearing down their similar additions first. Down they all came at the first blow of a sledgehammer and in their place were erected splendid constructions of glass. We mustn't complain, said Stanley. But why not? Why shouldn't she complain?

The garden was a consolation. Washing the dishes she looked out on it and sniffed and felt better. She had seen them admiring it from their patios and she had felt scornful that none of their money could give them what she had built over all these years. The oval of grass at this end hadn't a weed or bit of clover in it, only a sprinkling of daisies at the top. The lilac and japonica bushes had been tended so carefully and trained so skilfully from young bushes that now they formed a hedge all along the left-hand wall. The apple trees and roses were pruned every season and the borders kept clear for the small flowers to grow. Yet in spite of the hours and hours spent on it, the garden looked natural. There was nothing stiff or geometrical about it. It was mature but gay, organized but artistic. The house might drive her mad, but the garden never.

She promised herself a half-hour walking about in it after the dishes were done. She would manage it before Stanley came back, before he was there to bumble about and spoil everything, scattering his horrid cigarette ash everywhere. They were too much together since he had retired. She had known he would get on her nerves with his getting up at all hours as though *she* didn't still have *her* work to do. Today, Tuesday, was the only day he went out on his own to the Club. On Tuesday afternoons they had a bingo afternoon for pensioners at the Community Centre (he always called it the Club) and he enjoyed that. He'd tried to get her to go but she was furious at the suggestion. She had always hated games, always hated get-togethers, he knew that. She wasn't sociable. She had other interests – let him go if he needed it. She would please herself.

The little yard, when she finally stepped out into it, was full of sunlight. She blinked, and shaded her eyes with her hand. Not only was her sight not so good – she had also noticed that any strong light made her eyes water. Bouncing off the concrete ground the sudden sunlight was very powerful. She had always planned to cover in the yard. A bare six feet by four, it filled the space between the two additions before the garden began. The living-room window looked out on to it so that it was like looking through a tunnel to the open air beyond. In winter it gave her the creeps – she was always expecting somebody to come round the corner and surprise her. In summer, the sun was kept out of the house by the shadows cast on either side. She hated the yard.

Head bowed, she was about to rush through it when clear and strong she heard a voice say, 'Who do you suppose lives next door?' Unaccountably, her heart began to thud and she found herself hanging back.

'What do you mean – "who"?' came the reply.

'Well – you know – a family, or flats, old or young, that kind of thing.'

'Should imagine an elderly couple by the look of the front.'

'That's a pity, isn't it. It would have been nice to have children next door.'

'Perhaps they'll babysit.'

'Who?'

'The people next door, if they haven't got kids.'

'The things you think of.'

The voices went on, but farther away. She waited until they had died out and then, in a hurry, trotted through the yard onto the grass. Keeping close to the bushes she walked as naturally as possible to the bottom of the garden towards the garage. There she tried the door to make sure it was locked. The garage was on a raised bit of ground from where she could look into the next-door gardens, which she did, furtively. They were empty. Relieved, she came down, the excitement passing. Nobody could accuse her of eavesdropping. Eavesdroppers quite rightly never hear good of themselves, but she had not eavesdropped. What could she have been expected to do – go back inside, not walk in her own garden when she felt like it?

When Stanley came back she was still trembling with indignation. She burst out immediately, 'You've taken your time coming home, I must say.' Stanley took his hat off and gave her a long look that annoyed her to death. It wasn't what one could call a searching or penetrating look – Stanley was much too blank to apply such adjectives to. It was, on the contrary, a vacant look, if anything. It had proved very useful to him over a number of years, saved him from making a lot of silly mistakes. He had always employed this delaying device to great effect with his wife. Though at first it would produce anger in her, if he kept it up long enough it resulted in her telling him what all the fuss was about without him having to ask a lot of tiring questions and, if he could get away with sustaining his dramatic pause even further, she could be depended on to solve the problem posed herself. Hopefully, Stanley held his hat in his hands and concentrated on The Look, taking care not to let the slightest glimmer of either amusement, boredom or bewilderment creep into his expression. He had only to move a muscle to bring disaster on his head. He had no wish for a late tea.

'You're not going to tell me it took forty-five minutes to walk from the Centre?' Rose shouted at him. 'You might be slow but you're not crawling, not yet, though when I look at you tottering along like an eighty-year-old, not a seventy-year-old, I sometimes wonder which side of the grave you're on. A man who leaves his wife that long when anything could have been happening, anything. I might be dead and murdered the time you take, but oh no, I don't matter – and now I suppose you'll be wanting your tea, won't you, you'll be wanting your tea unless you've been stuffing yourself with shop cakes up there, have you? More than likely, you've never known what's good for you. Well, do you want your tea or don't you? Don't just stand there like a tailor's dummy.'

Stanley knew it was vitally important that that was precisely how he should continue to stand. He might risk clearing his throat at this juncture, or very carefully putting his hat down, but that was all. His pale, watery eyes were fixed on Rose's chest, which soon began to heave as she got going again. She had dirty marks on her dress which she didn't seem to notice. She'd washed that dress only last week. He'd seen her scrubbing it furiously but somehow not where the dirty marks were. Now, with the rest of the dress so clean, they stood out even more, except to Rose. Well, let sleeping dogs lie.

It all settled down nicely. Contentedly, Stanley munched his chicken salad and listened. He never thought of Rose as a hen-pecker or a shrew. He never even thought of her as bad-tempered because he understood her. She only shouted when she was upset or frightened and he saw it as his duty to console her by his calm. He was rock-like. She could hurl herself against him and he wouldn't break. He would be just the same afterwards. Not many people had witnessed Rose's funny ways. She had funny ways in public too, but not this kind. Only Frank, before he left, had asked him, 'Don't you get tired of her going on, Dad?' and he had been truthfully able to say that no, he didn't. The fact that Frank did would have hurt Rose dreadfully. It was all Stan-ley could do, when she took on so at his departure, not to tell her. It was something she must never know. Frank had gone to further his career.

'We'll keep ourselves to ourselves,' Rose was saying as though it was a newly discovered text, 'and mind our own business. Though if I can't walk in my own garden in peace I don't know what I'll do.'

'Nobody can stop you doing that,' Stanley said, 'you walk in it as much as you please.'

'Easier said than done,' Rose said. 'We're exposed out there these days.'

'I could put up a fence,' Stanley suggested, secure in the knowledge that he would not be called upon to expend the energy this would entail.

'No,' said Rose, 'my garden isn't a prison. We'll manage with-out fences, thank you very much. We'll just face up to the worst and keep smiling. And keep our mouths shut.'

'Least said soonest mended,' said Stanley, happily.

Chapter Two

Rawlinson Road, for all Rose Pendlebury's criticisms, had become a friendly place. People knew each other, talked to each other, even helped each other. The fact that they were all much the same kind of people naturally helped this good-neighbourliness. Within days the latest arrivals had received many overtures of friendship – names had been exchanged, invitations issued, that kind of loose middle-class camaraderie. The child of the couple who had moved into No. 8, a girl of eighteen months called Amy, was at once seized upon by mothers with similarly aged offspring and initiated into playgroups. And yet there was a sense of disappointment on both sides.

Rose Pendlebury knew nothing of it. She saw them coming and going, heard the voices voicing in a way that set her teeth on edge, and retreated into the core of her house. She did not witness the partial rejection, was not aware that her new next-door neighbour stood apart, nor would she necessarily have been glad if she had. The whole business of flashing smiles and shouted greetings in the street upset her, always had. It had nothing to do with being neighbours, which was why she had always ignored anything of that variety directed at herself. All she noticed were two things – no builders and no parties. For both she was grateful.

There was an impression of poverty, she fancied, and scolded herself for thinking so. Just because they were not knocking the house about did not mean they were poor. Nobody who was poor could even buy a house in Rawlinson Road. Her curiosity was nevertheless aroused by the extreme silence next door. If there had been carrying-ons like those Stewarts she would never have given the new people a thought, she'd have shut them right out of her consciousness as they deserved, and been ready for them when they came, grinning and grinning and all Christian names like the Stewarts. She remembered what they'd said – 'We're Jeremy and Penny Stewart and we've moved in next door, how do you do?' How do you do and goodbye. She never wanted anything to do with them, not ever. Let Stanley chat to them if he had to, showing his weakness. That was for him to decide.

Perhaps the new people were stand-offish. Good for them, as long as it was for the right reasons. If they were, they'd exclude her too. They'd have nothing to do with her, if they'd have nothing to do with the rest. They were welcome. But the woman – the girl, she wasn't more – didn't look stand-offish. Rose was quite surprised to find she looked shy. She'd seen her going out and in with the child and she had no appearance at all. Pretty, but no presence: you weren't aware of her the way you had those others thrust in your vision. She was shabbily dressed too, or perhaps just old-fashioned with her gathered skirts and short-sleeved blouses. She walked with her head down, her shoulders hunched, and she had a twitch about the eyes. Rose saw nobody could be intimidated by her.

Working away in her own house each morning, Rose Pendlebury could not help wondering how the girl in No. 8 was making out. How was she managing with all that big house to get straight? A system, that was the only way, a system like she herself had had, starting at the bottom and working upwards because the bottom part housed everything that was important. There had been such pleasure in that organization. Never at any time had she felt overcome, not by that, not by getting straight. All that had overwhelmed her had been the strangeness of the atmosphere, the pungency of new smells, the coldness of a light she did not know. She had to learn the house and that had at times put her into a panic. It wasn't something you could do easily or quickly. Their rooms, two rooms, in Stoke Newington had been so utterly familiar, not a corner she didn't know, not a part not meaningful. Leaving had been like coming out of a shell – she felt naked and vulnerable and in a hurry to bury herself again but it couldn't happen like that, the new layers had to grow, one by one. Were they growing for her next door? Was she appreciating these houses, seeing what they had to offer? Time would show, as Stanley would have been bound to say.

They were quiet in everything they did. The child laughed and shouted sometimes – it was a shock, at first, but lovely – but she had never minded children. They could make as much noise as they liked. It was adults who annoyed, but not these adults. He seemed as considerate as her, no thumps or bangs, no coming in or going out like the devil himself. He had a car, she noticed, but he never started it up at inconvenient times. She had to give them full marks for consideration – if that was what it was. There was no fault could be found – except that they were neglecting the garden. The grass was long and thick, already covered in dandelions, losing the shape the Dalys had given it. The small flowers along the borders were choking with weeds and there would never be a second crop of roses if they continued to neglect the first. Since that first day she had heard nobody, only the child, in the garden, certainly nobody working as they should be doing.

Cleaning the bedroom windows three weeks after the new people moved in – something Stanley ought to do but never would – Mrs Pendlebury could not help seeing her new neighbours. As they came into the garden she almost dropped her bucket with fright. It was silly, but the garden had always been so quiet and empty, even when the Dalys were alive, that the invasion shook her. She didn't know whether to stop or not, but when the woman lay down and closed her eyes she didn't see why she shouldn't go on with what she'd been doing. Squeezing her cloth out she tried not to look at the figure in the yellow dress but her eyes kept straying back to it, and especially to the toddler climbing over it. It was a girl, she could see that now, a pretty little thing, dark-haired like her mother. Watching the chubby hands grasp the flowers and the frown of concentration on the small face as the child tried to pick them, Mrs Pendlebury smiled. She liked them that age, just learning to do everything and yet babyish enough to cuddle and cradle in your arms.

Slowly, she went on cleaning the windows, the child's chatter floating up to her. She tried to pick out words but it was all gibberish except for the persistent 'mama' and 'flowers'. After a while, the little girl stopped and sat down beside her mother, looking round the garden for new diversions. Mrs Pendlebury knew it was only a matter of time before she saw her – the moving cloth would attract her attention. Should she go away quickly? She wanted to and yet she didn't want to. Anxiously, she wiped away, debating with herself, half hoping the child would see her before she had time to move. She saw the little head go back and the large brown eyes looked up at an aeroplane in the sky and then found the windows glittering in the sun and Mrs Pendlebury's cloth going backwards and forwards. Hardly daring to breathe, Mrs Pendlebury went on steadily with her job. The eyes stared, then moved away, then stared again. She smiled and nodded her head. The eyes went on staring but there was no answering smile nor any sign that the child had seen her. Finally, the child turned right round and began picking stones out of the soil in the border.

Mrs Pendlebury felt disappointed. Her job was finished. She replaced the net curtains and took her bucket downstairs. Stanley was in the front room watching horse-racing on television. Typical – only someone like Stanley could shut himself up in a dark room on such a beautiful day for such a worthless reason. She clanged her old iron bucket as loudly as possible to register her disgust as she emptied it and washed it out, not that he would hear. He only heard what he wanted. She was going out in the fresh air now she'd finished, once she'd changed her dress. Without realizing it, she was hurrying. Up the stairs she went again and into her bedroom. The curtains needed adjusting. The child was still there. She chose any old dress – they all seemed the same now, drab and uninteresting – and pulled it on. She was getting too fat for everything but then they'd all been bought ten years ago. Couldn't be bothered with shops now. Down she went again, taking a pair of garden scissors from the hook beside the kitchen door on her way out. There were a lot of dead heads needed clipping off the roses. Humming, she clipped away, working nearer and nearer the gap between the lilac bush and the forsythia, where for a yard or so one could see quite clearly into the next garden.

The child saw her at once. She merely put her nose on a level with the wall, still holding a dead rose for an alibi, and it saw her. She smiled. The same stare. She dipped down and up again, playing peek-a-boo. To her tremendous pleasure the child smiled, such a beautiful, wide, crinkly smile, and began to get up. Just then Stanley appeared at the back door and shouted 'What you up to, then?' She could have wept with mortification. Pushing herself away from the wall, she rushed up to him, mouthing 'Shut up' and flapped her hands at him. He stepped back and she charged in, yanking him after her.

'How could you!' she shouted. 'How could you do a thing like that? Making a fool of me, your own wife, what will she *think*? You sit in there all this lovely day then you come out and do a thing like that. Oh, I could kill you. Don't you ever think before you speak?'

'I only said – ' Stanley began, breaking his rule, such was his bewilderment.

'That's the point,' Rose said, 'you don't think, you don't care what embarrassment you might be causing. What call was there for you to say anything at all? Why can't you leave me alone? Go up to your precious Club or somewhere instead of hanging about my house. You spoil everything.'

Stanley breathed deeply, rocking backwards and forwards on his heels. This was a turn-up for the books. What the devil *had* she been doing out there? She was a mystery, that woman. What was she rushing upstairs again for? Up and down all afternoon, ruining his programme. Whatever she did up there, it calmed her down. She returned to the kitchen looking much better, but nothing would persuade her to go in the garden again. He went on his own and thought about some weeding but in the end just sat in the sun.

Throughout the next few weeks Stanley became aware that his wife had a secret. She was up to something. He tried hard to think what it could be but his mind had never taken an inventive turn and at a time like this it let him down completely. Eventually, he ceased trying to fathom the reasons for Rose's behaviour and was simply glad that whatever it was that preoccupied her at least made her more cheerful. She sang more than usual – not the rather aggressive hymn-singing she often went in for (though she never went near a church) but nice old-fashioned melodies like 'We'll Gather Lilacs'. Stanley enjoyed that. He was even moved sometimes to hum an accompaniment but that didn't please her so he had to stop. He risked saying, when this had gone on some time, 'You're a little ray of sunshine these days,' but that made her huffy so he didn't chance his luck. All would be revealed, no doubt, in good time.

What had worked such a transformation in Mrs Pendlebury's mood was the daily game she now found herself playing with the toddler next door. She found herself, every day, looking out of the upstairs windows as a matter of course to see if she could see the child. Soon she learnt to expect to see her in the morning about eleven and in the afternoon about three. She must have a nap and lunch in between which showed a sensible mother. Quite often Amy – her name was called often enough to satisfy that part of Mrs Pendlebury's curiosity – was in the garden on her own, just wandering about, running into the house on her own. The very first day after she had first waved, Mrs Pendlebury saw Amy look up to her window. There was no doubt about it. She distinctly looked up. At once, Mrs Pendlebury drew aside the net and nodded and waved and smiled. Amy watched, as grave as before, and then came that huge, cheek-bunched smile that made Mrs Pendlebury's inside turn to water. She even found tears in her eyes and had to wipe them with a corner of her apron. Thank God Stanley was so unobservant, for her eyes often misted over after an encounter with Amy, and she had to rush away to hide if Stanley came upon her. She told herself off for being a silly old fool but it was no good. All Mrs Pendlebury wanted was a smile and she was content – at least for the moment. She knew about children. She had studied them and she knew it was important to gain their trust. Just to be a face that beamed and nodded in the same place every day was enough.

The only worry in Mrs Pendlebury's mind as she plotted her relationship with Amy was the mother. She could hardly become friends with the little girl over the garden wall without the mother knowing, and it made her nervous to think of that encounter. The mother might not like her. She might not think her a suitable person to be friends with her daughter. Mrs Pendlebury bridled at the thought, forgetting she herself had put it there. She had never pretended to be anything that she wasn't and that was nothing to be ashamed of. She lived decently and if that wasn't good enough it was too bad. There were enough airs and graces in Rawlinson Road these days to make you sick. Her at the end of the road, for example, with her la-di-dah voice and her *au pair* girl and her stuck-up nose as though there was a bad smell. Real quality didn't behave like that. Mrs Pendlebury had worked for a lord and lady and they were as natural and nice as you please. No condescension at all. If that muck down the road was what Amy's mother wanted, then she was welcome to it.

In fact, it was Stanley who spoke first to Amy's mother. He came in one day looking smug and self-important and over his tea brought it up that he'd been speaking to their new neighbour. Mrs Pendlebury choked with suppressed curiosity. She went on drinking tea and not asking all the questions she wanted so badly to ask. Let him be maddening, see if she cared.

'Yes,' Stanley said, 'she seems a nice sort of person. Had quite a chat, must have been all of twenty minutes.'

'I'm surprised you noticed the time if it was so fascinating,' Rose snapped.

'They have a youngster, you know,' Stanley said, 'a little girl called Amy, eighteen months old. Seems a nice little thing. I said she was welcome to bring her in any time.'

'You said *what?*'

'I said she was welcome to bring her in any time.'

'And what was that meant to mean?'

'Well, you like kiddies. I thought it might be nice for you to have one about now and again.'

'Oh,' Rose gasped, 'oh – you're so clumsy, you're so insensitive – what am I supposed to be, a silly old fool or something? Bedridden, am I? Deaf and dumb? I don't need you or anybody else to make advances for me, Stanley Pendlebury. I've still a civil tongue in my head and I'll use it when I want to issue invitations so keep your big mouth shut in future.'

'Have it your own way,' Stanley said, adding as he left the room, 'Storm in a teacup.'

'What?' Rose shrieked. 'What was that?'

'I was only trying to do you a good turn,' Stanley said.

'I don't *need* good turns,' Rose shouted, 'just you let me be, that's all. When I want your advice I'll ask for it.'

Afterwards, she worried that Amy's mother would come to the door and take Stanley up on his grand gesture. She worked out an elaborate plan for such an eventuality, but knew that as she had no intention of opening the door she would not be called upon to put it into operation. She would not be pitied. She didn't want anyone being kind to her. If Amy came into her house it would be naturally, in the normal course of events. Quite how this would happen she did not know but she had confidence it would, some day. It might take months or even years but she was prepared to wait. So she settled down, the quality of her life already enriched in a way Stanley was too stupid to appreciate.

Chapter Three

At two o'clock on a very hot August Sunday Mrs Pendlebury sat down in the sitting-room, where it was always cool, to write to her son Frank. By four o'clock she had written, 'Dear Frank, Thank you for your last sorry I have been so long replying only' – and that was all. Only what? Frank's last letter, or rather his wife Veronica's last letter, for she did all the writing except at Christmas, had arrived in March. How did she explain five months' silence? She hadn't been ill. She hadn't been what you could call busy. Nothing had happened to write to Australia about, that was the point. She had nothing to write. But you couldn't put that. You couldn't put 'only nothing has happened' after a silence of five months. It would be insulting and childish.

In front of her, propped against the Quink ink, was Frank's last letter. She was always reduced to going through the letters line by line saying, 'Glad to hear that you had a nice day out on the beach, glad to hear Carol's cold is better, glad to hear Paul is doing well at school, glad to know the baby is walking at last my how he is growing I wish I could see him.' But she mustn't say that. She'd been invited umpteen times to see the baby and all of them. Every year for the last ten years since he started making money out of his farm, Frank had invited both of them out, all expenses paid, for as long as they chose to stay. Always, they had replied, 'We'll see.' But it never went farther. They never did see.

Sometimes Rose wondered if the people in the coloured snaps they kept sending existed at all. Was that Frank? Two stone heavier, a big square confident-looking man of thirty-nine instead of the scared, thin-looking lad of nineteen who had emigrated so long ago? And the woman, this Veronica, this doctor's daughter, herself a nurse, with her long red hair and perpetual smile – who was she? Rose had studied her photographs with a magnifying glass and still she could get no clues. Her letters were warm and friendly enough but they were only words on paper. You couldn't tell from letters. At least, Rose hoped you couldn't. God forbid that anyone should judge her by her painful epistles. Only her grandchildren's notes had any intrinsic value. Surprisingly, the girl Carol, who was fourteen on Christmas Day, wrote a poor hand and never had much to say, but the boy Paul, who was ten, had a real gift for writing. She enjoyed his little letters and it depressed her to think he would never tell from her words how pleased she was. What a waste. Three lovely grandchildren growing up not even knowing their grandma. Frank talked already of Carol coming over on her own soon and it terrified her. What would she do with a strange girl? It was the baby she most wanted. Alexander, aged eighteen months, would be no problem.

She wanted to write, 'I wish you would wrap Alexander up in a big brown paper parcel and post him to me,' but she didn't. She wasn't sentimental. It would just be silly to write such sloppy things. But if she had no news and wasn't to be foolish what could she write? There were no events in her life. She sometimes had an outing to relate, or very occasionally a wedding or a funeral to record, or a purchase to inform them about, but this time there was nothing. Except next door. There was next door. She hesitated, uncertain. Did they want to hear about next door? Slowly, she wrote, 'Next door has been bought for a lot of money they say but I don't know about that but they seem a nice young family there is a baby about Alexander's age a nice little thing called Amy.' She stopped. It was the longest sentence she had ever written. Reading it over it didn't sound right. Stanley would know why but she wasn't going to ask him. It put her in a rage to think she couldn't write a proper sentence and he could. But then he had been lucky, staying on at school till fifteen and then going to night school later. She hadn't had the opportunities. Out at thirteen and glad to go, that had been her lot. Her pride in Frank's achievements scholastically had always been tinged with a fierce resentment that shocked her and made her feel ashamed. How could she begrudge her son what she longed for? But she had.

Compressing her lips, she managed a few more lines about the weather and being converted to North Sea Gas. Doubtless Veronica sneered at her poor English. She could just imagine her daughter-in-law, the nurse, daughter of a posh doctor, laughing at her letters. Probably Frank didn't even stick up for her. Probably he laughed too, quite forgetting her upbringing. Probably by now the children joined in. They never said anything, of course. They always thanked her most fulsomely for her letters, saying how lovely it was to hear from her, but she knew what they must think.

Stanley came in as she was sealing the edges of the airmail form.

'Finished then, have you?' he said, beaming his approval. 'That's a good job done.'

'One you should have done long ago,' she said. 'When did you last write to Frank?'

'It's you they want to hear from.'

'What rubbish. You're too damned lazy to put pen to paper, that's your trouble.'

'I've had a lifetime of it,' Stanley said, 'and that was enough.'

Rose made a scornful noise. To hear him talk you'd think he'd worn his fingers to the bone pushing a pen when she knew perfectly well that as a minor clerk in the Civil Service only an hour or so a day had involved any kind of writing. But she never dared call his bluff. His former employment was a matter he took very seriously. Every day of his working life he had departed for the office with the greatest gravity and to be fair she had admired such sense of purpose in him. She missed it now he slopped about all the time. The only bit of character in him had gone when he closed that front door at eight forty-three precisely for the last time.

'Sealed it, have you?' Stanley said.

'I have. Why? Did you want to censor it?'

'I might have added a line, that's all,' Stanley said, smiling at her joke, 'but it'll do next time.'

'And when will that be?' Rose asked.

'That depends.'

'On what, pray?'

'On when they reply.'

'Oh, they have to reply, do they, before you'll have anything to say to them. Why? Why should they? I don't know how they have the heart to keep up a correspondence with a miserable pair like us. It's a mystery to me, it is really. What was this line, anyway? What have you to say to them? Some silly remark I expect, something they can well do without hearing.'

'I thought I ought to mention going over.'

Rose stared at him. He liked saying sneaky things like that, very softly so you could hardly hear. She smiled unpleasantly, the corners of her mouth turning down immediately afterwards. There was only one way to deal with Stanley when he got big-headed.

'By all means,' she said, ripping open the letter she had just sealed. 'There you are – I've only used the half sheet. Plenty of room for all the details.'

'You shouldn't have done that,' Stanley said, 'now you've wasted it. You can't open those sheets like that, you won't be able to fasten it up again.'

'That's nobody's loss,' Rose said, grandly, and threw the crumpled ball of airmail paper into the fireplace among the red paper chrysanthemums. 'I don't need to write if we're going over.'

'You shouldn't have done that,' Stanley repeated. He wanted to retrieve the airmail sheet but knew if he kept out of the way she would do it herself, later.

'Isn't it time, then? Aren't we off to Australia tomorrow?'

'No need for that, either,' Stanley said, cross now. 'You're just showing off.'

'*I'm* showing off? Oh my word, the cheek of it. You're doing any showing off that's being done. Who just said we were going to Australia and now we aren't?'

'I never said that. I said I wanted to discuss it.'

'What's the difference. Anyway, what is there to discuss – we'll never go.'

'There's nothing to stop us. Never has been. If we've never gone it's for one reason and one reason only – you won't. You want to but you won't.'

Stanley was about to carry his accusation further but Rose suddenly sat down in that heavy what's-the-use sort of way that he knew so well and he kept quiet. She was upset again. Writing to Frank always had this effect, which was why he never mentioned it or encouraged her. He'd told her over and over Frank understood, he knew his own mother, he didn't expect a book, but she went on striving to imitate Veronica's six pages and blaming herself when she couldn't. She took everything so hard, that was the trouble, her imagination was fearsome. What she needed now was a cup of tea and something to take her mind off things.

Quietly, Stanley went into the kitchen and brewed a good strong cup. As he fiddled about there he wondered whether he should take the bull by the horns and go to see that travel agent in the High Street. Theoretically, there was no harm in it. He'd get a few leaflets, make contact, set the ball rolling. It wouldn't cost anything. Except effort. He'd have to think about whether it would be wise. Even supposing he made the trip to the agents the subject would need such careful introducing. Rose would have a fit if he were to brandish timetables and prices in front of her. She'd collapse on the spot. Anything new panicked her. Any journey, even out to Hackney to see his sister, had her in hysterics. She was timid to the point of hiding herself away rather than meet anyone. Frank had said it was an illness and that there was a name for it and that she ought to be treated, but he had pooh-poohed the idea. There was nothing wrong in being timid. Rose liked a quiet life, that was all.

Stanley carried the tea in with the pleasant feeling of doing the right thing. Rose was still sitting where he had left her. She hadn't moved a muscle. He poured her a cup how she liked it and was gratified when her inert-looking hands suddenly came to life and clasped the cup.

'I've got a surprise for you,' he said. She had once told him his eyes twinkled when he was up to mischief. He tried hard to make them twinkle now.

'Oh yes. That's a change,' she said, quite nicely.

'It's out in the garden. You finish that cuppa and I'll show you.'

He noticed she drank it quickly but with relish and got to her feet the minute she had finished. He only hoped the surprise hadn't moved on. Out they went into the garden with him giving her little nudges and her saying 'Go on with you', but pleased all the same. Down at the bottom of the garden was a patch they had once grown strawberries on but now had small shrubs. Searching carefully, Stanley found the surprise and set it down at Rose's feet. Her laughter was a treat to hear. She laughed and laughed and clapped her hands and got down on her knees to examine the tortoise they thought had disappeared for ever.

The sound of Rose Pendlebury laughing out in her garden made Alice Oram jump. She had been sitting under the apple tree for so long that she felt she had become part of the thick grass, until the great gust of laughter reminded her that she was merely surrounded by it. She and her daughter Amy had already spent whole afternoons lying or rolling in the green, strong-smelling, clean grass that parted to receive them and then sprang up again with only the faintest of indentations left. Looking at other people's shaven lawns Alice could only shudder and wince as her hand stretched out and felt what it would feel like to touch such stubble. Their grass could grow as long as it liked, as high as a jungle. Perhaps if it grew too high for Amy to see through they might clip the tops off in a delicate way, but lash and slash it with tearing metal blades – never.

She did not have to move because someone laughed. They had wanted a house, a cottage, out in the country with fields round it and views but there were no departments of the Board of Trade in fields and Tony had to work, it seemed, and she would have to cope with streets and neighbours and the city. She shouldn't complain: this garden was heaven, even with laughter on the other side of the wall. She was lucky not to have anyone leaning over at every minute, and she knew when the old lady spoke she would speak too and be friendly, as was her nature. Friendly but afraid, of herself. She could only ever overdo friendship and had to watch who she became friendly with, understanding something quite different by the term. It was such a responsibility, being friends, one had to cry and endure pain and worry for a friend.

It was a long time before Alice went inside. Her daughter slept, her husband was not yet home, and if the truth were told she was a little depressed by inside. She had no confidence in it, failing to recognize the ugly pieces of furniture that seemed to fit nowhere. Passing them, all heaped together till she decided where they should go, she was given to kicks and curses. Most of the stuff had been her mother's. Why, when she had had her pick, why she had chosen such horrid pieces she did not know. Laura, her sister, had gone with her to the house and told her to pick first, anything, everything she wanted and she had made all the wrong choices which she must now put up with, not having the skill to disguise her lack of taste.

There was, however, supper to make. She had to watch her dreamy state. Trying to overcome the dangerous apathy that could at times engulf her, she had trained herself to observe certain rituals that Tony and Amy might not suffer. Neither would complain if there was no supper but her own remorse would hurt her. So she chopped vegetables, liking the textures and colours, and trimmed meat and laid the table, an island of bare board among crowded surfaces. She liked doing it, it gave her an easiness she was always looking for. Without such tasks she was a mess, having nothing she wanted to do and watching always for the slide into listlessness. Everything was ready when Amy woke and Tony came home.

They were a silent, non-talking couple, alarming to be with, so little was said. Sometimes they talked in a stilted way as though talking was something that must be done or the art would be lost.

'Today,' Alice said, 'the lady on the other side of the wall laughed.'

'Oh yes.'

'She has a very jolly laugh, not frightening, but I jumped.'

'It was quiet, I suppose, when she laughed.'

'Yes. She waves to Amy a lot. She seems to want to be her friend.'

'Amy has lots of friends.'

'Yes. She likes company and talking, trying to talk.' They both smiled, over the child's head.

'What I wonder is,' Alice said, 'is it wrong not to be friendly? They embarrass me, all these people. I want to tell them to leave me alone but it seems rude.'

'It depends what they want. You have to decide what they want.'

'Not much, really. First names, food at each other's houses, swopping children. Not really caring or listening. Not changing, never that.'

'Well, that's easy.'

'It's tiring, it's worthless.'

'Costs nothing.'

'Oh it does – such energy, always backing out of what they want you to do, making excuses, and they won't take hints. The woman Charlotte, at the end of the road, you know – that block on the corner – she invited us for drinks.'

'When?'

'Tonight but really tomorrow or the next day or any day, she doesn't care.'

There was silence again while they ate.

'Sometimes,' Alice said, 'I worry they might be right, the Charlottes. I feel mean. What's the point of anything if human beings can't be bothered?'

'But you can, when it's necessary.'

'How do you know that?'

'I'd know, so would you.'

Hours and hours of quiet wrapped round their conversation while they thought and felt. Tony could feel the unrest in his wife over such a little thing. Nobody suspected her of turmoil. People wondered if she had a mind of her own, she was so insignificant and the shyness of her smile made them want to help her. Her rebuffs were never recognized as such and everyone thought they did what they liked with her. Except him, and her sister Laura. They respected her inner strength and were even a little afraid of it. He would have forgotten, or buried, what they had said by the morning but Alice would discuss with herself and come to conclusions and judge herself and open up more questions and finally act. Not many people were so conscientious.

Tony Oram was a simpler soul than his wife, though neither as bland nor as insipid as he appeared. His energies, which like hers were prodigious but unreleased, were centred on escaping the trap of work. He hated work, the necessity of earning money, the inability to find anything he liked to do that would earn money. All he could do was concentrate on rising above his daily toil, despising it into non-existence. Part of his technique with himself was deliberately driving into work each day, an act of almost criminal folly. He would not be herded, he would not cram and touch other slaves all going the same way. Driving to work ennobled him. The daily hassle to park only goaded him to greater efforts, the queueing and honking only released an embitterment he enjoyed. Other men asked him constantly why he bothered, how he could stand it, but he only shrugged his shoulders and left them to think what they liked. Getting into his car at either end gave him the advantage whatever happened afterwards.

He was thinking about advantage when he passed the old couple he knew to be his neighbours the following day. Knew, but did not know. They suddenly presented themselves to him as being a case of necessity and the importance of acknowledging this overcame all other considerations. He stopped and said, 'Hello. Would you like a lift?'

She said, 'No,' as he said, 'Yes.'

'I live next door to you now,' he said, feeling silly. 'I'm going into Whitehall. Any help?'

They got in, eventually, after a good deal of mumbling and muttering during which he saw he should have left well alone. Alice had scored, necessity was elusive. Then when they were settled they did not seem happy and he saw he had been presumptuous. There was nothing he could do, except drive, which he did. Their presence breathing behind him was annoying. He supposed they found his silence puzzling since they must have been bound to misjudge his offer. He yawned and raised his eyebrows and wished he had Alice's useful but misleading shyness. He heard them shuffling about and knew they would speak. The man, of course. He predicted the man.

'Did the move in go all right then?' he asked, finally.

'Yes, thank you,' said Tony.

'Settled in nicely are you?'

'Yes, thank you.'

'Think you'll like it in Rawlinson Road then?'

'Stanley!' Rose hissed. 'Leave the young man alone. Can't you see he's driving?'

Tony took a quick look through his mirror. The old dear looked very hot and bothered.

'I'm sure we will,' he said, 'it's a nice road. I expect you've been there a long time.'

'You can say we have,' said Stanley, 'twenty-six years to be precise. When was the date, Rose? She's a genius on dates. You ask her any date – knows all the Royal Family's birthdays and that.'

'Shut up,' said Rose, quite audibly.

Tony took another quick look in the mirror. The old lady was now quite white. Her lips were compressed and she was staring out of the window. It crossed his mind she might be sick, but it seemed unwise to ask her. He began to wonder if she was capable of a kind remark.

'What I like about Rawlinson Road,' he suddenly said, 'is the gardens. You can forget you're in London in those gardens.'

'My wife here is the gardener,' Stanley said.

'Used to be,' Rose muttered, 'but it's all gone to pot now. I haven't the energy.'

'Well,' said Tony, 'if I can get ours to look half as nice as yours I'll be quite satisfied.'

'It shouldn't be difficult,' Rose said, rather sternly. 'Your garden has been well looked after. It's a mature garden, only needs kept up. You'll have to watch the builders don't wreck it.

They lit a bonfire on the lawn next door – a bonfire, all the old rubble from the house, it burnt for a week, it's never been the same since.'

'There won't be any builders,' Tony said. 'We haven't the money for alterations. Anyway, I don't know that I like all this knocking walls down and this architect-designed bit. I suppose I'm old-fashioned.'

There was no need to look in his mirror. They were both purring. His amusement at his own playing of such a game was spoiled by the ease of it all. What a drag talking to people was, feeling your way along in order to say the right things and get the right responses.

'Where can I put you down?' he asked.

'Anywhere will do,' Stanley said.

'Here,' Rose said at the same moment. 'Here' happened to be half-way down King's Cross Road, a stretch where there was neither bus stop nor shop, an unexpected no-man's-land, but in her insistence to be let off the old lady already had the back door half open. Alarmed, he screeched to a halt and she leapt out. The old man took five minutes to follow.

'Thank you I'm sure,' she said, already setting off along the pavement.

'Thanks for the lift,' he said. 'We didn't introduce ourselves, did we? I'm Pendlebury.'

'Pleasure,' Tony said. 'I'm Tony Oram. Any time.'

Stanley was pleased with the whole encounter, especially that last bit. It was the army had taught him that. Everyone ran down the army but Stanley thought of it as the finishing school of life, any pun being unintentional. Officers always introduced themselves by their surnames, and they always introduced themselves. Your name was something to be firm about. Reflecting how useful this lesson had been, Stanley caught up Rose who was going at a fair old crack in a peculiar direction.

'Hang on,' he gasped, coming alongside her, 'where are you off to?'

'I couldn't care less,' she snapped.

'Well, I could,' he said, 'and it isn't this way.' He took her arm and pulled her across the road and back the way they had come.

34

She didn't resist. All traffic scared her silly and on outings like this he could do what he liked with her. Since she was very cross her eyes were likely to be misted over and she wouldn't be able to see where she was going in any case. He had it all his own way. He guided her gently into a tube station, holding her arm tightly near the elbow, and on the tube he didn't let go. Neither of them said a word. They changed tubes and came up at St James's Park in one long pause.

'Oh, isn't it lovely,' Rose said, the minute they were in the park.

'Yes,' said Stanley, accepting the compliment, 'very refreshing. Just what the doctor ordered.'

If the remark jarred, Rose did not allow herself to show it. She wasn't going to let any irritation spoil this lovely park. She was going to sit on a seat with her eyes feasting on all the greenery and the lake and the ducks and the flowers and not be bothered by anything. People were the trouble – if only there were no people, she would be happy.

In bed that night when as usual she could not sleep – an hour's sleep was the most she ever seemed to get – Rose, going over the events of the day, was bound to reflect that she had not been entirely honest to imagine a world without people was what she wanted. The early hours of the morning were conducive to total honesty. The park without people would still have been beautiful but she had also enjoyed watching what Stanley liked to call, in that silly way of his, the antics of the human race. She was curious about all those strangers. She liked to listen to their conversations and cast an eye over their clothes and just look at them. There were so many of them, all with places to go to, all with places they'd come from. She longed to follow each and every one through a day in their lives. None of them felt like that about her, but why should they? She was just a boring old lady sitting on a park bench with nothing to do.

In the twin bed next to her Stanley snored. She burst out laughing at the thought of his daily protestation that he hadn't slept a wink. One day she would learn how to work young Frank's tape recorder and tape his snoring. Probably by now the machine would be rusted up, if those things rusted, she didn't know.

She'd done nothing stupid like keeping his room untouched. Once she'd realized he wasn't going to come back, ever, she had torn into that room and scrubbed it from top to bottom and packed all his belongings in tea chests, ready for when he sent for them, only he never did. She was glad in a way, not because it meant a little bit of him was still there – stuff and nonsense – but because the sending of them to Australia would have been beyond her. The only thing she ever sent other than letters was a parcel for Christmas and that took weeks of organizing – but you had to send something for the children at Christmas – and, of course, a pudding. Veronica, the doctor's daughter, didn't look as if she knew how to make a proper Christmas pudding.

Sometimes, in the morning, Stanley asked her what she had been thinking of when she couldn't sleep. Usually he only asked because he had some rambling anecdote to tell her about a thought he'd had during his supposedly sleepless night. She always replied, 'This and that,' and he never pressed her for details. There was a part of her that wished he would. It would have been a relief to let spill out some of the horrible muddle that filled her head, to unleash upon his unsuspecting head the long string of incoherent, unconnected thoughts by which she was plagued. No wonder she was so exhausted each morning when every minute of the night had brought a new attack.

That night a new character had his say unendingly. Tony Oram was his name, according to Stanley. She could have done without knowing the name, she could have coped better with his image. She could also have done without Stanley pointing out that he looked like Frank, or rather like Frank used to look before he went off for the six months that turned into forever. It wasn't an observation she had needed made. The very fact that Stanley had noticed it was proof that the likeness was remarkable, but then she was sensible enough to know Frank was a common enough type. There were thousands of tall, middling fair, thin, blue-eyed, ordinary looking young men in England. Not all of them had sticking-out ears and uneven large teeth, but enough to be not worth noticing. Their voices were quite different. Stanley had said how could she know that, how could she remember Frank's voice, and she had shrieked with fury at him. How could she forget her only son's voice even if he had been gone a hundred years? She could hear his voice, feel his hand, see his expressions as surely as read his writing. She could have him right there in the bedroom with her any night she chose. Stanley had looked so alarmed she had to point out she wasn't suffering delusions – she could just recreate Frank. With her eyes shut, naturally. Any woman would have understood. But Stanley wasn't a woman for all his old-maidish ways. He was securely male, ungiven to fantasy. She often longed to have a woman friend to confide in, but she had never had one. Friends had never been her line, not even when she was young. Her grandmother used to say they would have to have a friend specially made for Rose. She often thought how surprised she would have been to think she ever became friendly enough with someone to marry them.

Tony Oram had a good opinion of himself, of that she had no doubt. She hadn't missed his frequent looks in the driving mirror. He also thought himself very clever, with all his talk of being old-fashioned. She hated people who sucked up to you. Flattery never fooled her. She would have liked to tell him not to bother but it seemed rude when she was sitting in his car. It had been a strange sensation, being in a car again. She reckoned it was four years since they had last gone out in theirs. Now it stood rotting in the strong brick garage, built by Frank the week before he left, his last job for her. If Frank hadn't gone she would have had a proper kitchen. He had all the plans ready. Stanley had later suggested going ahead and getting a builder but she had wanted none of it. Without Frank they would get in a mess. Stanley couldn't handle builders. He would let them run riot.

Next door, she suddenly heard a child crying. She sat up in bed and listened. The wailing was quite distinct. She had never heard any sound from next door in the night. Anxiously, she waited. First it died down and then it came again, stronger, more insistent. The windows were all open on a hot night like this. She slipped out of bed and went to her window, but the sound seemed fainter there. She retreated to the wall and it grew immediately louder. Pressing her ear to the party wall, she strained to hear the sound better. Amy was not in that room, she was sure, she was higher up. Softly, Rose crept upstairs to the top floor and into Frank's old room and across to the far wall. There, the child was up against that wall as sure as she was standing next to it. Where were the parents? Below, or next door? Surely they would come. Her brows furrowed with distress, she crouched in her nightdress muttering, 'There, there,' pointlessly to herself. It seemed an age before the crying stopped and when it did she could not tell whether it was because someone had lifted the baby or she had just stopped of her own accord. But it had stopped. There was no need to worry any longer.

The first bird sang as she wandered into the kitchen to make a cup of tea. It occurred to her there might be lights on next door that would tell her if the child had someone with her. Quietly, she unbolted the door and went into the yard. There were no lights on at all. Since she was already outside she thought she would take a turn round the garden, so fresh and cool after the house. The grass soaked her slippers and wet the hem of her nightdress. If Stanley was observant what a lot of explaining she would have to do, but of course he would notice nothing. To test him, she deliberately left the back door unbolted. It was one of his jobs to lock up at night and open up every morning which he always did with maddening thoroughness. She must be sure to be there when he did it, to enjoy his consternation. Unfortunately, she fell asleep after her exertions. All the next day she had to put up with Stanley's odious jokes about some people sleeping well in this house, for it was ten o'clock and he had been up an hour before she stirred. Her only consolation was knowing about the door and knowing he hadn't mentioned it and knowing how perplexed he would be.

Chapter Four

Rose Pendlebury spent a lot of time in her garden any day of the year but that summer, the summer the Orams moved into the road, she almost lived in it. She had her favourite times – first thing in the morning and then again just before dark – but there was no time, apart from the hour after midday when the sun was hot and the shade poor, that she did not like. Her own ingenuity amazed her. There was hardly a job she did not manage to do in the garden from cleaning the shoes to scraping the potatoes. Over the weeks she accumulated a great assortment of basins and buckets and household impedimenta which stayed on the flags out at the back, everything propped up against the greenhouse wall after it was washed to bake dry. She even scrubbed the clothes in an old tub using a washboard dug out from under the stairs where she had providentially stored it after Frank insisted on buying that machine she had never wanted.

She was not altogether comfortable washing the clothes like that, knowing it was perverse when with a whiz and whirl they could all be done in a hurry. Defending herself against ridicule that was not likely to come from any quarter, she pleaded that all over the world women washed clothes in the sun and that it must be good. Though she had never travelled herself she had seen them, big gangs of them, on the banks of rivers with the washing spread out all round, white and opaque near the glittering water, somehow dramatic, however humble the setting. So she scrubbed and rubbed in her little dolly tub in the back garden and sometimes sang, pushing bits of hair behind her ears with wet rough fingers.

But she was suspicious. Her eyes would dart this way and that among the trees and bushes looking for interlopers. A change in the direction of light between the leaves could convince her that someone had broken in and was watching and she would rush towards them waving her scrubbing brush, scattering the grass with soap suds. At least she could laugh at herself when, as always, there was no one there. Laugh, and shake her head, and stand awhile looking back at the house.

Spending, as she did, all those hours in the garden she became attuned to all the noises. Within a very short while she knew someone – the mother – was in the garden next door almost as much as she was. When the child was with her the woman's presence was plain, but even when she was alone Rose's sensitive antennae picked up her neighbour's movements. She did not work in the garden, that was for sure. She sat, idle. For a young person it was strange. Rose wondered if she had a bad heart or consumptive tendencies – she looked weak enough. Catching herself speculating, she would sniff and cough, as though interrupting a conversation she disapproved of.

The child was different. She was nosy and determined. Rose could hear her all day long asking endless hardly formed questions that only her mother could understand. 'What dis? What dis?' floated over the wall and if she failed to hear the answer Rose would become quite distracted trying to decide what 'dis' had been. It was a lovely age. You could keep your newborn babies. She was moved to getting out old snapshots of Frank at that age and given to staring at them trying to bring back out of the muddle of shadows and lines the times she had had with him. All useless. There was no going back, not that way. She didn't know what people were talking about when they said they could bring it all back. Perhaps with that child in her arms something would come back, but not otherwise.

There seemed little chance of that. For weeks she had waved from the window and been waved back at, but where did that get her? Not far. Oh, the child knew her face well enough, but not who she was. That was up to the mother and the mother wasn't budging. Rose felt aggrieved by this state of affairs but as usual she sat on the source of her discontent and refused to examine it. There was no doubt at all that, her creed being what it was, this state of affairs would have gone on for ever if Amy had not broken out of her own accord.

It was a little enough thing. One day, about two months after the Orams' arrival, when Rose was settled at the card table polishing her brass bits and pieces, she heard the child's voice shouting, 'Amy's here, Amy's here,' right next to her wall. Putting the rag and candlestick down, Rose kept very quiet, hardly breathing. 'Amy's here,' the shrill voice repeated, followed by a scrabble and scratch at the wall. No other sound, no restraining adult. She could, of course, get up and look over the wall. Could, but wouldn't, but could and would do something or be damned for a fool. Throwing her head back, but not moving otherwise, Rose sang, 'Yes I know, yes I know, Amy's there, Amy's there,' There was a pause and then a shriek and a giggle and a rush. Away from the wall, to the house.

It was little enough, but a start. The game never palled, not for Rose Pendlebury or Amy Oram. They played it every day thereafter until one or other had to go. There were variations on the same theme, different parts of the wall to call out from, different words to call out with, within Amy's limited range. Always the concealment of both parties and the excitement of running away, Rose fearful of discovery and Amy of disillusionment without knowing it. The temptation to look over the wall was naturally strong. Rose saw it as a test. Should she give in to the desire, she might lose the child for ever.

Amy solved the problem herself. Bored with the game, she began to ask, 'Up? Up?' Rose did not know what to do. She could not lift her up, only look over, and would the mother, who had done nothing at all, approve? Anxiously, she tried to sing to the child but Amy began to cry and shout, 'Up! Up!' and Rose was afraid the mother would come and take her away. So she looked over the wall.

'Hello,' she said. 'Who are you?'

'Me Amy.'

'Hello Amy.'

'Hello Amy.'

They beamed at each other. The little face was funny, so inquisitive and twitchy, ready for a hundred different expressions. Rose talked to it a while and then said goodbye. Every day after that they had a chat over the wall, a time of suspense and anticipation. She had ready little gifts of flowers and apples which were eagerly taken and hugged.

The mother must know, with the child not yet two, if so advanced. She must be letting it go on. Rose was troubled by the etiquette of the situation, with which she was unfamiliar. All that was clear to her was that it was up to the mother, knowing what was going on. She would have to lay down the law, but no law appeared. Their delightful interludes went on and on with never a break. They grew longer and longer, more daringly jolly, with balls thrown backwards and forwards and peek-a-boo until both participants were exhausted. Rose went on worrying but playing, and then a sign came, as she had known it must. Amy gave her a rose, a wrapped rose, wrapped by an adult in silver paper with a white ribbon tied to it.

'What you got there then?' Stanley, smiling condescendingly. 'Been picking yourself a nice rose, have you? A rose for a rose, eh.' He chuckled.

'No I have not, and you crack that one every year. I'd be pleased if you'd desist.'

'No offence,' Stanley said, still smiling. 'Aren't you going to put it in water? Must look after it – roses don't just drop from heaven every day of the week.' He laughed at his own wit. 'Want a jam-jar or isn't that good enough for our heavenly Rose?'

'When have I ever used jam-jars for flowers I'd like to know?' Rose snapped. 'Never, so there's no need to think you're funny.'

'What are you going to put it in then? Your best Dresden vase?'

'Oh shut up about it. What are you so interested in it for I'd like to know? Mind your own business and if you've finished your breakfast I'd thank you to carry your dishes into the kitchen.'

Humming, Stanley did as he was told. He put the dishes in a pile on the draining board the way she liked them. It never entered his head to go further and wash them. If there was one thing Rose could be relied upon to do it was her work. He earned the money, she looked after the house. It had always been seen by both of them as a fair division of labour, mutually congenial. Rose was perfectly content with her lot, always had been. The fact that he now no longer worked did not seem to him sufficient reason to alter their routine. He was, therefore, thunderstruck when, as he came back into the living-room, glowing, Rose said, 'Didn't take you long to wash them pots I must say.'

'I haven't washed them. I've piled them up nice and tidy like you like them.'

'That explains it then.'

'If you want me to wash them I will. I thought you liked them piled tidy that's all.'

'I like them clean too.'

'You want me to wash them, then?'

'No I do not. You take an age and you break half the things. Keep out of my kitchen.'

'That's what I thought,' Stanley said, relieved.

Rose had always been contrary. It was part of her way. Just when you thought you'd misunderstood her it all came right in the end. She wasn't one of your straightforward types. Her mind was like the inside of a car engine, all little nuts and bolts and wires that looked a terrifying tangle until you knew how it worked and which bit operated what. Thinking about the car made him want to look at it. Without telling Rose, he went down to the garage and opened the door, with difficulty. The hinges had rusted. He was afraid he would pull the whole door off if he opened it too wide. Luckily, he was thin and could squeeze in through the slim gap. There was a tar-like smell inside, a combination of the sun on the creosoted roof and decaying rubber. Anxiously, he bent to look at the tyres and his worst fears were confirmed – they were beginning to perish. Shaking his head, he reassured himself by feeling the body. She had a lovely body. The shine on her bonnet had hardly dimmed, the chrome was rust-free. Saving the tyres, she was as good as new, better than half the rubbish you saw on the roads these days. Such was her magnificent condition he told himself he wouldn't be a bit surprised if she started at the first touch. The temptation to try was too great to resist. The door squeaked as he prised it open. Anxiously he looked at the frame but it seemed sound enough. The leather gave squeakily to his body as he sat on the seat and a small cloud of dust rose. He coughed a little, pleasurably. Out of his inside jacket pocket he took his car keys. He was never without them, though he had not driven a car for nine years. Strangely, Rose had never sneered at his clinging on to them, changing them from one jacket pocket to another. She often said 'Got your car keys safe?' and grunted with satisfaction when he jangled them in front of her.

The Riley didn't start at the first touch, nor at the second or third. It was to be expected. The petrol gauge registered a half-full tank but the leads were probably seized up and the battery flat. He sat for a while longer with his hands on the wheel, and then slid out of the seat into the lighter gloom of the garage. It was no good being sentimental about a machine, no good remembering all the good times they'd had in it. One day, he'd get it out again and take Rose for a spin. He should never have allowed her to make him stop driving but then he was never aware that she *had* stopped him or that he had stopped. There was no one day when he had put the car in the garage knowing that was that. There had been no conscious decision, which was the trouble as you got older – you drifted into habits without realizing it. He wondered if Rose had been quite so haphazard. Perhaps she had known what she was doing. Certainly, she had gone on for years and years about the traffic and how she was sure he couldn't cope – which was ridiculous. She had started getting the tube out to Barnet or Edgware or the Oval or the last station in the direction they were going and meeting him there because she couldn't endure the drive through London. It made him laugh just to remember it. But then there had come a time – he didn't recall when – that she discovered the traffic in suburbia was just as bad and then there was no persuading her.

The last time they had gone anywhere in the car was very early one Sunday morning, in late summer. She had him up at five in the morning and they were on the road before six, heading for Cambridge. He had thought an early start meant about eight and had at first been cross at her interpretation of the phrase, but as they sped along totally empty roads he was pleased. Rose was more than pleased. She sat at his side quite relaxed, looking out of the window, her hands folded quietly in her lap. Every now and again – she believed talking distracted the driver – she whispered, 'This is the way to do it,' and he nodded his agreement. Of course, the roads hadn't stayed empty and she began to tense up long before they got there, but she had still been fairly happy when they reached their destination. It was on the way back the trouble began. He took some care to stick to B roads though it made their journey much longer, but even so, since it had been a sunny day, there was a good deal of traffic and a lot of congestion at crossings. Rose said nothing until they were half-way home and then, on a completely empty stretch of road, she had suddenly said, 'I want to get out. Let me out.' To his horror, she had begun opening the door and it had been all he could do to restrain her. 'What's up?' he had said. 'There's not another car for miles. What's the matter?'

'I want to get out. I want to walk.'

'But we're miles from anywhere.'

'There's a big hill coming up. I remember it. We came down it, now we're going to go up. I want to get out. You can wait for me at the top.'

Once he'd known that was the trouble and that it was nothing to do with the traffic, he had been so relieved he'd let her out. This had proved a mistake. Every hill after that was a signal for Rose to jump out. Soon, she was walking more than driving. The humour of the situation sustained him for a while but then he found himself losing his temper which he had only done about twice in his equable life before. 'You'll sit there and keep still,' he had shouted, and reaching across had wrenched the door handle to the locked position. It was a stiff handle that they had a lot of trouble with and he doubted if he would ever be able to unlock it again, but at that moment he didn't care. Funnily enough, it had calmed her down. She sat as good as gold all the way home even though the road was practically solid with cars for the last few miles, all of them hooting and blaring in a way that would normally have had her in hysterics. But after that she never went with him again. He'd gone on his own several times, on short trips, but when they had stopped, or how many he'd made, he couldn't recall. They'd simply started taking trains and tubes and buses, and that had been that.

Closing the garage door, Stanley reflected something ought to be done about the car. He would have to have it out with Rose. If he wasn't going to use it again they should sell it. He believed he had said something to her to that effect before and she had come out with some ridiculous idea about having to ask Frank's permission – as if Frank would be interested in what happened to an old car! He had pointed out to her that Frank now had two cars and a truck – what did he want with half a 1949 Riley? But out had come all the stuff he'd heard so often about honesty and fair shares and the principle of the thing, and their discussion, the discussion he had intended, had floundered in his exasperation. Easy enough to write to ask Frank's permission had been her last remark. He would do nothing of the kind. He couldn't remember the exact details of the transaction between Frank and himself but he was sure he had put down by far the larger amount. It was only on the licence and tax and so forth that they had gone strictly halves, and since Frank left he had paid all that himself, including all the years it had been in the garage.

With thoughts of advertisements in the *Exchange & Mart* buzzing in his head, Stanley ambled back down the garden, pulling here and there at a more obvious weed just to show willing. She would have him out again that afternoon working away in the garden, he had no doubt. She was a terror for hard work, especially in the garden. He had only to stand and admire how lovely it was for her to point out that there was this to do and that to do and it was all a mess. But he had no real objections to her insisting he served his time. On went his hat and his old trousers and he took up his trowel or fork or whatever she wanted and said, 'Right boss, what now,' and did what she said. Lawn mowing was his speciality, and rolling afterwards. They tussled briefly over minor points like should the grass box be on or off, but, on the whole, harmony prevailed. After two hours, on the dot, out would come the card table and they would have tea under the laburnum, a salad usually, home-made veal and ham pie and tart of some sort to follow.

Rose was standing at the back door with white gloves on and a white handbag dangling from the crook of her arm. An alarm signal was triggered off in Stanley's head just at the sight of all the white. 'Won't be a sec,' he said as he drew nearer. 'Just got my trousers to change.' She glared at him. As fast as he could, he went upstairs wondering what the hell they were supposed to be doing. A wedding? No, that was so rare he would have remembered. But the word wedding kept coming into his head with irritating persistence. On his bed, however, lay his second-best suit and a clean striped shirt, which set his mind at rest. Weddings meant best suit and white shirt. Still, it was pretty serious, whatever it was, to call for such smartness. He dressed with what speed he could muster, not forgetting a clean handkerchief, and then hurried downstairs. There was no sign of Rose. The back door was closed and locked, the curtains slightly pulled. He knew what she'd done and it annoyed him – she'd set off on her own just to show him.

He pulled the front door hard behind him. Her white hat was clearly visible, on the other side of the street. There was little traffic at any time in Rawlinson Road, and rarely any mid-morning, but she'd taken a big risk by her own standards crossing on her own. Her eyes weren't up to it, he knew. He felt immediately sorry that he'd pushed her so far and instead of keeping on his own side of the street as he'd intended he crossed to join her. Neither of them said a word, but he took her arm and she let him. Handicapped by not knowing where they were going or why, he could not make conversation. All would be revealed, presently. Whatever their mission, she was nervous yet not unpleasantly so. Her step was firm, her brows not too furrowed. Looking at her face, he was saddened to see the hard lines between her eyes that never lifted. She wasn't frowning or scowling, it just looked as if she was. Once, when you pointed it out, she had been able to arrange her brow, but now she couldn't. The last time she had stopped to speak to a child, which she often did if they were far enough from home, the child had cried and run off and Stanley had known it was Rose's frown that had done it. However much she smiled and smiled, the frown was frightening.

It had the same effect on salesgirls, as Stanley had plenty of time to observe during that day. They started at Selfridges and finished at D. H. Evans and worked their way through some two million salesgirls, it seemed to him. What they were after was an outfit for Elsie's daughter's wedding – ah, he'd known wedding came into it somewhere – which was next month. Other seventy-year-old husbands might have quailed at the prospect of such a shopping expedition, but not Stanley. He was never embarrassed nor saw any reason why he should be. He was perfectly happy to look through rack after rack of women's clothes and stand outside changing-rooms while Rose tried them on. It was Rose who was embarrassed, yet she always took him, always had done. She used to take Frank, too – all three of them on a Saturday morning – until he had found ways of getting out of it. Stanley had never tried to get out of it. He knew what Rose wanted was a display of solidarity at what was for her an important and nerve-racking occasion. It wasn't that she wanted him to tell her what to buy, but just to be there, as a support, so that she didn't feel totally intimidated. All he had to do was keep saying, 'Very nice,' each time she appeared and keep in reserve a decisive, 'Now that's *very* nice,' if she appeared in the same thing twice.

He was aware quite soon that all was not going well. Rose grumbled that October was the most difficult month in the year to dress for, especially late October. It could be still summer, or, without warning, autumn. If it had been August a nice frock would have been sufficient, if November a costume. But October meant if she bought a frock she'd have to buy a coat and if she bought a coat she'd be positively obliged to buy a frock. But Stanley wasn't fooled. The trouble was also that Rose had lost her shape. When? He didn't know, hadn't a clue. She'd been so neat at the waist when they were married, like a bird. Now the only bird she resembled was a penguin. Her behind was huge and so was her bosom and her waist was just something that joined the two. It had been getting more of a problem every year to find something to fit her – not that she regularly bought new clothes: in fact, the dazzling white of hat, gloves and bag apart, he saw for the first time how shabby his wife was. A new outfit was essential, wedding or not. Concerned, he tried to be a positive help, which was more than the salesgirls were. They had always made Rose cross, but he had told her she took offence where none was intended, that she looked for slights. Now he wanted to help Rose, he found she had been right. They were insulting in their directions. – '5 ft 2 and under over there, outsize over there,' with an offhand nod in both directions. An occasional one would make an effort and inquire what exactly they were looking for, but since they did not know, beyond something for a wedding, that did not get them very far. Stanley thanked God for his own four suits, that were never going to wear out, and his shape, which never changed.

They had lunch in the cafeteria at John Lewis. It meant queueing for a short while and being told which table to go to instead of choosing their own, which Rose hated, but there was no alternative. It was one o'clock and they were there and exhausted. Rose was nearly in tears and gulped tea with her chicken salad to console herself. She hid her unhappiness under an aggressive front, making bitter remarks about the quality of the goods in the shops and the inferiority of the assistants, but Stanley did not heed her. He was thinking. What they needed was some personal service.

'The trouble is,' he said, 'these shops are too big. What are we doing in big shops? You want to try a small shop that specializes in your type and size.'

'Nobody specializes in freaks,' Rose said.

'There must be small shops,' Stanley said.

'No,' said Rose, 'just boutiques. Nothing my sort.'

'That can't be true,' Stanley remonstrated mildly enough but she burst out – 'There *aren't* any small shops these days' – so he kept quiet. Better leave well alone. Perhaps at the next place they'd have some luck, and even if they didn't it wouldn't be long before they set off home to avoid the rush-hour Rose was terrified of. He'd tried to do his bit and been repulsed. She would have to suffer for her own stubbornness.

It was a weary couple that Tony Oram passed on his way home that night. They were walking very slowly near the kerb edge down Rawlinson Road. She seemed to be staggering. If she hadn't looked so fierce he would have stopped to ask if anything was the matter, or to offer to carry the large paper carrier-bag that seemed to burden the old man so heavily. As it was, he drew up his car and was in the house before they reached theirs, to avoid the drag of having to exchange pleasantries with them.

Rose was relieved. The last thing she wanted to have to do was even say so much as good evening to a single soul. The ordeal over, she wanted to find sanctuary. Standing on the doorstep while Stanley fumbled about for his key such a longing overcame her to get in the house and never leave it that she whimpered with impatience. Every time she closed her eyes with exhaustion she saw hundreds and hundreds of people as they had walked past her, trapping her, in Oxford Street. None of them cared. They were all busy, all rushing, all trampling her down. The only sanity was inside her own front door minding her own business, or out in the garden playing with that child.

'Oh for heaven's sake hurry up!' she shouted and banged her fists in Stanley's back.

Chapter Five

The postman did not call often at No. 6 Rawlinson Road. Most mornings, he walked straight past, hardly troubled to check that he had indeed nothing for Mr and Mrs, or S. J. and R. B., Pendlebury. When he did have something to put through the letter-box it was usually a dull, buff envelope obviously containing either a bill or some kind of official information. Occasionally there was an airmail envelope, postmarked Australia, but they were few and far between. The postman actually did notice these airmail letters – the same man had been doing that street for ten years, to his own surprise – and if he had been on better terms with the Pendleburys he would have enjoyed giving them a bit of a rat-a-tat to herald the arrival of an important-looking letter. But he had only seen Him twice and Her never, so no special fanfare was called for.

The Pendleburys had never had much mail so they were used to this situation. Not many people they knew wrote letters. Once Stanley had finished work there was little to communicate with anyone about. Nevertheless, Rose always listened for the flap of the front door letter-box going, and always went immediately to see what had arrived. Without exception she was always disappointed. Even the Australian letters – though she loved them – were an anti-climax. Sometimes, she had been standing at a front window when the postman went by and she had been astonished at the number of letters the people across the road got – they had to be positively *shovelled* through the large brass letter-box which looked in any case as though it had been purpose-built. She imagined what it must be like to have to gather up the letters in armfuls and sit down at a table and open them all.

The letter-box at No. 6 was small and neat, painted the same pale yellow as the door. Behind it was a little box, like a bird's nesting-box, into which any letters were meant to plop. They could then be withdrawn through the iron grille at the back – in all, a complicated procedure that would have annoyed most people. It had annoyed Frank, who took after his father in that he was rarely annoyed. During the last two years of his residence in the house there had even been talk of changing both the style and the size of the letter-box, but it had come to nothing. It was well down the list of things that needed doing, way after a garage and a new kitchen and new guttering. Since Frank's big, bulky envelopes full of technical farming stuff no longer arrived there had been no problem.

One morning in September, Rose heard the postman and the flap going and was instantly alert from the half slumber she fell into around dawn. It could not be a letter from Frank – even Veronica was not so punctilious as to reply within a month. She hoped not, anyway, for she had not begun to look forward to one yet. Some dreary handout she supposed, or a card saying Stanley's new dentures were ready and would he please collect them. There was no point in going down at 7.30 specially to get whatever had come, but she undoubtedly felt parched. It had been another hot night, not a breath of air stirring the light net curtains. She needed a cup of tea.

The letter was the invitation to Elsie's daughter's wedding. The fact that she had known it was coming did not spoil Rose's pleasure one bit. It increased it, for there was no edge of apprehension about opening a strange-looking envelope that might contain anything. She made her cup of tea, then sat down to open the square, thick white envelope. Nice bold handwriting on the outside, not Dolores' she knew. Dolores could hardly hold a pen, as Rose had contemptuously remarked to her husband many times. She was pretty enough in the same kind of flash way as her name, but she hadn't stuck in at school and had ended up what they called a receptionist in a hotel. Elsie, her mother, seemed to think that was a good job, but Rose wasn't taken in. Dolores had no qualifications, not like Frank. Stanley excused her on the grounds that she was a girl, but Rose said Ellen would have been made to get some.

All mention of Ellen was banned. If her name slipped out, as it sometimes did, it was tacitly agreed that the culprit be excused, and no further word uttered for half an hour. Thoughts of Ellen were also banned but since they lurked in funny corners of one's head, they were not so easily dealt with. Dolores always brought Ellen to mind which was natural since they had been born within a week of each other, Elsie's first and only and Rose's second. After it was all over – *it* – Elsie had said she hoped Rose would look upon her niece, her Dolores, as a daughter in Ellen's place. She had urged Rose to have her as often as she liked – which years later Frank had made his mother see might, in the circumstances, have been rather courageous – but the offer had never been taken up. Rose had watched Dolores grow up from afar. There was no knowledge between them and no affection.

The invitation was very impressive. No expense had been spared as far as size and thickness of paper and gold lettering went. Rose admired it unreservedly and made a mental note to tell Elsie so. Praise where praise is due, as Stanley could be relied upon to say. She envied her sister-in-law the satisfaction of sending out this kind of high-class card. Frank's had been a shabby affair. He and Veronica had got married in a registry office and, from all accounts, had only two friends to a lunch afterwards. Once it was clear there had been no *need* to get married like that – and Rose had been terribly afraid there was need – it had been unforgivable. She quite saw she couldn't have gone to the wedding but to have had some lovely pictures and a photo in the local paper and perhaps been sent snippets of the dress material – these would have been such comforts. There had been nothing to show Elsie and her husband George – nothing at all. It had choked Rose even to tell them. Now Elsie was having all this satisfaction. She knew children weren't competitions, but it was hard.

It was a church wedding, of course. Rose was sure Elsie had kept going to St Anne's in Highgate specially so Dolores could get married there, for they had moved to an area where the churches were not pretty places. Every other Sunday, Elsie had trailed over from Hackney to go to St Anne's and now her years of devotion were repaid. St Anne's would make a nice background for the photographs. Well, let her have her hour of glory. She was welcome to it. When it was over she would be left with nothing, like them, unless Dolores proved more devoted than she had ever seemed. She would need to be to bridge the distance between Edinburgh and London. Elsie couldn't bear to talk about it, but she would have to face up to the unpleasant truth that she would hardly ever see her daughter, once married. She had said hopefully to Rose that once Alan was qualified they might move back south, but Rose had replied, rather cruelly, that pigs might fly.

Now that she was up, Rose felt she might as well have her breakfast and listen to the wireless. She was snobbish about the wireless and at the same time forgetful. She was in the habit of putting it on and forgetting about it – just as Stanley did with his television – but, whereas she stormed and raged at him for the waste involved, she excused herself on the grounds that, since she had it on very low, no harm was done. That was how she put it on now – very low, a bare hum, enough to make her feel part of the busy world of outside news, and yet without it being an intrusion. She couldn't hear a word that was being said but that didn't worry her. It was all bad news. Nothing nice ever seemed to happen. It was all killing and violence and strikes. She only felt safe when she could hear music coming through and then she turned it up.

It was such a lovely morning she decided to have breakfast in the garden: the idea excited her. She bustled about laying a tray and setting up the card table and a chair in a sunny spot. Only one spot was sunny at that time of the morning, down on the right near the japonica bush, where the sun just hit their garden as it rounded the end of the terrace. She felt worried about being so far away from the shelter of the house, but the earliness of the hour consoled her. Settled there, with her tea and toast and marmalade, she lifted her face to the sun and smiled. It was all so quiet and green. Dappled was the word, the day was dappled all round her. Her tiredness after the long night lifted. She could feel the sun warm the wrinkles on her face and persuaded herself some at least were ironed out. This was all she wanted to do, just sit somewhere quiet and green and not have to bother about anything.

Rose clung desperately to her contentment as the first cloud of anxiety came up. A present for Dolores and Alan. She said the words to herself then squeezed her eyes tight in an effort to blot them out. A wedding present. It had to be faced. More shopping, more getting Stanley into a decent suit, more trailing about. And what to get? They would have everything, all young couples did these days. She and Stanley had had so little, they were glad of anything. Sheets. That was traditional – or a blanket, or crockery. Sheets would be best, but coloured or plain? Coloured, she supposed. But what colours? She jumped up and went into the house to pour another cup of tea. Quietly she said out loud, 'Now stop it, my girl, just stop it.' She knew she said it out loud. She was pleased with the firm tone she managed to adopt towards herself. It cheered her. That was the way.

Her second cup of tea in her hand, Mrs Pendlebury did a tour of the garden. It was too early to think of playing with Amy. There was no noise at all from that garden, though on the other side she could hear clattering beginning. She patrolled up and down the lawn for a while and then drew her chair into a larger patch of sun that had appeared near the raspberries. As she did so she heard a voice say, 'You're sunbathing early today.' She remained half bent, her hands still gripping the chair she had been about to set down, the back of her neck suddenly cold and clammy. Carefully, she released the chair, her free hand going up to her hair to tidy it. She almost ran back into the house, but with a great effort turned and faced the voice. Amy's mother was peeping over the wall, her long dark hair tangled in raspberry canes. As though dazed, she heard herself say, 'Yes,' and then repeat it, 'Ye-e-es.' Her alarm grew as the girl's face disappeared, though the voice continued, 'Say hello to your friend, Amy,' then back came the face with another beside it.

'Amy's here,' Amy said, wriggling in her mother's arms.

'Yes, I know, Amy's there,' Rose said, slipping into the patter easily.

'There,' Alice said, 'I told you your kind lady was there. Say good morning Mrs Pendlebury.'

'No,' Amy said and slipped from view to run shrieking round her own garden.

'You have been kind to her,' Alice said.

'That's all right,' Rose said, stiffening slightly. 'Well, I'd best get on.'

'I hope I haven't kept you back.'

Rose looked sharply at the girl. Her face was scarlet, her eyes worried.

'That's all right,' she said again. 'It's going to be another nice day.'

'Hot.'

'A bit muggy.'

'Perhaps we'll have a storm later.'

'We need the rain.'

'Well, I'd best get on.'

'And me.'

They both nodded, and drew back from the wall. Rose deliberately stayed in the garden a few minutes longer before going in. Her heart had quietened down. She had said nothing she regretted. For a moment she had thought she was being patronized but had realized her mistake in time. The girl only wanted to be friendly and she had been friendly back. There was neither need nor likelihood of it going further.

But it went further, gathering momentum with each day. Now that they knew each other it was surprising how often they met going in and out of their houses, and always they saluted each other and exchanged words. Rose felt a little awkward, partly because she did not always see Alice and Amy before they saw her and was genuinely taken aback by their greetings. Her eyes simply weren't up to recognizing new shapes in a hurry. It was because of this slowness on the uptake, which she felt might give offence, that she was careful to be enthusiastic when she did see her neighbours. She always put down her shopping basket or her milk bottle and said, 'How is Amy today?' very cheerfully. The child's babble in return delighted her. She sifted the sounds cleverly and soon came to recognize the key words so that after a month Alice was assuring her she was the only one who could understand what the child said.

The only part of this new harmony that Mrs Pendlebury didn't like was the questions. Amy couldn't phrase proper questions but in her fashion she demanded to know Mrs Pendlebury's name, where she was going, where she had been and so on. The inquiries were easily evaded, but the day was not far off, she felt, when they could not be. Then what would she say? It wasn't that she minded Amy knowing but she minded Alice. It was while she was anticipating this situation that another one arose she had not even thought about. Amy began to want to come into her house. She would strain and pull at her mother's hand, jabbing her finger at Mrs Pendlebury's door and making her meaning quite clear. Luckily, Alice was firm. 'No, you can't go in there, Mrs Pendlebury's busy,' she would say without the trace of a hint in her voice. 'Yes, well, best get on,' Mrs Pendlebury would say, but afterwards she wondered about it. Why *not* let Amy come in? Doubtless she'd be out again in a second, no harm done. But her mother might come too, and that was different.

She supposed she'd been preparing herself for it for a long time but nevertheless Mrs Pendlebury took herself by surprise when one afternoon in early October, she peered over her garden wall and interrupted Amy's screaming with 'Hey, madam, what's up with you today? I won't let you come and see me if you scream like that.' The screaming stopped. Amy came to the wall and stretched on tip-toe shouting, 'Up! Up!'

'Where's your mummy then?'

'Mummy house.'

'Go and get mummy and ask her to come out. Go get mummy, Amy.'

The child ran in shouting and soon reappeared with Alice, who was wearing an apron and rubber gloves covered with soap suds.

'I knew you'd be busy,' Mrs Pendlebury said, quickly, 'so I thought she could come over to me for a few minutes, just for a minute or two, to give you a chance. That's if she'll come.'

'Oh, she'll come all right,' Alice said, 'but — '

'Of course, if you'd rather not, if — '

'No, no – here, Amy' – and she lifted Amy on to the wall, unable to say what she wanted to say which was that such a habit once begun might prove impossible to break.

Rose enveloped Amy in her arms to lift her down from the wall. Oh, the feel of her! The small fat tummy pressed into her chest and the soft arms rubbed her neck and the tiny toes curled into her waist. She felt intoxicated and longed to bury herself in this warm flesh and smell it and luxuriate in it, but Amy was all kicks and punches, longing to be free, so she set her down, keeping only the hand in hers and even the hand thrilled her. She ran to keep up rather than let it go. Amy made straight for the back door, though she had thought of them playing in the garden, and was inside before she could be stopped.

Rose was nervous. No need to apologize to a child, of course, but she found herself saying silly things like 'It's a bit untidy' and 'It's not like your house Amy'. But Amy wasn't listening. She accepted the fact that the door into the rest of the house was closed, to Rose's relief, and then turned to all the cupboards she could see. Laughing, Rose ran round closing the ones with dangerous things inside until they came to the shoe cupboard and there she left the doors open. Amy was already half inside, pulling out shoes and slippers and shoe-horns and shoe-trees in a frenzy of exploration. When she had everything out including some boxes, she sighed and sat and looked at the mound around her and began turning over each item. Rose sat and watched her. Each time Amy showed signs of boredom, she selected something different and quietly slipped it to her. And she talked, as she hadn't talked for years.

'Shoe? Yes, that's my shoe, and what a good one it's been. I bought those shoes ten years ago Amy and they aren't done yet. I've had them mended often enough but the uppers are still good. Yes, horn – that's a horn, a shoe-horn, can't you say horn? It's for putting your shoes on properly, look, you put it behind your heel like this, see, and it slips into the shoe and Bob's your uncle. Now, what have we got in this box? Do you want to rattle it? Eh? There, a lot of old dominoes, that's what's in there. It's a game but we don't play games now. Mind that lid, it's sharp, it should have been thrown out but my husband won't throw anything out, it's hoard, hoard, hoard, till I'm sick of the sight of all his rubbish. Now you know what that is, Amy? What is it? Ball, say ball, that's right, come on, we'll go and play ball.'

They played ball till Amy got bored and Rose was exhausted with all the running and catching. They made a lot of noise as they played, each of them outdoing the other in shouts and squeals. Rose was breathless and giggling. She kept saying, 'Oh dear me,' and, 'Oh goodness,' and shook her head a lot. Her hands got scratched with all the times she had to delve among the brambles for the ball and her stockings were dirty at the knees where she'd knelt to get underneath them. When Amy lay down in the grass and began to close her eyes and suck her thumb, she was glad. Tenderly, she gathered the small hot bundle into her arms and went to the wall. 'Hello,' she called. Should she add Mrs Oram or Alice? She was relieved that neither was necessary – the girl came running out at the first sound, effusive in her gratitude, falling over herself to express it. 'That's all right,' Rose said, graciously. 'I thought it would give you a bit of a break.'

Alice could hear her singing as she went back into the house. She put Amy in her cot, trying to stifle the vague irritation she felt at Mrs Pendlebury's attitude. Why did she have to pretend that she'd had Amy over to do her a favour when it was quite obvious she'd had her over for her own pleasure and loved every minute of it? It made her cross, but then she knew she always expected other people to be as open as she was herself and that was a mistake. One must be charitable. If Mrs Pendlebury needed such an excuse then she must grant it to her. Old people, she had noticed, needed to keep their pride even more than children. She carried on washing down the kitchen walls, reflecting on the hypocrisy underlying all relationships. Except marriage. That, she decided, was the true virtue of marriage – within it there was no need for pretence or pride-saving or any other of those exhausting social practices. At least Mrs Pendlebury had Mr Pendlebury. It was the old ones who weren't married that worried Alice. She saw them everywhere in this neighbourhood, tottering about half-crippled, with nobody to talk to. At least Mrs Pendlebury had Mr Pendlebury.

At the precise moment that Alice was drawing comfort from this thought, Rose was lashing into Stanley on his return from his Club on exactly the same subject.

'I've talked more to that child this afternoon than I have in a year to you,' she shouted at him. 'You won't never discuss nothing. I say things to you and you pay no attention, there's more response from that baby. I get sick and tired of it, there now.'

The 'there now' was accompanied by a slap as she slammed down Dolores' wedding invitation.

'We've had this three weeks,' she said. 'When are you going to do something about it?'

Stanley stared at the invitation. Slowly, he reached into his inner jacket pocket and took out his spectacles but before he could put them on Rose had snatched the invitation away again.

'What do you want to read it for? You know it off by heart or should do the times you've looked at it. What I want to know is when are you going to have the courtesy to reply to it, eh?'

'I don't see there's any call to reply,' Stanley said, 'seeing as how they've been told we're coming.'

'Oh!' gasped Rose. 'Oh! Stanley Pendlebury, you're the limit. Have you never heard of ordinary good manners? Have you never heard of decency? I want that invitation replied to at once, sharp. So there.'

Stanley took his time getting envelope and ink and pen and paper. Watched by a fierce Rose, he spread it all out on the table and coughed. He knew better than to ask what he should write, but he was damned if he could find the right words. It seemed silly going all formal to his own sister. Did Rose really want him to put 'Mr and Mrs Stanley Pendlebury have great pleasure in accepting . . .' and so on? A note would do. 'Dear Elsie,' he wrote, 'Thanks for the very nice invite and of course we are glad to accept.' He signed it with a flourish and handed it to Rose. She took it disdainfully.

'I don't want to see it,' she said. 'I should hope you would know how to reply to an invitation.' But she peered at the sheet and something about it disturbed her.

'Just a minute,' she said. 'What's this?'

'Read it,' said Stanley, rather rudely.

'I can't, you know I can't, but it looks funny – what have you said? – you've put dear something, I can tell – '

'You want glasses,' Stanley said.

'I may want glasses and if I do it's my business but I don't need glasses to see that's not right.'

In the end, he did it as she wanted and took it to the post to post it at once. All that fuss. Life with Rose was one long fuss. He didn't need anyone to tell him that she didn't have enough to do, not enough of the right kind of things that is. If only they had grandchildren near, that was what she needed, somebody to do something for. Once, he'd suggested she might help out doing the tea trolley at the hospital because he'd heard somebody at the Club talking about them needing help. She'd been furious – said he'd be wanting her to go round giving bread to the poor next. All day she'd kept exclaiming, 'The very *idea*, the *very* idea,' over and over. It had puzzled him. She liked helping people, nobody was kinder, but when he paused and wondered who Rose helped he discovered to his amazement it was only himself. It disturbed him to have to admit it. He listened more carefully at the Club and was astonished at all the things Rose's counterparts seemed to do. A lot of their activities centred either on the Club or the church, which of course explained it. Rose hated clubs. Stanley knew if only he could get her down there she would love it but he'd never manage it in a month of Sundays. The church was impossible. Neither of them had ever had any truck with churches. Rose thought all parsons interfering snobs, and though he wasn't prepared to go that far he wasn't drawn to them either.

On the way back from the post-box, which was a mere two streets away, Stanley was seized with a small fit of rebellion. He wouldn't go home straight away even if it was nearly tea time and even if he had just got back from the Club. He fancied a walk. Assuring himself that he wanted and needed the exercise, he about-turned and walked in the direction of the High Street. He'd look in a few shops, might even buy something. It was nobody's fault except her own if Rose couldn't also wander off on her own to the shops. If she had glasses she'd be able to. At the thought, he had another daring idea – he would make an appointment at the optician's for Rose, then she'd have to go. With a smile of triumph he did just that. It took two minutes of decisive action. Afterwards, he stood and smirked on the doorstep of the shop and then, in the same mood of resolution, stepped out into the street not knowing what he might do next.

What he did shattered him. He walked into a travel agents and got all the particulars on going to Australia – all the leaflets on boats and aeroplanes and prices and times. They made a big bundle for his now sweating hands to carry. He kept clicking his tongue to register his admiration at his afternoon's work and was so excited that he actually went into a pub that was just opening and had a whisky. There'd be hell to pay but there was going to be hell to pay anyway. Rose wasn't against alcohol but she *was* against pubs. Too bad. He might as well be hung for a sheep as a lamb. With that comfortable platitude on his lips, Stanley sauntered home.

Chapter Six

The rain began on the twentieth of October, causing great excitement everywhere since it ended the longest dry spell for thirty-seven years. Everyone remarked they'd had a good run for their money (especially Stanley Pendlebury) and must now expect to pay for it. They paid for it. Three inches of rain fell in twenty-four hours. There were floods in Cornwall, floods in Wales, and the M4 was closed to traffic. Naturally, the temperature also dropped, first five, then ten and finally, by the end of the third day, twenty degrees. In one brief week summer had given way to winter.

The Oram family were hard hit by the transformation. Their doors and windows were closed tightly for the first time in four months and immediately they were aware of the smell – a fusty, musty, *old* smell that spoke of dirt and rot and general decay. Floorboards that had been pleasantly cool to bare feet were suddenly cold and rough. The lack of curtains mattered when the scene outside was so dreary. Eating outside, they had not realized how makeshift their kitchen arrangements were, and now they fell over boxes and bags that cluttered every available floor space. Amy cried because she could not go out and talk to Mrs Pendlebury and when in desperation Alice rushed out with her to prove there was no one there she cried all the harder. It was horrible. The roof let in on the second night and they had to put buckets under the worst leaks. In the night, Alice forgot about the buckets and tripped over then and cut her head on a nail. She sat and cried in the swamp she had created.

There began a long, depressing series of phone calls to builders. Six promised to come. None came. The family across the road gave them the name of their builder who did come, but that only made them more miserable because he rhymed off a terrifying list of all that needed doing and said, proudly, he was much too busy to tackle it. Doggedly, they kept on asking and searching until a man was found to do a temporary job. The rain stopped coming in. Thankfully, they paid sixty pounds – which brought their bank balance down to fifteen pence – and closed the door on him.

Rose Pendlebury always went crazy when the first rain of the winter cascaded through the ceiling of the top room, where the distemper was discoloured brown, but Stanley calmed her with his commonsense approach. He pointed out the damage never got any worse and it was in a room that was never used, so why worry? The time to start worrying was when the downstairs rooms were affected. That was a cue for Rose to rush and show him the big damp patches all the way round the living-room skirting-board but he explained, as he always did, that that was *rising* damp. All these houses had rising damp. Nothing could be done about it, Stanley assured her. Rose wished Frank was at home. It made Stanley irritable. Frank was handy, Stanley had never denied that, but to hear Rose talk one would have thought he was a miracle worker. He could do just as well as Frank himself but she wouldn't let him. She maintained he would fall off the ladder and other unlikely disasters. Her attitude was very useful all the same – he saw no reason to decorate: what was on the walls was perfectly all right.

The mention of Frank's prowess almost put him off wanting to go to see him at all, but then the knowledge that the actual going was such a long way off cancelled out his reluctance. He brought the matter up after breakfast on Monday morning – a silly time to choose, as he later realized. Rose was always depressed in bad weather and never more so than at ten o'clock in the morning, when a grey, dismal day with nothing to do stretched ahead. At least in the evening the edge of her gloom had been blunted and, however much she said she hated it, there was always television to look forward to. Nevertheless, he had broached the subject and must take the consequences as, by midday, he was doing.

He'd taken the brochures out of their envelope and spread them on the white tablecloth. They looked gay and exciting. He just left them there, to speak for themselves, while he finished his third cup of tea. Rose was taking dishes into the back kitchen. Every time she lifted a dish she couldn't help touching one of the leaflets but, without the glasses she was sorely in need of (and, he smiled to himself, would soon have), they meant nothing to her.

'What's all this rubbish come through the door then?' she grumbled. 'You shouldn't even look at it – straight in the dustbin, that's what I do.'

'It isn't rubbish,' Stanley said, for a starter.

'You wouldn't know the difference,' Rose scoffed. 'They can take you in with any cheap offer. It's all a con these days if only you had the wit to see it, but of course you haven't. Put them in the dustbin.'

'You might be sorry if I did that,' Stanley said, enjoying being enigmatic.

'Oh might I indeed? What's so special about this lot then?'

'I'll tell you in one word,' Stanley said, 'Australia.'

'What?'

'I've been to the travel agents. This is all the literature on Australia – how to get there, how much it would cost and all that. I thought we might go in the spring.'

'Pigs might fly,' said Rose, but it was an automatic response. She seemed quite calm as she sat down at the table and spread out all the booklets. 'Now then,' she said sternly, 'where do I start?'

It was all going so well Stanley was lulled into a false sense of security. Down he sat with her and with great patience read through all the information. The enthusiastic blurbs sounded ridiculous read out in his flat, monotonous voice – so much so that Rose laughed out loud and said he would be the death of her and wiped the corner of her eyes with the edge of her apron. Outside the rain attacked the windows like a swarm of bees, bouncing angrily against the panes, and inside Rose and Stanley sat and read about the golden sunshine of Australia. When finally he had finished, she made another pot of tea.

'This is unexpected,' said Stanley, happily.

'About time,' Rose said. 'We're in a rut. We've been in a rut ever since Frank left. We never do anything unexpected. I'm sick of it.'

'Well,' said Stanley, drooling over what was to become his fourth cup of tea in an hour, 'at our time of life.'

'And what do you mean by that?' Rose asked, crumpling a list of prices.

'Well,' said Stanley, 'when you get to seventy you should be slowing down, taking it easy.'

'When have we ever done anything else? When have we ever just got up and done what we wanted? Never, that's when. I tell you I admire these young folk just going after what they want, not getting in a rut. If I was forty years younger I'd do just what they do instead of always playing it safe. That's been our trouble – we've always gone for safety, never risked a thing.'

'We haven't done so badly,' Stanley said.

'Haven't we? You call this not doing so badly? Stuck in here like two animals, nobody caring, never seeing anybody, never doing anything?'

'We're going to Australia,' Stanley said. She was hurting his feelings and didn't seem to care, but she'd run on like this many times before and he knew it would be fatal to mention feelings. The thing to do was distract her before it got to tears.

'All right then,' she said loudly, 'when are we going? What day? How? Tomorrow?'

'Don't be silly,' Stanley said. 'You know it will all need arranging. It will take time. You can't go to Australia just like that.'

'Why not? Other people do, other people just turn up and buy their tickets and off they go, other people – '

'You need passports for a start,' shouted Stanley. Her voice was getting on his nerves. Every word she spoke was more shrill and piercing than the last. 'And maybe a visa, I'm not sure. Then there are vaccinations and health certificates – oh, there are lots of things, lots of paperwork to be done.'

She was silent. Slowly, she gathered up all the leaflets into a neat bundle, then she put her head in her hands and looked at the tablecloth. The parting in her hair showed pink as she bent over. Now that she was quiet, he regretted slapping her down. He had overdone it, forgetting that quietening her down was so much easier than cheering her up.

'I'll get cracking today,' he said. 'We'll get the forms from the post office for passports.'

'Don't bother,' she said, her voice muffled by her hands.

'We'll fill them in and get them off straight away. It's the quiet season now, we'll have them in no time.'

'Don't bother,' she said again.

'I'll do yours,' he said, consoling her, thinking it was the writing involved that worried her.

'There's no point,' she said. 'They aren't likely to give me a passport, not in my state of health.'

'Don't be foolish, Rose – anybody can get a passport, anybody at all. They can't refuse you.'

'Health certificate then, I'll never get that.'

'I'm not sure you need one, I'm not sure *what's* needed, I told you.'

'Stands to reason there'll be some health check and that'll be that.'

'But you're in good health. You always have been.'

'Little you know, just because I don't go on about what's wrong with me like some people I could mention.'

'I'm the one more than likely not to get through a medical.'

'That's what you think.'

'Anyway, it's for the doctor to decide.'

'I'm not going to any doctor.'

'Now you're just being awkward. You've been to a doctor before.'

'And I'm not going again. He didn't know who I was last time, just a name and number that's all I was and he couldn't care less.'

'He's a good doctor, that Dr Thompson. He's done a lot for me. I find him very pleasant.'

'Tell me who you *don't* find pleasant. You find everyone pleasant, can't see farther than the end of your nose.'

'No harm in that that I know of,' said Stanley, with dignity.

She was rushing around now, grabbing the cloth from the table and shaking it into the fireplace. 'Steady on,' he said, 'you'll have us up in flames if you don't watch out with that cloth.'

'That wouldn't be a bad thing as far as I'm concerned.'

'Speak for yourself,' Stanley said, trying to humour her, but she wouldn't be humoured. It would be black looks and black words all day now. He sighed, and sighed again.

'What you huffing and puffing for?' she snapped at him. 'What have you got to worry about? You lead the life of Riley as far as I can see.'

He left the kitchen and wandered into the sitting-room where it was cold and dark. He sat in an armchair all morning looking at the wallpaper and listening to Rose hurling chairs and tables about as she pushed the Hoover from one end of the house to another. She never spared herself. When she hoovered, every bit of furniture was pulled away from the walls and she shaved the skirting boards so close that there was a mark all the way round. The whine of the machine gave him a headache but there was no question of lodging a complaint. What made him cross, though, wasn't the Hoover – he'd sat quite happily through Rose hoovering before – but the way he'd brought all this on his own head. He'd always believed, all his life, in letting things take their course. There were too many hustlers in this world. If a lot more people would be content to let things take their course, everyone would be a lot better off. Now he'd broken his own code he could expect instant retribution. This damned Australian thing would cause nothing but bother. Rose hadn't even started on the subject. She would alternately pick it up and worry it like a dog, or throw it away all winter long. If only she didn't have so much energy to waste, that was the trouble. There was so much violence in her, all squashed down, only coming over the edge of the pot every now and again, making ugly spill marks when it did. He wished the telly would start – what a godsend. In fact, he told himself, there might be no harm in just switching it on now in case there was an interesting schools programme.

When the screen remained blank, Stanley didn't at first worry. The socket was faulty, he knew that. The wiring in the house was old – a deathtrap Frank had called it when he put in the plugs, much too rotten for him to contemplate anything ambitious.

Rose was always on at him to do something about it, but electricians were hard to come by. Stanley confidently expected one to come his way sometime or other, but so far none had. Meanwhile, they observed a few elementary precautions and nothing had gone drastically wrong. He knew how to mend a fuse, which was all he had ever been called upon to do. They had few electric appliances, except for the fires which Stanley blessed as frequently as Rose cursed. Frank had warned them never to have more than two fires on at once because the circuit wouldn't stand it and, if possible, not more than one bar on the kitchen fire if two bars were on in the sitting-room. He sometimes reminded them of this in his letters and said how it worried him and that he'd be glad to pay to have the whole place rewired – but they wouldn't dream of it. They never forgot to turn one fire off if the other was on, never. It had become a religion with both of them and they meticulously observed all the rites.

The socket, however, might not be the trouble this time. Stanley began to worry. The set was old and it wasn't rented – Frank had bought it for them several years back. It had just arrived from the shop one Christmas Eve, the best Christmas present they'd ever had. But it wasn't rented and servicing had proved difficult and costly. They'd had a new tube two years ago which had entailed a lot of to-ing and fro-ing with the shop. Stanley was still exhausted at the memory. Surely the tube hadn't gone again? Rose swore he never had it off, but that wasn't true and, even if it had been, a tube only two years old ought to have been able to stand up to a bit of pressure.

The thing to do was check the socket. As Stanley unplugged a lamp to test it with, he noticed the fire was off. He'd had it on, he knew that, just one bar but the warmth had been the one comforting thing of the morning. Slowly, he plugged the lamp back into the socket he'd just taken it from and put it on. No light. With some excitement he shuffled over to the main switch and pressed. No light there either. At the same time he heard Rose cursing and shouting that there was something wrong with the Hoover. She came bursting in while he stood with his hand still on the light switch.

'Get yourself up out of that chair,' she said, even though he was standing up, 'there's work to be done, damned Hoover's gone west – it's been threatening to go wrong for months. Go on, get your tools, I'm only half-way through the house and it's the wedding tomorrow.'

'What's the wedding got to do with it? It isn't in our house, it's nothing to do with us.'

'We're going, aren't we? Or so I understood – and if we're going to be out all day who'll finish the hoovering? Anyway, never mind the wedding, just get on with it.'

'Hold on a minute.'

'No I will not – what's your excuse this time with your hold-ons?'

'I may not be able to mend that Hoover.'

'You can at least try.'

'It isn't a matter of trying. The light's gone too, and the television and the fire.'

'Oh God, that's it, we're sunk. Well, Frank told you, he's been telling you for years – the house needs rewiring, that's what.'

'Now wait a minute. It may just be a fuse. I'll have to look.'

She held the ladder for him while he climbed up and looked at the fuse box which, like everything else in their house, was inconveniently situated – above the front door. It took him half an hour to go through all the fuses, and that wasn't counting the ages he spent having a rest at the bottom of the ladder, coughing and spluttering and generally wasting time. She wanted to pick him up and shake him, she was so angry.

'Well?' she said, rattling the ladder.

'Hey, steady on,' Stanley said, not yet properly down, 'you'll have me breaking a leg next.'

'What's up?'

'Nothing. I can't work it out at all. None of the fuses have gone, everything seems fine.'

'You don't know what to look for more than likely. If Frank was here he'd – '

'He'd say what I say,' Stanley said, sharply. 'There's nothing wrong with the fuses. I can't understand it.'

'What are we going to do then?'

'I'll have to think about that.'

He sat and thought while Rose got out a small hard brush and dustpan and went through the house on her hands and knees scratching away like a badger in its hole. She said there was no time to waste, no point in hanging about, she knew they'd had it. Stanley tried not to be irritated by her almost joyful assumption that there would never be any electricity in the house again, but he resented her attitude and showed it by replying to none of the silly questions she threw at him from time to time. Gradually, he came to the conclusion that he would have to get an electrician. He recalled a notice on the newsagent's board – which he spent many hours looking at – advertising electrical work done in the evenings. He would go and look at it and ring up.

'Just popping out a jiffy,' he called to Rose. Her red face appeared over the banisters instantly.

'Where are you going?'

'Just popping out to see about getting an electrician.'

'Leaving me like this? In this state? Without a light or a fire.'

'But it isn't dark,' Stanley said.

'I don't care. I'm not being left like this. I'm coming with you.'

'But I won't be a minute,' Stanley said. He didn't want Rose with him, watching him copy a number off a board. Her opinion of such methods was well known to him. 'You'd best stay in,' he said, as soothingly as possible. 'It's pouring with rain and you'd just get soaked. No sense in two of us getting wet now is there?'

But she came with him. He stood miserably in the hall, his raincoat buttoned up to his neck and his cap pulled well down on his forehead, staring at his shoes, while Rose changed her skirt and got ready. She would never so much as step to the end of the street in a skirt that she had been working in. Even if she was staying at home and not intending to go anywhere there were morning clothes and afternoon clothes. When she came down the stairs he would see no difference, but then the two sets had always been indistinguishable to him. On went her poplin mac and over that a Pac-a-mac, and a rain-square over her head and finally she was ready. At that precise moment, when Stanley opened the front door knowing there was no reprieve, the lights went on.

'Well now,' said Stanley, smiling, as though he had engineered it. 'What do you think of that?'

Rose squinted up at the hall light. It flickered. She looked accusingly at Stanley, who was already unbuttoning his raincoat.

'What are you doing?' she said.

'What do you think I'm doing?' Stanley said, relief making him rude. 'I'm not going to sit down for my lunch in my raincoat, now am I?'

'You're not going to sit down at all,' said Rose, 'not if you don't carry out your intention and get that electrician.'

'There's no need now,' said Stanley, firmly, his raincoat off. It crossed Rose's mind that there was an example of him being nimble enough with his fingers when he liked. How long had it taken him to button those twelve buttons up and how long to unbutton them, that's what she wanted to know.

'How do you know it won't happen again?' she said. 'That was a warning, that was, and if you pay no attention you might not get another. Next time it'll be the dead of night and then what will you do?'

'I'll be asleep,' Stanley said. 'I won't know anything about it.'

'It'll worry me to death,' Rose said, 'not knowing when it's going to happen again or why.'

'It was your Hoover,' Stanley said.

'I beg your pardon?'

'It was your Hoover, you had it running too long when there was a fire on as well.'

'Who had the fire on? You had it on, sitting twiddling your thumbs at eleven o'clock in the morning instead of working to keep yourself warm. There should be no call for fires at eleven in the morning, so there.'

'Anyway it was that Hoover of yours did it.'

'Since when was the Hoover mine? It's yours too.'

'I never use it.'

'More's the pity. But you dirty the rooms that it cleans – oh yes, that's different. I suppose I'm only cleaning up my dirt, am I? Oh yes.'

'There isn't any dirt. You just wear the carpets *and* yourself out with that thing.'

'It's you wears me out, never doing anything that should be done. This damned house is falling about our ears and you don't do a damned thing.'

Then she burst into tears. Her Pac-a-mac scrunched and creaked as she sat down on the bottom set of stairs and cried, funny little gasping sobs. She shook her head from side to side and screwed up her nose and beat the air with her fists until an outsider would have been unable to tell whether she was laughing or crying. Stanley was appalled. He promptly sat down beside her and tried to put his arm round her, but she pushed him away, with a strength that amazed him and he toppled to the floor. Getting up his back hurt and he knew he would have to go to the doctor's the next day. At the sight of him clutching his back Rose's sobs redoubled and she covered her face completely with her hands.

'Come on now, old girl,' Stanley said, 'it's not that bad. I'll go and get that electrician chap all the same if it'll make you happy. Come on, up you get, you sound like a packet of crisps in that coat.'

He coaxed her up and out of her clothes and as he had hoped her position as housewife soon made her feel called to her duty and she was in the kitchen getting the lunch in no time, doing a lot of nose-blowing but otherwise all right. Nothing more was said about him going out. Daringly, he took a chance and sat down at the table after putting her radio on nice and low and laying a new cloth. He was remembering times when she had often had spells like this – times so long ago that he had been quite shocked at their recurrence. It had all been Women's Troubles then, which he didn't know much about and had kept well away from finding out. She'd been given to regular bursts of weeping and bad temper for a week at a time every month, and then there had been a couple of years once when the bouts never seemed to stop, just run in to each other. He'd tried mentioning doctors but of course she wouldn't hear of it. Said there was nothing the matter with her, it was just Nature. Stanley had been more than satisfied with that answer, as it had fitted in with his own diagnosis. Was it now Nature again but, if so, what aspect and, if not, was she sickening for a cold or flu?

All speculation was driven from Stanley's head by lunch and the news. He praised the warmed-up steak and kidney to the skies and Rose's sniffs grew less frequent. Food was such a comfort. He thanked God they both liked their food and that Rose was a good cook. Just sitting down with everything on the table nice and a steaming dish between them gave him such a good feeling. He knew Rose felt the same. She often sang or hummed as she got up afterwards and was always in a better mood.

They listened to the news, as they always did, in complete silence. Some of these new announcers didn't read the news as they had been used to having it read, but they couldn't rob the event of its sacred quality. It was Rose who picked up the vital information first about the strike. The power workers were going on strike. Negotiations had broken down. As an example of what would happen they had already shut down for an hour this morning. Industry had ground to a stop and domestic users in most regions had had cuts lasting up to two hours.

'Well I'm blowed,' Stanley said. 'So it wasn't our electricity. Well I'm damned. I would have looked funny going for an electrician.'

'No excuse,' Rose said, but absent-mindedly. 'We're all electric,' she went on, 'light, fires, the lot.'

'And the television,' Stanley said.

'That'll be a blessing,' Rose said, 'being warm's more important than telly. What will we do?'

'It may never happen,' Stanley said. 'We've had enough for one morning without worrying about that.'

Rose let him off, but her post-lunch glow gave way to a new and deeper misery.

Chapter Seven

The wedding could not have taken place in worse weather. It rained torrentially the entire day and no amount of pretence could have disguised that. Rose, drawing the curtains on another grey sodden garden, felt sorry for Elsie. The awfulness of the weather quite removed the tiny splinters of jealousy that had been pricking her ever since the invitation came. It wasn't even soft summer rain, that the sentimental could call romantic and claim made all the green seem translucent, but hard, driving stuff that almost seemed sleet. It was cold, too, shivering cold for those who had not yet donned their winter woollies, not at all the climate for thin wedding dresses. Rose was glad she had chosen a costume after all.

Stanley had booked a mini-cab to take them to the church, after a good deal of hesitation. He had expected to have a car sent but as the day drew nearer and they were not informed of any car coming, other arrangements had to be made. He was still convinced a car might have come, but Rose was adamant that it wouldn't. They didn't rate a car, she said. They weren't good enough. Stanley thought that was nonsense and was all for asking Elsie straight out if they were to be conveyed to the church or not, but Rose wouldn't allow it. By chance – a most remote chance – it was Rose who answered the telephone when Elsie rang the night before and he could hear how gratified she was to be able to say they had a car booked, thank you very much, and had never expected one being sent for them. That Elsie had been apologetic was a source of great pleasure to Rose. She went on and on about it all night in a way Stanley found distasteful, but he said nothing.

They were ready by eleven – the wedding was at midday – and the cab was booked for eleven-thirty. Rose, of course, had fretted about whether that was early enough but even she had to admit that, with the church only ten minutes' drive away, allowing half an hour was ample. If the worst came to the worst, they could even hop on a bus. It was Stanley's opinion that they could have hopped on one anyway, but he had had more sense than to say so. Now, watching the rain, his restraint was rewarded. They would have been like drowned rats walking two yards.

'Well I must say we look very smart, the pair of us,' said Stanley, as they waited.

'Speak for yourself,' sniffed Rose, but smiled.

'I am. All dressed up and somewhere to go. I like that.'

A flicker of lines appeared across Rose's forehead but she controlled them and sent them scudding away, contenting herself with, 'Yes, well, that's been up to you, hasn't it. It's what I've been saying, we've become stick-in-the-muds. Another few years and we won't even be going to weddings like as not – that's if there are any left to go to.'

'I'd always go to a wedding,' Stanley said, 'or a party.'

Rose laughed, quite good-naturedly. 'When did you last go to a party?'

'Christmas.'

'Christmas? Where for goodness sake?'

'The Club.'

'Oh, *that*. I thought you meant a proper party.'

'It was a proper party. We had good food, good entertainment and good – well – good company.' He felt guilty about that last bit. What a way to start off such a promising day. 'I'm looking forward to this do,' he said quickly. 'I can tell I'm going to enjoy myself.'

'No doubt,' said Rose, a little grimly. 'Just don't overdo it that's all. You may be seeing yourself home. I don't know that I shall be staying that long.'

Stanley didn't take her up on that because he knew perfectly well it was more likely to be the other way round. There was all this agonizing over going and then once there she was the life and soul. Rose was transformed in company. Thinking about it he realized what a very long time it was since he'd seen that happy transformation, and he looked forward to it all the more. She was looking nicer than she'd done for ages, but at the same time as he saw that he also saw how much nicer she could have looked if she hadn't put all that stuff on her face. Her hair didn't matter – it was hidden by her hat – but her face was unfortunate. It looked as though she'd dipped it in a flour bin. He had a feeling that the box of face-powder she kept in a drawer for special occasions had gone mouldy through lack of use – either that or the powder-puff had gone matted. There was no question of putting her straight, it would upset her dreadfully, nor could he mention the brilliant red of the lipstick she had seen fit to use for the first time. Veronica had sent it. At the time, Rose had exclaimed at the silliness of such a present, but he had noticed how carefully she put it away, and had known really she was flattered.

The mini-cab didn't come at eleven-thirty. At eleven-thirty-two precisely Stanley was made to ring them. They said the cab was on its way. When it still hadn't come at eleven-forty and Rose was threatening to take her finery off and go to bed, Stanley rang them again of his own accord. They couldn't understand what had happened, presented their apologies and said they would send another. Not knowing the ways of mini-cab firms Stanley was reassured, but Rose not at all so. She staggered him by snatching the telephone directory and hurling it at him with instructions to find a taxi-rank number and she'd ring them herself. They were still arguing over this when the cab arrived and the commotion began. Things they'd been sitting ready with had now disappeared – gloves, umbrella, bag – and had to be gathered up again. Rose shrieked at Stanley and Stanley went into long explanations to the driver about the mix-up. They departed in the worst possible style.

The church soothed Rose's nerves in spite of the fact that she had never liked churches. She never felt comfortable in them. They seemed full of snooty people looking down at you with posh accents and smart clothes and, if they weren't, then they didn't seem churches. The singing had always appealed to her but that was about all. The rest was mumbo-jumbo, either stories or lectures or endless prayers that bored and irritated her. Religion itself had by-passed her, though she was a baptized and confirmed Christian. She supposed she believed in God but to ask herself whether she did was too embarrassing. If anyone else asked her she was furious at their impertinence.

She and Stanley were seated four rows from the front which Rose found satisfactory. Elsie turned and nodded and smiled at them as the usher showed them to their place, which was thoughtful of her, Rose thought, considering how much she must have on her mind. She didn't recognize the couple on either side of them but that didn't matter. It was a wedding. Everyone was very friendly. Rose sat and admired the flowers and the way the little light there was outside managed to come through the stained glass as though it were sunshine. Only the noise of the rain on the roof told a different tale. Here, inside, it was sheltered and calm and everywhere you looked you saw something pretty. Rose looked cautiously, without craning her neck. She didn't want to make an exhibition of herself.

Dolores was fifteen minutes late, which Rose thought over-doing it. Five minutes, perhaps, though two was enough, but fifteen was showing off. Her poor mother was wringing her hands in anguish and the bridegroom looked about to faint with standing so stiff and still for so long. It made the opening chord of the Wedding March all the more thrilling of course – it caused a positive sensation. Rose had been determined not to turn round but such was the drama of the moment she found herself auto-matically wheeling round. The first thing she noticed was how flushed the girl was, as though she'd run all the way. Not the manner in which to arrive at the altar Rose thought and pursed her lips. She wouldn't look round again, nor did she, but the white, airy presence of her niece made her tremble as she wafted past. She felt intoxicated with her lightness and sweetness and the tears that gathered in her eyes were for the beauty of it, a beauty she herself had always found unobtainable. She had never, she was sure, and sad to be sure, gathered to herself such a beauty. She had never been blessed. She half turned to Stanley to beseech him to tell her if she had but, before she could even try to communicate what she felt, which she knew an instant later was impossible anyway, she saw that he was totally absorbed in un-wrapping a barley sugar and putting it in his mouth.

The rest of the service and all the business afterwards of sign-ing registers and what-have-you passed Rose by. She felt about to burst with suppressed feeling. There were things she wanted to say and do that crammed her senses with aches. All her features hurt – her lips were painful, her head throbbed, her eyes burned. She looked about her wildly and they were all so placid and relaxed and unmoved. Some cried – Elsie cried – but what were tears compared to how she felt? The pressure inside her made her feel quite faint and she was glad of the long sit. It gave her time to compose herself and behave as she knew she ought.

Elsie, Stanley's sister, had her under close scrutiny. That was the point of weddings for Elsie. It gave her a chance to gather together all the far-flung members of the family and put them under observation in a confined space – not that Stanley and Rose were exactly far-flung but they might as well have been for all they saw of them. Once upon a time, they used to have supper at Stanley's every Friday night and then Stanley and Rose would come for tea every Sunday, but the arrangement had fallen by the wayside. Perhaps that wasn't quite what had happened; perhaps they had cancelled a couple of Fridays and a Sunday or two and Rose had taken umbrage. Elsie couldn't remember, but it seemed more than likely. Rose was forever taking umbrage. Ever since Stanley had brought her home – a half-starved waif of a thing – she'd been taking umbrage and he'd been defending her. Elsie, though she was only ten at the time, could well remember how he had told them all before he brought her that she was very sensitive and they'd soon see why. Well, she had certainly proved sensitive but none of them had ever been able to fathom why. As another sister of Stanley's said, she had two eyes, a nose, was sound in wind and limb, if a bit on the frail side, and had a tongue in her head, so why should she be so touchy? Stanley had replied they'd understand in time – but they never came any nearer to doing so.

Watching Rose at the reception, as she did in between watching everyone else, Elsie thought how tragedy was stamped on Rose's face. It annoyed her. What had she to be so tragic about? Stanley had worked hard to give her a good home and an easy life. She'd never wanted for anything even when times were tough. There was the business of Ellen but that was so long ago, and then Frank leaving them on their own was bad luck, but a regular enough occurrence in lots of families. Of course, Rose took everything to heart. It was wrong to offend her when she brooded on slights the way she did. Elsie had tried to jolly her out of taking offence many a time but it was never any good. She shut up like a clam. Only Stanley knew her mind. They were a devoted couple, you had to admit that, but Elsie had a hunch that if that was devotion she didn't want it. Togetherness, in her opinion, could be carried too far, especially among married couples.

At least today the pair weren't together for long. Elsie saw one of her brothers go up and ask Rose to dance after the meal and to her surprise Rose agreed, and then as they waltzed round Elsie remembered what a good dancer Rose used to be. She groped in her memory but the details of a picture she was looking for had gone. All she could recall was Rose in red chiffon dancing with someone she'd forgotten, in a dim sort of place, and everyone stopping to watch and clapping – yes, she was sure, standing round and applauding. Elsie blinked at her sudden vision. Rose's legs were the only things that hadn't changed. Instinctively Elsie drew her own fat calves under the tablecloth as she concentrated on Rose's neat ankles and slender legs. Lovely legs, covered now in support stockings, but doing the Charleston how they'd flashed and twirled.

Stanley didn't dance. He'd met Rose at a dance but he never danced. Couldn't get the beat in his head and he was so slow partnering him was agony. Elsie could well remember the hours and hours she'd spent going round the living-room with him, turning him round forcibly when they reached the end. He was hopeless. It was hard, she thought, for any young man today to realize how important dancing had been in his position in the twenties and thirties. If you couldn't dance, you were a social outcast. Perhaps that was a bit strong. Stanley certainly hadn't been cast out of anywhere, but then he made up for his clumsiness with his nice manners. Girls liked him because he was reliable and nice and didn't take advantage. They made the mistake of thinking he was shy and he encouraged them, enjoying the sensation of being put at his ease. But had Rose done that? Elsie couldn't imagine it, Rose was a bundle of nerves, brittle as thin toffee, she couldn't put anyone at their ease.

When Rose was sitting down after three dances on the trot, quite red in the face, gasping and laughing and fanning herself, Elsie took her over a drink and sat beside her.

'Here,' she said, 'you need a drink after that.'

'Ooh, I should think I do,' Rose said. 'Thank you, Elsie, what is it?'

'It's a wedding,' Elsie said smartly, 'so never you mind – just drink it.'

Rose drank the gin and tonic and smacked her lips. 'Very nice,' she said, 'very refreshing.'

'You haven't lost the old skill,' Elsie said.

'Oh I don't know about that,' Rose said,'I'm out of practice.'

'You should take it up again.'

'What, at my age?'

'Why not? You enjoy it, you know you do.'

'Oh, I don't know. I wouldn't have the energy.'

'Course you would. If I can start something new, you can pick up something old.'

'What have you started?'

'Cookery classes, and pottery.'

'What kind of classes?' Rose asked, astounded. Elsie could not be imagined going to school.

'At the Institute, in the evenings.'

'But you can cook anyway, you've always been a good cook, and whatever do you want with making pottery?'

'I know I can cook but I'm sick to death of all the things I can make. I want to learn new things and I haven't the patience to learn it from books. And I've always fancied doing pottery – you know, with a proper wheel and clay and all that. You should see me having a go – scream, you'd die!'

Rose was silent. She simply couldn't see how Elsie had brought herself to do such an enterprising thing. Elsie was stupid, always had been, and she'd no initiative at all. But out she'd gone –

'... sick and tired of sticking in every evening with George messing about tinkering with his car or Alan's car or somebody's car and that telly driving me mad, and I thought, how can I get out, what can I do? And thinking about Dolores going and not even having her coming in and out – actually it was Dolores put me on to it. She was going to cookery herself, though I could have taught her the things she needed to know at her stage but she said she couldn't so much as learn how to tie a knot from me, so anyway I went and I liked it and there you are. There's a lovely crowd goes, young and old, and we have a grand time ...'

They always, Rose reflected, went on about these grand times. Stanley was the same about his wretched club. They were like children with their gangs, trying to make you feel out of it if you didn't belong then, when you did, you had to get in on the act and conceal the emptiness there. But still, Elsie was learning something whereas Stanley was just playing. She would like to learn something, but what? Art, she'd always liked art, but she couldn't draw – though that was the point, you went to learn what you didn't know – but her fingers were too stiff, surely?

Rose flexed them and looked at them critically. A foreign language – French – she'd always longed to understand French: not speak it, just understand it.

All afternoon and evening while the reception went on Rose's glance kept straying to Elsie, disbelieving. As she danced and sang and had several gins and tonic it seemed to her that her life was going to be full of conversations in French and pretty pictures on the wall. When they went back to Elsie's house later on, the first thing she saw among the litter of wedding presents was a small blue jug with a card propped up against it saying 'For Dolores and Alan my first pot from your potty mum.' Rose stood and looked at it for ages. She asked Elsie if she could pick it up if she was very careful, and Elsie giggled and said it was only a joke, and her real present was a dinner service. Rose picked it up. It was heavy and a little squat. The handle had a bump in it and the lip would never pour milk smoothly. The glaze was too thin and had cracked in several places, but it was a real jug, not just an ornament. Rose forgot her lifelong antipathy to her sister-in-law. She made a point of congratulating her very loudly and dragged a befuddled Stanley over to look. When he made jokes about it she became quite upset and insisted that his admiration should be unstinting. It was fortunate that it was impossible to embarrass Stanley.

Somebody they didn't know took them home at midnight. They were profuse in their thanks. Rose stood quite calmly and happily while Stanley went through the normally maddening routine of fiddling for his key. She didn't care how long they took to get in. There was nothing, for a change, that she wanted to be inside for. The world at large was not such an unfriendly jungle. It might contain things worth discovering. She didn't feel the urge to bury herself in her home and never go outside again. Once inside, she was in no hurry to go to bed either, though Stanley said he was dropping. Instead, she put the kettle on and the little lamp above the fireplace that gave such a nice glow. Stanley put the centre light on too, but she told him to put it off at once. He was an expert at destroying atmosphere. She made some tea and took it through to him. 'There now,' she said, 'a nice cup of tea to round things off.'

'Could have done with some of this hours ago,' Stanley said, rather gloomily. 'One thing they were short of, spoiling the ship for a halfpennyworth of tar in my opinion.'

'Nonsense,' Rose said, briskly, 'it didn't spoil nothing. A very nice wedding, very nice. I shall write and tell your Elsie so.'

'Why?' said Stanley.

'Because it shows appreciation and that's what this world is short of these days. Thanks where thanks are due – you should try it some time.'

'I thanked her already,' Stanley said. 'No call to overdo it.'

'It's tomorrow when it's all over that the thanks will be appreciated – and the effort. It takes *effort* to write and thank somebody, easy enough to *say* thank you but writing is effort.'

'Oh, all right,' Stanley said crossly. 'You've made your point. Well, I'm off.'

'Good night,' Rose said, settling back into her chair.

'Aren't you coming?'

'No.'

'I don't know,' Stanley said, sighing, and sitting down again himself. 'I'm dropping.'

'Go to bed then – I'm not stopping you.'

'You'll just wake me up when you come.'

'What wicked lies, Stanley Pendlebury – I've never in my life woken you up and you know it.'

'I can't understand why you want to stay up anyway – it's nearly one in the morning. What's up?'

'Nothing's up.'

'I would have thought you'd be exhausted the way you were carrying on.'

'I *beg* your pardon!'

'All that cavorting around at your age, it wasn't decent.'

Rose turned towards him, her brow creasing into frightening furrows of such depth and strength that her skin might have been corrugated iron.

'I shall treat that spiteful remark with the contempt it deserves,' she said, very grandly, and then added, triumphantly, 'thank goodness I can still recognize jealousy when I see it.'

'Don't talk ridiculous,' Stanley said, but feebly. He was

already stricken with remorse and only glad that Rose had taken it the way she had.

'You never could dance, or even cavort,' Rose said.

'I think I'll go to bed,' Stanley said. 'Try not to wake me up.'

Rose sat and listened to him shuffling off. Such an age he seemed to take with all his pottering about – so many doors to bang, so many boards creaking under his weight, though that was little enough. She wanted the house to herself. At last, all the noises stopped. Stanley coughed a couple of times, and then all was still. The electric fire made a strange noise, it needed seeing to, but she wasn't going to spoil things by that train of thought. Tomorrow was going to bring a new era. She was going to be determined, take life by the scruff of the neck and shake it, instead of sitting in terror. She felt quite relaxed, but resolute.

But next morning Rose could not even get out of bed. The minute she woke, she knew something was the matter. Even lying quite still, the room swam before her eyes. When she tried to lift her head from the pillow, a pain shot up her neck and she had to let it fall back again. She pressed her lips together with anger and tried to lift her legs, but they were dead weights. Closing her eyes, she concentrated on getting control of herself. Still with them closed, she sat up and swung her legs round till her feet were on the floor. The pains everywhere were dreadful, and as she levered herself onto her feet nausea overwhelmed her. Desperate, she clung to the back of the chair at the bedside and heaved herself up. Groaning she staggered across the floor and made her way all the way down the stairs to the toilet. There, she was sick. Being sick jarred her everywhere but she felt a little better, well enough to make some tea, and sit beside the fire. She sat crouched over it, miserable but scolding herself into holding on, and the thin red bar gave her some comfort – for a few minutes. Then it faded to gritty grey. Rose closed her eyes in despair. The damn fire now – everything was going wrong. Even as she thought that she remembered about the last scare, and switched the radio on. The eight o'clock news summary was just beginning. Strikes. The power workers were on strike in earnest. There would be cuts everywhere of up to six hours. Electricity would be rationed, domestic – she switched off.

Back in bed, Rose thought how nice it would be to die, quietly, without any fuss. Perhaps if she lay still enough death would claim her, but when, after another hour, her brain still seethed with rage at the power workers, she gave up all thoughts of a peaceful death. She wasn't the dying sort. She was too busy. Death would need a sledge-hammer to knock her out. Stanley, still snoring across the way, was a more likely candidate for a quiet end. The fact that he was still sleeping so very soundly drove her mad. Here she was, ill, in need of care and attention, and all he did was sleep. But he was better asleep. She'd rather lie here neglected without a bite to eat or a drop to drink for days if necessary than have Stanley acting as nurse. She knew what would happen. This combination of rheumatism and flu had attacked her before. It would take her a week to get over it, a week of messy, unappetising meals on trays, of Stanley moping about getting everything in a state including himself, moaning on at her about getting the doctor she refused to have. She didn't want him to wake up.

It all happened as Rose had known it would. She lay in bed most of the first week of November while Stanley tried to cope. The only thing she hadn't foreseen was that there would be even the faintest ray of sunshine, but there was. The rain still poured down, but the black gloom of it was lifted by the kindness of Alice Oram.

How she got to know, Rose was not certain, but suspected that Stanley, though under strict instructions to do no such thing, had gone and told the girl of his wife's illness. Probably he had laid it on with a trowel. He must have, for the bunch of grapes he landed in with the second day was enormous. She was angry and embarrassed, but the accompanying card slightly allayed her worry. It was prettily decorated with hand-drawn pictures of flowers and said 'To help Mrs Pen get better with love from Amy who misses her very much'. Nonsense, of course. Just a way of speaking. Amy didn't miss her – she wasn't old enough to miss people – certainly not people so removed from her – but it was a nice thought.

More nice thoughts followed. Some flowers were delivered on

the third day – anemones, only a few, but so attractively arranged in a blue jug that reminded her of Elsie's. She would have to return that, which might lead to complications, but she felt too awful to foresee them. Then, on the fourth day, Stanley appeared with some magazines which he announced he'd told the young lady she wouldn't be interested in. This so annoyed Rose that in spite of a horrible headache she sat up in bed and deliberately made an effort to read them. They were lovely magazines – *Country Life* and *The Field* and *The Geographical Magazine*. She thoroughly enjoyed them and made a point of telling Stanley so at repeated intervals. On the fifth day she assured herself enough was enough. Nobody could keep this sort of thing up indefinitely – in fact, she hoped they didn't. She was already overwhelmed. But promptly at eleven o'clock in the morning the doorbell rang and she heard Stanley, after the usual inexplicably long interval, answer it. She lay waiting, a feeling of excitement warming her as none of the hot water bottles tucked round her had managed to do.

He trudged in – why did he have to shuffle about like that? – a little later carrying a small packet.

'I don't know what this is,' he said, 'but it rattles. Shall I open it for you?'

'No,' Rose snapped, 'you're too clumsy. You'd harm what's inside more than likely. Give it here. I can manage to untie a parcel I should hope.'

She had, though, quite a struggle doing just that. The red ribbon was so cunningly tied and the gold paper securely Sellotaped. She felt tired when at last she had all the wrappings off. Inside was a box, an ordinary white cardboard box. She opened it, wishing Stanley would go away, but he stood and stared foolishly at what was inside.

'Funny sort of present,' he said at last. 'What's she given you shells for? Seems silly.'

'It isn't silly at all,' Rose said, 'they're beautiful – look at that one. Have you ever seen anything like it?'

'Plenty,' Stanley said, 'the beaches are covered with them.'

'But we aren't on a beach, that's the point,' Rose said.

'Seems funny to me.'

'Oh, you've got no imagination, go away.'

Rose lay and looked at the shells for a long time. Nobody had ever honoured her by assuming she had any imagination. Without putting it into words, she was proud to have been given such a present. How had that girl known, on such a slim acquaintanceship, that she wouldn't throw shells in the dustbin and think them silly? It was extraordinary. She huddled down under the blankets and thought about it. It was almost, she felt, as though she was being courted, such was the care and love – yes, it was not out of place, that was what she felt it was – the love with which these gifts had been chosen. Even the grapes hadn't been just grapes shoved in a paper bag or enveloped in scruffy tissue paper. Each one had looked clean and firm and the cluster hadn't been broken. They had been handpicked, none of your I'll-have-a-pound-of-those-how-much. It was strange to be the recipient of all this thought. She hoped Alice Oram hadn't felt she had to pay back all those trifles she had given Amy – that would be absurd. Stanley had suggested as much but withdrawn the suggestion when he saw how much it upset her. It couldn't be true. She consoled herself with the thought that the girl couldn't have gone on giving her things, not to that extent, if she had been prompted merely by a sense of justice.

When she was up and feeling stronger, if not actually well, Rose carefully put away all her gifts with the little cards that had come with them. She ate the grapes, of course, but pressed the flowers before they died. She had drawers full of those kind of mementoes going back years and years. There were very few things there that Stanley had given her, but then he did not bother with presents. That was the operative word – bother. Stanley was opposed to all bother and could not understand that present-giving could ever be a pleasure.

Frank had been better, but not much. Most of her mementoes were things like Dolores' wedding invitation and the ribbon from her bouquet that she had given her. And the little blue jug. Elsie had insisted and so had Dolores and Alan. She must have it. Dolores swore she would only throw it out anyway – she liked china jugs, not pot ones. They had compromised on Rose keeping it for her, until such time as she would claim it.

Rose was left with the other jug, that the flowers had come in. When everything else was put away, she washed the jug with great care and dried it and put it high up in her kitchen cupboard where Stanley couldn't knock it over. She didn't know what would happen. She was too weak to think straight. Would it be claimed? Or would she take it back? It would have to be decided, she told herself, together with a lot of other things.

Chapter Eight

The minute Rose felt her old self, which took another couple of weeks, she started on the Christmas pudding. Every year she sent Frank a pudding, the real traditional sort that he loved. By rights, she should have made it in October but Dolores' wedding had mucked all her plans up. Most of the summer seemed to have been dominated by Dolores' wedding, what with the buying of the present and the choosing of the outfit and – well – in general. So it was now nearly the last week in November and no pudding. It would have to be done at once and parcelled up and, if necessary, sent at vast expense by air. Stanley would have to see that this was done, for she would immediately move on to Christmas presents proper.

The day she made the pudding she got up bright and early and put the oven on to warm the kitchen. She thanked God the strike had proved a three day affair after all, or she'd have been sunk. She'd told Stanley they ought to look ahead to next winter and another spate of industrial action, as they called it on the wireless – they ought to buy a couple of paraffin heaters and get a gas ring fixed up again where they still had the old gas pipe – but of course he saw no reason to look to the next day, never mind next year. She had a good mind to buy something herself and hide it in the garage. In fact, she just might do that. She smirked to herself at the thought of Stanley's face.

Singing a hymn, she took the fruit from the sieve and examined it carefully. Each raisin and sultana and currant had to be fat and juicy and ready. They said 'ready washed' on packets these days but when you took it out it was as dry as if it had come across the Sahara. All the other ingredients were in the bowl on the table and the aluminium tin was standing alongside with the right length of string coiled on top to tie it with. It annoyed her that she was sweating as she began the careful mixing. There was no effort needed to mix, goodness me. She must be getting old if making a pudding brought her out in a sweat. Yet at the same time as she felt this irritation with her body, she was also pleased. It showed she still cared. Lately, she had begun to wonder if she hadn't been affected by everybody else's don't-care attitude. There had been a listlessness in everything she did which she hated.

Stanley came trailing in just as she was at the crucial transferring of the mixture to the tin stage.

'What are you doing then?' he asked, standing so near the cooker she knew he was going to knock the pan of boiling water over.

'Get out,' she screamed at him.

'Temper,' he muttered.

'It is *not* temper. How can I make this pudding if I have interruptions all the time? I can't concentrate with people chattering away.'

'You've been making it for fifty years,' Stanley said. 'Wouldn't think you needed much concentration. It's only a pudding.'

'It may be *only* a pudding but I *only* want to make it properly, something *only* you wouldn't understand.'

'No breakfast then.'

'There'll be breakfast in due course.' Her fingers slipped on the string and she cursed.

'I have trouble with my bowels if I don't eat the minute I get up.'

'Oh, you and your bowels.'

'All very well for you to say that, you don't have that trouble or – '

'How do you know? How do you know what trouble I do or don't have? Just because I don't broadcast it. There's food on the table to start with but of course you didn't look.'

'I need tea.'

'You'll get tea.'

Stanley sat down and looked at the bowl in front of him. He hated cereal. Slowly, he put two large spoonfuls of sugar on the All-Bran and drowned it in milk. It made him feel sick but he had to have bulk. He munched the tacky mess thoughtfully.

'Talking of Christmas,' he said, when he'd finished, more to remind Rose tea was needed than anything else.

'Nobody was,' she called back, but in better humour. He could hear the pudding boiling away. Everything must be under control.

'Well, with you making the pudding. Talking of Christmas, or anyway thinking of it – '

'I wasn't. Christmas is nothing to me.'

'You can't ignore it.'

'Why shouldn't I? I'll ignore it if I want. Once the pudding and the children's presents are off I'll ignore it. It's a lot of commercialized nonsense these days.'

'Oh, I don't know. You have to celebrate a bit.'

'What? What would I be celebrating? What's there to celebrate about two old folk sitting over one of those tasteless chickens?'

'That's it – that's the point. Are we going to Elsie's?'

'No.'

'Why not? She'll be mentioning it soon.'

'Let her mention it. I'm not going, not this year.'

'What's different about this year? We've always gone.'

'This year I'm not.'

'Then I can't.'

'Oh, you're off again. You're the silliest man I ever met. What are we – Siamese twins? You've no independence. You go to your wretched club on your own – why can't you go to your own sister's? Eh?'

'It would look odd.'

'Fiddlesticks.'

'You're getting cantankerous in your old age,' he said. They glared at each other for a minute and then suddenly Rose burst out laughing. He didn't mention Christmas or Elsie's again.

But the following day they had a terrible argument about it – or, at least, Christmas and Elsie's lay underneath what they actually argued about. It started with what Stanley had the temerity to refer to as 'that bloody pudding'. Rose woke him just as he was going off into a much needed extra sleep at eight o'clock to tell him to get up and get off to the post office and weigh the pudding and bring it back and tell her the weight so she could calculate how much wrapping to put on. They had this palaver every year. There were no weighing scales in the house – Rose used spoons for all her measuring, or else guessed – and every year there was the worry that the pudding plus protective coat would weigh over two pounds and therefore cost at least fifteen bob more to send to Australia. Well, he took that quite well, he considered, but when she wanted him to go, in the first instance, without any breakfast so as to be there when the post office opened, he rebelled.

'Fifteen minutes won't make any difference,' he said. 'I'll just have my breakfast.'

'You will not. If you delay there'll be a big queue and you'll be hours. You'll have your breakfast when you come back and not before. Then while you're having it I can be doing the parcel up for you to take back.'

'No,' Stanley said.

Rose compressed her lips. 'Right,' she said, breathing hard. 'Right. Now we know where we stand.'

'I'll go the minute I've had my breakfast.'

'Don't bother.'

He sat down and began the hateful business of eating his All-Bran. He could hear Rose clattering about in the hall. Presently, she came back with her coat on, her face as red as a turkey-cock's. She went into the kitchen and came back with the pudding. As she passed him again she paused and said with great emphasis, 'Just don't ever ask me to do anything for you again that's all. I'll remember this.'

'Sit down,' he said. 'I've nearly finished. All this fuss.'

'Don't speak to me like that, I'm not your chattel.'

'Now sit down Rose. You're getting excited over nothing. You always do at Christmas.'

'I do not! Oh, how dare you!'

She was gone with a rush, literally trotting down the hall to the front door. He half got up from his chair, milk dribbling out of the corner of his not-quite-closed mouth. She would only upset herself. But then he sat down again. It had begun to occur to him lately that there might be a case here for being firm. There had been too much talk about independence, or the lack of it. By giving in to her like a spoiled child he was making a rod for his own back. He intended, for example, to go to Elsie's for Christmas, come what may. He would be firm. When she came back – she'd probably get to the end of the road and wait a bit and come back – he'd be as nice as pie. He'd say nothing. Without trying to score, he'd quietly take the parcel from her and off he'd go, meek as a lamb. That was the best idea. He wouldn't rub his victory in, no need for that, but it would be remembered. Having to make his own tea and toast and an egg was the penalty he would have to pay, but it was cheap at the price, so he set about it with a will, hoping she wouldn't be too quick about coming back or there'd be another row about the few crumbs he'd left which would be condemned as a mess.

Outside, Rose had got no farther than the gate where she stood, irresolute, her eyes misted over with tears. The post office could only be reached by crossing a main road and she knew she was not up to it. In a quiet street like their own it did not much matter if she misjudged the distance from kerb to street, but the High Street was a different matter. But she would not go back in there and be treated like a baby, so off she set, thoughts of following a crowd across a zebra crossing filling her head. She heard rather than saw someone coming towards her, and ducked her head instinctively. She had no desire to talk to anyone at this moment of crisis.

'Hello, Mrs Pendlebury. Are you feeling better?'

The mild, musical voice of Alice Oram floated into Rose's consciousness and panic seized her. She had not returned the jug. She had not said thank you, and now she was caught.

'Yes, thank you,' she said, abstracted, her eyes fixed on the road ahead, her feet already moving.

'Oh, good. It's nice to see you out and about, isn't it, Amy?'

'Out,' Amy said, and at once wriggled from her pushchair and snatched at the parcel in Rose's hand.

'Careful,' Rose said, crossly, and then, realizing how cross she had sounded, 'that's precious.'

'Ta?' Amy said, hopefully.

'No, Amy, it isn't for you,' her mother said.

'It's to go to my son, in Australia,' Rose blurted out, and blushed. It sounded to her ears like boasting, and she hated giving away information especially in the form of a boast.

'How exciting. Is it for Christmas?'

'It's a pudding,' Rose said, by now rigid with embarrassment but unable to stop giving away such intimate details. 'Sounds silly I know, but he always loved my puddings.'

'Doesn't sound silly to me,' Alice said, 'it sounds lovely. Does it always get there in one piece?'

'Well if it doesn't nobody's told me,' Rose said. 'Of course, I wrap it carefully. This isn't it wrapped properly, it's just so I can weigh it at the post office.'

Alice looked blank, and so intense was Rose's mortification at seeming odd that she had to volunteer further news. 'I haven't got any scales, see,' she said, 'and the weight has to be right.'

'I've got some,' Alice said, 'come in a minute and we'll weigh it.'

Horrified, Rose saw her, in one quick movement, fling open her gate, get a key out of her bag and open the door. She disappeared inside, leaving it open for Rose to follow. There was no decent alternative in the circumstances than to accept the invitation of someone to whom one was currently obliged.

Once inside the front door, Rose proceeded with extreme caution along the hall. It was as well she did so, for the floor was littered with Amy's toys and stacked all along one wall with wood, planks and planks of it. She stood, hesitant, at the first door, trying to work out from Alice's voice where she should go. The house was a mirror image of her own but she didn't seem to be able to get her bearings. Indeed, she felt slightly frightened and was relieved when Amy toddled up and held out her hand. Together, they went to the very end of the hall and into what was Rose's living-room in her own house.

'Here we are,' Alice was saying, holding up some scales. 'Now where's the pudding? You sit there and I'll put them on the table.'

Rose didn't dare look to right or left. She was trying hard to be poised in this unexpected situation but it was a struggle. She wished she had her best coat on, and pulled the one she was wearing closer over her knees.

'Well then,' said Alice, 'is that all right?'

Rose peered at the scales and said, untruthfully, 'I don't have my glasses.' The minute she'd said it she wished she hadn't. Liars were always found out. The girl would wonder how she could have been going to read the scales at the post office. Explanations began to flood into her mind, but Alice had already read out, 'One pound twelve ounces.'

'Oh,' Rose said, 'half an ounce less than last year. That would be that extra few nuts.'

'Nuts? In a pudding?'

They chatted about puddings and nuts for a few minutes and the next thing Rose knew there was a steaming cup of tea at her elbow and sugar and milk and biscuits being offered. 'Oh,' she kept saying, unable to conceal how startled she was, 'Oh,' over and over again, but she was consoled to see that the noise Amy made masked her inarticulate squeaks. Slowly, she began looking about her, slyly at first and then with more boldness.

'Do you like it?' Alice asked her.

Immediately, Rose's eyes dropped to her cup. She had been caught in the act. 'Very nice,' she murmured.

'My sister arranged it,' Alice said. 'I'm no good at decorating, I never know what to do, but she's so clever. All I could think of was white paint until she came and made it look lovely. She said it looked like a hospital and she was quite right. Of course Tony – my husband – doesn't really like Laura – my sister – and he thought . . .'

An hour passed with no apparent effort. Rose by this time had her coat open and was settled more comfortably into her chair. She was deep in the problems of Alice's family and enjoying it all without absorbing any of it. She'd said very little herself but had managed every now and again to make what she hoped had been an intelligent comment. She had also used the opportunity to thank Alice for all the presents. The thanks came to her lips with difficulty. She was worried that she had sounded ungracious, even resentful, but it was hard to say thank you without sounding servile. She was out of practice, that was what it was. It was so long since she had said thank you to anyone, other than Stanley or Elsie, who hardly counted.

Rose finished her second cup of tea and began wondering how to manage the mechanics of saying goodbye. She couldn't sit here for ever, though Alice looked settled for the duration. The pudding was weighed, hospitality generously given – she musn't outstay her welcome. Should she just get up and say, 'Must be off now,' or what? Amy settled it for her by suddenly putting her thumb in her mouth and cuddling up against her mother, who announced that meant she was tired.

'I'd better go,' Rose said. 'Thanks for the tea and the use of your scales, very handy I must say. And I'll return that jug.'

'Don't worry about it – any time,' Alice said.

'It's all ready, washed and waiting,' Rose said.

'Pop in one morning then and have a cup of coffee.'

'Yes,' said Rose, carefully, as though she knew the habit well, 'yes, I will. That would be very nice.'

They saw her to the door and waved her off on her short journey. Smiling, Rose walked through her own gate and looked for her key. She'd left in such a hurry and in such a state that she wasn't surprised to discover she'd gone without it. Now she'd have to stand there for an hour while Stanley thought about answering the door – but the minute her finger touched the bell, there he was, peering out. It suddenly occurred to her how easy it would be just to push him in the chest and send him flying. A puff of wind would blow him away.

'Where've you been?' he asked her, 'I've been worried sick.'

'Serve you right,' Rose said, marching past him. 'It'll be a new experience for you anyway. I've spent hours worrying about where you were. Now out of my way. I have to get this pudding done up with four ounces of wadding and no more.'

He trailed behind her like a bewildered dog, not knowing whether to wag its tail or not. She was so pleased with herself yet he could not believe she had actually crossed the High Street.

Whatever her secret she would withhold it from him, only to let it out little by little, and then, when it was out, she would enlarge upon it a piece at a time for weeks on end. He must just have patience and be thankful she had come to no harm.

Next door, Alice too was reflecting that she must have patience. Mrs Pendlebury would not open out in the space of an hour drinking tea. It would still be a slow campaign. What exactly she was campaigning against Alice was not sure. She moved about the house thinking of Mrs Pendlebury for a long time, endowing her with all sorts of qualities she probably didn't have. There was about her face, Alice fancied, a violence that suggested a continual fight, but then faces could lie. Tony's face lied. Only the day before Alice had found herself admiring the cunning of nature. Her husband had an expression so mild and bland, the curves of his nose and cheeks were so soft and sweet, the large eyes steadfast and untroubled – what a lie. Night after night as he tossed beside her, unable to sleep or in the grip of some nightmare, Alice marvelled at the deception not only of his face but his whole demeanour. Nobody except her guessed at the twists and turns of his mind, nobody glimpsed his perpetual rage with himself and the way the world treated him. Most people even despised him as feeble, a yes-man, without character. His occasional flashes of temper were almost always mistaken for forced attempts at involving himself. He was altogether too detached and impersonal for them to be taken as real and symptoms of deeper anger.

Perhaps she ought to be devoting herself to converting Tony and not Mrs Pendlebury. Alice smiled as she made the bed at the hopelessness of such a task. For she and Tony ever to have married was enough of a triumph in itself, a minor miracle too intricate to fathom. He had sold his soul to another human being – there had been no cheating – and had never quite got over the shock. She had joined him on his erratic fight against the current struggle and it was all she could do not to become contaminated herself. He would go on through life outwardly conforming and inwardly howling with despair and misery at the waste of it all. He had no idea what he even wanted to do about his confusion should he be able to do it. He said he was happy, but if his state was happiness Alice preferred to be unhappy.

The routine of household tasks was soothing. Alice knew herself to be lucky that she did not find them, as her sister Laura did, irritating in their constant repetition. She did often stop to wonder whether they constituted happiness, this daily round of cleaning and putting to rights, and thought that, though happiness was too grand a name, they at least added up to contentment. It was when they were finished that the pricklings of uncertainty began, when the evening came and Amy slept and everything was tidy and Tony not yet home. The evenings held no promise, that was the trouble. It was nice to see Tony, nice to eat with him, nice to talk to him, but ultimately it left her with a sense of disappointment – not in Tony, but in herself. She felt traitorous that there should be even an element of dissatisfaction in their relationship, but what else could she call it? Sometimes she tried to talk to him about it, but he resented talk, even with her. It was all unnecessary. He would say they had been over whatever it was hundreds of times and would squirm and twist himself out of giving his opinion. But she would persist until he listened to her properly. After an hour or so of discussing whether it meant she should or should not have a career he would say he hoped she was satisfied that they'd wasted the best part of the evening. Usually, she then cried.

There was more point in talking to Laura, whom she either rang up or visited when she was at her lowest. Since this was not very often – Alice was an independent person – Laura didn't resent the time it took up, and it did tend, when it happened, to be very time consuming. Laura was so sensible and yet so *interested*. She never looked the other way when she was being told intimate things, never interrupted you, always listened properly and sympathetically and thought before she answered. She had told Alice many times that it was foolish of her not to do something about her life. She pointed out how bored she was going to become if already at twenty she felt restless. When Alice tried to explain that it was nothing to do with having or not having a job, Laura quite brusquely disagreed. It had everything to do with it. Alice was apparently what Women's Lib was all about – she had been so conditioned to accept her role that she felt guilty that she didn't like it. She wasn't discovering herself or extending her personality or even really living. All the solutions were neatly laid out for her by Laura – Alice knew them off by heart. She was grateful to her sister – at least she always felt better after talking to her – but was brought no nearer knowing what it was that really troubled her.

The first sun for five weeks came through the kitchen window as Alice put away the scales and washed the tea cups. How dirty the windows were with all the rain. She stood contemplating the job before her with a certain relief. She was not hiding behind the cleaning of windows, but it was true that she was glad they needed doing. The kitchen was now such a beautiful room that dirty windows were a positive insult. It would be a pleasure to clean them, a *pleasure*. Was it pleasure she needed more of, she wondered?

Stanley had, ultimately, heard the whole story and duly marvelled at the mysterious way things had of turning out. Who would have thought such good would have come out of what had started off so badly? He was pleased – more than pleased. The fact that Rose told the story as being against him in some subtle way did not trouble him at all. He was always wholeheartedly glad at her happiness.

And she was happy. He wished those who thought she had no fun in her could have seen her that morning. She sang, she smiled, she laughed until dimples he'd forgotten about appeared in the corners of her mouth. There was a swagger to her step as she went about her household duties and her body, bending and twisting as she scrubbed and polished, had never looked so supple. Sitting quietly drinking the extra tea that Rose didn't even realize he'd got her to make, Stanley wondered that so much could come out of so little. That girl next door was proving a blessing. He stirred four large spoonfuls of sugar into his fifth cup of tea and tried to decide whether Alice Oram knew what she was doing. Was all this friendliness a casual thing or planned and plotted? Knowing Rose as well as he did, he knew that eventually, in a black mood, she would herself begin to question Alice's motives, so he must be ready to parry her unfair thrusts. No, there could be no design in this neighbourliness. The Orams couldn't want anything he and Rose had, of that he was certain. What possible advantage could there be in being kind to Rose? None. Relieved at what he saw as a conclusion reached after deep study, Stanley supped his tea and gave himself up to the pleasures of the sweet, hot liquid.

Rose's gaiety continued well into the afternoon when she did a little gardening. Stanley stood patiently with string and scissors while she tied up fallen shrubs. He stared vacantly at her hands tying knots. She was slow, much slower than she had ever been with her quick, nimble fingers. 'Taking you a long time,' he commented. 'I could do it as quick myself and that's saying something for an old slowcoach like me.'

'Yes,' she said, pausing, 'it isn't my fingers it's my eyes. I can't seem to see the string.'

'Need specs,' Stanley said. 'I've said so for a long time. Why don't we go and get your eyes tested?'

'That would be just as well,' Rose said. 'I've nothing against spectacles. They do nothing but good that I know of.'

Carefully, Stanley sought for the right words to clinch it. 'Well,' he said, 'I took the liberty some time ago of inquiring about eye-testing and Maynards in the High Street can do it at half a day's notice. I thought that very reasonable. Costs nothing for pensioners. The only snag –' he paused, but best to confess it was a snag '– the only snag is you need a line from your doctor.'

'That's no snag,' Rose said, 'you could ring up now.'

'I could,' Stanley said.

'Go on then. Get them to leave a line out for me and then ring Maynards. I'll go tomorrow.'

Which she did. Dressed in clean clothes from the skin outwards, Rose presented herself at the optician's at three o'clock the next afternoon, clutching the line from her doctor. She wouldn't let Stanley come in with her. She wasn't a child who needed to be led by the hand. He could take himself off somewhere and pick her up later, after it was all over. He kept asking her if she was sure, which annoyed her to death, and made her give way to the first flash of irritation that she'd shown for thirty-six hours.

She sat waiting feeling brave and adventurous. She was quite calm, not a flutter of nerves anywhere, and she was well acquainted with all the places she would have got them if there were going to be any. It was all so simple and easy once you made your mind up to it. When the girl came to ask her to come through to the consulting room she walked with a firm, almost haughty air into it, and sat down in the right chair with no difficulty at all. The optician was very pleasant. He chatted away as he fitted the apparatus, exclaiming at her getting to sixty-nine without needing spectacles. She enjoyed giving him instances of how good her sight had always been until the last two years and he appeared impressed by her examples. 'That's truly magnificent,' he kept saying until she felt important and wise. It was a pleasure to answer when he turned the lenses this way and that and said, 'Is it better like this – or this – or this?' Her voice rang with authority as she pronounced her verdict. Each time she decided he would say, 'Good, very good,' so she knew she was making the right choice.

After a great deal of fitting, he came up with two lenses that made even the little letters on the board in front of her jump right up. 'Ooh,' she shouted, 'I can read everything now, that's marvellous.'

'Good, very good,' the optician murmured. Rose was so enthusiastic herself that she failed to notice he was not. He got out a peculiar instrument and spent a long time looking into her eyes – so long that her head began to ache. The game seemed to have stopped and a faint feeling of anxiety began to affect her.

'Good,' he said at last, to her relief. 'Well now, we'll get a prescription made up as soon as possible. It usually takes about ten days, then you'll be able to read the time on Big Ben from the top of Hampstead Heath again.'

She laughed with him.

'Just one thing I should tell you,' he said smiling, 'nothing to worry about but I don't think your vision has become cloudy just with advancing years. Spectacles will help a lot for reading and television and so forth but you'll still find your general sight might be blurred a bit.'

'Oh, I don't mind about that,' Rose said grandly. 'I don't complain about trifles. As long as I can see my way about and can read, that's all that matters.'

'Yes,' he said, 'it isn't exactly a trifle though. The point is, you've got cataracts on both eyes. It's very common at your age – they're very easily treated these days.'

'Treated?' Rose said, her voice a little high.

Mm. We can remove them easily in hospital under an anaesthetic.'

'Hospital?' There was no doubting the fear.

'A very simple operation – you can be in and out in a few days and your sight better than ever. But you may never need to have it done – it's impossible to tell. Yours are quite small yet. They could take another ten years or more to come up – or they may stay just as they are. But it's as well to know and have them looked at occasionally. Now, if you'd like to step into the next room my assistant will give you a selection of frames to choose from. It's been a pleasure attending to you. Good day.'

Rose stared at the frames spread out in front of her. The girl was talking but it was all a mumble to her. She didn't want to try any of the frames on, but after she'd stabbed a finger at the most ordinary pair she could see the girl insisted they must be fitted. Humiliated, Rose stood in front of the mirror having the frame measured. They needn't bother with all this fidgeting and fussing. Oh, she'd collect them, or Stanley would, and pay for them on the nail. She wasn't dishonest. But then she'd put them at the back of a drawer and forget about them.

That stupid Stanley was nowhere to be seen. She glared up and down the busy street but there was no sign of him. He'd be skulking in some television shop most likely, gawping at the colour set she'd no intention of letting him have. And what was she supposed to do? Stand here all day like a dumb duck till he remembered her?

'I was here all the time,' Stanley said, smiling, 'looking in the window.'

'You were a long time,' his voice said, close to her.

'*Where* have you been?' she shouted. 'I've been waiting and waiting.'

'How silly,' Rose stormed, 'as if I'd expect you to be looking in the window. Come on, let's get home, sharpish.'

They got home. Stanley was breathless with the rush. Tea was slammed on the table. He ate his fruit cake cautiously. Rose, he saw, was apparently ravenous. She devoured four big sandwiches and two pieces of cake with impressive speed and energy. He cleared his throat.

'What's the matter with you?' she snapped.

'Nothing. Just a frog. I think I'm getting a cold.'

'Oh, you and your colds,' she scoffed. 'You always think you're getting colds. Some of us have things a lot worse to worry about but we manage not to moan.'

There was a long silence. Stanley knew he couldn't stay at the table much longer. There could be no harder job in the world than extending sympathy to Rose.

'How did you get on, then?' he asked, determined to get it over with.

'I'm going blind,' Rose said. 'There's no two ways about it. Blind as a bat, that'll be me.'

'Is that what he said?' Stanley asked, shocked.

'It's not what he said that matters,' Rose told him, 'it's what he meant.'

Stanley digested this before he spoke again.

'All the same,' he said, 'what *did* he say?'

'I've got cataracts,' Rose said, 'both eyes.'

'Oh, them,' Stanley said, his relief making him forget to tread warily, 'they're nothing – half the Club have had their cataracts done, I'm sick and tired of hearing about them. A few days in hospital eating grapes and Bob's your uncle.'

Rose put her tea cup down with such care that Stanley found himself mesmerized.

'Stanley Pendlebury,' she said, with dreadful menace, 'never mention that club of yours to me again, or anybody what goes to it.'

'Anyway,' Stanley said, squirming, 'it's nothing to worry about. Cataracts don't make you blind, not in this day and age. You've got the wrong end of the stick. Didn't he give you any specs?'

'Yes.' She hated having to speak about them.

'Well then, there you are. You'll be right as rain when you get those. You scared me for a minute, Rose. Don't do that ever again. You brought me up short and, I don't mind telling you, I don't like it one bit.'

She went on sitting at the table, her hands clasped round the cup she'd so carefully lowered to its saucer. Her eyes misted over as she thought of what darkness lay before her and not all the reassurance in the world could have consoled her. Stanley was not worth arguing with when she saw how emphatically she was doomed.

Chapter Nine

It took Rose some time to grow accustomed to what she thought of as a death sentence, but once she had come to terms with the certain awfulness she must face, it gave her a sense of advantage that she almost relished. She never mentioned the cataracts again to Stanley – she didn't need to. Instead, she developed a way of looking at him through half-closed eyes whenever he grumbled about his colds or his back or his piles that silenced him at once. He might have proof that cataract operations were as common as tonsils, he might know there was nothing to it, but all the same it was an Operation. Did he have an Operation hanging over him? Well then. Rose's practised glare suggested both the question and the answer.

She didn't tell anybody else. George and Elsie came round one Sunday afternoon – they *must* be missing Dolores – and she didn't mention it to them though they remarked on her spectacles. Rose just said that yes they were a help and left it at that. She didn't want anyone to know and start making comments. They would know soon enough and meanwhile she didn't want sympathy. The only person she felt tempted to tell was Alice but she stifled the temptation. It would be unfair to burden a stranger with such miserable knowledge, though she was slowly beginning to feel that Alice was about as far from being a stranger as one could get. She was so considerate and kind, always so welcoming, and what Rose couldn't get over was that the girl seemed to like her company. When Stanley asked what they'd had to talk about in there all that time Rose said everything. They discussed everything. He could snigger at the thought but he would be astonished at the range of topics covered in their regular Wednesday morning sessions.

Quite how the sessions had become regular Rose didn't know. She didn't admit to herself that they had until Stanley began to refer to her being off on her 'usual' Wednesday jaunt and she had realized it had become a weekly event. It immediately worried her that she might be imposing, but Alice made such a point of saying, 'See you next Wednesday,' that she knew she was not. How a young girl like that could want an old fogey like her for coffee every week she didn't know, but for once she was not disposed to smack her luck in the face.

The first Wednesday she went – to return the jug – she had been so nervous again that she hadn't enjoyed it, but after that, knowing that she had been particularly invited – indeed, that she had what you might call an *appointment* – had helped her relax. But she never acted as though she owned the place, was never familiar. She always rang the doorbell even if the door was open, as it often was. She always waited to be asked to sit down. She never settled herself as though it was her own home. Though she might unbutton her coat and remove her gloves she never, ever, took off her hat, however much Alice begged her to. She knew, even if Alice did not, what dangers lay in being *too* friendly.

It was exciting being in Alice's house. All around things were happening at such a rate. Each week there was some new piece of decoration to admire or some new object to go into ecstasies over. Rose did not stint her praise. It was such a tonic to be surrounded by lovely things and her tongue tripped over adjectives she hadn't used in a decade. Then there was Amy, growing so fast with a new accomplishment to demonstrate to Pen each visit. Rose learnt things with her all over again and had infinite patience in teaching her long-forgotten skills. Much cuddling and kissing cemented the friendship until Rose felt an icicle had melted somewhere within her. It troubled her that she could not give more to Alice, the source of all her new happiness, when so much was being received and she began to fret over the lack of balance in their relationship, without putting such a label on it. What could she do? Gifts were out of place. Should she have Alice and Amy to her house? Etiquette might demand that she should but she shrank from it.

Alice unexpectedly gave her a lead. She confessed, in mid-December, to a great feeling of boredom with everything – she felt so dull and lifeless and couldn't be bothered to think about Christmas or Amy's birthday or anything. Rose was quick with her advice.

'You should get out more,' she said, briskly, 'a young girl like you. How often does that husband of yours take you out I should like to know?'

'Not often. It's Amy – she wakes up such a lot at the moment I don't like to leave her with a babysitter. She has such nightmares.'

'Leave her with me,' Rose said, promptly. 'She wouldn't mind waking up with me here, not Pen.'

Alice was silent.

'Of course, if you'd rather not – ' Rose said.

'No, no – it would be lovely – if you're sure it wouldn't interfere with your evenings – '

'It would be a pleasure,' Rose said. 'What's the use of us sitting in there with that damn telly on?' She had only lately felt free enough to swear in Alice's presence. 'We might just as well be here doing somebody a good turn.'

Alice again did not reply as quickly as Rose would have expected, but then she managed just in time to say, 'Thank you – that's very kind. I'll see which evening Tony can get home early. You're sure Mr Pendlebury won't mind?'

'Why should he?' Rose said. 'It doesn't make any difference to him.'

That was how she introduced the subject to Stanley.

'It won't make any difference to you, I should hope,' she said aggressively, 'but we're going next door one evening soon.'

'What?' Stanley said, 'Have we been invited to a do?'

'No we have not, don't talk so vulgar. We're going to do that girl a good turn. She's looking quite peaky so I told her to get herself out for an evening with her husband and I'd look after the baby.'

'Did you now,' Stanley said, 'quite right too. It's about time we were a bit more neighbourly.'

'I hope I've always been neighbourly,' Rose said. 'I hope I've always seen where my Christian duty lay and that you don't need to teach it to me.'

'No,' said Stanley, and, 'Do a good turn, that's my motto.' He paused. 'Only thing is – ' he began.

'Trust you to object.'

'I'm not objecting. What I'm saying is, where do I come into it?'

'I knew you'd try to get out of it. Full of words that's you but when it comes to deeds, oh no.'

'All I'm asking is why me? I mean to say, it's you that's baby-sitting, correct me if I'm wrong, so what do you want me for?'

'I can't very well go on my own,' Rose said.

'Why not?'

'It would look funny. And besides – '

But she couldn't finish. Stanley always had to have things spelled out for him, especially the things you were trying not to spell. She didn't want to tell him she wouldn't feel safe on her own in charge of a two-year-old. Anything might happen. With that Operation hanging over her she might go blind any minute. She might, with her dodgy legs, collapse on the stairs. Somebody might break into the house and she'd be defenceless. The telephone might ring and she was useless on the telephone – somebody might want to leave a message and Stanley with his office training would come in handy. Surely he could see why she needed him without her having to underline her own deficiencies? Perhaps he finally did, for he never mentioned it again, beyond inquiring whether by any chance that young couple had a colour set? Rose said she had no idea and would consider it an impertinence to ask. He would just have to wait and see.

The night duly fixed was Thursday. Rose was glad. She had never liked Thursdays, but now she would have something to do. She made Stanley have a bath on Thursday morning specially. It was ages since he'd had a proper bath, she knew that for a fact. He got himself in that bathroom and locked the door and the taps ran for ages but she knew perfectly well he hadn't soaked himself properly. This time there was to be no mistake – she wasn't going to take him next door not sparkling from head to toe. She ran the bath herself and put a little T.C.P. in the water to freshen it and then ordered him into it. She would have liked literally to stand there till he stripped naked and climbed in, but he refused and she did not push the point beyond making a few remarks about trusting him and not being easily fooled and so on. His clean underwear was all laid out for him, and his suit and shirt. He could polish his shoes himself – at least that was something he did do well. You could always see your face in Stanley's shoes even if the rest of him made your face burn with shame. He could do hers while he was about it and save her the trouble. She had enough to do in the circumstances.

Alice had said seven-thirty would be lovely, so at seven-thirty precisely the Pendleburys rang the doorbell. Rose felt a little tense and anxious, especially when nobody came to the door at once. Stanley put his hand out to ring again, but she stopped him. Once was enough. It was cold standing on the doorstep, and humiliating. The first doubts began to cross her mind. Well, whatever happened it had been her own fault, walked right into it she had, thrown over the principles of a lifetime ...

The door opened with a rush and Alice stood there almost sobbing with guilt.

'Oh,' she gasped, 'I'm *so* sorry – the telephone rang at the same time as the doorbell and I had to answer it because I knew it would be Tony – I'm *so* sorry – how dreadful to keep you waiting – please come in – '

They went in. The warmth from the newly installed central heating wrapped itself round them and made Rose breathe easier. There was a bustle of activity while Alice took their coats and then a moment of hesitation not knowing what to do. Stanley half turned to go through the wrong door and though she knew she had made the same mistake once Rose was hard on him.

'Not there,' she said, scathing, 'the kitchen's through here.'

'I wish we had the sitting-room ready,' Alice said. 'It seems dreadful sticking you in the kitchen but I'm afraid there isn't anywhere else.'

'The kitchen will suit us fine,' Rose said, pleased to be putting somebody at their ease. 'We don't stand on any ceremony.'

'You'll help yourself to tea, won't you?' Alice said. Stanley said yes at the same time as Rose said they wouldn't need any. 'I've put a tray out so you don't have to look for anything.'

'Very nice,' Stanley said.

'You shouldn't have bothered,' Rose said. Both their eyes took in the tray in the centre of the wooden table with all sorts of things on it. Stanley was fairly certain he could see chocolate Bath Olivers which he adored, though they threatened to split his teeth, and Rose didn't need her glasses to know homemade gingerbread when she saw it.

'Amy's asleep,' Alice was saying. 'You know her room don't you Mrs Pendlebury?'

'Course I do,' Rose said. 'Don't you worry. 'I'll keep popping up.'

'Well,' Alice stood in the centre of the kitchen, 'I'll be off then. I'm meeting Tony at his office to save time. We're going for a meal and then to the theatre – I've left both telephone numbers beside the phone itself just in case you need me. And we won't be late – eleven at the latest.'

'You be as long as you like,' Stanley said. Rose wished he hadn't and frowned.

'Right then,' Alice said, but still she didn't go.

'Off you go,' Stanley encouraged her.

Finally, the door clicked and she was gone. They both stood still for a few minutes looking about them.

'They've done it up nice,' Stanley said, admiring the white walls. He touched one to see whether the rough effect was paper or paint.

'Don't you touch a thing,' Rose warned. 'We haven't been asked in here to leave dirty marks everywhere.'

'Shall I take the rocking chair?' Stanley said.

'Take what you like.'

'My mother used to have one like this,' Stanley said, rocking gently, 'and President Kennedy I do believe.'

'Which do you fancy yourself as?' Rose said.

Stanley laughed. 'I don't know that I could sit in it all night though. Here, you have a try.'

Rose sat in it but her legs were too short to rock it with so she was permanently thrown back. 'I'll have this other one,' she said. 'Here, pass me that tea towel there and I'll spread it on the back. I don't want to mark it leaning back.'

'Should have those thingummies we have,' Stanley said.

'Nobody has those any more,' Rose said. 'They're out of fashion. Things aren't looked after any more, nobody cares about marks except me. It's the look of things, that's all anybody cares about.'

'I wonder,' Stanley said 'where the telly is?' He tried to sound casual and failed.

'Don't know,' Rose said, smirking. She had noticed the absence of the box before him.

'They must have one,' Stanley said.

'Why? Why must they? There's no law saying everyone has to be glued to that thing night and day like you. I expect they read a lot instead.'

'You should have told me,' Stanley said, angry.

'I didn't know.'

'You should have found out.'

'I don't see – ssh – listen – that's the baby. Right. Up I go. You sit here and *don't move*. You'll only frighten her charging about if I have to bring her down.'

The stairs made her pant, she took them at such speed. There were lights on all the way up but she clung to the banister all the same, not trusting her eyes. Outside Amy's door she stopped. Didn't want to burst in wheezing like that. Calmness was the thing – a nice feeling of reassuring calm. The crying wasn't too bad now but she thought she'd rather deal with it before it got worse. Quietly, she pushed open the door and peeped in. Amy was standing in her cot, thumb in her mouth, her eyes quite closed. Rose crept across the floor to her and went down on her knees. Singing softly, she pulled Amy away from the bars and when the little body collapsed onto the blankets she pulled them up over her, still singing, and patted her back. The crying stopped. She stayed there a while longer, and then got up. It was easy. She'd always had the touch with children. Even as a girl she'd been able to get other people's babies to sleep when she wasn't much more than a baby herself. The midwife used to say Rose Carson went in as she went out.

There was a lovely smell in the room that Rose couldn't quite define – a warm, powdery, sweet smell. She wanted to stay there, but she would have to go. Stanley could not be left to his own devices in a strange house. She pushed back the damp curls on Amy's forehead and went out. At the top of the steps, she paused. Unmistakable sounds of somebody's telly wafted upwards. Down she charged, bouncing on the stairs with rage, practising aloud what she was going to say to Stanley. God knew where he'd found it – it made her feel sick to think what trespasses he had committed – but need he have it on without any care or consideration?

'Stanley!' she shouted as she rushed through the door. 'What do you think you're doing?'

'It's your favourite programme,' Stanley said. 'Quick, sit down.'

He was sitting a few inches away from a portable television set that he had perched on the very edge of the table. Rose leaned over and moved it back.

'Put it off,' she commanded.

'Eh?'

'Don't you "eh" me – put it off. If you're clever enough to find it you're clever enough to turn it off for a minute. Now, where did you get it from may I ask?'

'It was in the bedroom,' Stanley said.

'*What*?' Rose was incredulous. 'In the bedroom – which bedroom? Oh my God!'

'Their bedroom, the young people's.'

'How *dare* you go in their bedroom – oh – what will we say – you'll go and put it back this instant.'

'But I want to watch it,' Stanley said.

'I don't care what you want – back it goes.'

'You're being silly,' Stanley said.

'Better silly than sly. What would they think knowing you'd

been snooping about the house prying into their affairs – and the nerve of it, pushing open doors, peering into rooms – oh – it makes me quite ill. I don't know how you could behave like that, I never thought it of you.'

'It was common sense,' Stanley said. 'We were told to help ourselves to anything we wanted and make ourselves at home.'

But he took it back. Rose went with him just to make sure he didn't perpetrate any more outrages, and also to see the bedroom. She wouldn't let Stanley put the light on but she could see well enough how pretty it was with some kind of flowered paper and a patchwork quilt on the bed.

'Well if I can't have telly because of your silliness,' Stanley said when they were back downstairs, 'I should hope I'm to be allowed tea. Using their gas isn't going to be a crime is it?'

Getting the gas lit was a problem all the same. It was a long time since they'd had a gas cooker and none of the controls seemed the same. Rose was so worried about Stanley either blowing them all up or else damaging the cooker that she would hardly give him a chance. Eventually they got it lit and the kettle boiled and the tea made.

'Pretty cups,' Rose admired. 'It's ages since I've seen any nice china. I wouldn't mind treating myself to a set of this.'

'You've got enough,' Stanley said, still smarting at her foolish attitude over the telly. At this very minute 'Sportsnight with Coleman' would be beginning, to which he was very partial.

'Good gingerbread,' Rose said, her mouth full. 'I'm glad somebody still makes cakes. Of course, Alice isn't typical of the younger generation.'

'Alice? Getting cosy, aren't we? I didn't know it was Alice and Rose.'

'Don't be rude,' Rose said, 'just because you're in a bad temper.'

'It's hardly surprising I'm in a bad temper,' Stanley said, 'with "Sportsnight with Coleman" just starting.'

'A change is as good as a rest,' Rose said, maliciously. 'I'll just wash these things and then I'm going to choose a book from those shelves and settle down for a good read.'

She washed the cups and plates with exquisite care, filling the basin with lukewarm water only and rinsing off the suds afterwards, not that there were many. She didn't want to be extravagant with other people's belongings. It was strange how she enjoyed using them though – even the sink and taps were different from hers and made the task an adventure. She'd always meant to have stainless steel, it was definitely superior. Enamel chipped and stained however careful you were. And a tap that mixed the water – that was clever and time-saving. Her eyes moved backwards and forwards all the time round the different fittings and possessions, taking them all in, finding even the most insignificant items of interest.

'Have a good stare,' Stanley said, watching her. Rose ignored him. She dried her hands on her own handkerchief and debated whether to put the milk jug in the fridge – the room was warm. There was still a lot of milk in the jug and it might go off, but if she put it in the fridge it might look as if she was being nosy, so she covered it and put it on the window sill and put everything else on the tray exactly as it had been. They'd eaten all the cake and biscuits, which might seem greedy. She wished she'd stopped Stanley having that third piece of cake and that fourth biscuit.

Stanley never kept a grudge up for long, at least you could say that about him. She saw, as she made a performance out of choosing a book, that his bad temper had spent itself and a great affection for him moved her to say, 'There's an evening paper there, shouldn't think it would do any harm to look at it.' He picked it up, pleased. Stanley dearly loved newspapers but they'd stopped getting them delivered some years ago in the interests of economy – an economy they both knew was unnecessary and in this particular case hardly worth the trouble but nevertheless they had gone ahead and done it. The fact that Stanley went to the corner shop every day and continued to buy the newspaper he'd formerly had delivered was neither here nor there. Rose saw how silly it was but reflected that it gave Stanley a much-needed purpose in life and also some exercise so she did not put a stop to it. These colder evenings, though, he often didn't make the effort to go out and get the *Standard*, so finding it was a treat.

He settled down quite happily after that. She took her book to the kitchen table where there was a strong light overhead – a lovely orange open shade it had – and began reading it, or trying to. She'd picked *Mary Queen of Scots* because she'd always been interested in history and because it looked such a lovely book, so heavy and glossy, not like some of the flimsy things she saw up at the library. The first sentence was beautiful. Rose read it twice – 'The Winter of 1543 was marked by tempestuous weather throughout the British Isles: in the north, on the borders of Scotland and England, there were heavy snow-falls in December and frost so savage that by January the ships were frozen into the harbour at Newcastle.' Rose stopped and thought about it. She could see all that snow – just like the winter Frank was born when a double-decker bus got stuck in a drift outside the house where they had rooms. And as for frosts, she knew what the writer meant. She'd never seen ships frozen in a harbour but she'd seen plenty of sheep frozen solid in the country when she was a child. It made her shiver and yet excited her – the warmth of the orange light and the wooden table and the burnt cork colour of the floor and the swirling brown patterns on the blind and Amy upstairs asleep in that sweet-smelling room and Stanley quietly rocking away and gingerbread inside her and the ships frozen into the harbour in 1543: Rose felt happy and tearful.

The second sentence wasn't so good, but Rose pressed on relentlessly, sometimes going back two or three times to overcome what she knew was her own stupidity. It wasn't the words – she was good at words, and she knew how to use a dictionary if they were too much for her. No, it was more than that – she couldn't seem to hold whole sentences in her head if they didn't paint a picture. Now that first sentence was unforgettable – she would remember every word years after because she *saw* the ships and frost. You couldn't expect a writer to be an artist all the time – she knew she was at fault and it saddened her. She wanted to know about Mary but she didn't seem able to cope. She would have to admit it was too hard. Sighing, she contented herself with looking at pictures and dipping into the text every now and again, wishing all the time that someone would write good books for old folk like her with no education and failing powers of memory and concentration. Frank would have understood all this straight away and she supposed Tony Oram did, or was the book Alice's?

She kept the book open in front of her but didn't look at it any more – she just liked it lying there, full of promise. It was getting on for ten o'clock. They'd be back soon. She hoped they'd had a good time. She herself had never gone out when Frank was little, never, but then she hadn't wanted to, no desire at all. She'd been quite happy to stay in at night. Thinking back, she realized they would have had nowhere to go anyway and no money to spend. Sometimes Stanley went out to the pub – he liked a drink in those days and the company of the pub – but he never had anything to spend. He went mostly to play darts and have one half-pint shandy. When he came back on Fridays he'd bring her a penny chocolate whirl. That was her treat for the week.

She turned round to say to Stanley, 'Do you remember – ' and stopped. His mouth was open and his eyes closed, but he still held the paper in his hands close to his eyes. Why bother him with such sentimental nonsense? Did it matter about that penny chocolate? She was furious with herself and turned back to the beginning of her book with determination. She'd master that second sentence, and the third and the fourth if it killed her. She wasn't going to slip into senility without a fight. She'd stop herself going soft in the head through sheer effort. Maybe she hadn't enrolled at classes like Elsie, maybe she had stopped Stanley taking them to Australia, maybe she was too timid and shy, but by God she wasn't going to become a bundle of wishy-washy stories about the olden times.

When Alice and Tony came back she was still bent double over the book and hardly looked up.

'Hello,' said Alice, 'has everything been all right?'

'Yes,' said Rose, vaguely. She was at page ten and didn't want to be interrupted just as she was getting the hang of it. She stared at Alice as though she had no idea who she was.

'Oh, good. Well, we had a lovely evening out thanks to you.'

'Any time,' Stanley said, grandly. Alice was grateful for his enthusiasm and said with great emphasis, '*Thank* you, Mr Pendlebury.'

'Well,' said Rose, banging the book shut, 'we'll be off. Come on Stanley, coats on, they don't want us hanging about now the job's done.'

'Oh don't go – Tony's just going to make some cocoa, aren't you, Tony? Stay and have some. You sit there, Mrs Pendlebury – look, use this cushion. That chair looks pretty but it's hell to sit in. I should have told you. What were you reading? Oh, that. That's Tony's – he likes big books, stays up half the night reading them because he can't sleep.'

'At his age?' Rose said, but softly. Tony Oram was still an unknown quantity. Best tread carefully.

'I know, it's ridiculous. Sometimes it's four in the morning before he sleeps.'

'He should see a doctor,' said Stanley.

'Doctors are no good,' Rose said.

'We haven't got one yet,' Alice said, 'not since we moved. Who should we sign on with? Who's your doctor? Is he good?'

'No,' said Rose, 'he isn't.'

'I find him very nice,' Stanley said.

'Well, you should know,' Rose said. 'You're the expert. Never away, he isn't. It's shocking – abusing the Health Service he is.'

Tony, measuring four mugs of milk into a pan, smiled at that. His back was to them as he fiddled about with the cooker and got the cocoa and sugar from the cupboard. Alice was working hard at chatting the Pendleburys up and succeeding pretty well. Stanley, of course, was easy enough – any old remark satisfied him – but Rose was more of a problem. He saw what Alice meant about her being on the defensive. Prickly as his beard before he shaved. He stroked his chin and felt pleased with his simile. The horror of a visit to the National Theatre must have shocked him into lyricism. Alice loved it though – the event, the people, the poetry of Shakespeare, all the things he hated, but he took her rarely enough so he musn't complain. Tonight he didn't feel disposed to complain about anything. He felt warm and mildly drunk and wished he could take Alice to bed straight away, without the necessity of drinking this revolting cocoa and getting rid of the Pendleburys. Since Amy was born their evenings out had been rare and ruined by Alice's urge to charm whoever was babysitting. Why she bothered was clear to him but he wished she didn't feel that way. If only she would use an agency and they could go out whenever they wanted and say thank you and goodbye the minute they came in.

'It's very kind of you,' Alice was saying for the fiftieth time in a tone that set his teeth on edge.

'Cocoa up,' he said, and came to sit beside them on the table. Beyond the barest pleasantries he had no intention of talking to them and thereby extending the conversation.

'Was it a good play?' Rose asked, stiff now that the young man had joined them.

'Not my choice,' said Tony, 'but very enjoyable.' He smirked into his cocoa to hide his derision.

'Tony hates Shakespeare,' Alice said. 'He won't make the effort to listen properly and so he gets bored.'

'You have to make an effort,' Rose said.

Tony successfully resisted the temptation to ask why.

'My wife likes a good play,' Stanley said. 'It's all she'll watch on television.'

'Most of it's rubbish,' Rose said.

'There was a good one tonight, I noticed,' Alice said, 'by Rosemary Ann Sisson. I thought Mrs Pendlebury might be watching it.' She paused. Rose and Stanley waited, smiling slightly. 'Oh, how awful – I forgot to bring the telly down.'

There were five minutes of apologies and protestations of it not mattering before all the squawking settled down. Tony could hardly bear it and had to get up and look for a biscuit to calm his agitation. At least it had the effect of breaking the party up. Another five minutes of profuse thanks and hold this coat Tony open the door Tony shine a light Tony help Mr Pendlebury with that gate Tony it's sticking and they were gone. Immediately, Alice's vivacity disappeared. She collapsed onto the bottom stair and leant back.

'I'm exhausted,' she murmured.

'Hardly surprising. That performance lasted all of forty-five minutes and was better than any I saw on stage tonight. You must be stark raving mad.'

'Are we going to bed or –'

'Certainly we're going to bed. I wanted to go the minute we got in, didn't I? Marvellous way to round off a lovely evening.'

'I had to talk to them, I couldn't just boot them out, could I?'

'They would have gone in two minutes if you'd let them.'

'And been hurt that we were just using them.'

'You just imagine all this sensitivity.'

'I don't. Mrs P. would have been dreadfully hurt, it would just have been exploiting her.'

'Rubbish. She was probably dying to get to bed or have a decent cup of tea to take away the taste of that disgusting cocoa you forced on them.'

'I didn't force it – they were thrilled.'

'Then why did they leave half of it?'

'They were thrilled at the *idea*.'

'You're crazy.'

'Let's not argue.'

'Let's not. But let's not have the Pendleburys to babysit. You can go on doing your bit every Wednesday morning when I'm at work and that's that. I don't want to get involved with them. Right?'

But it wasn't that easy. Alice knew she had already irrevocably committed herself to having the Pendleburys babysit again. Before Mrs P. said, the following Wednesday, 'I don't suppose you'll be wanting us to come in another evening and give you a break,' she knew she would have to say yes, she did want them, she was dying to have them, she couldn't do without them, Amy loved them, they were the only people she could trust ... All she could try to do would be to limit talking to them afterwards for ten minutes. Or twenty, at the most. The thing to do would be to have them in earlier than she needed while Tony was at the office and talk to them then, give them a glass of sherry and sit down and take an interest before she left. Then Tony needn't have them inflicted on him.

She felt so drained as she cleared up the cups and put them in the sink. She looked around to see if there were any more dishes and her eye fell on the tray she'd left. They hadn't had any tea, only the cake and biscuits. But then she saw the tray had been re-laid almost exactly as she had left it with the cups and saucers and teapot and plates washed, dried and put back. That was thoughtful, even Tony would have to admit that was thoughtful. She imagined Mrs P. doing it with such care and precision. It was the little things that mattered. Sometimes she thought Tony was right and she was quite mad wooing Mrs P. the way she was doing, but when she came across little things like that she felt reassured. The world *must* be a better place to live in because she gave the Pendleburys gingerbread she'd made specially and they washed the dishes it had been eaten from. She wouldn't have it that it wasn't. More cheerful, she went up to bed.

Chapter Ten

Amy's birthday was January 1st which, at the time, had given Alice tremendous pleasure. The obvious symbolic nature of being presented with a new baby on the first day of the year had delighted her. Explaining this to Mrs P. before Christmas she met with instant agreement. Mrs P. also liked birthdays to be on occasions. She told Alice in a rush how excited she had been that Frank was born on February 29th, making him even more special than he already was, and her great wish had been that Ellen should be born on Midsummer's Day but she had missed it by four hours. Who, asked Alice, was Ellen?

'My daughter,' Rose said. She didn't suppose the words had passed her lips more than a dozen times, ever, and certainly not for many, many years. Alice didn't know about Ellen. She wasn't looking sympathetic. Glancing at her, Rose was suddenly struck by the thought that she could tell about Ellen without any fear at all. Or could she? She had never tried. 'Yes,' she went on, dreamily but her eyes sharp, ready to pick up any hostility, 'yes, I had a daughter. She died when she was eighteen months old.' She waited to feel the cold, slimy wetness come over her skin, but nothing happened. 'It was an accident.' She put up her hand to her hat and felt it. 'They put natural causes on the certificate but nobody was ever sure. She was perfectly healthy. Then she just died.' There was no picture of Ellen's face in that pink bonnet. Rose blinked. Nothing she couldn't look at. Alice was sitting quite still.

Should she mention what the coroner had said about the pillow in the pram? The nice, soft, comfortable pillow in its scrupulously clean broderie anglaise case. A tightness came in her throat and she knew the pillow would always be a stumbling block. She was grateful that Alice hadn't pressed her, only listened, attentive and serious. What she'd always hated – the reason she'd stopped talking about Ellen – was people saying they were sorry, saying it till you wanted to scream you didn't care if they were sorry and how dare they inflict *their* sorrow on you when you were already bowed down with it. The sorrow had to be entirely hers. You wanted people to help you go on not pull you back all the time into your sea of misery.

'Well,' she said, brightly, 'is Amy having a party?'

'Yes,' said Alice, taking her cue, 'ten altogether.'

'My goodness, you'll be busy with ten two-year-olds.'

'They aren't all two,' Alice said, 'there's the boys next door, the younger ones, they're six and seven, I think, but she adores them – '

'I think I've seen them,' Rose said, 'has one got red hair, a bit chubby?'

'That's right, that's Rory. Then there's the Stewart girl, Sally, she's four, isn't she – or is it five?'

'I don't know,' said Rose, sniffing, 'never have nothing to do with them though we hear them enough. They don't have anything to do with the likes of us.'

Alice hesitated. 'And Sam at the end of the road, he's five and a half.'

'Him down the road?' Rose asked. 'Yes, I know him, friendly little kiddie, not like the mother.'

Alice stayed quiet. Charlotte Driscoll along the road had told her, quite matter-of-fact, how unfriendly Mrs Pendlebury was. She had asked Alice, too sweetly, what the secret of her success was? How had Alice won Mrs P. over when everyone else had failed? Alice had blushed and stuttered she didn't know. Questions like that were agony. Of course she knew, but Charlotte had not the patience to unravel it all. That was the point, as Mrs P. had divined – Charlotte and those like her were not interested in Mrs P., only in adding another scalp to their already crowded belt.

There was a distinct silence, full of tea pouring and biscuit munching. Alice felt this was a test case if ever there was one. If she let Mrs P. get away with condemning Charlotte, if she didn't tell her she also was at fault, then that was it. The level of her own friendship with Mrs P. would have been determined for all time. She would be stuck with a cardboard acquaintance when she had wanted to move towards reality and move Mrs P. with her. Breathing deeply she said, 'How do you know she's stuck up?'

'Her on the corner? You only have to look at her.'

'But she can't help how she looks.'

'You can't help your features but you can help how you arrange them,' Rose retorted. 'Oh yes, certainly you can.'

Alice stared at Mrs P.'s very crossly arranged features and the scowl that nearly always sat on them.

'Well, you know how it is,' she said. 'Often I catch sight of myself in a shop window and I think who's that bad-tempered girl and it's only because I've been thinking hard about something or worrying.'

'*She* hasn't got anything to worry about.'

'How do you know?' Alice asked, quite sharply.

'They've plenty of money, you can see that.'

'But there are other things to worry about apart from money,' Alice argued.

'That voice,' Rose said, 'it goes through me hearing her call that child, real lady of the manor she is. The little boy asked me once if I wanted a lift in the car to do my shopping – do you want to come in my mummy's car he said – and she said, *she* said not today darling another day. Oh yes, she wasn't too shy to say that – not today darling or any other day, not likely. I've never looked at her since and don't intend to.'

'But what good does that do?' Alice almost wailed with distress.

'Good,' said Rose, 'who's talking about good? I don't want to do her good, I just want to keep her out of sight and mind, thank you very much.'

'But then the world isn't a very nice place.' Alice didn't care how prim she sounded. 'It just gets worse and worse.'

'It couldn't get worse,' Rose said. 'It's as bad as it can get. All you get on the news is robberies and violence. There's nowhere safe any more. If it isn't bombs it's strikes. Most of those who strike are lazy good-for-nothings, they've never done a decent day's work in their life, they don't know what hard work is but then the State just encourages them. We had no social security or whatever it's called in our day. If you didn't work you starved and that was that.'

'Surely you don't think that was a good thing?' Alice asked. She was getting so nervous she found it a struggle not to shout.

'Work's always a good thing,' Rose said, sternly. 'If more people worked the country wouldn't be in the state it is.'

Alice had never been so glad to hear Amy wake up. She rushed upstairs and brought her down and positively flung her into Mrs P.'s arms, then collapsed exhausted into a chair. It was horrible hearing Mrs P. rant on like that, dodging this way and that, punches to the belly, punches to the groin and no time to recover in between. Now, she was all smiles and laughs, all songs and jests as she bounced Amy up and down on her knee. Was it the same person? There were whole areas of discussion it would never be safe to touch on. She felt tired at the thought of all the careful treading that would have to be done, and for what?

'I like to speak my mind,' Rose said, suddenly, literally in the middle of 'Baa-baa Black Sheep', 'and I like people to speak theirs.'

'Oh, good,' Alice said, weakly.

The minute Rose went back next door Stanley said, 'You've got a good colour. What've you been doing in there?'

'Arguing,' Rose announced.

Stanley looked shocked.

'You needn't look so horrified,' Rose said, 'we didn't come to blows.' She smiled at her joke. 'Yes, we have a good bit of give-and-take in there, I can tell you, we both say what we think.'

'What was it about?' Stanley asked.

'Politics.'

'How do you mean, politics?'

'Politics – something you've always been too lazy to find out about. You needn't look so dumbfounded.'

Stanley decided to keep quiet. It was all too complicated. 'As long as you enjoyed it,' he said.

'I did enjoy it, and I'm not ashamed to say so. It's a good thing to give your views an airing.'

'Be careful who you do it with that's all,' Stanley said. 'People can take it differently from how you think. You don't realize sometimes how you hurt people's feelings.'

'Rubbish,' Rose snapped.

But afterwards, for the rest of the day and night, she worried. Had she been too hasty? She tried to remember how Alice had taken her frankness. She tried to see the expression on her face but couldn't for the life of her picture it. That in itself made her anxious – she must have got carried away. How had it all begun? That Charlotte woman, her at the end of the road, that was how it had begun, she *would* be at the bottom of it. Well, she was unrepentant. She hated that woman and her sort. Alice was different. Come to think of it, she wasn't sure where Alice fitted in. She wasn't like that Charlotte or the Stewart woman, she'd seen that straight away even before they became friends, but she wasn't like her and Stanley either, even allowing for age. Where did Alice belong, whose side was she on? Pondering about this sent Rose very successfully to sleep at two o'clock in the morning and she had a splendid sleep till eight. She woke up full of energy and knew at once that this was a day to have an Outing.

It was a beautiful December morning with the finest of frosts covering the grass and the thinnest of mists masking a blue sky. By eleven it would be glorious. Rose rushed to get ready and lay the breakfast and get Stanley up and out. He grumbled all the time but she persevered with good humour and by ten-thirty they were standing on the doorstep, the front door shaking with the bang Rose had given it as it shut to.

'Ooh, smell the air!' she said.

Stanley coughed and muttered, 'Bit raw if you ask me.'

'That's because you don't breathe properly,' Rose said. 'Come on, best foot forwards.'

They nearly tripped over Amy, playing on the pavement in front of her gate with a tricycle. Naturally, they stopped and engaged in a long chat about Santa Claus and her birthday and so on and then when Rose said they'd better get on she said can

Amy come with Pen and when Rose said not today darling she began to cry. That did it. Rose felt brutal. Somewhere, someone had done that to her – not today. How could Amy understand not today? Why *not* today? Rose laughed out loud – she loved to feel herself about to do something daring.

'We'll take her with us,' she said to Stanley.

'Where are we going?' Stanley asked. 'How can we take her if we don't know where we're going?'

'We'll go to the heath, to Kenwood,' Rose said, 'it's just the place to be on a nice day like this.'

'That means a bus.'

'All right it means a bus,' Rose said, impatient. 'As if we haven't been on a bus before.'

'Bus, bus, bus!' Amy shouted.

'Yes, bus, bus, bus!' Rose shouted, laughing. 'Come on Stanley, ring that bell and we'll get a coat for her and a pushchair.'

Some twenty minutes later they stood in the High Street waiting for a bus, with Stanley holding the collapsed pushchair and Rose holding Amy's hand. Rose was not quite as euphoric as before. She kept telling Stanley to be *ready*, to step on the bus the minute it stopped and lose no time. She would hand Amy to him and he had to sit her on the first available seat and sit down *at once* beside her. Amy was in the seventh heaven. Half of what she said, or tried to say, was lost in the roar of the traffic but Rose kept beaming and smiling and it seemed to satisfy her. The traffic was terrible. Faint pricklings of irritation that children should be subjected to all this noise and dirt threatened to spoil the glow Rose had enjoyed since she woke up, but she stamped them out. Amy was oblivious to the dust and screech of brakes. When the bus duly arrived she was as good as gold and hopped on neat as you please and did what she was told. There were no problems, and when they got to Highgate it was the terminus so there were no problems there either. The conductor even set the pram up for them and, what pleased Rose most of all, told Amy to hold Grannie's hand while she got off the bus. She didn't contradict him. Why should she? She'd never see him again, there was no harm done letting him think what he liked.

Everyone thought the same, she could see they did. All along the front of Kenwood House when they wheeled Amy past people smiled and nodded. Amy was such an engaging little thing, so bright and perky, and Alice had her dressed just right. Rose approved, she liked the new things they had for children these days. Amy's scarlet siren suit lined with some kind of white wool was exactly what was wanted, it kept her warm and snug and it didn't matter how dirty she got it because it could be washed in a jiffy.

Stanley was soon left behind. Amy trotted this way and that, forever changing direction like a yacht in a gale, and Rose trotted with her, alternately chasing and being chased. Every now and again she would remove some dirt from Amy's hand, or check that she hadn't cut herself during some minor fall, and these were the moments she liked best. Then, she was claiming Amy as hers. People watching saw Amy belonged to her, that she wasn't an elderly woman on her own but responsible for a child, such a pretty child, and that felt good. Carting Stanley about with you was no source of pride. He was an encumbrance, like an umbrella on a sunny day, something you took because you were over-cautious and cursed all the time when you didn't need it. Amy was an asset. Rose felt, the child beside her, that she didn't look so bad after all. She felt healthy and vigorous, ready for anything.

They went into the café in the coach house and had coffee before they left. Rose was a little tense about taking Amy in. She would have preferred not to have a coffee and tried to persuade Stanley that neither of them needed a drink, especially a hot one, but Stanley would not be put off. He was dying for a hot drink. Typically, he did not care that satisfying his own wants might endanger Amy. She might pull the drink over – Rose could just see it happening. The minute Stanley put the two cups on the table together with Amy's juice, she was on to him. He must sit well away from Amy and if he put his cup down on the saucer guard it with his hands. She herself drank the scalding liquid in three quick gulps and then pushed the empty cup and saucer away. Even empty cups were dangerous – they might get pulled over and break and the jagged ends could cut if Amy touched them. Amy showed no signs of breaking anything. She sat quite still and self-important, sipping her juice through a straw and breaking off every now and again to beam at Pen. Rose beamed back and relaxed a little. The chubby legs in their red wellingtons were kicking her as they swung backwards and forwards but she didn't mind. Amy finished her drink and rubbed her eyes.

'She's tired,' Rose said, concerned, 'best be off.'

'Half a mo,' Stanley said, 'I haven't finished my coffee.'

'Can't help that,' Rose said. 'Come on, hurry up. When a child's tired you can't fret about coffee. Alice said to be back at twelve-thirty and back we must be. She has her dinner then and a nap.'

'Wee wee,' Amy said.

'Oh dear,' Rose said, 'where are the toilets?'

'Next door but one,' Stanley said. 'You take her and I'll finish my drink.'

There was no alternative. Rose took Amy's hand and hurried her along and was grateful to find the lavatories without any difficulty. Getting Amy out of her siren suit was much harder. Rose soon lost her admiration for the garment as she struggled with the zip and pulled off the arms and then underneath there were tights and pants and it was all a lot of bother. At last the little bottom emerged, like a white nut from its casing, and onto the lavatory went Amy. She was so small, Rose had to hold her steady. The look of desperate concentration of the child's face made her both laugh and cry. She was quick with her congratulations afterwards, telling her over and over again what a good girl she was. The minute Amy had finished, Rose realized she wanted to spend a penny herself, but she couldn't, not with the child there watching. It wasn't nice, she would feel embarrassed. Carefully, she explained to Amy that Pen wanted a wee-wee too and if Amy just stood outside the door and didn't move Pen wouldn't be a minute. Rose tried, while lifting her heavy coat and skirt with one hand, to keep the lavatory door shut with the other, but Amy thought it was a game and pushed hard against it. Rose was in such a hurry to finish that she emerged with her clothes all anyhow and a definite feeling of discomfort, but there was no time to put herself right. Amy had to be home by twelve-thirty.

She was relieved, when they got outside, to see Stanley waiting outside the café.

'You've been an age,' he said, 'been having trouble?'

'No,' said Rose. 'Now come on, best foot forward before she falls asleep.'

'Doesn't look sleepy to me,' Stanley said, and indeed Amy had revived – so much so that she refused to get in the pushchair.

'I'll go and get her a lolly,' Stanley said, 'that'll persuade her.'

'Indeed you will not,' said Rose, 'the very idea.'

'Lolly?' said Amy, hopefully.

'Now look what you've done,' said Rose. 'Go and get her an apple Stanley – they sell apples, I saw them.'

Stanley got the apple but Amy took one look and hurled it away.

'Now that was naughty,' Rose said. A woman passing was heard to comment, 'Poor little thing,' and Rose flushed crimson.

'I'll carry her,' Stanley volunteered.

'You can't carry her,' Rose said.

But he did. While she pushed the empty pushchair, feeling very foolish, Stanley carried her. Rose tightened her lips as she watched the little girl cuddle up against Stanley, shrieking with laughter as she examined at close quarters his funny hairy nostrils and flappy ears. He wiggled his eyebrows at her and she giggled fit to burst.

'You're spoiling her,' Rose accused him, 'she needs a firm hand. Put her down now.'

'She's all right,' Stanley said.

'You'll be in bed tomorrow with a bad back,' Rose warned, 'and then it won't be all right.'

He carried her all the way to the bus stop and only relinquished her when they got on. Rose took hold of her reluctantly, afraid she might not come, but Amy was just as happy to cuddle Rose as Stanley and immediately began playing with the buttons on Rose's coat. She smelled slightly of cigarette smoke which annoyed Rose. Stanley shouldn't smoke cigarettes if he was going to have anything to do with children. It wasn't nice. She'd never let him smoke when Frank was little, not until he was old enough for his lungs to cope, for it was Rose's considered opinion that babies' lungs were easily damaged. She'd made him go out of their bed-sitting room on the rare occasion when he had a cigarette.

They walked into Rawlinson Road in good order, Amy safely strapped in her chair, to Rose's immense relief. People she'd never spoken to spoke to them as they made their way and she found herself smiling back graciously. Stanley had his hands on the pushchair too but she gradually edged them off. Two couldn't push a pushchair comfortably, there wasn't room on the handle for four hands. It made her feel very steady having that handle to hold onto – it felt solid under her grip and gave her confidence, like holding onto a banister when you were coming downstairs did. She found herself trying to remember what had happened to their pram after Ellen died. A big Silver Cross thing it had been, much too big for their room, much too expensive for their purse, but she had been determined her children should have the best pram, even if she couldn't give them the best of anything else except love. It had taken up most of the space in their room and they had used it as a table, putting a board across the top and sitting on stools either side. She had kept it in immaculate condition. Often, when she read adverts put in by people trying to sell prams, she came across the phrase 'immaculate condition' and wondered if they knew what they were talking about. Her pram had gleamed. You could literally see your face in the navy blue side, and the chrome work glittered even without the sun on it. But it had become a coffin, that's what. Ellen had died in it. She'd told Stanley to burn it. As they were nearing home she turned to Stanley and stood still and said very casually, 'What did you do with our Ellen's pram?'

Stanley just looked at her.

'Ellen's pram,' she repeated calmly, 'that big Silver Cross pram – what did you do with it after she died?'

'I don't know,' Stanley said in a croaky voice.

'Clear your throat,' she said, 'too much smoking – clear it and have a think.' She waited. Stanley shifted from foot to foot. What an unexpected day of reckoning.

'I think I gave it to Elsie and told her to get rid of it as best she could,' he said at last.

'And did she?'

'I never asked.'

'That's not like you. Well, we must ask. I'd like to know. Now then Amy, where's your mum?'

'Here,' called Alice, at that precise moment so that Rose knew she must have been watching from the window. It made her happy that she must have seen them coming home in such good style.

'Did you have a lovely time?' Alice asked, unstrapping Amy and lifting her out. 'Thank you so much for taking her – it was a lovely idea, you are kind.'

'As long as it gave you a break,' Rose said.

That evening, they sat watching television in front of the electric fire. Snow was forecast for the Christmas holiday.

'Frank's well out of it,' Stanley said, 'they'll be eating that pudding of yours in a heat wave I expect.'

'They can keep their heat waves,' Rose said. She sat and thought about it. Often, Frank sent a snap of them all taken on Christmas Day on the beach with them all in bathing costumes and a picnic spread out in front of them, her pudding in the middle. She'd always meant to ask them how they got it hot on the beach and where was the white sauce? Surely they didn't eat it cold or lukewarm, surely Veronica made white sauce?

'Here,' she said, abruptly, 'what happened to those folders and things you had about going to Australia?'

'They're in the drawer,' Stanley said, concentrating, if you could call it that, on the news.

'*Which* drawer?'

'The hallstand drawer.'

'Of all the places,' Rose said. She sat a few more minutes and then went to look. They were all there, in a big buff envelope. She took them out and through into the kitchen with her. Now she had her spectacles she didn't need to rely on Stanley to find out the facts for her, not that he would ever falsify anything.

When Stanley came through an hour later looking for his supper she had all the leaflets divided up into three piles in front of her.

'What's this?' he asked, disappointed to find only paper on the table and no sign of tea.

'Those are no good,' Rose said, pointing at the biggest pile. 'I don't want to go by sea. You don't get cheap rates by sea and anyway I'd get fed up long before we got there. Those are too expensive, silly to spend more than we need. These are possibles, travel clubs you can join. Mind you, I'd want it to be above board – none of your fiddled charter flights – we'd have to join a proper club what we were entitled to join and wait our turn. They have meetings and things, we'd have to go to those.'

Stanley cleared his throat.

'Yes, well, let's get Christmas over first then the decks are cleared.'

'They're clear now,' Rose said. 'I've got all my presents ready, such as they are, and I'm not sending any cards. It's a waste of money.'

'Yes, well,' Stanley said.

'Yes well what? Are we going to Australia or are we not?'

'It's a big decision,' Stanley said. 'You said yourself there's forms and things.'

'Now I've got my spectacles I can deal with forms,' Rose said, 'and I dare say a medical or whatever you have to have will be no worse than an eye test.'

'Seems a funny time to think about it,' Stanley complained, 'bringing it all up again like this, springing it on me. What put all this into your head all of a sudden?'

'That's what you can't call it – sudden,' Rose said. 'It's been in my head for years, and well you know it. Every year at Christmas Frank and Veronica ring up and what do they say? When are you coming over, that's what they say. They put those children on and what do they say? When are you coming to see us, that's what they say. It's our duty to go. We owe it to them to at least turn up. I don't know what they must think of us. I'm ashamed to think how rude we've been. Wanting to go doesn't come into it, that's neither here nor there – '

'Steady on,' Stanley said.

'And there's that baby, same age as Amy next door and we haven't even seen him. Oh yes, we help out next door and I'm not saying I regret it but we don't help out there do we? How many grandparents have those poor children got? Only us. Veronica's parents are dead, aren't they, and even they made the effort before their time came – they went out when Carol was born, and I should think so too, but we didn't, did we?'

She was thumping the table sending the leaflets flying, and Stanley didn't like the look of her at all. He resolved that by hook or by crook he'd have a word with the doctor about her, see if there wasn't something that could be put right. She got so excited and worked up it frightened him – and not only that, she'd got it all wrong. They'd be going to Australia to enjoy themselves, wouldn't they? For a holiday, good times. She was making it sound like a prison sentence. If she was going to look at it like that he wasn't at all sure he wanted to go, not on your nelly.

'Yes, well,' he said slowly, 'I'll write off for particulars to those clubs you mention, see what we can do.'

That quietened her. He was relieved to see her put the kettle on and start getting some food out. That kind of carry on made him hungry.

'I'll tell Frank then,' she said, 'when he rings. It'll give us something to talk about for a change.'

There was never, in fact, much time for talking. When the phone rang at nine o'clock on Christmas morning, as it always did, Stanley was there in the hall, ready and waiting, with Rose at his side. There was always such a lot of interference and so many voices telling you to hold the line and then when Frank did come on he sounded so far away you had to tell him at once to shout and usually he couldn't hear you at all. Then it was Happy Christmas Grandad, Happy Christmas Grandad and Happy Christmas Grandma and the phone getting passed from one to another so that just as you'd got used to one voice there would be another and the air was full of people asking who they were talking to. When the big moment came and Frank duly said, 'When are you coming over?' Rose laughed and shouted, 'You'll never guess!' Stanley could hear all the crackling that went on as Frank presumably passed this onto his family, and then Rose was positively yelling, 'Next year, we hope, yes we've made our mind up at last!' The noise that followed was very gratifying to say the least. When she came off, Rose had to wipe her eyes.

'They seemed very pleased,' she said.

'I should think so,' Stanley said.

'Veronica was ever so nice about it, it's what I've always hoped for, that was what she said. I expect she was putting it on, but still. We'll give you a marvellous time, she said, and I said – '

'I heard you,' Stanley interrupted, 'and I don't think you should have said what you said.'

'Why not?'

'You made it sound as if you didn't really want to go. That wasn't very nice.'

'Of course I want to go.'

'Then say so.'

They argued all Christmas Day about that, off and on. Only going to Elsie's in the afternoon put a stop to it temporarily because on the way there and back they had Elsie's to bicker about. Stanley thought it was plain daft to miss dinner and just go for their tea. He couldn't see the point of such half measures. Why go at all if they weren't going to go properly? Rose called it a compromise but what for, that's what he wanted to know. They had a very nice chicken dinner, he had to admit, but it was hardly the same. They also went next door to give Amy her present, but what made Stanley even more annoyed, Rose refused a drink – Christmas Day and she wouldn't accept hospitality. They were in and out like a whirlwind, no point in having gone. Rose hissed at him that he was slow on the uptake, couldn't he see the young people had visitors? So what, Stanley had wanted to know, it's Christmas, people *do* have visitors, it's a time of good fellowship, haven't you heard? Rose replied she knew her place and no one would say she didn't, Christmas or no Christmas. But Stanley had the last word. Just before they arrived at Elsie's he said, 'Sometimes I think you need more than your eyes tested,' and she had no time to reply. He knew what *his* New Year resolution was going to be, anyway.

Chapter Eleven

There was only one guest Alice found difficult at Amy's party and that was Rose Pendlebury. She didn't misbehave in any way but the sheer strain of seeing that she was in no manner slighted, overlooked, ignored, left out, told before the celebration was half over. Stanley was no trouble. He sat in a corner slowly and carefully blowing up balloons with a pump as the children burst them. Nothing flapped him. He even managed to drink seven cups of tea without maiming for life the throng around him.

Rose too had been given her jobs. Alice had thought long and hard about what tasks would be considered menial and which an honour. She couldn't ask Mrs P. to make the tea – that would make her too much the servant-in-the-kitchen. Nor, she felt, could she ask her to answer the door. She finally settled on Mrs P. being in charge of all the little presents and giving them out. They were all wrapped up in layers of coloured tissue paper and tied on to the Christmas tree. Every time a game ended Pen untied a present for everybody and gave it to them. It would all probably have worked perfectly if the children hadn't got over-excited and rushed for the tree each time, but such was the state of permanent confusion that there could be nothing orderly about the process. Mrs P. got quite flushed and Alice worried about her welfare. She wasn't wearing her new spectacles and seemed to take an age to untie the little gifts. The children became impatient and the older ones shouted while the younger ones cried. Alice decided it was time for tea half an hour before she had planned.

Tea was a success. Nobody ate very much except the two boys from next door but they all sat quite still and stared at each other. Mrs P. of her own accord went round pouring out orange juice and clearly enjoyed the clamour for more. It was, Alice thought, lucky that the children were so young and not a smart-alec among them. Otherwise the sight of Mrs P. complete with black fur hat and garish make-up might have proved irresistible. As it was, she was accepted as part of the furniture, at least until the grown-ups came at the end to collect their offspring.

The minute the first person came into the room Mrs P. started to say she'd better go and to call for Stanley to get her coat which she now clearly regretted having taken off at all. But Alice was firm. It was her solemn intention to introduce Mrs P. to every single parent. She would do it loudly, with pride, so that Mrs P. would get the message. She would involve herself publicly – no more of this slipping in for coffee as though on a secret mission. Mrs. P was her friend and must meet her other friends on equal terms before their friendship went any further. Luckily, the first parent happened to be the mother of a little boy who lived across the road and had moved in even more recently than Alice herself, so Mrs P. could have no preconceived ideas about her. Alice introduced them to each other and was agreeably surprised to hear Mrs P. begin to chat quite freely and civilly. She promptly left her to answer the door and was reassured by the laughter that followed her.

By the time Charlotte, Sam's mother, arrived Mrs P. had met and appeared to charm some dozen of the road's inhabitants, many of whom she had been meeting and ignoring for anything up to ten years. The technique, Alice observed, was for her to look vague as vague and murmur something about not seeing too well these days and then hope the person she was talking to would leave the subject alone. They all did so, even the Stewarts, who had actually been emphatically snubbed many times. As Alice had hoped, they welcomed the opportunity to catch Mrs Pendlebury with her guard down and establish themselves as the nice people they were and not the ogres she had cast them as. They, and others, were fulsome in their praise for her garden and Alice even heard her assure Jeremy Stewart that he could certainly come and get a japonica cutting when it was the right time to take it. It was, she thought, really quite funny to see Mrs P. being courted by all these terribly smooth prosperous couples so terrified that she might condemn them as snobs. She was definitely the star of the occasion and rose to it with zest. Alice caught Stanley's eye at one point and distinctly saw him wink.

But Charlotte was another matter. Mrs P. had already said she hated her, had already pigeon-holed her feelings. It was up to Charlotte, who knew nothing of how she was rated, to persuade Mrs P. otherwise and Alice found she had not the nerve to do more than introduce them and then gratefully submerge herself in the surrounding hubbub. When she looked round again, as the first people were beginning to leave, she saw rather than heard that everything was going reasonably well. True, Mrs P. was no longer laughing and her smile was more forced, but she was talking to Charlotte and that was something. Charlotte herself was on the other hand smiling too much, that particularly glacial smile that Alice too found irritating. Her mouth smiled, the corners of her eyes crinkled authentically, but the eyes were hurried, wanting to do anything but smile, wanting to be away from such intimacy. Alice suddenly felt as worried for Charlotte as for Mrs P., which she knew was silly. Nobody could be more detached, stronger, more confident than Charlotte. Socially, she had no problems, where beside her Mrs P. was a mass of complexes and nerves.

When everyone had gone Alice sat down amid the wreckage and closed her eyes. Her legs ached, her head ached and she was quite hoarse with shouting against the clamour. Mrs P. had offered to help tidy up, saying it was a shame to leave her with all that mess, but Alice had been insistent – she would do it herself, when Tony came home. She wanted more than anything just to be on her own, to have the luxury of flopping and not having to talk. She felt, indeed, a bit like Tony himself for once – people were a bother, entertaining them was striking attitudes. She wished she hadn't offered all the parents a drink when they arrived at the end, but it had seemed such a nice idea, a way of returning the hospitality extended to her but never accepted. All her ideas were nice, all her motives warm, but the reality proved so tiring.

At her feet Amy played with some of her new toys, most of all with Pen's train that whistled as you pulled it along, the train that had been so minutely examined to see that there were no sharp edges, so anxiously scrutinized to see the paint was lead-free, the parts securely welded together. Tony scorned toys for children – they were supposed to like wooden spoons and pan lids just as well – but he would like this one. He should really have been there but he didn't think there was any need for a party – Amy was too young, he said – and they had quarrelled so much about it that Alice deliberately organized it for when he would be at work. The Pendleburys had obviously thought that very queer. There had been remarks about a father's what you need here every time the boys next door fought. It had made Alice spring to his defence in spite of herself.

Tony was a good father. She needed to reassure herself that he was. He loved Amy, he was devoted to her, it was just that he didn't do so many of the things her own father had done. He wouldn't take Amy for walks on any account, maintaining against all the evidence that they bored her as much as they bored him. He wouldn't see that she had plenty of fresh air and any sunshine going. He wouldn't make her eat things that were good for her that she didn't necessarily want. For two weeks she ate nothing but ice-cream and tomatoes and he only laughed. He wouldn't supervise her manners, he wouldn't insist on please and thank you, he wouldn't stick to her nap routine at weekends. He wouldn't follow the pattern Alice had followed and was trying so hard to recreate.

She wondered, as she rested, about Rose and Stanley as parents. Rose was full of advice about every single aspect of bringing up children. Nothing, it would seem, had ever been too much trouble, too much effort, she had disliked nothing about it, found nothing annoying. Alice knew, at a distance of some forty years, Frank's routine from cradle to manhood. 'I always used to' was Mrs P.'s favourite opening. Alice was given to understand that theirs had been an idyllic partnership, never marred by ugly arguments or scenes. It somehow depressed her, and then the fact that she could be depressed by such a happy thing depressed her even more. She felt, always, inadequate. Amy required her to reach heights she did not feel equal to scale. Every day of motherhood found another fault in her. She would never be able to look back, like Mrs P., and glory in her perfection.

And Stanley? He made no claims. Being a father seemed to have made no impact at all on him. She had watched him while Rose launched into some long saga about Frank's childhood and he had been blank. Frank apparently stirred no chords in his memory. Without saying a word, it was obvious that Rose was the only one he had ever cared about. Alice wondered if Tony would be the same, or would everything change when Amy grew older? She shivered at the thought of the years ahead and the state the Pendleburys had reached and was glad to hear Tony's voice in the hall.

'The Pens must have enjoyed it,' Tony said, 'they've got every light in their house on. It's like Blackpool illuminations.'

But Alice, for once, did not have the strength to be curious.

Every light was indeed on in the Pendleburys' house. Rose had started at the top and gone right down the whole house putting lights on, main lights, lamps, every blessed light they had. She left all the doors open as she went and when she arrived back at the kitchen she thrust a writing paper at Stanley and said, 'Get a pencil.'

'What's going on?'

'Never mind, just get a pencil and follow me.'

'I'm tired,' Stanley objected.

'I can't think why. You've been sitting on your backside as far as I can see all afternoon. Nothing tiring about that so stop moaning and get that pencil.'

'What's it for? Pencil's no good for most things, ballpoint's better.'

'Oh, anything, just come on.'

He got his ballpoint, the one he kept for going to the Club, where you needed it for bingo sessions, and grudgingly followed her. His neck, still encased in the stiff white starched collar she'd insisted on, hurt him. He wished she'd give him time to change back into his own clothes but she wouldn't hear of it.

'Let me look at you decent for another hour or so, for goodness sake,' she said as he suggested it on the way up the stairs. 'I get sick and tired of you in that baggy cardigan and no collar on. You just stay as you are and mind you don't dirty yourself.'

'What we trailing up here for? I'm out of breath.'

'Out of breath going up your own stairs, that's a fine kettle of fish that is, it's pathetic that's what. When did you last climb your own stairs? When did you last look at your own rooms? It's a disgrace, I'm ashamed.'

'There's no call for me to go up there,' Stanley said, defiantly resting on the second landing.

'Is this your house or is it not?' she shouted at him. 'Well then that's call enough. Anything could be happening in those rooms and you'd never know about it. I know about it because I'm the muggins who cleans them but not you, oh no. Well, there's going to be a few changes. I'm going to be able to hold my head up in this road or know the reason why. Now, have you got that blessed ballpoint? Come on, you'd think it was Everest the carry-on you're making.'

But she was panting too. There were forty-one stairs to the top of the house and they were steep. They both stood on the top landing gasping, and then Rose led the way into Frank's room.

'We'll start here,' she said, her voice losing some of its sternness through lack of air. 'A clean sweep, that's what's wanted here. He doesn't want any of these things so out, the lot.'

'Some of those things are quite valuable,' Stanley objected.

'Then you sell them. Now, write that down.'

'What shall I write?'

'Dispose of contents of Frank's room, that's what.'

'Not the bed or the chair.'

'No, we'll keep those.'

'I should think so.'

'Clean walls thoroughly and distemper.'

'What?'

'You heard.'

'Are we decorating then?'

'Yes we are. We're doing this place from top to bottom then I can hold my head up.'

'But nobody *sees* it.'

'I see it, don't I? And I'm pig-sick of looking at it. When I go next door it's like a tonic, that's what – like a breath of fresh air, all those colours and that white paint – and then I come in here and it's all dark and dingy and they're the same house, just the same, but I couldn't have anybody in, could I, not with the place like this. I'd be embarrassed to let them farther than the front door let alone up here.'

'Who were you planning to let in?' Stanley insisted, latching on to that as the weak point.

'Alice for one,' she said. 'How many cups of tea have I had in her house? Scores. She's never so much as been invited here and it's not right.'

'I invited her,' Stanley said, 'when you were ill, but she wouldn't come.'

'Of course she wouldn't, who would?'

'That had nothing to do with it.'

'How do you know? Who would want to come into this hole? They all throw open their doors, wide open they do, and I'm ashamed to open mine more than a crack.'

'All right,' Stanley said, 'but she won't be coming up here will she?'

'She might. You have to be prepared with guests. Amy might trot up and she'd follow. You can't be too sure.'

He was silent. Laboriously, he wrote on the paper, then waited.

'What you writing?' she asked suspiciously.

'Just what you said dear.'

'Take that silly smile off your face. There's nothing to laugh about. I'm trying to be orderly and you smirking and sniggering doesn't help.'

'Especially if I'm doing it,' Stanley said quietly.

'What? What you muttering about now? Come on, out with it, say your piece.'

'I said there's nothing for me to laugh about if I'm going to do all this decorating.'

'*You*? Who said anything about you? You couldn't do it, it would take till doomsday. No, it'll be done properly. We'll get estimates.'

'Who's been putting ideas into your head?' Stanley asked. 'Estimates, it'd cost a fortune.'

'Estimates don't cost nothing.'

'Who said?'

'Somebody I was talking to. You can ask anyone for an estimate and it doesn't cost a thing, then you look at them and pick the cheapest.'

'That's a laugh,' Stanley said, 'now that *is* a laugh. I'm entitled to laugh there. Do you think we've come into a fortune?'

'We can afford it.'

'Who says?'

They both stood in the middle of the room, Stanley stabbing at the air with his ballpoint, Rose with her arms akimbo. Their finances were rarely discussed. Together with the subject of Ellen, there was a tacit agreement that they would not be delved into. Stanley had control of them – he had the bank account – but Rose had a quicker head for figures than he had. He was the writer, she was the arithmetician, doing it all in her head, of course. A mind like a computer, that was what she had, all dating from the days when they made you stand up on wooden forms in the classroom and if you couldn't answer the rapid tables that swept from row to row like machinegun-fire then you had to keep standing until you towered over everyone in your ignorance and your legs trembled with the desire to sit. Rose had always been first on her bottom, no bother at all. Stanley couldn't compete and he didn't try. Once he discovered Rose's bent he made shameless use of it, reciting out all the figures for her to do his income tax returns.

He knew, therefore, that she was aware down to the last pence how much they had in the bank, whereas he couldn't have said without taking a squint at the book. Somewhere about sixteen hundred pounds he reckoned, somewhere in that region. He knew it was under two thousand because once Rose had worked out what their income from interest would be if they had two thousand, and it had seemed the right sum to aim for. Two thousand would yield them a nice little addition to their pension, but they had never managed to make it, and of course now there was no more saving. Their money could only shrink unless they had another windfall. The thought caused Stanley the mildest tremors of anxiety about once every five years but otherwise he was resolved to take things as they came. The house, after all, was theirs, and how many people could say that? Mortgages had not been the Pendlebury style. They could have had their house ten years before they did if Rose hadn't been firm about not borrowing. In vain Stanley had tried to explain a few economic facts to her about the nature of money but it had been no good. Rose's house had to be hers, owned lock, stock and barrel. It meant now, of course, that their outgoings were quite small and almost met out of their pension. They paid electricity bills out of the interest on their sixteen hundred but otherwise managed on what they had, except for rates. Rates depleted their capital each year, even with the pensioners' rebate they were entitled to – and what a battle he'd had to get Rose to agree to that with her no-charity ideas. It was still supposed to be a dreadful secret that they applied for and got that, but without it they really would have been making inroads.

He didn't dare mention windfalls. Rose was still sore on that point, still not reconciled to the manner in which they had gained one thousand of those sixteen hundred pounds. She did not approve of gambling, that was the trouble, not in any shape or form. Only mugs gambled. When he'd realized he had eight draws he'd been more terrified of what Rose would do and say than thrilled at the prospect of a fortune. It was in a way merciful that it had turned out not to be a fortune but a modest enough sum that could be kept quiet – from everyone, that is, except Rose. What a how-do-you-do that had been. He'd waited days and days for the right moment to tell her, but it never came, and then, with him being so careless, she found the cheque and the whole thing blew up. It was the deceit, she said, which hurt her most, to think he'd been doing those disgusting pools half his life and concealing it from her – that was what rankled. Snaffling the coupons from under her gaze every week, filling them in secretly, creeping off to post them – oh, he was one for MI5 he was. No, he couldn't mention the windfall, couldn't claim the money as his when any discussion came up about what they were to do with their savings. Suddenly, he had an inspiration. Putting his ballpoint away he said, 'What about Australia, then? That's what I want to know.'

'What about it?

'Well, it'll cost a pretty penny as I see it.'

'Seven hundred and fifty pounds,' Rose snapped.

'There's spending money – '

'Included.'

'Well then, that's not much change out of sixteen hundred pounds is it?'

'Sixteen hundred and sixty-seven pounds. Take away seven hundred and fifty leaves nine hundred and seventeen, approximate cost of decoration as compared to others two hundred and thirty pounds leaves six hundred and eighty-seven.'

Stanley stared open-mouthed.

'Now wait a minute,' he said.

'No. I've waited too damn long as it is. These other two rooms up here, they don't need stripped, it's only plaster, they just need washed and a coat of emulsion and the woodwork done. They should come up very nice. I think I'll have white.'

'Shows the dirt,' Stanley said.

'There isn't any dirt to speak of, not up here. I'll have white. The staircase is a problem. I'll have to think about that. Something nice and warm is what's wanted, a nice warm paper. I'll have myself a trip down to Sanderson's and look through a few books. Put "paper, question mark" next to "staircase". Down we go, look lively. I've changes to make here. We're moving up for one thing.'

'Up?'

'Yes, up. I've always fancied a first-floor sitting-room like they all have. This room is wasted. Look at those lovely windows – let's have that stuff off for a start, silly idea, don't know why I put it up, just habit.' With one quick movement Rose ripped the net curtains down from both windows, standing between them and tugging with all her might. 'Let the sunshine in,' she said.

'It's night time,' Stanley said, 'and this room doesn't get any sun, not that I know of.'

'Don't carp,' Rose said. 'I'm having this all white, walls, ceiling, everything. And a new fitted carpet, a nice plain red.'

Stanley had had enough. He threw down his precious ballpoint, which he had taken out again at her insistence, and followed it with the pad of paper. He left her ranting on and went downstairs, switching off lights as he did so, leaving her stranded in one pool of lamplight. She could stay up there till she came to her senses – he was going to make himself some tea. Sipping it, he felt better, was even able to see the funny side. He'd been wanting Rose to socialize for years but if half an hour's party talk produced this kind of thing, then he'd be better off keeping her under lock and key. On his second cup, he regretted not keeping his temper and going along with her because he now saw it was all part and parcel of that daft evening-class idea: given time it would come to nothing. He should just have let her run on and written whatever she wanted. Thinking there was still time to do that, he left the teapot on the hot-plate and went to climb the stairs again.

Rose was standing where he had left her, still under the gold standard lamp that his mother had given them as a wedding present, her arms full of white net. Clearing his throat, Stanley bent down and picked up the pad of paper and his ballpoint, examining it anxiously to see that it hadn't been damaged. The little point flicked in and out quite satisfactorily.

'Now then,' he said, 'everything white and fitted red carpet. Right?'

She didn't reply, just stood there. It made his flesh creep. He cleared his throat again.

'Sorry about that incident,' he said, 'I was a bit parched to tell you the truth, that was all. Shall we get on?'

Still she didn't reply.

'No hard feelings,' he said, hopefully. He went slowly over to her and peered at her to see if she was crying but her cheeks were quite dry.

'Here,' he said, 'I'll take those.'

He thought she might hang on to them, but she let him take the curtains and he tried to fold them tidily to please her, but knew he'd made a mess. Her arms remained cradled as though she was still holding them.

'Come on, Rose,' he said, his anxiety beginning to give way to exasperation, 'get a move on, it's cold up here, there's a nice fug up downstairs, let's go and have some tea. You're like ice.' And she was. He touched her hands and they were icy. He was dreadfully afraid there was something the matter with her but at last she closed her eyes and dropped her hands and said, 'I'm tired, I feel very tired, I'm going straight to bed. You can do what you like.'

She trailed across the floor wearily and he walked beside her with his arm about her saying, 'There now, old girl, take it easy.' He went with her to the bedroom to help her get into bed until a flash of her old petulance reassured him and he went back to his tea and the telly. There'd been enough excitement to last him a long time. He wondered only vaguely what had come over Rose up there. Whatever it was she would snap out of it better on her own.

The events of New Year's Day were not referred to again in the Pendlebury household. Stanley woke the next day with slight twinges of foreboding but a glance across the room showed him Rose was up and when he came to listen he could hear all the normal household noises, so all was well. He said nothing and she said nothing. They had their meals and watched telly and did all the usual things and the even tenor of their day was restored. Everything was perfectly all right until they got to the next Wednesday, and even then he suspected nothing until it got to eleven o'clock and Rose was still in the kitchen. For some reason this worried him. He thought hard about it until he realized the significance of it being both Wednesday and eleven o'clock and then he hurried to find her.

'Here,' he said, 'do you know what day it is?'

'Wednesday, unless I'm very much mistaken,' she said quite calmly, continuing to clean the cooker.

'And do you know what time it is?'

'Eleven o'clock by my clock and it won't be far wrong. I set it by the news each morning.'

'Well then – what about your date?'

'I'm not going.'

'Why not?'

'Why should I?'

He thought about that. Her jaw moved as she shifted her teeth about inside. What should he say? After due consideration he came up with, 'Well, be like that if you want but it seems a pity. First time I've ever known you let anyone down, that's all.' He had the wit to turn his back as he said it.

'I beg your pardon – who have I let down I should like to know? Don't come in my kitchen saying things like that and then turn your back.'

'You know very well,' he said, knowing that would madden her.

'I'm not letting anyone down, it isn't a definite arrangement and never was. I shan't be missed, you needn't worry yourself.'

At that minute the telephone rang.

'There you are,' Stanley said, 'that'll be her.'

'She hasn't our number,' Rose said, above the noise. 'I've never given it to her, unless you've given it to her.'

'There are directories,' Stanley said, scathing. 'I shall leave you to answer, any road. I've a call of nature to answer.'

'Don't be vulgar,' Rose snapped.

'Vulgar or not, I have.'

The phone rang and rang. She was determined to ignore it but it brought her out in one of those sweats she couldn't stand. There would be no rest from the dizziness until she answered. Half sobbing, she went into the hall and sat down before she lifted the receiver.

'Hello?' she said.

'Oh, hello, Mrs Pendlebury?'

'Yes.'

'Oh, it's me, Alice, next door. I just wondered if you were going to pop in or not, or are you too busy?'

'Yes, I am rather busy,' Rose said, vague as vague. 'Yes, I'm very busy this morning.'

'I thought you might be,' Alice said, cheerful, hearty, her voice uncommonly loud. 'I thought things had probably piled up after the holiday. Never mind – just thought I'd check. How about tomorrow?'

'I don't know,' Rose said, her voice wandering all over the place.

'Oh, well, some other time, when you're not so busy – just when you feel like it. Amy's dying to show you all her new toys properly.'

'Yes,' Rose said, flatly, 'right then. I must get on.'

'Sorry to have kept you back. See you soon.'

After all the buzzing and booming of the telephone the house was deathly quiet. The chair creaked as she stood up. She passed a duster over it, then tucked the duster back into the pocket of her apron. She sniffed and looked at herself in the hallstand mirror. It was hard to make anything out. The mirror was a small dark patch between shrouds of raincoats. She couldn't see herself properly but then why bother.

'I heard that,' Stanley said. He was sitting in the lavatory with the door open, a habit she hated. 'I don't know what you're up to but I think it's a disgrace, that's all.'

She rushed down the hall and slammed the door shut, hoping she bumped him somewhere, then she went on into the kitchen and slammed that door shut too and went on with the cooker.

All she had said was that she was busy. That was nothing to be ashamed of, nothing she couldn't get out of. Nobody could take offence at that, surely, and Alice hadn't taken offence. She had sounded perfectly happy about it. No harm was done. She wouldn't go in again but had nothing to reproach herself with, she hadn't said anything unkind the way Stanley was trying to make out. She would tell him so. Decisive, she marched out into the hall.

'I said nothing unkind,' she said through the closed door, 'it was the simple truth. You stop trying to make something of it.'

He didn't reply. She banged the door once and said, 'Trouble-maker,' and went back into the kitchen. Slowly, thoroughly, she cleaned each hot-plate. Next door, Alice would have put away her particular cup, the one she had admired that had come from a pottery in the country somewhere. Alice always set it out for her, together with the plate with the flowers on that was like the first china she'd ever had when she and Stanley were married. No harm was done. It didn't take two seconds to put a cup and saucer and plate away. It was just they were always put out so nicely and now they would have to be put away. What would have been on the plate today? Alice was very good at providing tit-bits, all homemade. She always told her not to bother but she couldn't resist the goodies put out, especially the wholemeal scones. She raved about the scones. Nobody made scones any more except from packets. It struck her as so amazing and wonderful that somebody like Alice should make these delicious scones, positively crumbling with goodness. She'd often told her she was a marvel – praise where praise was due, as Stanley would say.

He was taking a long time, on purpose to annoy her, to get at her. She wouldn't rise to it. He could sit there for ever if he wanted to and she wouldn't care. He was in love with that lavatory and his blessed bowels, obsessed he was. His whole day revolved round it. He kept trying to discuss his piles with her but she wouldn't let him, she didn't want to hear. He could go and bore the doctor if he had to, that's what doctors were for. Yesterday he had even tried to show her his underpants which he said were bloodstained and she had snatched them out of his hands and thrown them into a corner. He had no standards, no sense of what should be talked about and what shouldn't. Later, when she retrieved them to wash them, she had been quite alarmed to find he was right. With great disdain, feeling this was something he'd no business expecting her to do, she'd soaked them in cold water and then scrubbed them fiercely.

She was busy all the morning, extra busy, justifying her explanation to Alice. It was one o'clock before she allowed herself to pause and wondered that Stanley had managed to restrain himself from coming in to complain lunch was late. Perhaps he had – she had been banging and crashing about with her broom so that Alice would hear her. He could well have come in and she would never have heard him. He mumbled so anyway, you could hardly hear what he was saying at the best of times. She took the casserole out of the oven and lifted the lid – delicious. The meat and gravy looked beautiful, done to a turn. She marched through and put it on the table, which she quickly finished setting. 'Lunch!' she shouted, and sat down. With great fairness she divided the best pieces of meat onto the two plates. It steamed and bubbled most gratifyingly. Nobody could say she couldn't cook. It made her sick watching people buy terrible things like luncheon meat – luncheon meat! – when they could buy some cheap stewing meat and make a dish like this. All it took was slow cooking and a bit of this and that added to it.

Stanley was the limit. Well, if he wasn't going to come she

wasn't going to call him again and she wasn't going to wait. If he couldn't smell that smell he didn't deserve what was on his plate. He would come trailing in clutching that wretched newspaper of his and complain he hadn't heard her. More fool him. She ate some of the meat with relish. Very good, very very good. She couldn't wait for Stanley to tell her so. Up she jumped and rushed to the door, shouting his name. There was absolutely no reply. Angered she tore into the sitting-room but he wasn't there. Surely he hadn't gone out? Breathing hard, she checked the hall-stand. Both his raincoat and his overcoat were there and he was such a fusspot he wouldn't even put the milk bottles out without one or the other on. Surely he wasn't in that lavatory again? Back she marched and hammered on the door.

'Are you there Stanley?' she called. 'Eh?' There was no reply, but to be sure she yanked the door open. He was sitting there with his trousers round his ankles and his head on his knees.

'Oh!' she gasped, and closed the door quickly. 'I don't know how you can.' Then she remembered that blood and said, 'Your dinner's on the table anyway so hurry up.'

She sat down at the table again but didn't touch her food. She felt dizzy. Clearing her throat, in preparation she knew not what for, she got up again and returned to the lavatory. 'Stanley?' she said, uncertainly. 'Are you all right?' She would have to open the door again. With reluctance, she swung it open. He'd passed out. Biting her lip, she bent down and lifted his face up. If she wasn't careful she was going to knock him off the lavatory and never get him up again. The mechanics of trying to look at him and get his trousers up without looking at him and the shame of the meat steaming to waste so preoccupied her that the awfulness of Stanley's predicament took a long time to make any impression on her. Most of all she felt furious. He was a ton weight for such a small thin man. His inert body was so heavy and clumsy she could hardly manipulate it at all. It was only when she'd got his clothes in some kind of order and had him lying on the floor that she began to feel frightened. She wanted, rather late, to scream but knew she wasn't a screamer. She told herself that firmly. She wasn't a screamer. The lavatory was full of bright red blood which she flushed away with her eyes closed. What should she do? Phone the doctor of course. She stepped over Stanley to go to the phone, thank God they had a phone, in the old days you just ran for your neighbour. Her legs were weak. They would hardly take her down the hall. She was going to have to pull herself together. Trembling, she lifted the phone and dialled. They took a long time to answer.

'Dr Thompson's surgery.'

'I want the doctor,' she said.

'Doctor's out on calls, who's speaking please?'

'Mrs Pendlebury,' she said. 'I want the doctor.'

'Doctor *is* out, can you ring later?'

'Thank you,' Rose said, and put the receiver down. She was shaking all over. 'Oh dear,' she kept saying, 'oh dear, dear,' and her hands were up to her face, kneading it. That damn phone, she hated phones, in the old days . . .

She flung open the front door and ran down the path, her slippered feet skidding on the thin layer of ice. She rushed along the pavement grabbing handfuls of privet as she passed and then into next door's path and up it and a hard hand down on the bell. 'It's my husband,' she was saying, before the door opened. 'It's my husband.' When Alice stood in front of her all smiles and rosy cheeks and nods she just went on repeating it like an idiot, over and over again, and then she began to cry and clutch Alice and pull at her, like a dog unable to communicate anything except the terrible, urgent need to be followed at once.

Chapter Twelve

Rose went to bed that night on her own for the first time in fifty-one years of marriage, but she was glad to be alone. The whole day had been such a strain with all the different kinds of fuss that had gone on, so much coming and going and talking, talking until her very hearing seemed affected. All she had wanted for hours and hours was to be on her own, the very thing everyone seemed to be conspiring to prevent. Only Alice had been her ally, her protector, dealing firmly with the doctor and the hospital people and Elsie, all of whom thought she should have someone to stay with her. No, Alice had said, her clear voice cutting through the muddle, no, she wants to be on her own, let her be on her own, we're right next door and if she knocks we can hear. It had satisfied them, even Elsie who had looked daggers. She was on her own, and now, in the creaky quiet and the darkness, she could begin to go over everything and sort it all out.

She wanted to be chronological but no matter how she tried to begin at the beginning it was the end that filled her mind. Stanley, lying in that hospital bed like a shrivelled sparrow, his nose just peeping over the white blankets, his eyes heavy lidded and yellow. It had given her a pain in her inside just to see him like that, even though the doctor said it was nothing in the least serious. He'd had an internal varicose vein that had ruptured and caused a lot of bleeding and he'd passed out with the loss of blood more than anything. They'd deal with that and she'd have him home before she'd time to miss him. She believed them but at the same time resented their assurances. Who were they to say it wasn't serious? They talked as though passing out stone cold for hours on end was nothing. What *was* serious she would like to know? And why had it happened? That was another thing that needed going into – he'd been going to the doctor for months with those piles, why hadn't something been done? He hadn't been looked after properly, he was just an old man and nobody cared. It was a scandal, it made her blood boil, it made her want to shout at them with their smiles and their arm-patting.

She exempted the nurses. They had been lovely, everything they always said nurses were, regular angels of mercy, so kind and gentle with Stanley and so sympathetic with her. Even the sister, the one in blue, had been nice to her when she didn't know the ropes, no starch in her at all but sit-where-you-like and a cup of tea while she waited for them to see to Stanley. They had helped her get over her terror of the place. They seemed to know, without her saying anything at all, that she'd never been in a hospital before, not even to visit and that was the truth. She'd always managed to keep out of them, thank God. Just leaving flowers or a little gift at the reception desk had always been enough for her. The smell, the trolleys, the uniforms, the paraphernalia of illness, even at a distance, had sent her running out.

When her time came she had resolved to die at home rather than be meddled about with in there. Now, of course, she would have to get over it. Stanley must be visited. She mustn't shirk her duty, but even knowing about the nice nurses wasn't going to make it easy.

Rose moved about in her bed. She knew she always looked untidy in bed. Tossing and turning as she did the covers all came out and some fell on the floor, and the rest got pushed into a big bundle. Now Stanley hardly disturbed his bed. If it wasn't for airing it she need hardly have made it. He just lay there, rigid, his toes turned up at the end making a small lump, but otherwise the counterpane smooth and unwrinkled. When they'd had a double bed she had felt guilty messing the bed up so much when he lay there so neat. Often she would have heaved over and taken every blessed sheet and blanket with her leaving him totally uncovered, still lying there immaculate and immobile. At least missing him in the room wasn't as bad as missing him in bed. It had been a good idea getting single beds, they had both slept better at once and she had regretted it had taken them so long to get round to it. Convention, that was all that had kept them in a double bed, convention and economy.

Gradually, she began to settle down and feel more familiar with the events of the day. She could start to remember things people had said and think about them. Elsie had said Frank should be told. Typical, damn silly idea: she'd squashed it straight away. What could Frank do stuck in Australia? The doctors said it wasn't serious, so why frighten Frank? All drama, that was Elsie. Wait till Stanley was himself and heard about it, he'd give Elsie some stick. Trying to get in on the act, that was all. Who'd roped Elsie in anyway, who'd told her, how had she come into the picture? She must have done herself, she realized. It was that woman at the hospital, not the nurse, the one in ordinary clothes who took all the particulars, she'd asked about other relatives and Elsie had come up. She'd given them Elsie's name and address, she supposed. Now she thought about it, that person had asked her if she would like her sister-in-law informed and she'd said yes because she'd felt it would seem funny if she said no. They caught you out those people, caught you when you were least prepared and then there was Elsie and everyone watching. They had kissed – well, embraced. Awkwardly. Elsie had drenched herself in scent. The smell was so strong and fresh that Rose just knew she'd rushed into her bedroom and put it on before she came to the hospital. She despised Elsie for that, and for the state of excitement she'd been in. It hadn't fooled her, that little speech about being so sorry and anything-we-can-do. No, she'd seen through it. Elsie had come for the pleasure of it. She wasn't upset, not if she'd had time to put more scent on. George had had more decency. He'd held her hand really nicely and squeezed it and shaken his head without saying a word. Actions spoke louder than words.

Inevitably, after a lot more going over jumbled pieces, Rose had come to Alice, which she'd been trying not to. Her debt was so enormous she was scared to look it in the face. That girl had been a brick. Rose could still feel the relief that had come over her from the minute Alice took control, for that was what she had done. In she'd come, into this house, and pushed Rose into a chair (where she knew she'd sat and cried but she wasn't going to dwell on that) and then she'd lifted the phone and dialled 999 and given all the particulars so coolly. Yes, an ambulance please, a gentleman unconscious. No, I don't know what's happened, his wife is much too upset to talk about it. So authoritative, so calm, and referring to Stanley as a gentleman unconscious. She'd tell Stanley about that later. The whole embarrassment of how he'd come to be unconscious was avoided and she was glad. Then, in the few minutes before the ambulance came, Alice had been so quick-witted, packing a bag for Stanley – heaven knew where she'd looked and what she'd found – and finding the front door key and helping her into her coat so that when the ambulance arrived they were all ready. She'd closed the sitting-room door while they got Stanley into the ambulance too – *that* was appreciated. She didn't want to see him on the stretcher. Had she said that to Alice? She couldn't remember. Anyway, she never did. Alice drove her to the hospital in somebody else's car. Whose car? She didn't know, but it wasn't Alice's. And where had Amy been? She didn't know that either. Alice had arranged everything. Is this your daughter the person who took particulars had asked?

No, but it could have been the way she'd behaved, the way she'd looked after her. Who said young people didn't care these days? Rose squashed the feeling that she had.

Kindness. Plenty of it. Home again, the electric fire still on, running up terrible bills all that time but the warmth was welcoming. Elsie and George sent packing. Oh, she supposed she *had* been rude. Well then. Wasn't she entitled to be in the circumstances. 'I can see we're not wanted,' Elsie had said, 'though some people would have thought you'd prefer your own family at a time like this to outsiders.' Thank God, Alice had been out of earshot, putting the kettle on, or her feelings would have been dreadfully hurt. Fine repayment that would have been for all she'd done, hearing herself called an outsider. Rose knew she'd deliberately raised her voice when she told Elsie off and said, 'She's the best friend I've ever had and just you remember that with your outsider talk. Now then.' And Elsie had left, barely able to get out that she'd ring in the morning and if needed was there. Then there had only been Alice. And herself. Something had had to be said. Oh, she'd tried so hard to say it, to get it out. She'd struggled and struggled and sought for words but her mouth was full of saliva and they were drowned in it. All she'd said was, 'Thank you for everything, dear' – oh, so humiliating in its inadequacy! And *dear*, to call her dear! Such a sloppy, silly swipe at affection. Why couldn't she have found eloquence? Alice had smiled and said, 'Please,' and shook her head and then the tea was steaming between them.

Further back, Rose instructed herself, go further back. She screwed her closed eyes up and clenched her teeth. It was all a judgement, it had all happened because of her not going next door at eleven o'clock. There was no escaping the connection. 'They' had been watching. She'd been mean and spiteful and thought horrible thoughts and this had happened to punish her. She had spurned Alice Oram and kicked and reviled her and then this had been sent to make her crawl, to make her prostrate herself in the dust of shame. The irony was not lost on her for want of knowing the word. It was fitting, she saw that. Nothing could have been more just. She'd paid a great price for her nastiness and still hadn't done. Alice hadn't realized, though, that was one blessing – she didn't know Rose was never ever going into her house again, of that she was certain. She'd covered up well for herself. Alice had really believed she was busy, which was a mercy. She need never find out. Only Stanley was in on her secret and there was no one more willing to forget than Stanley.

Everything had changed, of course. She saw as clear as daylight the trap she'd been about to walk into. She'd even laid it herself. It had been set up after poor little innocent Amy's party when she had said to herself, I've been made a fool of. She'd thought she saw it so clearly. Those young people had been fooling about with her. She'd become a game, something to be taken out when things were dull. She'd got all puffed up and conceited, she'd been taken in and started copying them, getting big ideas, imitating them like a monkey in the zoo going through a human tea party. Stanley had pulled her up just in time that night when he threw his ballpoint down. She'd seen it then. Wanting white walls indeed! Wanting big bare windows! Wanting self-coloured fitted carpets in smart shades! Wanting pinewood in her kitchen! Wanting to have coffee mornings! And who, she had asked herself, is responsible for this ridiculous carry-on? Alice Oram. No hesitation – Alice Oram. She'd known there was something behind all that buttering up. A laugh, that was what had been behind it. She'd even remembered seeing her smile and *wink* at somebody across the room while she was talking to that Charlotte woman. She'd winked, proof as plain as you like. She'd scolded herself for being so slow to see it. Her love for Amy had blinded her to the obvious.

Rose lay alone in bed and wept, in a huddle of grief. She tried to tell herself no harm had been done but she felt ugly and soiled. Alice Oram had offered her simple loving kindness and she'd chosen to twist and mangle this gift into bitter pulp. Why did she always have to see evil when there was none? Why couldn't she be like Stanley, unsuspicious, never looking for motives, taking people on trust? Because nobody had ever convinced her that they were in earnest, except Stanley. She'd always got slapped down in the end, always been left in the lurch. She'd learnt the hard way that the only person you can trust is yourself. Until Stanley. And now Alice. Alice had proved herself a hundred times over just in one day. When her tears were finished Rose fell asleep vowing, 'I am going to *give*, that's what.' No more hostility, no more drawing herself into a shell. She was going to go out and *give*.

The miracle was not accomplished with the speed Rose would have liked. It was not really accomplished at all, but at least a change did take place. She tried, that was the difference. She fought her instincts like a tigress. When Alice wondered if she would like to come for a simple lunch – wondered, she realized, with great diffidence – she said yes, straight out, and went and enjoyed it and said, unequivocally, that she did. When Tony Oram offered to run her to the hospital she accepted and asked him in while she got her coat and the things she had to take. She told him how kind he was being – not in her usual aggrieved way, cross because somebody was being kind and making you beholden to them, but with real appreciation. When Elsie turned up and asked her to come home and have a bite with them, she said that would be very nice, and when Elsie said you may as well stay the night, she said yes, she might as well.

There was no doubt her new policy agreed with her. She felt much better, better than she had done for years. It was partly, though, that the new routine suited her. Having Stanley to visit gave her a purpose in life. The hospital was not far away and she quickly learned an easy route to it which she could walk in twenty minutes without crossing a main road once. Stanley had been worried about that and it had given her great pleasure, made her feel quite triumphant, to be able to tell him what she had worked out. The mornings were busy with preparing things to take in to him, and the evenings busy with people ringing and calling to ask after him. No end of people took an interest in his illness. She was quite overwhelmed by the notes and gifts and inquiries, and teased Stanley about being popular. She said she needed a secretary to cope.

In a very short time she grew to love the hospital and couldn't imagine how she could ever have thought it anything but cosy and friendly. Once she knew the way to Stanley's ward it was child's play and she assumed a proprietorial air that was so convincing that strangers chose her to ask for directions. She didn't restrict herself to Stanley's bed but when she saw something needed doing she popped up and did it. Sometimes she was rushed off her feet filling glasses with water and picking magazines off the floor and getting biscuits out of tins in lockers. Sister said she ought to be paid and she said in reply, quick as lightning, she couldn't repay by anything *she* did what *they* were doing for Stanley. 'Thank you, Mrs Pendlebury,' Sister had said, quietly, and she'd felt marvellous. If she heard anybody visiting in the ward grumbling about the nurses she was furious and took it upon herself to tell them straight that the nursing staff were beyond reproach and she'd thank them to shut up or get out. Stanley said she was interfering and wished she wouldn't, but she told him to shut up as well and carried on exactly the same.

Stanley, she could see, really was perfectly all right within a couple of days, just as the doctors had said he would be. He loved being in hospital. Whereas other patients fretted about being confined to bed, he revelled in it, so much so that he got a ticking-off from Sister for not trying to do more for himself. Rose could have died of shame, but Stanley was unperturbed. He took himself and his illness very seriously and was annoyed, after the first shock had made her sympathetic, that Rose reverted to her usual abrasive self. He was moved to remind her that he could quite easily have died. 'Oh no,' Rose said, 'you're not going to hang that over me for the rest of your natural. Died, indeed. Why, if you hadn't been so damned lazy you could have got up from the you-know-where any time you wanted.' She laughed loudly at his indignant expression and put another grape in her own mouth.

Watching her from his lovely warm bed Stanley observed the change in Rose but put it down to nearly losing him. That was what had done it, he was convinced. Nobly, he considered all that terrible pain had been worth it, if it had made Rose see how lucky she was. She joked now but he could remember her face as she bent over him when he came round from the anaesthetic and there had been no kidding – she was in a dreadful state. He'd only seen her like that twice in his life – once when Ellen died and once when Frank left for Australia. She was a woman who cried easily and often, but not like that, not with that pain in her eyes that hurt you just to recognize. She had held his hand for hours between hers, chafing it and patting it and saying his name over and over. He admitted he'd enjoyed it. Being Rose, of course, all that soon stopped but he wasn't fooled, he could see the transformation. He was valued now, that was what it was.

He asked her once if she was lonely in that big house on her own.

'Certainly not,' she said. 'I'd even go so far as to say I enjoyed it.'

'I needn't bother coming home then.'

'No need to be like that – you asked me a straight question and I gave you a straight answer. No need to take the huff. I'm too busy to be lonely.'

'You're not busy at night.'

'No, but I'm glad to rest my legs after all the trailing up here.'

'You don't have to come if you don't want to.'

'Here – what did Sister say? Help yourself more, Mr Pendlebury, that's what she said, and that includes not being all self-pitying. Of course I want to come, don't talk ridiculous, but I get tired, that's all.' She paused. He did look very pale and thin. 'I don't like going in on my own of an evening, I admit that. It's dark and gloomy with no lights on or a fire, it isn't homely. And I can't be bothered to make meals for myself. I miss you and I sitting down for meals.'

'I'll soon be home,' Stanley said, pleased.

'Mind you, Alice has been very good, and Elsie. I've had several meals with both of them and very nice too.'

'With Alice Oram?' Stanley inquired, delicately.

'Do we know another Alice?' Rose asked, not deceived. 'Yes, she's been very kind.' She selected another grape. 'She came in for a cup of tea last night, just to see how you were getting on.'

'A cup of tea,' Stanley said, casually.

'Yes, and a bit of that fruit cake. We just had it on a tray in front of the fire.'

'Very nice,' Stanley said.

'Yes, it was. Very informal,' Rose said, and then, 'We had a glass of sherry after.'

'Where did you get that from?' Stanley asked, no longer able to hide his keen interest.

'I bought it. At the off-licence.'

'You've never been in an off-licence in your life!'

'I've never done lots of things. Anyway, it was in the window, that Bristol Cream Frank used to get, on offer, 10p off, so I bought two bottles.'

'*Two* bottles?'

'Well, one isn't much good, is it? Two bottles will last. We had a glass after our tea as I was telling you. It was very nice, bucked us up. I was glad I'd got it in because, if I hadn't, I wouldn't have had anything to offer that Charlotte woman and I'd have looked a proper fool – she's not the tea type.' Stanley waited, hoping she would go on, not moving a muscle in case he distracted her. 'These grapes are from her, for you,' she said. 'Very nice of her, wasn't it?'

'Very nice,' Stanley said emphatically.

'Yes, that's what I thought, considering she doesn't know you or me.' There were bits of fluff to pick off the bedcover before Sister saw them. 'She's quite nice really, quite friendly. Did you know she's been married twice?'

'No,' said Stanley, politely.

'Yes. Her first husband was killed in an accident and she lost the baby she was carrying with the shock. Terrible, isn't it?'

'Terrible,' Stanley agreed.

'Everybody has their tragedies,' Rose said, 'if only you knew. It doesn't do to judge people by appearances.'

'No,' said Stanley.

Rose was glad he wasn't going to rub anything in. He knew it had been a confession of guilt, no need to say any more. She knew he longed to hear more about her evening but she was shy about telling. After all, it didn't amount to very much. She and Alice had had their snack and then their sherry and the doorbell rang and there was that Charlotte woman. She'd been so glad Alice was with her, had positively glowed with satisfaction at being able to show her visitor into a room with someone else in it. Then they'd all had another glass of sherry and talked. She couldn't believe, afterwards, how long they had talked with never a falter on her part, never a lull in the entire conversation. She could remember what Alice had said and what Charlotte had said, but what had she herself said? It was a mystery, but she had said a great deal, she knew that. All she could remember was the blitz being brought up and her telling them about what it had been like and how Stanley had run down the street with his tin helmet on and his gasmask flying out behind him because he couldn't get it shut up. They'd been so interested in knowing about it and then – oh yes – they'd got on to evacuees and what it had been like sending Frank, aged about eight, away. Now that had them really interested, they wouldn't let her get off the subject, she could hardly answer all their many questions.

After they had gone, the house had still seemed full. Clearing away the glasses and plates, plumping the cushions up, sweeping the crumbs from the floor, she still seemed to hear all their voices and feel the warmth of other people's presence. A faint scent of something hung in the air and she closed the sitting-room door carefully on it hoping it would still be there in the morning. The house was never like that when just she and Stanley were in it. It hadn't really been like that since Frank left. He used to have the sitting-room on Friday nights, for his friends. She and Stanley stayed in the kitchen and the living-room those nights, though Frank had always said there was no need to. Stanley had spent all his time trying to get himself in there on one pretext or another but she kept a sharp eye on him and wouldn't allow it. Those young people wanted to be on their own, as she told him. She herself kept well out of the way. At nine o'clock she prepared a delicious supper and loaded it onto the trolley and Frank came in for it. Through the open door she could hear them all talking and laughing and it pleased but frightened her. Sometimes she watched from the upstairs window as the guests came and went and they were such lovely looking youngsters. She did meet some of them, before Frank stopped having the evenings. He insisted. He said it was silly of her to behave like a housekeeper and he wanted to introduce his friends to her, so she went to the door, just once, and said good evening and that was that. Stanley had known them better with opening the front door. He knew all their names. Sometimes she'd envied him his familiarity. He'd been quite put out when the evenings stopped. They'd asked Frank after a while why he didn't invite his friends any more and he'd just said he was too busy. That was all – too busy. No more Friday evenings, no more suppers to make. Sad, really. She'd missed them coming and going. It had left her with an uncomfortable feeling, an unaccountable suspicion of guilt. But she'd done all that was expected of her, the suppers had been lovely, never the same thing two Fridays running, never. And she'd put fresh flowers in the sitting-room on Friday, every Friday, and polished the table with lavender polish so there was a lovely sweet smell. Frank couldn't complain she hadn't made an effort, every effort. Nobody could have put themselves out more, he couldn't have expected better treatment. But the trouble was she felt he had.

'Penny for them,' Stanley said.

'Oh, I was just thinking about Frank. Here, do you know your Elsie wanted to ring Frank and tell him about your illness.'

'No call for that,' Stanley said, but privately he wondered why this outraged Rose so much. He *had* been very ill, no good trying to minimize it.

'That's what I said. You could write to him yourself with all the time you've got lying there. I'll bring you an airmail in tomorrow.'

'I don't know that I could manage it.'

'Course you could. Sister said there wasn't anything you couldn't do if you put your mind to it. She notices, you know – she's told me how you're in that dressing-gown smart enough and down to the telly room the minute I've gone. You can't fool her.'

'I wouldn't want to worry Frank.'

'There wouldn't be any need to worry him. No need to go into details, just say you had a slight mishap – '

'That would be a lie,' said Stanley.

'Oh, don't be so silly. Tell him exactly what you're here for then. Frank's no prude.'

Rose was proud of that. She knew she was a bit of a prude herself but then that was her upbringing. She'd been determined her children should be brought up differently and call a spade a spade and not be ashamed of their bodies and natural functions.

She was proud to have been ahead of her generation in that. Right from the beginning she'd answered all Frank's questions properly and marvelled at what a straightforward attitude it had given him. She and Stanley could never have that freedom. It was too late for them. They got dressed and undressed either with the light off or on their own and their life was full of secrets and euphemisms that she despised. Stanley was either coy or coarse and she couldn't do with either.

'You can tell him about our arrangements,' she said, 'that'll give you something to say.'

'What arrangements?'

'Oh, don't be so annoying – going to see them of course. We haven't written have we? There's been nothing since that phone call, has there? They'll be wanting to know.'

'I don't know that I'll be able to go now,' Stanley said. 'The hospital will be wanting to keep an eye on me. I shouldn't think they'll want me to go far out of their reach.'

'My God,' Rose hissed at him, 'I don't often blaspheme but you'd make an angel swear. Not far out of their reach? They'll be glad to see the back of you. The doctor more or less said that if you'd been sensible and gone in time to your G.P. it could have been done in Outpatients or not needed at all. You've got very grand ideas of your own importance, my man. They won't want you back at all – they won't *want* you.'

'We shall have to see,' Stanley said.

'Rubbish!'

'Anyway, what arrangements? I haven't made any yet.'

'Then you'll have to get cracking.'

'How can I, here, like this?' said Stanley, getting cross.

'You can write off for details. I'll bring in all the leaflets when I bring the airmail. I should think September would be a good time. We'll go for a month, that's long enough. We'll have been in that club for nearly a year then. Yes, September or October. We'll book it and send a deposit.'

'You can't get a deposit back.'

'I know you can't. We won't want it back.'

'Anything could happen.'

'Anything could always happen. You must look on the bright

side, Stanley,' and she burst out laughing. 'You look as if you've eaten a sour apple,' she said, followed by more giggles, until her nose began to run with laughing, she was shaking herself about so much.

She laughed a lot these days. Alice had remarked on it, said she had a proper belly laugh when she got going. It was true. Stanley when he laughed could do it almost silently, just a sort of burr in his throat that got louder like a vacuum cleaner, but she opened her mouth and out came this great noise and for ages afterwards she was still exploding and working it off. She always had to wipe her eyes within minutes of starting and she could feel her cheeks burning and her whole face moving as though it was being pushed. She liked the feeling, it made her feel energetic, as though she could do anything. There were no limits to the possibilities once she started to laugh, it seemed to spark off a generosity in her that she had only suspected.

Out in the street, in Rawlinson Road, she smiled at people she had always ignored – still not readily but after a decent interval when she was sure they were looking at her, which was a lot easier these days now she had her spectacles. Smiling meant stopping and stopping led to talking which was easy because there was Stanley to talk about. Charlotte asked her in to tea and so did the Stewart woman but fortunately she was on her way to the hospital each time. Fortunately, because she knew she hadn't gone that far, not quite yet. Alice's was enough for the moment. Going further afield would be too much, too exciting, too disrupting when she was only a learner. When they asked her next time she would perhaps accept, if she was sure they really meant it. They must all give her time to cope, she had to walk before she could run, that was it.

That was what she did. While Stanley recovered, Rose persevered and gained confidence in her new self. Occasionally, she had lapses – moments of grumpiness for no reason, flashes of hostility that she failed to control, days of depression and gloom that just had to be got through. Those were the days when that nastiness inside her welled up and started saying all the horrible evil things it had always said and she had to be sharp with it. The only thing to do on days like that was get out of the house and among people as quickly as possible. This she learnt to do, though it was always an effort. Her new habit of self-mockery and raillery helped – how she went on at herself! How she heaped scorn and abuse on her own grumbling! But it worked and that was all that mattered. When Stanley came home he would find her quite a different person. He had something to look forward to, if he did but know it. She was enough of the old Rose, however, to make sure that he didn't.

Chapter Thirteen

That winter, the winter of Stanley's accident and convalescence, passed more pleasantly and at a faster rate than any Rose could remember. They were in April and some sunshine at last and the garden coming to life before she knew what had happened. She had a cold in February, soon after Stanley came home, but threw it off easily and felt no ill-effects. During the whole period she had no real downs at all, no dreadful weeks when the thought of seeing another set of days come up made her want to scream. On the contrary, she had so many good days to look back on that she didn't know which to choose when she wanted to indulge herself in a little nostalgic wallowing.

There was the day Alice took them to Whipsnade Zoo, a day so perfect that Rose never tired of reliving it. She told everybody about it until they were sick and tired of hearing it – or that was how Elsie felt, for she had heard it three times and each time it grew in the telling. She was given to understand that these young neighbours of Rose's that she set such store by were angels in disguise. The thoughtfulness, the consideration – those were the qualities Rose harped on about. Elsie thought it the daftest idea she had ever heard of – an outing to a zoo at their age *and* on a freezing March day *and* with Stanley only a few weeks out of hospital. As for the absurdity of having a picnic, well. No matter how much Rose went on about the novelty, and the steaming hot soup and the crunchy hot buttered French bread, Elsie could not accept that it had been in the least enjoyable. What amazed her was Rose's wilful distortion of the facts – Rose, who so prided herself on frankness and plain speaking. Whipsnade Zoo was only twenty-odd miles away and Elsie knew the weather didn't vary that much. The day had been freezing, frosty and freezing, with a cold, clinging mist. All right, the mist had lifted and the sun shone, but it was a March sun, no warmth in it at all. It was unbelievable that it had been so hot in the sheltered dip beside the kangaroos that they'd loosened their coats. And apart from anything else, what about the driving? What about the M1 that Rose had sworn she would never go on? Some people forgot things very quickly.

Rose knew, of course, how Elsie felt and made allowances for her. Elsie was jealous and jealousy was a terrible thing. She couldn't bear the Orams to have been so kind, she wanted to be the only one who was kind. Well, she had been. She'd given them a nice day too – not as spectacular as the brilliant one at Whipsnade but very nice all the same, just somehow more conventional, more the sort of outing you'd expect. Elsie and George had no imagination but you couldn't blame them for that. Who, on the face of it, would think an old couple would like a winter picnic at a zoo? No, Elsie's outing was more what anyone would have thought their cup of tea – a drive to Kew Gardens and a look in the greenhouses and then a drive to Richmond and a look at the river and tea in a very good-class hotel, then back to Elsie's and an evening watching colour television. No conversation at all. Bits of chat about Dolores but nothing to get your teeth into, nothing like the talk they had with Alice and Tony. Rose knew she would treasure the talk more than anything, especially the arguing.

They *had* argued, Alice and her against Stanley and Tony, a real set-to. Nobody had got upset, nobody had shouted or been unpleasant, they'd all abided by the rules of debate, but no punches had been pulled. Ding-dong all the time. She'd been pleased with Stanley's performance. He'd been most intelligent in his remarks. The young people had listened very respectfully and she could tell they were impressed. She'd been pleased with her own showing too, though she worried that she might have sounded more violent than she felt. Anyway, she didn't care. It had been so lovely not just having pleasantries thrown at you.

161

People were full of meaningless pleasantries towards the old, they thought that was enough – and if they did go any further they handled you so carefully, that was the most insulting thing of all. You weren't worthy of combat once you were over sixty, not unless you were someone famous like Malcolm Muggeridge. If you were just an ordinary old person nobody bothered to find out what you thought.

Rose would have liked, when she tuned in to her memories of this day, to have been able to go over the argument in detail. It worried her dreadfully that she couldn't for the life of her remember what it had been about. She was ashamed she couldn't remember the main topic. If only she could ask Stanley he would trigger her memory off and it would all come back, but she couldn't bring herself to ask him. Having to do that would nullify the whole experience. How could she relish the intellectual content of that day if it had apparently made so little impression on her brain that it couldn't retain it? It was too humiliating. She preferred to cling onto the certain knowledge that something worthwhile had been discussed than run the risk of finding out it had all been about nothing.

Stanley, she knew, had enjoyed it as much as she had, if for different reasons. It was difficult to make him see that the idea of a young couple taking an old couple out for the day was at all startling. Stanley saw nothing revolutionary about it and did not quite grasp Rose's point. He accepted other people's effort so easily, that was his trouble. But he had been grateful and it was he who had invited the Oram family for tea the following Sunday. Rose's heart had leapt in the old way when she heard him, but she had managed to back him up and sound convincing and squash her apprehension which was still real enough to make her dizzy. He was quite right. Hospitality must be extended and on a grand scale and at once. There was no reason whatsoever why not. They had no secrets from the Orams – who knew how shabby and dull their house was. Nothing would be a revelation, and she didn't need to feel they didn't really want to come because if they found their company boring they wouldn't have asked them out for the day.

All week Rose worked hard in preparation for the tea. She

spring-cleaned the house, paying particular attention to the bathroom and lavatory. If they stayed a couple of hours, as they were bound to, these areas would be visited and they must be spotless. She felt some of her former resentment as she cleaned them – those places were so old-fashioned. Nowhere was the contrast between Alice's house and hers more stark than in this area. She loved the lavatory in their house. Everything was white – white basin, white pedestal, white tiles on the floor, white paint on the walls, all so hygienic and pure and what a lavatory should be. It always smelt fresh and airy and faintly antiseptic, whereas her own, no matter how many bottes of bleach she poured into the bowl, always smelled funny – fusty and earthy and generally not clean. But it *was* clean, she knew it was, scrupulously clean, it was just that it was old and probably lined with rust or something. She hated the clangy old chain you pulled – Alice's had a button – and the green paint and the old dark wooden seat and the brown pipes everywhere. She really had to take a firm hold on herself to stop getting upset.

About the tea itself she had fewer worries. She baked three kinds of cake, made her own biscuits and boiled her own ham which she was going to have on the table on the big oval plate with the willow pattern. The ham wasn't really an extravagance for she and Stanley would live off it for weeks. Well, a week. There were lots of things you could do with cooked ham and the soup at the end would be delicious. Pea soup with ham stock took some beating. She almost made soup but decided it was too heavy for tea time, and then there were such a lot of plates involved with soup. She wanted to be sure she could cope without getting flustered.

It all went off very well. They couldn't have been more appreciative, and what a tea they had eaten! It was a good job she hadn't been counting on the ham for it took a beating. Stanley carved it beautifully in long thin slices, just a rim of white round each. Tony Oram had six and Alice four and even little Amy managed a whole one to herself. She was glad, of course. She hated people to pick at their food, she liked hearty eaters. When Alice remonstrated with Tony she was fulsome in his praise. The cakes vanished too and really the only thing they left was the jelly and custard at the end which had been made for Amy. Afterwards they retired to the sitting-room and played games – I-spy, that kind of thing. Stanley had kept looking towards the television set but knew better than to put his longing into words. They'd finished off with a glass of sherry and then they'd gone home: a success, but very tiring. She could hardly clean up the mess afterwards, she felt so drained. It wasn't the work, it was the strain of having guests. She shouldn't have felt any strain but she did, she didn't feel natural, not yet. She'd found herself watching for things going wrong all the time and couldn't really relax. She kept jumping up to go and get some missing item from the table and then overdoing the apologies that it had been missing in the first place. Not the way to behave, but there you are. She half thought of confessing these feelings to Alice the next Wednesday morning but stopped herself just in time. It would only be embarrassing.

The Wednesday morning sessions were now a firm fixture, and so was the once a week babysitting. In addition, Rose had Amy in on her own when Alice went shopping on Tuesday morning, and also took her out for a walk on Monday afternoons when Alice's sister Laura came. Altogether, it was a full week. Elsie was right to comment that they were getting very thick. What Elsie didn't understand was that any services rendered were reciprocal and that there was no obligation on either side. Rose liked looking after Amy, she was glad to give Alice a break after all she'd done for her. The girl never took advantage which was what Elsie couldn't see – Alice was always scrupulous to ask, every time, if it was convenient to have Amy, convenient to babysit and Rose was always scrupulous to say, 'Are you expecting me?' when she went for coffee. They had the ideal relationship, they were what neighbourliness was about. Rose, standing in her garden the first real spring day, looked towards next door with her head high and a smile on her face. She looked forward to summer and chats over the wall and Amy in sight and hearing every day. There was nothing – or only a very little thing – to mar her pleasure.

'I can't stand it any longer.' Tony felt justified in being more emphatic than he normally allowed himself to be, even if it brought down on his head the kind of long-winded discussion he went a long way to avoid. 'It's driving me completely and utterly mad. If you don't get somebody else just every now and again I'll never go out again. What's the point? If we have a bad evening it makes it a million times worse having it dragged out another hour, and if we have a good evening it spoils it totally. And Amy sleeps now – when did she last wake up? Since she was two she's slept like a log.' He was standing at the window of their new grand sitting-room on the first floor. 'There's the Stewarts out again – no problems. They go out about four times a week, no fuss, twenty pence an hour and goodbye when they put their key in the front door. That's what I want.'

'We're very lucky to have the Pens,' Alice said, 'they're very good to us.'

'Bloody hell – *they're* good to *us* – we run a one-man charity for them. When I think of the endless bloody boring hours – days – I've put in amusing them to please you – you're raving. They're not good to us – it's the most one-sided business I've ever come across. Look, what would happen if we went out of the Pens' lives – what, eh? Total collapse, the light going out, whatever you like. What would happen if they went out of ours? Relief, that's all I'd feel, bloody relief.'

Alice carried on ironing. She knew he didn't like her ironing in the evenings but Amy was so dangerous to have around when irons were on and there were so many other things to do when she had her nap.

'The point is,' Tony was saying, more patiently, 'you don't like it either, do you?'

She kept quiet, sweeping the iron across the wrinkled sheets and folding them with great precision.

'She gets on your nerves,' Tony went on. 'You're so careful with her the strain exhausts you. I just don't know why you bother.'

'We've had all this before,' Alice said.

'True. But you're getting more and more involved with them, you can't do what you want any more – there are so many trumped-up reasons for leaning on the Pendleburys, you've worked so hard to make them feel indispensable you've come to believe they are.' He stopped and looked at her, then took the iron out of her hands. 'Stop ironing. Sit down. You look like a bloody drudge.'

'Well I'm not.'

'Let's go out and have a meal. I'm going to go and ask that *au pair* girl the Stewarts have if she'll come in for a couple of hours.'

'We can't – it would hurt Mrs Pendlebury's feelings dreadfully.'

'Why? For God's sake – she can't take offence because we ask somebody else in to babysit, what the hell has that got to do with her?'

'She thinks she does it to give me a break, but if we get somebody else then we could always get somebody else and not need her.'

'Good idea.'

'We can't, it's not worth it.'

'But I *want* to go.'

'I've got a perfectly good meal ready.'

'Keep it for tomorrow. Please, Alice. It's ages since we just went out without any fuss. After September we'll hardly get out again anyway. I'm going to ask that girl.'

She let him go, out of weakness. The truth was she never wanted to go out enough. Even working herself up to go out when the Pens came in was an effort – and yet once out, she enjoyed it, it was good for her. And as Tony said, after September when the new baby was born, they would hardly get out at all. They must make the most of their comparative freedom, before they were back to three-hourly feeds. She dressed in something Tony liked and tried to stimulate some enthusiasm. She wasn't fair to him. Charlotte was always reading her little lectures on keeping herself young and fresh and lively for her husband. This, according to Charlotte, meant not doing any housework or cooking or other demeaning tasks – demeaning to the body and the intelligence – but getting other people to do them so that you remained beautifully preserved for your husband. It was useful to be able to say to her that they couldn't afford chars or *au pairs*, but it was a cheat to get out of the argument that way. She was always teasing Tony and saying wouldn't you like to be married to Charlotte? – teasing because he couldn't stand her. She was the epitome of the middle-class graduate wife that he loathed. He had only to see her, in all her six o'clock finery, lolling on a chaise-longue in the drawing-room windows, Sam safely with an *au pair* girl, glass of sherry in her hand, ears pricked for dear Richard to enter, to maintain he wanted to vomit. Alice thought she could well remind him of that if he spent the rest of the evening nagging her.

But he didn't. They went to an Italian restaurant near by and had a meal and she had to admit it was relaxing and enjoyable. Usually they were so keen to get the most out of the Pendleburys that they crammed a film and a meal into the time and ruined both.

'Did you know,' she said over the coffee, 'the Pendleburys have a flat on top of their house.'

'They can have a penthouse for all I care.'

'Their son, Frank, the one in Australia, used to live up there with his own little kitchen and it's all equipped.'

'You fancy moving in, do you?'

'Don't you think,' she went on, ignoring his attempt at facetiousness, 'that it might be a good idea to get them to rent it to Jane?'

He said nothing at all, just looked at her until she blushed and bent her head.

'You won't be able to ignore her,' she said, 'we'll have to have her to stay. In fact, I'm surprised your mother hasn't pointed out we have enough room for her to live with us. It might be very clever to forestall that.'

'It might also be very foolish, and bring all kinds of things down on our innocent heads. I don't like Jane, you don't like Jane, Jane doesn't like me and she certainly doesn't like you. To invite her to live next door would be ridiculous.'

'She is your sister.'

'That doesn't make me responsible for her welfare. If she comes to London it's under her own steam.'

'Your mother thinks – '

'I don't care what my mother thinks.'

'But you do. You *do* care what your mother thinks, even if you don't like her either. She only has to get on your back and you can't get her off it.'

'I might if you'd let me.'

'It was like that long before I ever appeared on the scene.'

'But I was just about to break away.'

'Again?'

'I really would have done, I'd have emigrated.'

'Like Frank.'

'Who?'

'Frank Pendlebury, he emigrated.'

'Sensible bloke. I'm not surprised. If Mrs Pendlebury was my mother not even you would have stopped me emigrating.'

'I bet she was a marvellous mother, you've got her all wrong. She's not in the least like your mother, she's got a spirit of adventure about her.'

'That wine went to your head.'

'Yes, it did, it always does when I'm pregnant.'

She looked very pretty, flushed and soft, her cheeks full of curves and hollows.

'Let's go home,' he said. 'No big bad wolf tonight.'

'You're very unkind.'

They didn't discuss Jane any more, but by the time the following Wednesday came round Alice had made up her mind to ask Mrs Pendlebury if Jane could have their flat. The more she thought about it, the more attractive the idea seemed. If Jane was next door she wouldn't ever need to stay the night. She would be distinctly useful for babysitting – Amy liked her if nobody else did – and she was not the sort of person who would hang about them. That was not her technique. When she came to see them it was always resentfully, a visit she imagined was a duty one to keep her mother quiet. Alice knew Mrs Oram pushed Jane into it with her 'Haven't you been to see Amy this week?' and then she felt obliged to come and to stay. She was a funny girl. They were a funny family, not at all Alice's idea of what a family should be. No bonds except blood seemed to unite them and yet none of them broke free. Each of the three grumbled about maintaining contact with the others and yet they all did. Alice wished she'd known Tony's father, for whose memory they all seemed to have great admiration. Daddy had been dead ten years yet they all constantly referred to Daddy approving or not approving of something.

Mrs Pendlebury would like Jane. She would automatically approve of her because she was a nurse and hard-up and hard-working. Her excessive neatness and orderly behaviour would instantly recommend her, and the frigidity of her emotional responses would be labelled keeping herself to herself, and applauded. Jane would be quiet, modest in her needs, would speak when spoken to and not otherwise. Her insipid nature would be read as shyness and her apathy on every subject except dieting called gentleness. Jane, no matter which way one looked, was tailor-made for the Pendleburys. And it would be doing everyone such a favour. Jane would get cheap accommodation and the Pendleburys would get company, just enough to make the house feel lived in without intruding on their peace and quiet. It would also make them feel they were being public spirited and there was nothing Mrs P. liked better. Alice could already hear her saying they were just doing it to help out, housing being in the state it was. The fact that Jane would only be with them for two years, the length of time her diploma would take, would be an enormous asset – a short-term investment giving them a let-out should it all not work. She would go home to her mother in Chelmsford every weekend and do all her laundry there and not bother them at all.

Alice could hardly wait to broach the subject and yet at the same time knew how important it was to do just that – wait.

The negotiations were as delicate as those involving a multi-national agreement and Alice proceeded with the finesse of a diplomat. Easily half an hour was spent on preliminaries, on working Mrs Pendlebury into a good mood. There were certain topics Alice knew produced a Pavlovian reflex and she introduced them one by one. Head of the list was a boring saga about Amy's doings – Mrs P. could not get enough of them. It was the next best thing to having Amy on her lap. So Alice laboriously retold the incident of Amy locking herself in the bathroom and how Tony had had to be brought home from work and climbed the drainpipe and got in the window and all the time Amy sang songs through the keyhole but could on no account be prevailed on to go and look for the key which it later transpired she'd covered with soap and thrown down the sink. Amy's cuteness had to be admired, her mischievousness exclaimed over, her bravery acknowledged, then, as always, there was a parallel incident from Frank's past to be dredged up and swopped.

By the time all this had gone on, Mrs P. was on her second cup of tea and laughing a lot and her coat was undone. With great skill Alice moved nearer her prey.

'I suppose,' she said, 'your grandson will be up to these kind of tricks now. He'll keep you going when you get out there.'

'I expect he will.'

'Won't it be exciting seeing him for the first time?'

'Well, I've seen photographs, Frank's kept us well supplied with those, but they aren't the same, are they? Yes, I expect we'll notice a difference.'

'When are you going?'

'About September. Stanley hasn't seen to it yet but he'll have to get cracking soon. He's so slow he makes me scream.'

Alice smiled sympathetically. Mrs P. had only lately brought herself to criticize Stanley openly – it was part of their new intimacy.

'How long will you stay?' Another much-asked question begging another much-enjoyed answer.

'A month I should think, mustn't outstay our welcome. Of course, Stanley would stay for ever but as I said to him, quite apart from anything else there's the house to consider.' Alice held her breath and felt suddenly nervous. 'It can't be left indefinitely, nor the garden.'

Alice knew any offer to help would be haughtily refused. Instead she said, 'It is a worry.'

'Yes, but he doesn't see it is. It's a worry anyway.'

'So's this one. Tony thinks we should let the two top rooms now we're all straight. The rent would pay for the rates at least.' She paused. Had she imagined it, or was there just a flicker of suspicion in Mrs P.'s eyes? But she had to go on, it was now or never. 'Have you ever let any of your house?'

'No.'

'I don't fancy it either,' Alice said, quickly, 'but men don't understand, do they?'

'We thought about it after Frank left,' Mrs Pendlebury said, quite relaxed, 'but it would be such a lot of bother.'

'Wouldn't it,' Alice said.

'Mind you, it's wicked us having all that room.'

'I don't see why. You're entitled to it.'

'That's what Stanley says.'

'Do you know anyone who does let rooms round here?' Alice asked, knowing damn well Mrs P. knew nobody.

'No, I don't, not these days.'

She would never ask why, that wasn't in her code.

'It's Tony's sister,' Alice said. 'She's a nurse and she's coming to London for two years to do a special diploma. She'll be at U.C.H. and wants somewhere in this area, just a room, cheap – you know nurses get paid so little. We've said she can live here but she wants to be independent. She doesn't want a flat – she'll be going home every weekend – and she doesn't want to share. I can't think how she's going to find anywhere.'

Mrs P. was sipping tea in quick little sips, the cup effectively masking her expression.

'So if you hear of anything,' Alice finished, 'you might let me know.'

'Yes, I will,' said Mrs P., vague as vague, which was a sign that the point had been taken.

'I've been sewing,' Alice said. It was time to leave well alone.

She left it at that for another two weeks, but brought in mentions of Jane haphazardly. Each time she did, she saw Mrs P.'s face register the reference. How long before she dared tackle the subject again? It was so hard to know if the idea really had taken root. She could expect no open indication. But in this she was proved wrong. Another week later and Mrs P. came in – marched in – looking very perky and announced, 'I've been thinking about that nurse.'

'Jane?'

'Yes, I believe you said she was called that. I was thinking we ought to take in somebody like a nurse in our house.'

'What a *good* idea, I never thought of that.'

'Well, I put two and two together and I thought what are we doing with that flat of Frank's when a nurse could be having it.

Course, it might not be to her liking, it's not smart, it's shabby really – '

'She'll be thrilled,' Alice said.

'I don't know about that, she'd have to see it.'

'Of course, but I know she'll be thrilled. What kind of rent were you thinking of?'

'That would be between her and us,' Mrs P. said, quite sharply. 'We'd have to sort something out, that's Stanley's department.'

Alice felt she'd won a great victory and sensed an elation too about Mrs P. Yet, as the morning wore on, she observed a change take place in her neighbour. She began to frown, to clutch at things anxiously, to bite her lip, and at last she blurted out, 'It isn't a flat, you know. You mustn't tell her it's a flat.'

'No, of course not.'

'It's just two rooms and a kitchen, not even a proper kitchen, just two hot-plates and a plug for a kettle. Frank didn't do any proper cooking, it was just for when he came in late and wanted to make himself something. I always said to him I'd be willing to get up any time and cook for him or he could always use my kitchen but he said he felt he was disturbing us and it made him feel happier, he's very considerate, not like Stanley. So it isn't really a kitchen.'

'She eats at the hospital,' Alice said, soothingly, 'and the rest of the time she has snacks – apples and cheese – she's always slimming.'

'Oh well then.' But a minute later – 'There's no bathroom you know, it wouldn't be very suitable, being a nurse, would it, not having a bathroom, being a young lady. There's only a sink and she'd have to share the bath and the other. When Frank was here we had an arrangement – he'd have the bathroom certain times before he went to work and we'd have it before or after and then having the other downstairs – you know, where Stanley ... having the other was a help. But a nurse – '

'It sounds fine,' Alice said cheerfully, but Mrs. P. was in full flood, getting more excited every minute.

'The furniture isn't up to much, it would need a proper going over, not that I'd mind that.'

'Jane can clean it herself.'

'Oh it's *clean*, goodness me, it's *clean*, I wouldn't have dirt in my house anywhere – '

'I only meant – '

'It's clean but it's old and there isn't much of it.'

'We could lend her some things.'

'I don't know if Stanley would like that, he's funny about borrowing.'

Alice knew exactly who was funny about borrowing.

'Well,' she said patiently, 'Jane might not think she needed to borrow anything.' She tried to think of something comforting to say. 'She's a very tidy person, my sister-in-law, very quiet too. You'd like her.'

'I don't suppose we'd see much of her.'

'She does work hard and long hours.'

'These nurses do, it's a scandal.'

Alice knew she was winning, but then another panic.

'All the same, they like to enjoy themselves when they can, I've seen that, she has to have her leisure moments, she wants to be with people her own age doesn't she, what about entertaining?'

The last word was a screech. Patiently, Alice said, 'Jane doesn't entertain. She can't afford it. I've never ever known her have a party or even a group of friends home. She sometimes goes out to the pictures or for a meal but that's about all.'

'Oh, well.'

'But if it worries you, perhaps it would be better if I didn't mention it to her?'

'It's up to her, isn't it?'

Alice wanted to say no, it's up to you, but restrained herself.

'She's coming over this Sunday. Could she pop in then, just to see if you liked her?'

'I don't need to like her.'

'No, but you know what I mean.'

'I don't know about Sunday, Sunday's difficult.'

'Never mind, then, some other time.' Alice felt it was important, even though she didn't want to put pressure at this moment, to get an unequivocal answer. 'Shall I mention it to Jane?' she asked.

'Yes, if you like,' Mrs P. said, grandly, offhand, 'no harm in mentioning it.'

'It's just I wouldn't like to raise her hopes if – '

'If what?'

'Well, if you might change your mind.'

'*I* won't change my mind.'

'Oh, good. I'll send her in then, the next time she comes, but not this Sunday, if it isn't convenient.'

There was a pause. They were both exhausted. Alice searched around for a subject that would reduce the emotional pressure.

'It looks as if we're in for a lovely spring,' she said at last.

'Yes, yes, it does. A man on the wireless was saying it would be a good summer too, but I can't see it happening, not after the scorcher we had last year.'

'We've got daffodils out in our garden. Would you like to come and see them?'

They went out into the garden. Against the wall of the kitchen the sun was hot.

'That's better,' Mrs P. said. 'You get stifled indoors.'

They wandered round the garden as though it were a sizeable estate with Mrs P. bending down to look at flowers and shrubs and to poke at weeds. She kept turning and lifting her face to the sun and sniffing and smiling, with her eyes closed. Alice noticed how very white her skin was, a real parchment pallor made worse by the dull white-grey of her hair straggling from underneath the eternal hat. She really didn't look well, whereas Stanley was nut-brown and bright-faced. But to pass any comment on Mrs P.'s appearance was strictly taboo. She didn't like to be told she didn't look well or that she was drawn or haggard.

They were still examining the borders when Charlotte walked into the garden, round the side entrance. She smiled her hard, impersonal smile and said wasn't the weather lovely and then in a voice that set Alice's teeth on edge she said she was longing to show her garden off to Mrs P. and to ask her advice. Alice expected Mrs P. to refuse abruptly or to take refuge in vagueness, to start mumbling excuses and find she had to get back to Stanley. But not a bit of it – Mrs P. was all laughs and charm and shall I come now and off they both went leaving Alice also smiling and nodding like a clockwork toy, alone in her garden.

She went inside and watched. Charlotte's house was right at the end of the road, a dozen houses away but at an angle. She could see the two of them walking round the much larger garden over there and presently, as they stood talking, the *au pair* girl brought a tray out and put it on a garden table and Charlotte and Mrs P. sat on a wooden seat under a tree and drank from the china cups. Both of them smiled all the time. Charlotte's cat came to the table and Mrs P. took hold of it and cradled it in her lap and stroked it and the cat was quite happy, curled up and slept. Alice turned away, unaccountably depressed. It was good of Charlotte to bother – it was nice for Mrs P. to have another friend – but she felt sad and excluded. Charlotte had specifically asked her to come too, had even consulted her about whether she thought Mrs P. would come, this feeling of hers was too silly to analyse. But she knew she was worried. Mrs P. was her responsibility. She was the one who had nurtured and cared for her, she was the one who had endured the downs as well as the ups, she was the one who had extended love and friendship to Mrs P. Did Charlotte know what she was doing? But wasn't that what she had been working towards? Hadn't she been trying to bring Mrs P. into fellowship with others? Why then did she tremble at her own success? Why should she behave like an anxious lover?

When the doorbell rang Alice was lying on her bed at the back of the house waiting for Amy to wake up and trying to control her own unworthy feelings. She almost didn't answer it.

Mrs P. was standing on the doorstep.

'I think I forgot my gloves,' she said.

'Oh, I hadn't noticed.'

'I had them in the garden.'

'Let's look then.'

There was an embarrassment between them. Neither spoke as they went back into the garden. The gloves were lying on the path. Alice picked them up and handed them to Mrs P. Her face felt red.

'There you are.'

'Thank you. They're only an old pair but they fit well. I'd have been sorry to lose them. Well, I'd best get back, Stanley will be wondering where I've got to.'

But she went on standing there, searching for something to say.

'I like your garden better than hers,' Mrs P. blurted out, 'it's cosier somehow, more friendly.'

'A mess, though. Charlotte really looks after hers. I'm ashamed of ours.'

'Oh, but she has a gardener and plenty of time to work in it herself with that *au pair* to do the house.'

'Still.'

'It's not my sort of garden, hers, too formal, too laid out. I shouldn't feel comfortable in it. I've often looked at it from our windows and thought well, she can keep it. Ours are smaller but they're nicer.'

'Perhaps. Her house is lovely.'

'Yes, very nice. She asked me in to look round but I didn't have time.'

'You should have looked, it's beautiful, it's like my sister Laura's, all architect-designed.'

'There's nothing wrong with your own.'

'Oh, it's all anyhow.'

'I think it's lovely, you've done wonders with it, what do you want to run it down for?'

'I don't really, it's just – I don't know.'

'Here, are you all right? You seem a bit low. I thought that last week. I said to Stanley, Alice seems off colour, excuse me mentioning it.'

'I'm having another baby.'

'Ooh!' It was exactly that sound. 'Oooh! How lovely! Oooh! Isn't that nice. When's the happy event?'

'The beginning of September.'

'And you're not showing at all, you'd never guess. Well then, that *is* nice. It'll be a boy, I'm never wrong.'

Everything was fine again. They parted glowing and Alice sang as she ran up the stairs to get Amy. Only a small part of her registered with unease the fact that her happiness these days seemed dependent on Mrs P.'s approval.

Chapter Fourteen

Rose knitted a great many things for Alice's new baby. She sat all summer in the garden knitting away, pleased to be doing something both useful and enjoyable. All her garments were blue, a soft sky-blue that nobody could help but like, bonnets and jackets and leggings. She edged many of them with satin ribbon and bought tiny pearl buttons that were the devil to sew on. As she finished each article she washed it and dried it and pressed it and folded it and wrapped it in tissue paper and put it in a box. Amy loved to peep in this box but was never allowed to take the contents out so that it became a game of great excitement just lifting the lid and peeping between the folds of rustling paper. To please her, Rose also knitted some clothes for her doll, in blue, and wrapped these up and gave them to her and Amy positively shivered with pleasure.

Sometimes, Alice came and sat with her but more often she went and sat with Alice. It was more suitable, in the circumstances, for her to do that. They'd built a stile over the wall at the bottom – a makeshift affair of boxes and bricks – which she could get over quite easily but which might have been dangerous for Alice to attempt in her condition. Amy soon learnt how to negotiate it and came over on her own whenever she liked. She did it when Elsie was visiting and Rose showed off about it no end. She laughed when Elsie suggested her life wasn't her own with a two-year-old popping over whenever she felt like it and wrecking the place. 'Who wants their life to be their own,' she said, and laughed again at Elsie's expression. She was so proud when, in front of Elsie, Amy climbed on to her lap and cuddled her and gave her a kiss and afterwards wouldn't even look at Elsie.

'My goodness,' Elsie said, 'that's cupboard love, if ever I saw it.'

'Whatever do you mean?' Rose asked.

'Well, she's after something isn't she? Sweets I expect.'

'Sweeties,' Amy said, helpfully.

'There you are, what did I say? She knows you spoil her with sweets, that's what it's all about, isn't it, young lady.'

'I'd thank you not to put words into children's mouths,' Rose said, furious. 'Amy's never in her life had sweets from me.'

'Sweets,' Amy said again.

'Hasn't she?' Elsie said, 'Doesn't sound like it I must say. Knows the word well enough.'

'Of course she knows the word, she's not stupid, not like some people, nor jealous.'

'I beg your pardon?'

'How's Dolores? Anything on the way yet?'

'Give her a chance, it's only June, they were only married in October.' Elsie was successfully side-tracked, but not without realizing it. 'They aren't properly settled yet. I wouldn't want them to have a family, not yet, not till they have a house and they're all set up.'

'Like you,' Rose said.

'Yes, well, we had the sense to wait.'

'You can call it sense, I'd call it something else.'

'Oh you would, would you, and what might that be may I ask?'

'You ended up with just the one. You left it far too late.'

'That had nothing to do with it.'

'Hadn't it? I'd say it had. You were lucky the one you did have wasn't a mongol. Better to have them when you're young without all this waiting for washing machines and things, better to have another like Alice's doing, like I did, before the first's too old.'

She was always, Elsie thought, so full of herself when she was handing out advice. There was no puncturing her vanity, never had been. Shy, she had said to Stanley many times, shy? Rose didn't know what shyness was. She could get on to topics that made you blush and you were prevented from arguing, just out of decency. She was blunt and crude, barged on regardless without taking any account of your feelings, but *her* feelings, that was something else again. Elsie felt a growing desire to get her own back, she didn't care how. For a time, after Stanley's illness, Rose had seemed a different person, kind and considerate, not so sharp, but now she was worse than ever, really puffed up with these blessed neighbours of hers, as if nobody else had neighbours, as if there was anything special about them, as if they *were* anybody.

'Thank you for the tea,' she said, putting her cup down, 'very nice. And the cake.'

'That was Alice's,' Rose said, 'she made it for me yesterday.'

'Oh, did she. Very nice too. I wish I had neighbours who made me cakes.'

'You'd go a long way to find one like my Alice.'

'Your Alice?'

'Well, she's like a daughter to me, like Ellen would have been.'

'You hope.'

'What do you mean by that?'

'Things don't always turn out as we expect, do they? Look at Frank, never thought he'd leave home, did you? And he did, at eighteen, soon as he could.' Elsie was frightened the minute she'd said it – glad but frightened. It would be no good pretending there hadn't been implications in what she'd said – Rose was quick on the uptake. She was glaring at her now fit to terrify anyone. 'Of course he needed to go for his job,' she found herself saying. Rose could be violent when roused.

'Yes, he did. You can't farm in England, not today, not unless you're in a farming family. That was the only reason Frank left home.'

'Yes, of course, Rose.'

'I'm taking Amy back now, I might get her pushchair and take her to the swings. Do you fancy coming?'

'To the swings?'

'That's what I said, don't look so shocked.'

'What would I want with swings?'

'It's not what you want, it's what Amy wants – she likes swings, children do.'

'Oh. No, thank you. I've got better things to do.'

'I'm glad to hear it.'

'What?'

'I said I'm glad to hear it. I've got nothing more worth doing than helping a friend out by taking her child for a walk. We could all do with helping each other a lot more. Some of us are too wrapped up with ourselves.'

Elsie hated her. 'Well then I won't keep you back from your good deed,' she said, 'just mind it doesn't rebound, that's all. Mind you don't regret all this coming and going. I only hope it all turns out all right, I only hope you're not wearing rose-coloured speactacles, that's all.'

'Oh, get on with you,' Rose said, quite good-humouredly.

'My conscience is clear.'

Rose laughed. 'That's nice for you,' she said.

Afterwards, she tried to tell Stanley what Elsie had said, how silly she'd been, but to her surprise Stanley's reaction wasn't quite what she had expected.

'She might have a point,' he said, warming his feet in front of the fire the way she had told him not to.

'What point?' Rose was so amazed she let him go on doing it.

'Well, you think the world of Alice.'

'Certainly I do – and with cause. You might not be sitting there tonight doing that dangerous thing if it hadn't been for her.'

'Yes, well.'

'You're not getting out of it that easy – yes, well. I'll yes well – what are you getting at? What's that sister of yours been saying? Out with it, I'm waiting.'

'She hasn't been saying anything. She said it to you. I'm only saying she might have a point.'

'What point?'

'Well, the girl's only human after all.'

'Whatever are you getting at now – '

'She's only human,' Stanley repeated, 'that's the point. You expect too much of her maybe with liking her so much. She isn't perfect, that's the point.'

'I never thought,' Rose announced, at last taking a swipe at his slippered feet, 'I never thought I'd live to see the day, I didn't. You're as wicked as that sister of yours, both of you are wicked, you can't see good when it stares you in the face without wanting to spoil it. I'm disgusted, that's what.'

'I didn't mean that. I like Alice as much as you do. It's only – '

'You're jealous.'

'Now don't be silly – '

'It's not silly. I can see it plain as plain. You like to be cock of the walk, that's what it is. It was the same with Frank, you couldn't bear me to do anything for him, you wanted me all to yourself and now it's Alice you've taken against in just the same way.'

'Nonsense.'

'Nonsense is it? We'll see. And we're letting those rooms to that nurse. That's final.'

Stanley wondered, not for the first time, if Rose's brain was differently constructed from other people's. He had been all for letting the rooms to the nurse, she must know he had. It was Rose who had hummed and hawed and first said yes and then said no. He'd just let her twitter on without interrupting, agreeing with what her final verdict of each day was. Yet now she was pretending that he had somehow been against it. Perhaps Alice understood her better than he did. He hoped so. Since his illness he didn't seem to be able to cope the way he had once done, which was strange because he knew he hadn't so much to cope with.

'I'll tell her tomorrow,' Rose said, 'I'll get her to bring that girl round and we'll fix it up.'

'You do that,' Stanley said.

'Yes, I shall. I shall. It's a scandal having those rooms empty. One thing, it'll leave somebody in the house when we're away. I didn't ever like the idea of leaving it empty all that time.' Stanley kept very quiet. 'Have you fixed it up yet?' He knew she would say that, he had been waiting.

'No,' he said, straight out.

'Why not?'

'It's complicated. They're always so busy down there. But there's plenty of time, not as if we're emigrating.'

'That's what you always say. Just don't you go letting me down that's all. I only hope Alice's has her baby before we go. I shouldn't like to be away then. There'll be a lot to do.'

'I expect she'd manage.'

'Of course she'd manage.' She was angry with him for pointing this out. 'We all manage if we have to, but there's no need just to manage.' Stanley was silent. 'She isn't looking well, you know.'

'Who?'

'Alice. She looks peaky. She needs a holiday.'

'Maybe she'll have one. Maybe she'll go and stay with her mother.'

'Her mother's dead,' Rose said, scathing.

'I didn't know,' said Stanley, huffed.

'You didn't know because you don't listen, you don't care what people are telling you. You've been told umpteen times her parents are both dead, killed in a car crash, dreadful. She's only got that sister of hers, Laura.'

'Oh. Well, maybe she'll go and stay with her.'

'Don't be silly,' said Rose vehemently. 'I'm going to tell her she needs a holiday. I am.'

But there was no need. Alice told her the very next day that she and Tony were going off for a week to Rye in Sussex while Laura looked after Amy – told her with apprehension in case she disapproved but Rose was emphatically encouraging. It was just what she needed. Amy would be quite happy with her cousins, it would be good practice for when the baby was born, the weather was lovely, Rye was lovely, everything was lovely. Rose glowed with approval and became quite excited herself. Of course she would come in and water the plants, of course she would let the window cleaner in, of course she would open the windows now and again, of course she would check they'd put things off, of course, of course, of course . . .

When she left the house, with Alice already packing, Rose remembered she hadn't mentioned the nurse. But it didn't matter, there was plenty of time. Her own relief made her feel guilty, but she tried to ignore it. She must concentrate now on the job in hand. As soon as she got in she laboriously wrote down a list of everything she had to do for Alice. Stanley asked her what she was doing but she shushed him at once, and said it was private. Well, she knew it wasn't private but Stanley was such a gossip and Alice didn't want the whole road knowing about her business. He would tell everyone, not honouring the implicit trust in the job. These days it took him half an hour getting along the street with all the people he talked to. That Charlotte was his boon companion – hours and hours he spent at her gate droning on about his blessed operation. It was a wonder she could put up with it. Stanley, of course, could never see when someone was being patronizing, just humouring you, just letting you fill in time. It was the greatest of his many failings.

So Stanley was excluded. Rose went next door on her own every day and did all the necessary things. She loved it. The very first morning when she went in the house was full of sunshine and the colours everywhere dazzled her. She stood with her back against the hall door and a great feeling of peace and sweetness seemed to flood from every corner towards her. Slowly, she toured the rooms and the sun played like music everywhere she went, rippling in giant scales from one end to another. She was careful to touch nothing but she noticed everything and sometimes longed to pick up this or that. Alice was clean but not tidy. She herself could never have gone away leaving clothes festooned everywhere and drawers and cupboards open. But she didn't condemn Alice for that – it was right, she had her priorities right. Now Elsie wouldn't have seen that, she would have been horrified, she had no imagination at all and Dolores was the same. You wouldn't catch either of them having less than an immaculate house and not a scrap of enterprise between them.

The day the window cleaner came Rose went from room to room with him, never leaving him alone. It annoyed him but she didn't care about that. She wanted to do her job properly and all he had to do was do his. He was a cheeky young fellow, told her Alice – yes he called her that – Alice usually gave him a cup of coffee, but she told him smartly that what Mrs Oram did in her own house was one thing but what *she* did in somebody else's was another. He also said Alice just left him to it and he pulled the door behind him when he'd finished. She told him she'd wait and see him out, though she didn't disbelieve him. Alice was very casual. She left the key in the door all the time, that's if it wasn't wide open anyway, and her shopping lay in the car with the boot open to the world for everyone to see till she had time to bring it in. All very well, but she was putting temptation in people's way and that wasn't right.

The best morning was Thursday when Alice had said Mothercare would be delivering a parcel of things for Amy and for the new baby and would she – if she had time – unpack it and check off the items and – if she had time – put them in the airing cupboard. The parcel duly came and Rose unpacked it in the bedroom where she could spread things out on the bed and keep them clean. She'd put her spectacles on and brought a pencil and she ticked all the items off – all correct – and unwrapped them. The prices fascinated her and she wished she had somebody with her to exclaim to. Putting the goods in the airing cupboard was fun too – such beautiful sheets there, such beautiful towels. She had to move some of them to make room and did so reverently, tidying them without realizing as she did.

On her way out she heard a voice shouting, 'Hello, Mrs Pendlebury,' and peering along the road saw Charlotte unloading her car.

'Oh, hello,' she replied, but distant, cold. She didn't like calling attention to the fact that she was coming out of Alice's house. Charlotte had put her bag down and was coming along the pavement. Rose trotted quickly to the gate, preferring to meet her there.

'I hear you've got a caretaking job,' said Charlotte, with that smile.

'Oh, yes,' Rose said, vague, looking over her shoulder.

'I was wondering whether I could leave the key of our house with you too – we're going away tomorrow and it would be so nice to know somebody was popping in.'

'Well I don't know really,' Rose said, seething at the impudence.

'You have enough to do, have you?'

At least she could take a hint.

'Well, I am a bit busy.'

'Another time then. Will you come and see Jemimah's new kittens? She's had six and they're adorable.'

'Oh, yes, yes, I will,' still very vague.

'When can I ask you – let me see – how about this afternoon for tea – just a cup of tea, I'm not a good baker like Alice.'

'I don't know about this afternoon.' Immediately Rose heard herself she was sorry. There was no need for her to be like that. Hurriedly she said, 'Well just for five minutes.'

'Lovely. About four o'clock?'

'Yes, that'll be all right.'

'Bring Mr Pendlebury with you. He hasn't seen my garden.'

'Yes, all right.'

They went dressed in their best clothes, Stanley reflecting that it was a sign of how far Rose had progressed that they no longer wore them to go to Alice's. He'd been allowed for some time now to go next door with his ordinary trousers on, as long as he put on a tie and jacket with his shirt. But it was the old Rose that afternoon, fussing away, getting herself into a state over nothing, suspicious about the reasons she'd been invited. Stanley was glad when it was all over. Charlotte was very kind but Rose didn't seem to take to her in the way she did to Alice. The difference, as he saw it, was that Alice was soft, full of anxieties herself, full of worries and self-deprecation which Rose knew about and could respond to. Charlotte was not. Whatever she was really like, she appeared confident and clipped. Her conversation sounded artificial, rehearsed, and there was nothing more likely to make Rose uneasy. She strained all the time to keep her end up with Charlotte and the strain showed.

'I'm worn out,' she said as soon as they were home. 'That's done me for today.'

'Very nice,' Stanley said, abstracted.

'Oh, she means well, but she's not my sort. Oil and water don't mix, no good trying.'

Stanley sneaked a look at her.

'What's up?'

'I've got a headache.'

'Have a lie down.'

'Yes, I will' – but she didn't move. She felt so depressed she didn't dare go and lie down. She must distract herself before the 'What's-the-use?' feeling swamped her. Why? Why on this lovely sunny day of all days? She roused herself from the chair and went, a little unsteadily, into the garden. Always better outside. She felt lonely and sad but not so persecuted. There was a newspaper lying on the garden table. Stanley left them any old place. She picked it up and sat down where he had been sitting and tried to read it. Her eye was drawn to a heading:

'70-Year-Old Woman Dead 6 Weeks.'

That was her age next birthday. She read the line several times,

saying the words to herself, before she went any further. The
report said:

Mrs Janet Barber was found dead today in her third-floor flat. Aged
70, Mrs Barber had been ill for many years with chronic arthritis but
had refused offers of a ground-floor pensioner's flat. The medical
report stated she died of a heart attack at least six weeks ago. Neighbours in the block said there was nothing to make them suspicious.
Mrs Barber spoke to nobody and rarely went out. She had no milk
delivered and few letters. Her only living relative was a sister-in-
law, herself an invalid, who visited from time to time. It was this
relative, Mrs Anne Barber, who found her sister-in-law.

Rose let the paper fall out of her hands. She was crying, her
body shaking. The sun shone very brightly but it was a menacing brightness, hard, metallic. She wanted to run screaming
from it. Stanley came out slopping tea all over a saucer.

'Here,' he said, 'have a cup of tea.' He was so unobservant,
never seeing her tears. 'You should wear sunglasses,' he said, 'that
sun's strong. What have you been doing with my paper? It's all
scrunched up.'

'I was reading it.'

'That makes a change. What were you reading?'

Rose jabbed a finger at the item. Stanley peered at it.

'Oh that,' he said, 'I don't read those bits. Nothing of interest
there.'

'Nothing of interest?'

'No, not to me. You'll always get silly people like that, not
looking after themselves.'

'She had arthritis, she couldn't get about.'

'Well, she should have looked after herself.'

'But she didn't know anybody, she hadn't any family, nobody
came near her.'

'I expect it was her own fault. Look – it says – "refused offers
of a ground-floor pensioner's flat". There you are, what did I tell
you? Some people are just stubborn.'

'Like me.'

'You're not stubborn. Anyway, you're not living on your own
in a third-floor flat with arthritis and you've got family and
neighbours.'

'Family? Frank's in Australia, what good would that be?'

'There's Elsie.'

'How often does she come? Every six weeks, like the sister-in-law in the paper.'

'What are you getting at?'

He stared at her, belligerent, his lower lip sticking out. He didn't like the way things were going, not at all. Here they were in the middle of a lovely summer day and this had to happen, a bolt out of the blue, as surprising as if it started to snow at this very minute. He scratched his head. What was needed was a diversion, something to take her mind off things before that hunted look claimed her face.

'I was thinking,' he said, 'we should have a day out while the weather lasts, a day by the seaside. We could go to Brighton, tomorrow, first thing, have our lunch and tea out and a walk on the pier?'

She shook her head, still crying, and he felt frightened. He wished Alice wasn't away. There must be something the matter with Rose, something he didn't know about, something serious.

'I'm sending for the doctor,' he said, but she at once cried harder and shook her head and got in such a state that he had to take that back.

'Quiet then,' he kept saying, 'quiet then, or I will send for the doctor,' and bit by bit he edged her into the house.

In bed, alone, Rose slept. The sun was still shining when she woke up. At first she was alarmed to be in bed with the sun shining but then she remembered. The sheets were cool and she felt comfortable. She had a strange feeling of lightness and distance, as though she wasn't really inside herself, but on the outside looking in – strange, but not unpleasant. The drowsiness that made her eyes heavy was hard to fight but she felt it was dangerous and must be controlled and fought it hard. Eventually, she got out of bed, amazed to find she still had her clothes on, even her shoes. Stanley must have been in a right old panic. It made her smile to think about it but then memories of how she'd disgraced herself took the smile off her face. Stanley would want to know what had been the matter. He had a right to ask but she wasn't going to be able to answer him. It would be no good appealing to any powers of intuition – Stanley had none – nor could she ask him to identify with her sense of the supernatural. The nearest she would be able to get would be to tell him she'd felt as if someone was walking over her grave. He would understand that, and put it down to the piece in the newspaper on top of feeling depressed. That would have to do. Digging deeper was in any case painful, but she knew that feeling, that state of terror, had nothing to do with newspaper stories or depression or tiredness. She'd had that feeling since she was seven and had learnt to live with it, until recently. It was only now that she was old that she couldn't deal with it.

There had never been any telling when this vision of her own mortality would strike. If anything, she had it worst when she was happy. She remembered particularly the day Stanley had said he loved her and asked her to marry him and her happiness – such a physical ache of pleasure – had been pierced by a terror so acute that she had clung to him and cried. He had been amused. She couldn't make him see how happiness was so near tragedy, she couldn't tell him how afraid it made her. Then again, when Frank was born, the sweetness and relief mixed with misery until she crouched under the sheets and wept and wept. Stanley said she was morbid, that was all. Morbid? She knew what the word meant and she wasn't, she wasn't preoccupied with death, death had nothing to do with it. It was just happiness made her shiver. Not always, of course, just sometimes. Everything seemed pitiful. The only release she had ever found was a few times in – she found it hard to find words to use even to herself – in love-making. She often felt guilty and furtive when she came across references in newspapers or the occasional magazine that came her way to what they called the ecstasy of an orgasm. She tended to frown when she read them and made sure Stanley wasn't about, but she knew that was what had happened to her. It was a horrible word, but that was when – when she was having one – that was when she felt at peace. Happy but at peace in one split second, the whole process – happiness, terror and then the most marvellous peace.

Well, that was a long year ago. She stood and looked at the single beds before going down. She couldn't remember the last time they had made love but she recalled feeling ashamed that they still did whenever it was because it seemed indecent at their age. Her mind told her not to be so silly, but she couldn't help feeling it wasn't very nice beween people over fifty. She looked at Elsie and George, that was the trouble, and the idea revolted her, but then the idea of Elsie and George even when they were young had revolted her. Love-making was for young couples like Alice and Tony, begetting children, making love to some purpose. Anyway, it had faded out and they had both been quite happy about it. An arm round each other's shoulder was enough, a kiss on the cheek sufficient, but she had never found any substitute for the peace.

She went next door into the spare room and stood at the window. Across the road two cars pulled up outside the house and the next minute the woman who lived there was standing at the open door smiling and her children were running down the path to greet the people getting out of the cars. Rose saw at least two of them were much older than she was – a really bent old lady who had to be levered out of the car and a white-haired old man who walked with two sticks. They were ushered into the house with great care and attention and everyone kissed each other and then the door closed. The lights started to go on all over the house and there were people at every window and then they all trooped downstairs and gathered round a table and the curtains were drawn. Rose thought the woman looked up at her as she drew them, but wasn't sure.

Downstairs she was very civil to Stanley. She told him about the party across the road and what a lovely time they were all having and how nice it was to see a family gathering like that. Rose even went so far as to say that woman, whom she knew by sight but not name, had her good points if she could be so kind to older folk, and Stanley was quick to agree. But even while she was admiring the family scene Rose reflected that there was a lot of nonsense talked about families. They were always supposed to be happy but there was a lot wrong with the phrase one big happy family. Her family had been big. She'd had five sisters and three brothers and it had been far from a happy experience. She never talked about it, not even to Stanley. The memory of how cruel they had all been to her could still make her cry. She'd been the second youngest and nobody ever had a kind word for her, whatever they said about everyone loving each other and helping the little ones. Nobody helped her. She had to struggle to do everything – struggle to get her boots on with all those buttons, struggle to get her clothes on and all the tapes tied, struggle to get enough to eat and a place in the bed she shared with four others. The only person who ever tried to help her or give her any affection was her grandmother who regularly wept tears for the state they were all in. Her mother never wept. She was tough and strong, working as hard as her father, and there was nothing motherly about her except the bearing of the children she resented. One by one they'd all left home and Rose had never heard from them since. She and little May went to live with Grandma when she was eight and May six and things had been better after that, but in many ways it was too late, she couldn't seem to trust anyone. Until Stanley.

'It might be a good idea, your idea,' she said, pouring him a cup of tea.

'What idea?'

'Forgotten already have you? Just humouring me were you?' – but she was laughing – 'A day at the seaside, that's what.'

'Oh. Right. We'll have a basin of that. There's a 10.10 train from Waterloo if I remember rightly. How about that?'

They caught the 10.10 with ease. They both loved trains. Rose would trust a train anywhere and Stanley still had a small boy's hankering after driving one. They each had a corner seat in a non-smoker – Rose couldn't bear a smoke-filled carriage and Stanley managed to last that long without – and settled themselves nicely for the hour and a half that the journey took. Nobody bothered them. They each had a magazine and a bag of barley sugars, enough to make anybody happy. Rose sat swinging her legs – a fraction too short to touch the floor – with the magazine spread out on her lap and a sweet in her cheek. The countryside flashed past outside, the sun zipped in and out, and she felt content. There was nothing she liked better than a nice journey.

'I like travelling I must say,' she said to Stanley after a while. The ticket collector had just been and was most affable.

'Can't call this travelling. It's just a dawdle. You wait till Australia, then you'll be travelling.'

'I dare say.' Rose's heart beat faster. That might be too much of a good thing. 'How will we manage?' she asked.

'What do you mean, manage, there won't be anything to manage, it's all done for you these days. A cab to the airport and Bob's your uncle, you're in their hands then.'

'There'll be luggage.'

'All taken care of. You have it weighed and a label put on it and then that's that. All done by conveyor belt, untouched by human hand.'

Rose was impressed in spite of herself. Stanley might be slow but he was thorough. If he went into a thing you could depend on him to get it right. She sat and thought about what he had said and about Australia and she saw them in her mind's eye leaving the house, locking it and leaving it.

'We could give the key to Alice,' she said. Stanley just grunted. 'She could pop in now and again. What do you think? We've never given the key to anyone before.'

'What about the nurse?'

'I forgot.' It was good to have the train window to look out of. 'I don't know about that. We shall have to see.'

'You can't keep them hanging about.'

'Who's keeping them hanging about? It's up to her, isn't it? Anyway, what did you mention that for? Let's enjoy ourselves for goodness sake, for one day, surely we can enjoy ourselves for that long.'

They did, but the pressure was there. She wouldn't forgive Stanley for that.

Chapter Fifteen

Alice brought Mrs Pendlebury some cups and saucers back from their holiday – large, grey stone ones with a darker grey swirling pattern on them. She didn't take them in to her but waited until Wednesday morning to make the presentation. There were exclamations of 'You shouldn't have', but they were finally accepted enthusiastically. Then Mrs P. in turn gave Alice a memento from Brighton, some pot-pourri in a little jar. Like children, they clutched their respective gifts to each other and wondered what to say and do next.

'And how did Amy get on?' Mrs P. asked.

'Splendidly. Laura's bringing her back this morning – in a few minutes I think, she said elevenish.'

'Oh well then I'll go, you don't want me about, I'll be off.' There was a frenzied search for gloves.

'But I do, I've been dying for you to meet my sister, she's heard so much about you. Sit down, please.'

But Mrs P. would have gone in a panic if Laura hadn't that minute rung the bell and then there was no way out. Rose stood grunting to herself as the voices in the hall mingled with Amy's shrieks of joy and then, as she still stood immobile, Amy came running in and flung herself at her and the confusion helped her get over her fright. All the same, she was quick to go. Alice's sister was smart – hair, clothes, make-up, everything. They couldn't have been more different. She had such a haughty look about her too and a smile almost as meaningless as Charlotte's. Alice asked her to stay and have coffee with them but she knew when she wasn't wanted, knew when she was an embarrassment. Best to get out in that situation. Scarper, quick.

'You're early,' Stanley said, which only made matters worse.

'Are you still sitting there with that damned paper?' she shouted at him. 'Get moving – you know what the doctor said, not enough exercise. You can get down to the shop and get me a loaf.'

He went, after a tussle over who was paying for the bread, and she was left in possession of the house. She made a good deal of bustle tidying up, including sorting all the papers out. They should have salvage like they did in the war, she thought. It was a waste putting newspapers in the dustbin. Everything had its use then, even old newspapers, every scrap was significant, people cared for things. They cared for each other too. She knew it was wrong to find anything good about the war – Frank had always said she romanticized it but he knew nothing about it – yet it was true that it made people care. A common aim, that was it, all pulling together. It was your business, your duty to look after other people. After an alert had sounded everyone rushed into each other's flats seeing that the old folk and babies were helped to the shelter. Nobody was left out. She and Stanley had regularly helped the elderly couple downstairs into the shelter, holding them under the elbows to keep them steady. Sometimes they didn't hear the siren and then she or Stanley would knock on the door and get them up, even walking right into the bedroom if necessary without so much as a by-your-leave. It wasn't interfering, not in those circumstances. Nobody thought you were being nosy. There was a lot to do in the raids, everyone had to help out in an area like theirs. They were all working people round there, all with jobs to do, not like this area they lived in now. Stanley gloated over how Rawlinson Road had come up but she sometimes wished it hadn't. They were among the nobs now, not like in Stoke Newington in the old days. Perhaps they should never have moved, perhaps they should have stayed where they were, among people who knew them – except most of them were dead now, or moved away.

It was not surprising that with her mind running on such topics Rose's eye should be drawn to the advertisement on the front page of one of Stanley's newspapers. 'Help the Aged' it said and there was a picture of an old lady wearing a shawl and those old-fashioned gloves without fingers.

Mrs Macphail is 82. Her sight is failing and she suffers from angina. She has been living for twelve years by herself in one small room without heat of any kind and only a single gas ring to cook on. She is one of the lucky ones. Under our care she is now well looked after, but there are many more like her. Help us to help them.

There was an address to send money to.

Her fingers trembling, Rose tore the advertisement out and crumpled it up and then straightened it out again and reread it, and then systematically tore it into tiny strips, and using Stanley's lighter she burnt it in the sink and then ran the ashes down the drain. She wasn't crying, she was angry. They shouldn't put things like that in the papers to upset people. What good did it do? None. And those old folk shouldn't let themselves be used like that. She wouldn't, never, no matter what happened.

The telephone rang while she was still clinging on to the taps watching gallons and gallons of water cascade down after a few flimsy ashes. It brought her to her senses. She turned the water off but not before she'd soaked a dishcloth and put it to her forehead to cool her down.

'Hello,' she shouted down the phone. It buzzed and crackled and she yelled hello again, ready to be furious with anyone or anything. Very faintly she heard a voice say, 'Hello, Mum.'

'Wrong number,' she snapped, and had almost put the phone back down when 'Frank' drifted into her ear. She jammed the receiver back to her ear.

'Frank – oh – I thought it was a wrong number – is everything all right, can you hear me?'

'Yes, just. Now listen, Mum. I've got the tickets for you and Dad, to come out to us, bought them today. It's October 1st for a month. I'll be writing but I wanted you to know. Here's Veronica.' . . . 'Mum? Hello – isn't it exciting . . . all looking forward . . . Frank couldn't wait . . . exciting . . . here's Frank' . . . 'Mum? You'll get your passports and everything won't you . . . only three months . . . letter . . . good-bye.'

Had she said anything at all? Rose, still with the dishcloth pressed to her forehead, couldn't remember. The water dripped down her face running down her neck and all she could think of was that she would have to change her jumper.

'What's up?' Stanley said, coming in with the bread. She didn't answer. She wanted to torment him, to channel her mixed-up emotions into something positive.

'Hot are you?' he said. 'It is hot, roasting out there. Last summer all over again if you ask me. Not the weather for working.'

'You'll be all right then.'

'I've been for the bread, haven't I?'

'Have you done anything else?'

'What's that supposed to mean?'

'Did you get it at Barkers like I said?'

'I did – there you are, it says Barkers on the bag. If that isn't proof I don't know what is.'

'Well then, Barkers is next door to the travel agents.'

'I know it is.'

'Did you call there?'

'What for, you said a loaf and I got a loaf. Why should I call at the travel agents?'

Rose let him think about that for a bit. While he was thinking, she got the lunch going and set the table. Stanley stood still looking stupid for a while and then sat down.

'I suppose you mean about Australia.'

'Give him a banana.'

'No need to be rude. Well, there's no hurry for Australia. I can go in there any time.'

'Or no time.'

'No need to go in on a roasting day like this.'

'Or a cold one, or a windy one, or a wet one. Excuses, excuses, excuses. Eat your lunch.'

'You've put me off, being nasty.'

'That'll be the day.'

She watched him take the knife and fork up and begin to eat in his slow thorough way. It would drive Veronica mad.

'It might be better to wait till next year,' he said. 'I was talking to a chap at the Club and he was saying they're clamping down on these charter flights. You have to be careful, we could get caught.'

She regarded him with quite naked contempt. Her face was ugly. It scared Stanley just to look at her.

'Now what's up?' he asked. 'You look enough to frighten the devil. I don't know what's got into you lately, you're back to your old ways.'

'I was reading in your paper about an old lady of eighty-two who lived in a room with no heat.'

'Not that again.'

'I'm seventy next birthday, I thought. I've twelve years. With a bit of luck you might fix up for us to go to Australia by then. If I'm dead you might get cheap rates for my coffin.'

'No need to be sarky,' Stanley said.

'No need for anything,' she said.

He wished she would shout. That quiet voice was the one he hated.

'How was Alice and little Amy?' he asked.

'Don't hide behind them.'

'I'm not hiding, I asked a civil question.'

'They're all right.'

'Did they have a good holiday?'

'Yes.'

'When's she coming over? It's a while since I've seen her. I expect she's talking ten to the dozen.'

Amy did come over, later in the afternoon. Rose kept out of the way, deliberately, watching Stanley with her. He was soon bored. His one ambition was to stay in his chair. He wouldn't get up and look at anything, he wouldn't get up to play, he wouldn't fetch balls when they got stuck or chase butterflies or pick flowers. He was a dead loss. All he wanted to do was sit on his beam end. When she reckoned he was really fed up, when his bluff was called, Rose trotted out and launched herself into strenuous romps with Amy. How the child came to life! See, Stanley, she wanted to shout, see how she laughs, how her cheeks glow, how she jumps and claps her hands? You can't do that, can you, you and your I-haven't-seen-the-little-thing-for-ages. You've got no give in you, no go, no interest. For an hour Rose gave an exhibition of such amazing versatility that Alice was moved to look over the wall. There was no doubt Mrs P. was in her element entertaining Amy – more than entertaining, participating at a two-year-old level. No wonder the child adored her. Mr P., sitting in his chair, must be highly diverted.

But Stanley was not. He was uneasy. Rose's performance frightened him, that and her funny look over lunch. There was a shower over her head, as his mother would have said. There would be tears before nightfall at this rate, and just when she seemed on an even keel. What had gone wrong lately? Nothing. He couldn't put his finger on a thing. The weather was lovely, she had her garden, she had him better and Australia to look forward to. Australia couldn't possibly be it. She hadn't mentioned it for ages till today. Anyway, he wouldn't be rushed, not at that price. Besides, if she was sickening for something it might be wise to wait. Frank wouldn't thank him for taking her out there not in A1 condition. But she seemed healthy enough – she couldn't run round like that if she wasn't. It was just in her ways she was odd.

Odd. Queer. A bit funny. Stanley fought the words. It was Elsie who had first put the notion into his head. 'Rose can be a bit peculiar these days,' she had said, 'a bit disturbed. You should get her seen to.' He had been as close to furious as he knew how, but the observation had stuck. Elsie meant sick in the head. He had watched the same telly programme himself, about mental breakdowns. What he would have liked to have pointed out to Elsie – a busybody as Rose had always said – was that Rose had no pressures on her. That was the point. She might be a bit moody, a bit eccentric now and again, but she was stable enough. The chap on the telly had made it plain that it was pressure pushed people over the edge. They might get there themselves but pressure of one sort or another pushed them over and to get them back again you had to isolate and remove the pressure.

Rose had everything she wanted. He was quite confident about that. Naturally, if Frank could have lived next door and Ellen the other side that would have been better, but this side of that kind of heaven she had everything she wanted. They led a quiet life which suited her perfectly. They had their little pleasures – the garden, good food, outings – they were quite content. No pressures at all. Health might be a worry, but he couldn't see that it was, not really. She had her aches and pains, there were her eyes, but that was all. There was nothing to account for this lapse of behaviour, but that was assuredly all it was.

All that evening Rose barely spoke to Stanley. She did her duties as she ought – a meal was provided, cleared away, washed up, tea given – and she spoke when she was spoken to. He could fault her on nothing, she took good care to see to that. Meanwhile, she hugged to herself her secret, endlessly debating when she should tell him. She was tempted to wait until the letter arrived, which could be anything up to two weeks the way the posts were. She pictured Stanley's amazement as he read the letter: probably he would still be in bed when the post came and when he came down he would say, had he heard the postman and she would say, very casually, that he had and that there was a letter from Frank but she hadn't had time to open it. That would surprise him but he would see it was still stuck down. He would open it, making a mess of the envelope as he always did, and then he would read the news and his mouth would drop open in that silly way and his lips move and then he would say she didn't know what Frank had gone and done. That would be her big moment. She would say she'd known for two weeks and then what a retracing of the intervening time there would be.

Well, it was one possibility. There were others. She could tell him now, but he didn't deserve it. She could tell him tomorrow. If she waited longer than tomorrow she would have to wait two weeks. She couldn't decide. Sitting watching him slumped in front of that goddamn telly she was waiting for a sign, and thinking that anyway she could tell Alice.

'I don't really think I want to go out tomorrow night,' Alice said. 'I'm too uncomfortable. I can't sit still and I can't eat and I don't see the point.' Tony shrugged. 'I'll drop the Pens a note,' she went on, 'otherwise I'll have to talk to Mrs P. for hours telling her not to come.' Listlessly, she picked petals off a rose. 'It seems such an effort lately. She will go on about what I ought to be doing about Amy's tantrums, it drives me crazy. And it's such a strain letting her pretend she's broad-minded and frank and honest when she's so bigoted. Today she said was Charlotte a Catholic, and when I said I'd no idea she was full of significant nods. Makes me sick.'

'What did Laura think of her?'

'Laura hardly saw her – she jumped up like a frightened mouse and ran for it. She's so annoying when she does that very humble person act. I can just imagine the rage she was in when she got home, persuading herself she'd been slighted when she was doing the slighting. Then in the garden – it made me feel ill watching her, she was hysterical rushing up and down with Amy, showing off like a child. I could see old Stanley didn't like it either. I wanted to go and drag Amy away.'

'But you can't do that, it wouldn't fit in with your image as a shining saint.'

'Oh, don't be horrible. I'm fed up.'

They were sitting in their splendid sitting-room, idle. Outside the sun still shone but the garden seemed to have lost its charm for Alice that year. Everything had lost its charm. Looking at her, Tony thought that though the line of her pregnant body was beautiful as she lay on the sofa, her long sprigged dress dropping on either side, her face was drawn. She didn't stand up to child-bearing very well. He would be glad when the child was safely born and she regained her energy and bloom – except that itself only came back slowly.

'Laura's made a good job of this room,' he said. 'Couldn't have done better myself.'

'Tell her.'

'She couldn't care less whether I like it or not as long as it's to her own Good Taste. Actually I think she must have had a minor lapse when she was organizing this floor and those curtains – it's not her at all. That's what I like about it.'

'Mrs P. chose the curtains. Laura wanted plain white and I didn't know what I wanted as usual and Mrs P. happened to be in the day I had to decide between the six samples Laura left and she just pointed to the brown and orange and I thought, she's right. The funny thing was, Laura thought so too in the end. I cheated of course – I pretended I'd chosen them all by myself.'

'I didn't know Mrs P. was so decisive.'

'Oh, she's decisive. She makes all the decisions next door. Stanley just does what she wants.'

'Like I do.'

Immediately her eyes filled with tears.

'Oh now come on – it was only a joke.' He came over to her and held her hands. 'Hey, come on, I was teasing.' But her tears fell without stopping. 'I do exactly what I want to do,' he said, 'You're the most unbossy woman I've ever met in my life. I was just trying to make a cheap joke.' Still she cried and he had to let her and hold her until she had finished. He felt shocked and could not stop himself saying, 'How could that make you cry so much?'

'Oh, I don't know. I'm sorry. It's thinking about us being old, being the Pens. It's so pathetic.'

'But we won't be pathetic, we'll be lovely. You'll be a gorgeous old lady and I'll be a dapper old gent and it'll make people feel good just to look at us, proper Darby and Joan stuff.'

'One of us might die.'

'Oh for God's sake, Alice.'

She was crying again. 'Rose might die and what would Stanley do? Imagine his life. Or Stanley might die and she'd just shut herself up like an animal.'

'Now look – stop it – you're getting ridiculously upset and it's not all pregnancy blues. You'll have to stop having anything to do with the Pendleburys if you're going to let them get on your nerves like this. We never seem to talk about anything else except those two.'

But she wasn't listening.

'It's like you've always said, there isn't any point to anything.'

'That's only half – there isn't any point so you might as well enjoy yourself, be the complete hedonist.'

'Like Stanley. Mrs P. is always saying all he does is enjoy himself.' Her sobbing came on again like a gale.

'What's wrong with that?' said Tony, exasperated.

'His – enjoying – himself – it's telly and bingo – and – and – being nagged to death and a day at the seaside – oh it's *awful*.'

'Sounds lovely to me.'

'Don't say that! Don't! Stop it!'

Tony stared at his wife with total disbelief. Her face was scarlet, her features contorted, tears streamed from her eyes and she drummed her fists viciously on his arm. He freed himself and got up and went to the window. Such ugliness was unfaceable. He didn't want to turn round until silence told him that she had composed herself. But he waited a long time. The sobs still came in gusts, and then there were long drawn-out hiccups and groans and endless snuffles and sniffs before the attack was over. When only the smallest of rustles could be heard he looked over his shoulder, determined, until he saw her, not yet to go to her. But when the extent of her misery showed itself in the damp hair and blotchy face and pinched mouth, he went across and knelt down beside her. She started to say she was sorry but he shushed her and eventually she went to sleep.

He felt exhausted, as though he had done all the crying. What made him angry was that it was all about nothing. It disturbed him that Alice could be capable of such lack of proportion, that all this could have started from one innocent remark. She felt so deeply about even the most shallow things, that was the trouble, and hardly anyone guessed. Watchdog Laura, so intent on taking her mother's place, knew and protected her sister in a way that had always surprised him. He had resented Laura's care as interference until he realized it was genuine solicitude and then he was touched by it, though his ego was hurt when he appreciated that Laura only carried out her self-appointed task because she didn't trust him to do it. She was right. He might love Alice but he couldn't handle her at a time like this – he couldn't give her confidence as Laura could. This distressed him. When an outburst was long over he had ventured to tell Alice how helpless he felt and confessed to her the pain his inadequacy caused him, but she was always embarrassed and liked to pretend it had never happened so they never got very far.

Next door, the Pendleburys had their television on very loudly. He felt irrationally angry. Alice was asleep, they had no consideration – he longed to bang on the wall or ring up and complain. They took his wife for granted – she was always so bright and cheerful with them, so kind, so anxious about their welfare and they didn't give a damn, not a damn. He found himself actually standing with his hand on the telephone until the sheer absurdity of his attitude saved him from himself. Alice was soundly asleep, nothing would waken her. He would be better occupied putting her to bed than giving way to such pettiness. Alice was never petty. Her understanding never failed to shame him. With some difficulty he managed to lift her off the sofa and on to their bed. She stirred but put her arms round his neck like Amy did and he felt happy and proud.

Alice's baby was born that night, two months prematurely. He lived for three hours and then died. Tony came home at midday like a man shell-shocked, carrying Amy in his arms. Her hands were clasped round the back of his neck and it was that which made him cry the minute they were home.

*

Rose had rung Alice's bell three times but there had been no answer. She could not believe it. Wednesday, eleven o'clock, and no answer. She had been stood up. The pain of it made her tremble. She charged off the doorstep as though jet-propelled and rushed round the corner to the shops where, in her distress, she bought a great many things she did not need. Coming back, she could hardly bear to look at No. 8. Her head down, she scurried past, hurt and upset. Alice had forgotten, probably gone out and forgotten. It was easily done, she supposed, though she had never done it herself, people did forget. But what could have made her forget? She wouldn't call again – let Alice come to her senses and realize. Oh, she'd be round quick enough then apologizing, but the damage was done. She'd been treated like dirt, made to look small.

She said nothing to Stanley. There had been such queues at the shops it had taken her the best part of an hour shopping. He thought she had been next door and she wasn't going to tell him she hadn't, why should she. He would just drive her mad thinking up excuses for Alice, as if she cared. There were now so many important things that she couldn't talk to him about that she had to keep her mouth firmly shut. Working helped, as it always did. She cleaned her kitchen cupboards out, singing loudly to drown her own thoughts. The singing was harsh, out of tune, but in the mood she was in she took pleasure in mauling the tune. She had been too happy this year. They – They, whoever They were – They had seen this and were cutting her down to size. She'd gone all sloppy after Stanley's illness, really soft in the head, lost her wits as Elsie had tried to tell her. She'd overstepped the mark in trying to change. Change was all very well but it could be carried too far. She had got dependent on next door, that was it. Well, when Alice came she wouldn't make a fuss. Definitely not – no sulking. She'd say it didn't matter a bit and be gracious and laugh. But she had got the message, thank you very much.

It did enter Rose's head that it was very quiet next door and had been since first thing. Usually, there was a certain amount of noise, what with Amy running in and out banging the back door and Alice calling to her and crashing and banging as things fell over under the impetus of a two-year-old's clumsiness. That morning, there hadn't been a sound, except for her own clatter. Under cover of putting crumbs out for the birds, Rose surreptitiously looked up at the windows next door. They were all closed, all the curtains were closed – Amy's bedroom at the top, Alice's below and the kitchen blind. Now a little disturbed, but still aggrieved, Rose went to put empty milk bottles out though she knew the milkman had been and gone. His car was there. Furthermore, the three daily pints of milk still stood on the doorstep and the newspaper was stuck in the door. Now why hadn't she noticed that before? She'd been looking the other way when she rang the bell, that was it.

The situation needed rethought. Rose felt muddled. Something was up, that was clear. Perhaps she had been too hasty in her judgement, but whatever it was that had happened it wouldn't have taken a minute to tell her. Her anger started working itself up again, just as Stanley came in from one of his silly errands. He immediately irritated her the way he stood in her kitchen looking like a bag of bones.

'You look like a wet week,' she snapped.

He just looked at her. She was more annoyed than ever when she saw he really was for some reason shaken.

'Oh come on,' she said, 'what is it now – what moans have you got today?'

'I just met Tony next door,' Stanley said.

'What of it? I expect you've stood gassing for hours.'

'No, we haven't, he wanted to get inside.'

'Huh, he hasn't time for anyone that young man, can hardly pass the time of day.'

Stanley sat down, putting the tobacco he'd just bought onto the table. Slowly, an idea was building up in his head.

'How did you find Alice this morning?' he asked, looking hard at Rose, his voice surprisingly firm.

'That's my business,' she said.

'I don't think you went in at all,' Stanley accused her. 'I don't think you put a foot in the house. I think you didn't get an answer and jumped to conclusions and took the huff. That's what I think.'

'What if I did – it's none of your business.'

'You led me to believe you'd been in there.'

'I did nothing of the kind.'

'I think you did and I think you should be ashamed of yourself. We have our faults but we've never lied to each other.'

Rose's heartbeat quickened. Stanley couldn't say boo to a goose but he'd made her sweat. It was no good glaring at him – his eyes were quite fixed and steady and she was losing. He had the advantage and he knew it. He was showing off, bullying her. She started to cry. He did nothing and said, 'I don't know what you're crying for. You've nothing to cry about. When you've heard what I've just heard then you can cry.'

'Oh, get *on* with it.'

'Alice had her baby last night. It's dead, and she's very ill. There.'

The tears dried up at once. Rose felt waves and waves of heat passing through her, strong as an electric current. Her head sang and she literally staggered. Stanley was satisfied. He helped her to a chair and went to put the kettle on. Had he been cruel? Yes. Well, there was a use for cruelty sometimes. Cruelty cauterized. There was that meanness festering in Rose and it wanted burning out, the iron put straight on it for a minute. That's what he had done. For years he'd stood by and let Rose go her own peculiar way, but not any more. This was the way to deal with her.

He made the tea good and strong and took it to her.

'Yes,' he said, sitting down, 'came on very sudden, in the night. He said they hardly had time to get her to hospital. It was all over very quick.'

'A boy?' Rose asked, whispering.

'Yes.' She nodded her head, gratified. 'Only two and a half pounds.'

'Stillborn?'

'No. He lived three hours in an incubator. They did everything they could.'

'Alice?' She felt unable to look at Stanley and was glad he was generous with his information, that she didn't have to plead.

'She'll be all right. She lost a lot of blood, had to have a transfusion. Of course, she's upset.'

Rose nodded, her hands clasped in her lap.

'He went with her, Tony did, took Amy and went with her. I told him, I said you should have given us a ring and we'd have come in and stayed with the little thing.'

'Oh, I wish he had!' Rose said. 'Oh, I'd have given anything to help.'

'Well, he said there wasn't time to think, it was all a panic. Anyway, I've told him, he's to bring Amy straight round to us any time he likes, and if there's anything we can do he only has to ask. That's what I said.'

'I'm glad you thought to say that.'

'We owe that young couple a lot. It's our chance to be good neighbours.'

'It is.'

Rose's misery ate into her all day. Stanley continued to be stern and his sternness acted as a brake on her emotion. She didn't dare cry. She wasn't even sure that she wanted to cry. Remorse was so much stronger in her than grief. The phrase 'I denied her twice' kept going through her head. If Alice had died, how would she have lived with it? The thought took her breath away. Thank God Alice was all right and amends could be made. Uneasily, she wandered about the house, her forehead permanently creased in lines, picking things up and giving them a perfunctory dust and putting them down. Whatever could she do? Stanley had offered their help, but should she go and knock on the door and offer it again? She shrank from contact with Tony. You didn't want outsiders when you were upset. But should she go? Should she impose the ordeal on herself as a penance? He wouldn't want her, he might close the door on her face. It was that possibility that convinced her she must do it.

An hour later, she stood on the doorstep of No. 8 dressed in her best clothes with a bunch of white roses in her hand for Alice. She had tied them up with ribbon and put a card saying 'Hoping these can say what words cannot'. She wasn't at all sure it was appropriate but wanted to say something. She rang the bell and waited stoically, not flinching, glad to wait, to be kept waiting. She would ring once more and then leave the flowers on the step. The whole street could see her but that was part of the bargain with herself. Her humiliation must be public. At her second ring, she heard footsteps and trembled. The door opened and Tony Oram stood there. She couldn't look at him.

'Come in,' he said, tired, not opening the door wider.

'No, no I won't, thank you,' she said, very quietly. 'I don't want to intrude. I just came to say how sorry I am and if there's anything I can do . . .'

He cut her short, 'That's very kind.'

Awkwardly, they stood there. She pushed the flowers at him, saying nothing. He took them reluctantly.

'I'll take them to Alice this afternoon,' he said. 'Thank you.'

'How is she?'

'Oh, pretty low.'

'Yes. Well, I won't keep you. Give Alice my best wishes and tell her to get well soon.'

He said he would and closed the door. Rose walked the few yards back to her house, remembering after Ellen's death. She'd hated all the people who said they were sorry, each and every one of them. She hadn't given a thought to how they felt, to their sorrow. It had been suspect, affected, a millionth part of hers. Her suffering now opened her eyes. She felt so helpless, so unable to communicate her sympathy, to do the right thing. She hadn't even been able to look at Tony Oram, such was her agony of doubt, but how she'd longed to cry with him and share his burden and how much more she would long to do it with Alice.

She went back into her house and told Stanley that Frank had rung up and that their tickets were in the post.

Chapter Sixteen

Lying in bed looking at Mrs Pendlebury's flowers and reading the message Alice thought how they meant nothing at all to her. 'Hoping these can say what words cannot'? Well, no, they couldn't. They said nothing at all to her. She felt a hardening in her attitude towards Mrs P. which she knew was unfair but which was real all the same. The surgeon had been most emphatic that the premature birth of her son had been a technical fault, as it were, hinging on the state of the placenta, and had nothing whatsoever to do with any emotional factors. Alice accepted this, but rebelliously went on connecting her scene with Tony with what had happened, and the scene had been about the Pens. Tony thought so too. He was adamant that this was her big chance to make a clean break with Mrs P., or at least put their relationship on a different footing. She could hide behind her weak condition to stop all the traditions of a year – stop the babysitting (Charlotte's *au pair*, not to mention the Stewarts', was available), stop the coffee mornings, stop the taking out of Amy. Stop it, and don't start again. Be friendly and firm. Chat over the wall, chat in the street, wave and smile, occasionally have her in: but no more responsibility.

Alice agreed. It had all gone sour. What she had hoped for when she first set out to convert Mrs P. to human fellowship had backfired and she had become a martyr. She lay in bed the second day she was home waiting for Mrs P. to come in and practised what she would say. Nothing much, really. She would simply say the doctor had told her to be very careful for a couple of weeks and not have visitors and generally be as quiet as possible. Mrs P. would take the hint. It was worrying that she might have noticed they had been out to celebrate her homecoming under Charlotte's auspices, but that couldn't be helped. She must be resolute.

Her resolution vanished the minute Mrs P. put her head round the bedroom door. Her knock was so timid, her eyes so anxious, her whole demeanour so genuinely shy, and when she smiled and asked how Alice was it was like Amy smiling for forgiveness after a tantrum and a smack and tears.

'I'm fine,' Alice said, 'just a bit weak. Come in, sit down, thank you for the lovely flowers.'

Mrs P. came in and perched on the very edge of a chair. Then she said something that completely threw Alice's prepared words to the winds, that made the very thought of what she had been about to do repugnant.

'I *have* missed you,' she said. She shook her head and repeated, 'I've really missed you, Alice. I can't tell you how I've missed you and your friendly face.'

Alice was appalled. It was a departure so new and shattering for Rose Pendlebury to confess to affection and dependence in one breath that she could not take it in.

'It hasn't been the same without you. Charlotte down the road invited me for coffee on a Wednesday but it wasn't the same. I appreciated the gesture, but it wasn't the same. We aren't the same sort. And the garden was that quiet – dreadful it was.'

'I missed you too,' Alice found herself saying but Mrs P. wasn't listening, she hadn't finished.

'It made me appreciate the interest you've taken – no, I know not all young people are so considerate and it's no use you saying they are. I want to get this off my chest, it's been bothering me for a long time. It was the happiest day in my life when you moved in here and if anything had happened to you I don't know what I should have done. There.'

They both cried, Mrs P. on a tide of high emotion and Alice in self-defence. Then there was a good deal of mopping up to be done, a searching for handkerchiefs and a disposing of them, followed by smiles and laughs at their own expense and big sighs when it was finished.

'I shouldn't stay too long,' Mrs P. said at last, 'not in your condition.'

'Oh, I'm just pretending,' Alice said.

'Where's Amy?'

'Charlotte has her. She's going to have her every morning just for this week. She's spoiling me.'

Mrs P. looked a little taken aback. 'Oh, well, that's very nice. I was going to say I would have her but if she's being looked after – '

Instead of saying that yes, she was, Alice found herself making excuses. 'Well with Sam almost the same age – and the *au pair* is very good – '

'It's only natural,' Mrs P. said. 'Children like to be with children. When my Frank was little I used to take him to the park, rain or shine, just to be with other children and when he started school they couldn't believe he was an only child. He isn't an only child, is he, the teacher said to me and she wouldn't believe it when I said yes, as a matter of fact, he is. You should do the same with Amy.'

'I do,' said Alice.

'It's difficult for only children. Of course Frank wouldn't have been an only . . . nor would Amy . . .'

'I hope she won't be for long.'

'So do I. That's what I hoped after my Ellen died but nothing ever happened. Well, there you are, that's life.'

Alice did not feel like saying that yes it was.

'How's Mr Pendlebury?' she asked instead.

'Oh, he's all right, grumbling as usual, slow as a snail. I had to drag him to the passport office.'

'Passport office?'

'Yes,' said Mrs P., vague, spots of pink in both cheeks. 'We've left it a bit late to go through the usual channels so we had to go down. We're off in three weeks.'

'No! How exciting – tell me about it. When exactly do you go – by air or sea – how long for – oh I *wish* I was you.'

Mrs P. tried hard to seem casual but failed miserably. She told with pride of Frank's gesture, of how he had paid for and organized the whole thing and had their tickets sent and all they had to do was get passports. She told of the telephone conversation and the excitement at the other end and how none of them could wait. She rhymed off the magic list of place names they would visit and recited their itinerary for the journey with relish. Alice responded with animation. Together they pieced together what they knew about Victoria and Adelaide, about kangaroos and aborigines, about surf-riding and sheep and the outback.

'I'd give absolutely anything to be you,' Alice said when they'd exhausted their common knowledge. 'Just imagine – to be going to a whole new continent and not even as tourists but going to see your family, all those faces you've never even seen.'

'Yes, well,' said Mrs P. She frowned and played with her gloves. 'It won't all be plain sailing of course, there'll be snags, drawbacks. Bound to be.'

'What do you mean? There won't be *any* snags, it'll all be lovely. They've asked you to go, they've pushed you into it, they're all *waiting* for you.'

She knew she had divined exactly what the matter was. 'She sounds such a nice person, Frank's wife, and the children too.'

'Oh, I expect she's nice enough. She's a doctor's daughter you know, a nurse herself. She's very clever, writes good letters and lovely clear writing, much better than Frank's. He thinks the world of her of course – "You couldn't have found a better wife for me yourself, Mum," that was when he rang to tell us he was getting married.'

'There you are then.'

'But you can't live in another woman's house and not have differences, can you? And there won't be any getting away if anything goes wrong, we'll be stuck. I don't like the feeling that I won't be able to get away.'

'You won't want to get away, you'll see. They'll spoil you, it will be the most marvellous rest.'

'Oh I don't want any rest – I want to muck in and help. I hope she won't make me rest.'

'She won't if you don't want to.'

'She doesn't do her own housework you know – they have help. Veronica works mornings in the hospital, I don't know how I'll get on with help, I'm sure.'

'Like a house on fire,' Alice said promptly.

'Of course, I can take care of little Alexander – he's Amy's age. I don't suppose he'll be fussy.'

'He'll adore you, he'll dote on you.'

'Two-year-olds can be funny.'

'Not with their own grannie.'

'Well, we shall just have to see. It's three weeks away yet. Anything can happen.'

'Nothing will happen – you'll go and you'll probably love it so much you'll never come back. After all, you've nothing here to keep you, have you? I mean, no family or ties of any kind.'

'It depends what you call ties,' said Mrs P., visibly offended. 'We've lived in London fifty years, thick and thin. That's a tie in my opinion.'

'Yes, but it's not flesh and blood, is it?'

'There's a lot of nonsense talked about flesh and blood, to my mind. I get sick to death of hearing about flesh and blood and then reading all those scandalous stories in the newspaper. You can't open a paper these days without reading about old folk getting neglected. Now then.'

Alice hesitated. It was no good pointing out to Mrs P. she wasn't being logical – it would be like persecuting her.

'Well, I'm glad you'll want to come back,' she said, quickly. 'We'll miss you quite enough as it is – a month will seem an eternity.'

'Oh, you won't miss me like I missed you.'

'But I will, it will be dreadful. Amy will be lost without you.'

'She'll manage. She's hardly been near me for weeks and weeks.'

'But she hasn't been here – '

'Memories are short.'

'No – no they aren't – ' Alice spoke louder and more forcefully than she had intended. 'I think the opposite – memories are long, they last for ever, it's just finding them sometimes takes time. I don't think I ever forget anything really.'

'You're young. It's different when you're young. Stanley can't hardly remember what happened yesterday and he's got me nearly as bad. Well, I'd best be going. Can I get you any shopping? I don't expect I can. Charlotte's doing it in her car, is she?'

'Yes, she is, but there are some things I forgot to put on my list – but Tony could get them.'

'If you'd rather he did of course – '

'No, I'd rather you did, but it might be a bother or make your bag too heavy – '

She made out a list, not entirely faked but full of items that could have waited indefinitely.

'I shall have to do some shopping myself,' Mrs P. said, happily waiting. 'We can't go to Australia with what we've got, Veronica would have a fit.'

'I don't suppose she cares two hoots what you wear,' Alice said, absent-mindedly.

'Oh won't she – well I would and I do. She doesn't want to take a couple of tramps around now, does she? She wants us to be a credit to them, doesn't she? I should think so. My goodness I wouldn't like it if my in-laws showed me up. No, there'll have to be some shopping done from the skin out, no good shirking it. And suitcases to put it in. We haven't a suitcase between us, not what you could call a suitcase.'

'I'll lend you one.'

'I wouldn't dream of it, thank you all the same. I should hope we can afford decent luggage.'

'But there doesn't seem much point just for one trip.'

Mrs P.'s face was fierce. Alice felt tired suddenly. Ashamed, she took refuge in falling back on her pillows and saying feebly that she didn't feel well. Instantly, Mrs P. was solicitous, blaming herself for talking too much, scolding herself for not noticing the invalid was getting tired. She insisted on making Alice some tea and on straightening the bed and drawing the curtains and finally tiptoeing out with the hoarsest of whispered goodbyes.

'Everything all right?' Stanley said as she came in. 'I thought I might pop in as well and cheer her up.'

'You'll do no such thing,' snapped Rose. 'She's in no fit state for visitors. I don't think she's at all well. They should never have let her out of hospital.'

'They turn everyone out before they're ready these days,' Stanley said. 'Take me – I needed another week but – '

'Oh shut up, turn everything to yourself you do. There was nothing wrong with you so don't you go comparing yourself with a woman who's just lost a baby. I won't have it.'

'Anyway – ' Stanley said, feebly.

'Mind you,' Rose went on, 'knowing what I know I'm not surprised. The very idea of going out at that time and just out of hospital. What can you expect? Of course, I didn't say nothing, I don't want to know their business. But to go gadding about like that – it's not right. What's the good of all those doctors and nurses putting her right if she doesn't take care of herself? I can't get over her wanting to go out, I can't really.'

'You don't know where she went,' Stanley said, 'there is that to consider. All you saw was them getting into a car, that's all.'

'It was enough – and coming back, I heard them coming back, after eleven it was. Oh there's no doubt where they'd been.'

'Where?'

'The theatre or the pictures of course.'

'They could just have been having a meal.'

'From seven o'clock to after eleven? What kind of meal is that?'

'They might have been at her sister's.'

'I don't want to discuss it. The harm's done and she's paying the penalty. White as a sheet she is.'

'I'll wait till she's a bit better then before I go in.'

'If at all,' Rose said.

But Stanley was determined. He liked Alice, he was very fond of her – in a different way to Rose of course but nevertheless he had a soft spot for her. She was always so cheerful, that was what he liked, always a smile and a cheery word for him. Besides, they had a lot in common. He knew she must have put up with Rose's peculiar moods just as much as he had. Rose might pretend all was sweetness and light in there, but he was no fool. He didn't believe it. He wouldn't be a bit surprised if there hadn't been plenty of sticky moments, and he owed it to Alice to let her know in his own way how he knew what she had to put up with. So he would go and see her, take her some grapes, pass the time of day. Rose could say what she liked – she knew perfectly well that once his mind was made up there was no stopping him.

He arranged the visit himself. Catching sight of young Tony coming home from work he nipped out without Rose even being aware of it and asked him if he thought it might be convenient for him to pop in and see Alice for a few minutes the next morning. Tony said that would be fine, he would leave the key in the door and Mr Pendlebury could come in about eleven. Pleased with himself, Stanley said nothing to Rose. Luckily the next day was a clean shirt day so he felt quite presentable when he gave the bell a touch so she would know he was coming and went straight in. Rose thought he'd gone for his paper – which he had in a manner of speaking. He had it under his arm and grapes in his other hand.

Alice, lying waiting for her second Pendlebury visit, was intrigued at the idea of Stanley coming on his own. She had, it was true, visited him in hospital so perhaps he was merely returning the courtesy. She hoped so – to endure another agonizing session of the sort she had spent with Mrs P. was too much. It was not, she reassured herself, in Stanley's line. He would stick to platitudes and the only difficulty would be to get him to go. Once settled in a comfortable chair in a warm room he was hard to shift. But Stanley surprised her. He refused a seat and insisted on standing to attention at her bedside, his small brown face creased in smiles.

'I'm not stopping,' he said at once, 'just come to pay my respects and see you aren't fading away.'

'No fear of that – I'm too well looked after.'

'You make hay while the sun shines,' Stanley said. 'Once you're on your feet there'll be no going back.'

'Oh, I've been on my feet,' Alice said, 'I've even been out, wasn't it wicked? We went out to the theatre and for supper the night I came home.'

'I should think so too,' Stanley said. 'Cheers you up, an outing, I always say.'

'Do you know, it did. I felt human again. Just getting dressed made me feel better. But I would never have thought of it – wouldn't have dreamed of it – if Charlotte hadn't arranged it. Wasn't she kind?'

'She was,' Stanley said. 'She's been very kind to my wife too, but you know Rose.' He paused, still smiling. 'She's a bit prickly but her heart's in the right place.'

'Exactly,' Alice said. 'But she worries me sometimes.'

'Oh, you don't want to let Rose worry you. You just have to take the rough with the smooth.'

'I was wondering – ' Alice stopped.

Stanley was bland, placid, determined not to see malice even when it was intended. He would not misconstrue anything she might say, he would not doubt her motives were honest. But would he ever admit to difficulties, real difficulties, with his wife? Might she not presume too much?

'I was just wondering,' she went on, 'whether sometimes she's quite well?'

'Oh, she's as tough as an old boot. It's me has the troubles.'

'Yes, but – well, she gets more than depressed, don't you think?'

'We all do sometimes.'

'True.' Alice thought she detected the merest glimmer of warning in Stanley's small, pale eyes. 'Anyway, Australia will cheer her up.'

'Yes, that'll keep her going.'

'Wasn't it good of your son to arrange it?'

'He's a good boy, Frank. Never gave any trouble. Always thoughtful.'

'Just like his mother.'

'Yes.' Stanley sucked his cheeks in and let them go with a pop. 'Of course, he's the spitting image of me really. Except for height. Where I'm average he's tall – easy 5 ft 9 he is. It seemed to happen all of a sudden – one minute he was going to be average and then it was like the beanstalk, just shot up.'

Stanley straightened his 5 ft 5 inches and, 'I must get on or I'll catch it.'

'Thank you for coming to see me.'

'Now don't forget – the minute you feel like an evening out again you let us know. We've missed babysitting.'

'I will, but at the moment – '

'That's right, slow and steady wins the race. You stay in for a while, but when you're ready, tip us the wink.'

Rose hardly let him in the door before she was on him like a terrier.

'You're *sly*,' she hissed at him, 'sneaking off like that – that's what you are, sly. If there's one thing I hate it's slyness.'

'I wasn't sneaking,' Stanley said. 'You never asked me where I was going. I would have told you if you had.'

'Butting in where you weren't wanted.'

'I only stayed five minutes. You were in an hour.'

'We had things to talk about.'

'And I took a present, some nice grapes.'

'Grapes?' Rose laughed scornfully. 'She has any amount of grapes, cartloads of them. Didn't you see them in a big dish on her dressing table? Trust you – can't think further than grapes.'

'What did you take then?'

'That's my business but I can tell you it was a damn sight more interesting than grapes.'

Stanley took his coat off and prepared to go into the sitting-room to read his paper. To his annoyance Rose followed and sat down too.

'Aren't you busy?' he asked, hopefully.

'I'm always busy, unlike some people I could mention.'

'Don't let me keep you back.'

'You already have with me having to worry about where you were.'

'What's worrying about that?'

'How was she then?'

'She was all right. I thought she looked grand, a lot better than I did after I came –'

'Did she say anything about babysitting?'

'No, but I did.'

'I *told* you never to mention it! I knew it! That's done it! That's torn it!' Rose was up, attacking the china cabinet with a duster.

'I only said to let us know when we were wanted and she said she didn't feel like it at the moment.'

'Oh no! Doesn't feel like it! But we know different don't we, we know she's been out behind our backs.'

'Yes, she was telling me about that,' said Stanley, taking care to be offhand.

'She admitted it, did she?'

Stanley thought about that. 'No,' he said, 'she just told me, in the course of conversation.'

'And what did you say? I hope to God you didn't say we'd been watching?'

'I wasn't watching,' said Stanley pointedly. 'You were. But anyway I didn't say. I just said I was glad she enjoyed herself. Now can I get on with my paper?'

'You haven't got time for reading papers. There's a lot to be done. We've only three weeks and not a thing bought, not a blessed thing. We'll go out straight after lunch and again tomorrow and again the day after that if necessary.'

'It won't take me five minutes to get what I want.'

'What *do* you want? You've no idea, have you, it's all up to me, isn't it? You want pyjamas for a start off, you hadn't thought of that, had you? And underwear and socks and a suit –'

'I've plenty of suits.'

'Not for travelling you haven't.'

'What do I want to be buying suits for at my time of life? I've enough to see me out.'

She whirled round, knocking the lamp off the top of the cabinet, and snatched the paper out of his hands.

'I won't have that!' she shouted. 'That's enough – no more talk about one foot in the grave. I've had enough of it, it's disgusting that attitude.'

'All right then,' he muttered, 'now look what you've done – I shouldn't be surprised if you've ruined that lamp.'

'What if I have – I'm sick of the sight of it. It's been there twenty-five years and I'm sick of the sight of it. I could do with breaking a few more things. That'd show you.'

Stanley noticed, against his will, little bits of froth overflowing from her moving lips, globules of spit that gathered, hung for a moment and then dribbled down her chin.

'Here,' he said, sternly, handing her a handkerchief, 'wipe yourself,' but she dragged a sleeve across her mouth instead and he put the clean square of white cotton back in his pocket, glad she had not sullied it. 'You've got yourself in a state,' he said, 'and there's no call for it. Now take it easy for a bit.' To set her an example he sat down himself and spread his newspaper out on his knees. She stood still for a while and then picked up the lamp and slowly dusted it and replaced it on the cabinet. Then she left the room, her feet shuffling instead of trotting.

It was hot and still in the garden. Rose couldn't claim it freshened her up. She walked round a few times, tending to things as she went, and then came to rest near the low part of the wall. She looked over quite openly, not caring who saw her. It already seemed an age since Amy had sat pulling daisies and looking up at her. She had a great yearning to see the little girl, but there was no sign of her. She was always across the road these days, or out playing with other children. She didn't need Pen any more. Rose's eyes filled with tears. She didn't need the insufferably complacent Stanley to tell her that was the way of the world. Of course it was, she understood that, but it didn't mean to say she couldn't grieve if she wanted to, did it? It was usually the winter when she got these feelings but there was nothing wintry about this humidity. Perhaps there would be a storm and that would help. Sadly, Rose trailed her hand through the leaves, plucking a few and scattering them as she went.

There was a storm and it did help. Rose woke up feeling quite gay and jolly. So different was her mood that she actually apologized to Stanley for her 'temper' the day before and not even the graciousness of his acceptance annoyed her. In such a mood, there were no problems – everything fell into place. She saw quite clearly what they needed for Australia and how she could get it, and how the house could be cleaned in time and arrangements made to have Elsie pop in occasionally. She didn't want to ask the Orams, not with all the trouble they'd had.

She rang Elsie first thing and laughed a lot while she talked to her.

'I'm going to ask you a favour, Elsie,' she said, her voice loud and cheerful.

'I'd do anyone a favour,' Elsie said, mournfully, 'you know me. If it can be done, I'll oblige.'

'Yes, well, it's about the house being empty while we're in Australia.' There were loud exclamations at the other end which only increased Rose's happiness. 'Yes, I've been meaning to tell you but it's all been that sudden. Frank arranged it all at his end. We're off October 1st.'

'Fancy you wanting to go all that way. You're not flying I hope?'

'Yes, we are. It's never too late to start.'

'Well you're welcome I must say. Rather you than me. I only hope everything's all right.'

'What I wondered was if you could pop in occasionally and open the windows and that?'

'Certainly.'

'If it wouldn't be a bother.'

'No bother. You'll tell your friends, will you, so they won't think I'm breaking in?'

'I will.'

'They won't be offended will they? I mean, me coming in with them so near . . .'

'They've had a lot of trouble,' Rose said, just a little sharply to show she'd registered the insinuation. 'Alice's baby died.' The exclamations this time made Rose impatient, 'So you see they've enough on their plate.' She was ready to ring off. Elsie was a trial even at the best of times. 'We'll bring the key round before we go,' she said. 'You'll be in Sundays will you? Not going away?'

'No. Dolores and Alan are moving flats or we'd have gone up there.'

'Nice place is it?'

'We haven't managed up yet. George has been busy.'

'Doesn't seem a year.' Rose immediately felt unkind. She needn't have said that. 'Time flies,' she said. 'Anyway, I must be off. I'm rushed off my feet what with getting ready.'

They managed to buy the suitcases that afternoon without too much bother, and very satisfactory they were. The price was scandalous but she had made it clear to Stanley before they ever entered Selfridges that on this point she was immovable: good luggage they must have. Forty-seven pounds each they were, big black leather things with scarlet silk lining and two handles and strong all-round zips and locks and keys. She tried carrying them as well as Stanley – back and forward along the basement floor – and found them easy to manage. Then the assistant kindly filled them with tennis rackets and things so they could get the weight and back and forward they went again. No bother.

Rose didn't feel at all tired when they got back. She took the cases up herself to the bedroom and opened them and had a practice pack. She was in the middle of this when the doorbell rang and was down the stairs, as nimble as you like, in a flash. She was delighted to see Charlotte there with Amy.

'Hello,' she said, expansive, beaming, 'now I haven't seen you for a long time, young lady.'

'Alice left her with me till four o'clock, Mrs Pendlebury,' Charlotte said, 'but I've just had a phone call to pick up my husband from his office and I didn't want to drag Amy down and miss Alice so – '

'Yes,' said Rose, 'I'll have her.'

'It's only a matter of ten minutes really.'

'Come on, Amy.'

There was a fraction of a second during which Amy hesitated

but then she was running down the hall and Rose closed the door and followed, chasing her through the house. There was the old cupboard to be pulled out and the usual objects to examine, only this time Amy was cleverer and not so amazed. She put a pair of Stanley's shoes on and clumped around the kitchen and then had to have one of Rose's aprons to complete her outfit. The bell went again before they had time to really begin to play.

Alice came in with some embarrassment. Almost the only time she'd ever been in the Pendleburys' house, apart from high tea, was at the time of Stanley's accident. But Mrs P. was in no mood for remembering such painful moments – it was all shouts and laughter as she led her through into the back and showed her Amy in all her splendour.

'Me cook,' Amy said.

'What shall we cook?' Mrs P. asked.

'Pastry.'

'Right. Where's the flour? Look – isn't she smart, she remembers it's in that bin. Right. What next? Where's the lard? Where does Pen keep the lard?'

'Actually,' Alice began, 'we'll have to go – my sister's coming to take us to the zoo. It's her youngest's birthday and that's his treat.'

'Oh well,' Mrs P. said, but quite nicely, 'we can't compete with that, can we? Are you going to see some monkeys Amy?'

'No,' Amy said, scowling. 'I want to cook.'

'She's getting a will of her own,' Mrs P. said.

'Come on, Amy,' Alice said, 'you can cook another day if Pen will let you.'

'She's always welcome, though we haven't seen much of her lately, but she doesn't forget, do you, Amy?'

'I want to cook,' Amy said. Mrs P. smiled.

Alice had to pick her daughter up and carry her forcibly out of the house screaming all the way and Mrs P. following, enjoying every minute of it. She felt sick with the physical effort by the time she got her outside and even then Mrs P. stood at the door watching as though enjoying the spectacle. Though this was how she felt, Alice was aware that she was reacting exactly as Mrs P. herself would have done – attributing nastiness to somebody when they felt none. She wished Charlotte had dumped Amy anywhere except next door, she wished she had got back just ten minutes earlier, she wished she'd taken Amy with her – anything to have avoided that scene. As it was, Amy would have to be allowed to go back and cook or she would never be forgiven.

On the way to the zoo in Laura's car Alice suddenly remembered the Pendleburys were off to Australia. Immediately her depression lifted. It would provide such a break, such a valuable block of time for them all to find a perspective they never had. And the trip was bound to affect them. They would come back quite changed, better able to cope with what were quite ordinary problems of day-to-day living. There was even the possibility that they might not come back at all, whatever Mrs P. said – and if they couldn't go back and couldn't go forward wasn't that the best thing to hope for? Wouldn't it be better to part than mark time for ever in a bog of misunderstandings? She would let Amy go in tomorrow. She would make an effort to be forthcoming again herself. She ought to be able to manage any strain for less than three weeks.

Chapter Seventeen

Amy went to make pastry with Mrs Pendlebury the next morning, and then the next and the next after that. Each time she was collected by her mother she would announce the time she was going to come the following day, and when Alice demurred Mrs P. would say, wearing her best grand duchess look, 'Yes, that's all right, I'll take her off your hands for a bit,' and all Alice could do was thank her and remember Australia was only a matter of days off. Occasionally she tried to say that she was sure Mrs P. was very busy getting ready for her trip but Amy was convinced she was helping. Packing was her favourite game. She recited a list of all the things Pen had in her case, stringing them into one long word.

Alice was grateful that at least Mrs P. seemed cheerful about it all. There were no signs at all that any kind of panic had set in as the time dwindled to a week. She brought in to their re-established Wednesday coffee mornings letters from Frank and letters from Veronica and letters from the two older children and had Alice read them all several times. They were exemplary letters. Alice found the ones from Veronica particularly enlightening and couldn't help remarking to Mrs P. that her daughter-in-law seemed to know her very well considering they'd never met. All Mrs P. said was, 'She's a doctor's daughter – they know how to go about things. I expect there's more to her than meets the eye.' 'What do you mean?' Alice asked. She hardly ever asked Mrs P. that, for it was when she was at her most enigmatic that she was also most sensitive, and did not like to be pushed or made to explain.

'Well, she's clever, isn't she?' Mrs P. said. 'No point in putting my back up. I'm Frank's Mum, he wants me over there and she knows that, doesn't she?'

Alice read both Frank's and Veronica's last letters again. It seemed quite obvious to her that it was Veronica who was the more enthusiastic.

'Is there anything I can do while you're away?' she said instead of what she wanted to say.

'No thank you. My sister-in-law will be looking after the house.'

'Really? But she lives at Hackney, doesn't she?'

'Yes, but it won't be any bother. She'll see to it.'

'I'd be only too glad, you know.'

'No, that's all right.'

But it was not. Remembering Mrs P.'s awkwardness Alice was not surprised that when she had to re-open the subject she did so in a state of considerable agitation.

'We've had a bombshell,' she announced, marching into Alice's kitchen and hurling her gloves on the table. 'It's the absolute limit. I shan't get over it easily I can tell you that. That's her finished as far as I'm concerned. Finished.'

'Have some coffee,' Alice said, turning away to the cooker to hide her smiles.

'She rang up last night,' Mrs P. said, snatching the proffered mug and swilling it down without seeming to notice it was boiling hot (though normally her sips were so ladylike the liquid must have been freezing by the end), 'and said she was sorry but it wasn't convenient to have my key. Wasn't convenient! And the things I've done for her, the trouble I've taken – I was speechless.'

Alice drank her own coffee. She had heard all about Elsie many times.

'Perhaps she's ill,' she suggested.

'Ill? Not her, she's not ill.'

'Well, she must have had a reason. What did she say when you asked why it wasn't convenient?'

'I didn't ask, I wouldn't dream of giving her the satisfaction. Oh no, if that's the way she wants it she can have it. Nobody gets a second chance with me.'

They both heard the coffee going down each other's throats.

'I rang off,' Mrs P. said. 'Of course, she rang back but I was ready for her. Stanley answered. You can answer that phone, I said, because it's your sister, I said, and you can tell her from me I don't want to know.'

'Did he?'

'Course he didn't. Started trying to tell me a lot of old rubbish about them going on holiday and not liking the responsibility while they were away – ridiculous. On holiday for a month, I said – they saw you coming.'

'What a pity,' Alice said, trying to adopt Mrs P.'s own attitude of extreme vagueness when embarrassed.

'No, it isn't,' Mrs P. said, loudly. 'Is there any sugar in this? It's bitter to my mind.' Alice leapt to get the sugar. Mrs P. had been having coffee for fifteen months with exactly that amount of sugar. 'No, it isn't a pity. I like to know where I stand with people. It's better to know. But we're sunk now – the place will go to rack and ruin.'

'Don't be silly,' Alice said. 'I told you ages ago it would give me the greatest pleasure to have your key and see your house and garden are looked after. I was quite hurt you'd asked your sister-in-law instead of us, really.'

'You've got enough to do,' Mrs P. said, 'and with not being well.'

'But I *am* well, I feel fine.'

'You don't look it. No, I know what it's like, I lost a little one too. I couldn't ask you to take on my house in your condition.'

'Mrs Pendlebury,' Alice said, stiff and even sharp, 'it really wasn't at all the same. I had what was really a late miscarriage. I never even saw the baby. Your daughter was a person to you and the way she died much more – harrowing. I'm not in the least haunted by my bad luck. I've wiped it out of my mind.'

'You can't,' Mrs P. said. 'You can't ever wipe it out. I couldn't even say Ellen's name for ten years, not even to myself.'

'But I didn't even *have* a name – don't you see, I haven't any associations at all.'

'It's putting too much on you, in your condition.'

'But my condition is splendid.'

They argued at a tangent for some minutes more and then Mrs P. suddenly gave in with a completeness that showed she had always intended to. The key was produced that very second, together with a list of what had to be done, neatly printed by Stanley. 'You don't want to bother with that,' Mrs P. said, 'that's just Stanley's office training. All I care about is letting some sunshine in now and again, that's all, especially in the bedroom. I hate a stuffy bedroom. We once went for a week to Bournemouth and when we came back it was like the Black Hole of Calcutta. Just fling open the windows on a good day – but be careful, some of those frames stick. They're not safe. I've told Stanley to have them seen to but he never does. Don't let Amy near them or they might catch her little fingers.'

'Tony will cut the grass,' Alice said.

'He needs to cut his own first,' Mrs P. said, but laughed. 'No, he isn't a gardener. Just you leave it. It won't grow too much at this time of the year and we should be full of energy when we get back.'

There was about her, Alice thought, an intensity that was startling. Her eyes, normally rather watery looking and slightly hooded, seemed to have taken on a brightness and above all a concentration they had never had. Instead of darting about uneasily from object to object, never coming to rest for more than a few seconds on the person she was talking to, they had recently become fixed. She looked somehow transported – not necessarily with delight but just not there. She talked quite normally but her eyes were somewhere else and the lurking smile playing about her wide, usually grim mouth added to the unnerving effect.

'I haven't seen him for twenty-four years,' she said, drinking from an empty cup. 'You don't know what that's like.'

'No,' said Alice.

'I knew he'd grow up and go away. I wasn't stupid like Elsie. It was only common sense. I never expected nothing. But when he went away there didn't seem any point any more. Of course, I never said nothing. I wouldn't have held him back for anything.'

'It's hard,' Alice said, 'but you had Mr Pendlebury. If I had to choose between Tony and Amy I'd have to choose Tony.'

'What a dreadful thing to say!' Mrs P. stood up. 'That's dreadful, dreadful. You should take that back at once or you'll regret it – something terrible will happen.'

'I'm sorry,' Alice said, 'it's a silly thing to bring up anyway. I only meant – '

'I should think so,' Mrs P. said.

They kept to trivial matters from then on, Alice working hard at it. There was, she decided, no real communication possible with Mrs P. It was better to talk endlessly of shoes and ships and sealing wax than risk confusion and offence. She ignored the mystic quality about Mrs P. and settled for the larger prosaic part. They talked about clothes for the voyage and packing and getting the house to rights and Alice made several appreciated suggestions. She confined herself to admiring new dresses and shoes and helped to suggest presents. She went with Mrs P. to the optician's and arranged for another pair of glasses to be made up with tinted lenses. She went with her to the dentist and arranged to have another set of upper teeth made in case the worst should happen and the existing ones break. One by one she unravelled Mrs P.'s deepest darkest fears and helped her deal with them. She was a tower of strength and all the time she was counting the days until Mrs P. would go, longing to be free from the peculiar kind of strain put upon her.

Stanley felt it too. He had been minding his own business steadily for the last month but even so Rose's exalted mood could not pass him by. He was quite willing to be pestered about tickets and timetables but she left him alone, seeming to have a confidence in his capacity that she had never had before. She left him, in fact, altogether to his own devices and that annoyed him. She was acting as if only *she* was going to Australia. Sitting with that soft sick-cow look on her face she was given to little speeches about where Frank was going to take her and what she was looking forward to most and when he chipped in with his expectations she didn't listen. It was as though she was constantly having a vision. However hard and matter-of-fact the things she was saying, the look on her face told another story. He felt she wanted brought down to earth with a bump.

'Only three days left,' he said, over their supper. 'I see you've got everything packed. Do you want me to do the cases up and bring them down?'

'Plenty of time,' she said, looking over his head and stirring her tea with that faraway look. 'I might put some tea in,' she said, 'you never know. I might want a cup of dependable stuff.'

'So might I,' Stanley said.

'What?'

'I said I might want a cup of tea in Australia, a cup of our own stuff I mean.'

She stared at him blankly.

'I'm going too, you know,' he said.

'Course you are,' she said, 'but I don't suppose we'll see much of each other.'

'Why not?'

'Well, Frank mentioned taking me for a few outings on our own.'

'He meant me as well.'

'No he didn't.'

'Yes he did. Here, I've got the letter to prove it.'

'Oh, put it away. Think I don't know what he said? My own son? You're forgetting how well we got on, aren't you? We could do telepathy Frank and I. I haven't felt that way since except sometimes with Alice next door.'

Stanley was so cross he said, 'I'm surprised to hear that. Telepathy, eh? Reading her thoughts? I bet there are a few you haven't read.'

'Such as what?'

'You must have been getting on her nerves if you've been behaving with her anything like you've been behaving with me.'

'Sometimes I think you're a very nasty man, Stanley Pendlebury.'

The excitement of the actual day approaching banished any bitchiness between them. They were up by seven each morning, both of them, scurrying around doing jobs that should have been done weeks ago. Rose was happier than she had ever been, conjuring up reserves of strength she didn't even know she had. Last-minute visits to the doctor for Stanley's medicine were managed without fuss, and a hair appointment the day before taken in its stride. The furniture in all the rooms except the kitchen and their bedroom was covered with old sheets and every ornament put away. Stanley didn't understand the reasoning behind this but Rose seemed to think it necessary. They had a whole day in the garden giving the lawn the closest shave it had ever had, trimming the grass edges and tying up the bushes. All the garden tools were scrupulously cleaned afterwards and put in polythene bags and then in a sack and brought inside. And still Rose had not spent her energy.

'Well,' she said, the night before, 'everything's done, everything's shipshape.'

'You must be worn out,' Stanley said. 'I don't know where you get the energy from. I'm beat.'

'Don't you say that – I don't want any moans this trip. You just keep your mouth shut if you don't feel well. No fussing – now remember.'

'I don't fuss, but if I feel poorly – '

'Just go and lie down if you feel poorly, don't go broadcasting it and casting a blight on everything.'

'That's easier said than done.'

'Oh, look on the bright side for heaven's sake. This is going to be a happy time.'

'You've changed your tune.'

'I beg your pardon?'

'It's not often you're looking on the bright side.'

'It's not often I have the chance with you nagging.'

'Me nag? Me nag?'

'And that's another thing – we don't want any arguing. Let's keep our arguing for when we're on our own. Now, do you want a sandwich to use up that last bit of ham?'

'Yes,' said Stanley, glad everything was on a level he understood.

They had a pleasant supper, eating up all the odds and ends. Stanley did rather well – not only did the ham stretch to four sandwiches but there were pieces of Madeira cake and a currant scone. He ate them all, washed down with several cups of tea, to a background of the radio news. Rose listened with him and they both nodded at each other when the announcer said that the power workers were again considering strike action which could lead to blackouts within a few weeks. Stanley remarked they were well out of that and Rose that she was sick of hearing bad news. Both of them agreed that the news in Australia was bound to be more cheerful.

Going to bed was a sentimental business. Stanley said, 'Last time I'll lock up here for a while,' and Rose, obviously feeling this was a sign he was taking it as seriously as she was, was pleased. She cleaned the cooker meticulously, leaving the door a little ajar. They would only need the electric kettle for the morning, barely time for a quick cuppa before the off at eight o'clock. Stanley said they would have breakfast on the plane but she knew she would be too nervous. Food was unimportant – she didn't seem to need it at the moment. They went upstairs together for once and lay for a while chatting. The excitement was a physical thing – they swopped stories of butterflies in stomachs and clammy hands until Rose burst out laughing and said they were a couple of kids. In the end she told him to stop talking. They must get some sleep to face tomorrow. They promptly fell asleep and slept very soundly, so soundly that they heard nothing at all, neither the phone nor the doorbell nor the loud treble knock.

Alice knew the Pendleburys were leaving at eight in the morning. It was a sunny, mild morning so she opened the front door and told Amy to shout when the Pens came out of their door. So sure was she that the shout would come any minute that she didn't bother keeping an eye on the clock and was surprised when Tony came down to find it was almost eight fifteen. Amy trailed in dragging a toy at the same time.

'Amy, did you wave bye bye to the Pens?'

'Pens didn't come.'

'Are you sure, Amy? Were you watching all the time?'

'Yes,' said Amy, definite and bored.

Just then there was another bang next door.

'They're still there,' Tony said, 'you must have got the wrong time.'

'But I didn't – I know it was eight. Perhaps their taxi hasn't come. Oh how awful – you know what they're like about taxis. Do you think you should – '

'No. They'll ask if they need me. You surely don't think even the Pendleburys would risk missing a plane to Australia just because a taxi hadn't come, Stanley's not that bad.'

Alice spent the rest of the morning alternately listening to sounds next door and rushing to the front of the house at the slightest noise of a car. Nothing conclusive happened. When Amy went for her rest at eleven she was no wiser. The soothingly practical Charlotte who came along to borrow something couldn't see why Alice should be agitated but then she never could. Agitation was an emotion Charlotte had spent a lifetime suppressing and openly despised in others. Alice immediately felt ashamed. There was, of course, nothing for her to worry about whatever had happened. Telling herself this at five-minute intervals after Charlotte had gone in her antiseptic cloud did no good at all. She was frantic with anxiety. Twice she went into the garden and peered over. Not a sign of life – everything still and sterile after the big clear-up.

In the afternoon, she took Amy out. They passed the Pens' house but there was no indication either that they had gone or were still there. All the way to the park and back Alice was distracted by the thought that one or other of the Pens might have collapsed. Another of Stanley's attacks, she decided, would be preferable to it being a case of Rose simply having cold feet. Perhaps the calm of the last few weeks had all been a subterfuge, perhaps her contentment had only been a pretence and underneath fear had all the time been preparing to pull her in and down. Alice thought about the consequences if this were so and felt sick. Her face assumed a drawn, grey look that made acquaintances think she must be ill or moping after her miscarriage and, without realizing it, she was shunned by several.

Tony came home to find her wandering about the house unable to settle to anything. He was hardly through the door before she was saying, 'I'm sure something dreadful has happened.'

'Rubbish. Their light was on when I came in.'

'Was it? Which light?'

'The lamp they have in the front room on top of their telly.'

'Are you sure?'

'Of course I'm sure – go and look for yourself.'

'No, I don't want to.'

'Then stop worrying. They'll come and tell you eventually and if they don't I can't see it matters. It's none of your business.'

But neither Mr nor Mrs Pendlebury did come. Alice found herself standing in her own hall clutching their key several times a day. From being an ordinary dull brass Yale key with a bit of string tied round it the object became as menacing as a weapon. If she wasn't going to use it she must return it and there was no way of returning it without facing Mrs P. She couldn't just put it through the letter-box as the cool Charlotte advised – it would be sacrilege. She became convinced the Pens were waiting and watching for her, and her head was full of scenes in which they accused her of fraud. The scenes turned into nightmares and she woke twice in a state of sweating terror that roused Tony to a stiff and unsympathetic anger.

'I'm returning the key myself tomorrow,' he said, after the second occurrence.

'No, you can't.'

'I can. You're working yourself into a panic over nothing. We've been through all this before.'

'But you – '

'I don't want to discuss it. Good night.'

She waited, terrified, for him to come back. He was very quick.

When he came in again, looking for his car coat to go to work, he was brisk and cheerful.

'Mission accomplished,' he said. She looked at him appealingly. 'All right, a blow-by-blow account. I walked up the front path, rang the bell and waited. After a couple of minutes Stanley opened the door and I said hello Mr Pendlebury how are you everything all right I hope and he said yes thanks and I said we thought we'd better return your key as you didn't seem to have gone off and he said yes thanks we had a cancellation my daughter-in-law's ill. Oh, said, I, what a pity, yes he said but that's life I expect we'll go in the spring instead and I said might be a better time to go even if it is a disappointment now and he said that's what I say and I said well I must get off to work be seeing you and that was that.'

'How did he look?'

'Like he always looks – no collar, sleeves rolled up, old suit waistcoat – '

'You *know* what I mean.'

'Like Stanley – dozy. He never changes his expression anyway, not that I've ever seen. He was in a hurry, for him – dying to get back either to the lav or English lessons for Pakistanis on telly.'

'Did he say how Mrs P. was taking it?'

'He said exactly what I've just told you he said – no more, no less.'

'It must have been literally at the last minute – can you imagine – '

'No. You can keep your imagination to yourself and divide by two.'

'Imagination?' Alice said, and stood still in the hall while he left for work. He kissed her but she hardly felt the kiss. Imagination didn't come into it. She knew for a fact that Rose Pendlebury would be going through the tortures of the damned – and let Tony condemn that for a high-flown phrase if he liked. Mrs P. might well be damned. The disappointment, quickly followed by retribution as it surely would be, could only weaken the last strands that had kept her believing in the human race at all, strands of hope, strands of anticipation, binding her to other people. They were so very thin and fragile anyway, so easily severed, leaving her bitter and betrayed, feeling she had tried but that it was hardly worth while. And Alice found she cared more than she would have admitted before this happened – Mrs P. must not cast herself off. It mattered that she should feel wanted and cherished. She could not, as Stanley would say, be left to stew in her own juice.

Wednesday came and went and no Mrs P. Alice had hardly expected there would be. She was ready to go next door before it was past eleven, before it was decently certain that Mrs P. would not be coming. She didn't expect, either, that Mrs P. would open the door and was ready for Stanley.

'Hello. Is Mrs Pendlebury all right?'

'Yes,' Stanley said, 'but come in, she'd like to see you.'

Alice was sure she heard a scuffle and even a cry of some kind from the back room at the end of the passage down which she followed Stanley.

'Yes,' he said, 'she's all right. A bit disappointed, of course, but she'll get over it. It was a bit of a shock.'

'I should just think it was. It must have been literally at the last minute.'

'Yes, yes it was. We didn't hear the phone – Frank phoned you know – and we didn't hear the telegram boy. Of course, that upset my wife, not hearing them, that upset her as much as anything. Now where is she?'

They were in the back room and it was empty. Stanley looked amazed. He shuffled into the kitchen and called, 'Rose?' but even Alice from where she was could see there was nobody in the tiny room.

'She was here a minute ago,' he said, 'where can she have got to? She must be in the garden.'

'Never mind,' Alice said, 'I only came to say how sorry I was about Australia. I'll pop in another time.'

'No, you stay there,' Stanley said. 'I know she'd like to see you. I'll just look in the garden.'

He found her in the garage, sitting in the old car, crouching down on the back seat.

'Whatever are you doing?' he asked. 'I've been looking everywhere, calling your name and everything. I've got a visitor for you.'

'Then get rid of her.'

'It's young Alice, come to see how you are.'

'Get rid of her. Go on – get rid of her. It's your doing, you can get out of it.'

'But she's come to – '

'I know why she's come and I don't want to see her, I don't want to see nobody.'

'Don't be silly – '

'Don't you call me silly, I'm not silly, I've got all my wits about me, you needn't worry about that.'

'It isn't polite just to send her away. What's she done to deserve that?'

'She knows.'

'I don't know what bee you've got in your bonnet now but – '

'You get rid of her.'

'But what am I to tell her?'

'Tell her what you like for all I care.'

Stanley stood and scratched his head, but refused to move. He couldn't see his wife's face very clearly in the half-light of the garage, but her voice was one he knew well enough, one half-way between hysteria and rage that told him more than any arrangement of her features. She wasn't to be trifled with, not in that mood. Best leave her alone, to get over whatever it was by herself. He went out into the garden and slowly retraced his steps down the path. He could see Alice standing obediently by the window. She was a nice girl, he wouldn't want to see her feelings hurt. He would have to invent a story though he wasn't good at that kind of thing. What should he say? What the devil could he say? He cleared his throat in preparation for a good deal of mumbling, but Alice saved him the bother and he blessed her for it.

'She's busy unpacking all the garden tools, I suppose,' she said.

'Yes, that's right.'

'Well, I won't interrupt. I must get back anyway – I've left Amy asleep.'

'It was very nice of you to call. I expect my wife will come round shortly.'

'You tell her to come in any time.'

They both smiled.

'You're quite sure she's – all right?' Alice asked.

'Well,' Stanley hesitated, 'she's a bit low, in the circumstances.'

'Couldn't you go away to cheer her up? I mean, without being interfering, perhaps a little break by the sea would take her mind off things.'

'You might be right there.'

'I mean, with winter coming on – Mrs Pendlebury doesn't like winter, does she, and if she's depressed anyway – '

'Oh, she'll snap out of it before winter don't you worry.'

'But I do worry. I don't like to see her unhappy. We all think the world of her.'

Alice stopped, embarrassed by her own gushing words that were the only ones she felt might make an impression on Stanley. He said it was very nice of her but she could tell nothing had penetrated his thick layer of complacency. He showed her out, smiling and making remarks about the weather while in the garden she knew his wife was hiding.

But Stanley was slightly alarmed and by no means as impassive as Alice had thought. He watched from the back window to see Rose come out of the garage. She took her time about it, and when she did she had a ridiculous old straw hat pulled down over her face. She meandered between the bushes, pulling at things, sometimes literally going in circles. If only she'd had a good cry when it had happened. He'd known at the time that was what she'd needed, but instead she'd laughed and said things like, 'I knew it,' and been loud and raucous in everything she did afterwards. She'd tipped the whole of their cases out into a heap on the floor – just ripped them open and up-ended the whole lot and shouted, 'Waste of time that was!' He'd been furious, absolutely furious, not prepared to make any kind of allowances for that kind of behaviour. The mess was appalling. She made no attempt to clear it up, just kept walking round it like somebody skirting a bonfire and she had indeed actually suggested burning everything. He sweated at the memory of it. There had been something wild about her all that long awful day, something unrestrained and vicious.

It had all settled down, of course. The next day she was quiet and moody. She said she didn't want to talk about it and he had respected her wishes. Naturally, she wouldn't talk to Frank when he rang again, and he'd had to deal with that himself. Frank was worried to death. Veronica, it seemed, had broken her leg in two places and fractured an arm and heaven knows what. She'd fallen from a ladder painting the outside windows for them coming. Frank kept saying she was just like mother, wouldn't wait till I got home, had to have it done. Stanley reassured him. It didn't matter the trip being postponed, they quite understood, and of course Frank had done the right thing no doubt about that, no point at all in them coming if Veronica was out of action.

Stanley was exhausted after that telephone marathon. He felt aggrieved that Rose didn't appreciate what he'd saved her. 'That was Frank,' he said, needlessly. 'It seems Veronica fell – '

'I don't want to hear. Don't mention her name.'

'Well that's very nice I must say. Your only daughter-in-law has a serious fall and you don't want to hear about the accident or – '

'It wasn't any accident.'

'How wasn't it? Did she break her leg and arm deliberately then? Eh?'

'I don't know what she did.'

'I've just told you – she fell off – '

'You don't know either.'

'Frank just told me, she fell off a ladder painting the outside windows for us coming.'

'So she says.'

'*Frank* said. Are you calling Frank a liar?'

'I never said nothing about Frank – it's her, I don't want to know.'

'I think you should see sense.'

'I can see what I want to see thank you very much and that's quite enough.'

There had been no moving her. He didn't dare wonder what

235

terrible thoughts she was harbouring. It was better to look the other way till her own common sense put her right. Nobody could help her, it would all take time. He felt sorry for himself having to put up with it and almost wished he could have another 'do' and get himself carted off to hospital for a few weeks. What did he have to look forward to here? Rose moaning, taking it out on him. Strikes any minute, seeing nobody, only the Club for escape and her resenting him going so much that it was almost more trouble than it was worth. What a life.

She came in at last.

'I hope you're proud of yourself,' he said.

She didn't reply, just pulled the dirty old straw hat farther down on her head. 'I'm going down to the Club this afternoon,' he said, 'get my name down for the functions as I told them to take it off. Do you want the news on?'

'It isn't time for the news, nothing like time. Why don't you think before you speak?'

'I speak anyway, more than you've been doing – been like living with a dummy this last week.'

'If you've any objections you know what to do.'

'Do I? What then?'

'Get out.'

'Don't talk silly. This is my house.'

'It's come to that, has it? My this my that. Oh well, it's better to know where I stand. I'll get out myself. When do you want me to go?'

Stanley was so irritated he was at a complete loss. He groaned and slapped the window sill with his hand and then laughed and said she was the limit.

'What a carry on,' he said finally. 'I think we both want our heads felt. What a to-do.'

Rose refused to laugh with him. She looked at him with hatred and cursed him for his attitude of acceptance. She'd wanted him to flare up and carry it a stage further, she'd wanted to be out on the street with her apron and straw hat and then she'd just wander like a tramp. How dare he mock her anger and misery by being reasonable, by ridiculing it. To show him how she felt she picked up the vase from the table and threw it to the floor and then left him staring in that stupid way at the pile of wet crystal and the puddle on the carpet and the yellow chrysanthemums splayed out everywhere. He could think about *that* down at his precious club.

Chapter Eighteen

Between October and Christmas, Alice saw Mrs P. only twice – once she met her head on in the street and had five minutes' desultory chat before a heavy shower of rain sent them both scurrying on, and once over the garden wall when they were both burning leaves towards the end of November. That was the most disturbing of the two encounters. Amy saw Pen first, standing as she was on the garden table looking over the wall. Mrs P. greeted her shout happily enough, and came to the wall with her rake still in her hands, but when Alice came too she at once became busy again and replied to pleasantries in monosyllables. Amy, of course, began asking if she could go over but Mrs P. didn't offer and Alice had to say Mrs P. was busy, wait till another day. They both went on working in the garden for another half-hour, Alice feeling distinctly uncomfortable.

As New Year approached, and with it Amy's third birthday, Alice felt an effort must be made. She and Amy made a splendid invitation asking the Pens to come to the birthday party. It was a giant card, covered in tinfoil and tissue paper, leaking glue everywhere, proudly special and homemade. They took it next door together and when no one answered the bell left it propped up against the milk bottles where it couldn't be missed. No reply came, but on the morning of Amy's birthday Stanley came in looking more dishevelled than Alice had ever seen him and said could Amy come in to see Mrs Pendlebury for her present. Amy was out of the door shrieking with excitement before Alice could ask if she could come too. Stanley trailed after her saying he would bring her back. They were gone a bare five minutes and then Amy was hammering at the door wanting to show off the big box of sticklebricks she'd been given.

'I hope you said thank you, Amy,' Alice said. Stanley had disappeared.

'Yes I did. I said thank you for having me.'

'Did Mrs Pen give you the bricks?'

'Yes.'

Alice wanted to ask so many things and gazed at her small daughter helplessly. She couldn't subject a three-year-old to an inquisition, however badly she wanted the information.

'Was Pen all right?' she asked, feebly.

'She was in her bed.'

'Really? Upstairs? Did you go upstairs?'

'Mm. Up twenty stairs.' Amy counted them as conclusive proof. 'Pen was in her bed in a blue nightie like your blue nightie with the strings on.'

'Ribbons.'

'Ribbons on.'

'What did Pen say?'

'Happy Birthday aren't you a big girl are you having a party what did you get for your birthday isn't that nice.'

'What did you say?'

'Thank you for having me I got a bike.'

'Did you ask if she was coming to your party?'

'No. But I saw my card I made.'

'Where was it?'

'I don't know. Pen had it.'

'In bed?'

'I don't know.'

A little ashamed of her eagerness, Alice let it drop. At the party that afternoon lots of people asked about the Pendleburys, remembering the year before. Some had seen her in the street and said how ill she looked, others had seen her at the window and had waved but she had not waved back. Alice tried to explain to the genuinely interested – among whom Charlotte was not one – what had happened, but she only had to embark on this explanation to find it impossible to continue. Nothing, after all, had happened. The Pendleburys hadn't gone to Australia, that was all, wasn't it? She couldn't expect anyone, on that basis, to feel as she did. One or two expressed sympathy with the old couple,

Penny Stewart even going so far as to say the anticlimax must have been awful for them, but Alice was left afterwards feeling the Pendleburys, even to those who knew them, were unimportant, not to say invisible.

She had, next day, her one and only row with Charlotte about them. Driven to confide in someone – Tony would not be confided in on this taboo subject – she in desperation blurted out to Charlotte how worried she was about Mrs P. It was, she knew, a mistake – Charlotte might brightly ask you what was worrying you but she never meant it – but once she'd started she had to continue.

'I know she's moping in there thinking nobody cares.'

'But you've been in, haven't you?'

'Yes.'

'And invited her to the party?'

'Yes.'

'Well then she can't think you don't care.'

Charlotte smiled with satisfaction at her neat, tidy solution.

'It takes more than that,' Alice said. 'She's so dreadfully unhappy.'

'She's always struck me as just rather a bad-tempered old woman – always so sour. She looks like a cross frog.'

'Maybe there are reasons why she looks cross.'

'Nobody *has* to look cross. Everyone can manage a smile surely?' – and Charlotte smiled to show how they could manage it.

'No, quite often people can't,' Alice said, flushed and obstinate.

'Mr Pendlebury does, poor old man. It must be dreadful for him putting up with her.'

'It's worse for her putting up with him – he doesn't help her at all, he just wants a quiet life.'

'I should think so too.'

'Well, I don't. I mean, if you love somebody – ' Alice flushed even redder, knowing one didn't talk about love in everyday contexts ' – you want to make them happy and help them get out of their depression.'

'He should pack her off for a week somewhere. They're not poor are they?'

'No, I don't think so.'

'Well, that's what he should do. I'll tell him next time I see him.'

'It wouldn't really help. It's inside herself, the trouble. She's gone all her life with these feelings of persecution and – '

'Oh goodness me, I must go, I've got to go to the hairdresser.'

'I'm sorry I bored you.'

'You didn't bore me, you just bore yourself. I'd forget about it, if I were you.'

'I know you would, but you're not me, that's the point.' A quick, brittle smile and Charlotte left it at that.

It was, anyway, impossible to forget. Quite apart from anything else, the banging started. Every night, about ten o'clock, there would be a horrible crashing against the wall where they had the sofa – a great, persistent thumping that went on and on. Not even Tony could ignore that. Alice was sure the Pens must be trying to attract attention and became unbearably anxious about them, so much so that Tony said he would ring up and find out, but as he went to the phone the banging stopped and they heard loud, angry voices instead. Tony said he couldn't now ring up – people were entitled to have arguments. It became a nightly occurrence – loud bangs for up to half an hour followed by loud voices. Tony was amused, Alice terrified. He made jokes like Stanley at last taking the stick to Rose which Alice hated. They decided the banging was caused by a poker or some other solid, hard instrument being knocked against the old chimney that the Pens had never boarded up. They themselves had removed the fireplace and there was now a ventilation brick at the bottom of the chimney breast through which the noise was coming. It was impossible not to hear some of the words being shouted after the banging subsided, and they scared Alice most. The Pendleburys were a respectable, elderly couple who never, ever swore – beyond a mild 'damn' – and held it in abhorrence, yet distinctly, among a jumble of speech, could be heard 'bloody' this and 'to hell' that and 'Christ knows' and other harmless, mild but unmistakably bad language.

Then, in February, the power cuts began, first only a couple of hours in the morning then another two or even three in the afternoon, and finally up to three lots of three hours each every day. The banging stopped, the shouting ceased, and instead, for hour on hour, Alice sat rigid listening to an endless wail. The wailing rose and fell, rhythmic, persistent, sometimes breaking off only to start again after a few minutes. 'I can't stand it,' Alice said after the third evening, 'it's terrible, awful – we've got to do something, I don't care if it is interfering.'

'Perhaps they haven't any candles,' Tony suggested. 'I expect they're in the dark and freezing cold.'

'Of course they are – that house is like a morgue even with their miserable little electric fires on. What do you think it's like now?'

'I'll take some candles round.'

'And that paraffin lamp – we can manage without that.'

'We might need that if – '

'I don't care! Go on, take them, go *on*, Tony.'

He went, at once, groping his way along the palings till he got to their hedge. The street looked pretty with all the candles flickering. In the Pendlebury windows no light of any kind shone. He knocked and rang but there was no answer. He couldn't go back to a half hysterical Alice with candles and lamp still in his hands. Kneeling down, he peered through their letter-box but there was a wooden box behind blocking any sound. He'd shout till doomsday and they wouldn't hear. Then he thought perhaps they were scared to answer the door whereas they might answer the phone, so he went back and rang them. The telephone rang and rang – they could hear it – but was never answered.

'Oh this is ridiculous,' Tony said, bad-tempered. 'What's the point of carrying on like this?'

'Please,' Alice pleaded.

He rang again and after five full minutes, just as he was about to hang up, Stanley answered.

'Hello, Mr Pendlebury,' Tony said, cheerfully. 'It was me ringing and knocking.'

'Oh,' Stanley said, quite calmly, 'we wondered who it was.'

'I was bringing you some candles and a paraffin lamp.'

'Oh. That's very kind of you.'

'Do you need them? Would you like them?'

'No, we're all right.'

'You don't seem to have any lights on.'

'No. We don't need lights really. Not much point is there? It isn't as if you can do anything.'

'Well, it helps to see your way about.'

'We don't mind about that.'

'I'm sorry to have bothered you then.'

'That's all right.'

Tony put the receiver down. 'Bloody hell,' he said, 'the old bugger – you'd think I was after him instead of trying to help. That's the last time I'm making a fool of myself for you. They can rot for all I care.'

'They're in total darkness,' Alice whispered, 'just sitting there, in the dark, crying.'

'Stanley wasn't crying. He was quite perky.'

'They must be so cold – and no telly and no light – oh God.'

'Shut up about them. It's entirely their own fault.'

They went to bed soon after, before the power was restored. Miserable, Alice stared at the ceiling in the candlelight while Tony undressed. It was so dramatic when the lights went off, so cosy being without them. But not next door. Next door, power cuts were a return to the Dark Ages in every sense. They might as well be in a cave, crying with fear while outside monsters prowled and there was no magic fire to keep them away. She began to cry herself and had to turn away so Tony would not see. He blew out the candle and got into bed beside her. They lay, drowsy, lightly breathing, bodies warmly touching – until with the most ugly suddenness there was a crash outside and another crash, and they both clutched each other and sat up. 'I've had enough,' a voice cried, 'I've had enough.' It was cracked and strained, a voice produced against tremendous odds.

'It's Mrs P.,' Alice whispered.

'Where?'

'Outside – in the garden. The noise was the door banging.'

Tony got up and went to the window. He could see nothing in the absolute blackness.

'She must have gone in again.'

'No – listen.'

They heard swishing sounds and sharp cracks as twigs snapped underfoot.

'She must be in the garden.'

Tony strained to make out any shape below. His breath steamed up the window pane and he kept having to rub it clear with his pyjama sleeve. His feet were cold and numb on the floorboards. Just as he was about to let the curtain drop, he saw a white, loose blob moving about in the next-door garden, floating this way and that, indistinct but unmistakable. He closed the curtain a fraction more as the moon came from behind a cloud and lit Mrs Pendlebury's swaying figure. She began shouting again, raising her fists in the air and stretching it seemed to the sky.

'I've – had – enough!' she shouted. 'Why can't you leave us alone? Two seventy-year-old folk – why can't you leave us alone?'

'Don't get up,' Tony said, sharply, and got back into bed himself. 'She's crazy – try not to listen.' But they listened as the threats began.

'It'll be the police tomorrow – that's it – I've had enough, I'm fetching the police, they'll get you, they'll have you – '

'Rose?' Stanley's reedy voice cut into the shouts. 'Rose? Are you out there? Come in – come in.'

'I've had enough, it's the police tomorrow – ' The rest was lost in muffled crashes and bangs and one final slam of the back door. Their ears ached in the reclaimed silence.

'He'll have to get a doctor now,' Alice said.

'Of course he will.'

'What do you suppose she meant, about the police?'

'Just wandering. She probably thinks someone's trying to murder her.'

'What will they do?'

'The police won't do anything – but Stanley won't send for the police. He'll get the doctor and they'll put her on sedatives.'

'Poor old woman. Do you think we should – '

'We should keep right out of it. It's just as well this happened – it's forced Stanley's hand. She'll get the medical treatment she needs now and Stanley will get some peace.'

*

Peace was a long way off for Stanley as he struggled with the demented Rose. His one aim had been to get her inside at all costs – in the house and the door locked and bolted and then he could breathe easier. It only needed somebody to hear her like that and they'd have her in the loony bin faster than lightning. She didn't seem to realize this, she thought everyone understood she was just a bit irritable.

'You should watch your tongue,' he said, when he had her inside, 'it'll land you in trouble. Now come to bed and be sensible. You'll get your death of cold wandering about like that in your nightie.'

But she stood with her back to the door, arms folded, her face somehow swollen and her eyes brilliant in the middle of its puffy redness.

'I want the police,' she said, her lips seeming to have difficulty with the words, which came out thickly as though she was drunk.

'Don't talk ridiculous. What's all this about the police? I don't know what's got into you.'

'I've had enough, they've broken things, they've stolen things, they've spied on me and interfered with my papers – '

'What papers? What the devil are you on about?'

'Frank's letters and things, they've been at them, I know how I left them and it wasn't like that, it could only have been them.'

'Who?'

'Those Orams, that's who, I never trusted him, it's him and her but he put her up to it, he came in and rifled through my things, he – '

'Stop it!' said Stanley, almost growling with anger. 'Do you hear me? Now shut your mouth, I want no more of that talk, it's wicked and dangerous. I don't know what idea you've got into your head but you can get it out, now.'

She was weeping, shaking with sobs. Stanley felt drained. She leant heavily on him as he half dragged her upstairs and into bed, and then he crawled into his own bed and tried to shut out the noise of her crying. It went on and on until, his sympathy spent, he wanted to hit her or put a cushion over her head, anything to stop that moaning. He hoped, with his talent for going off the minute his head touched the pillow, that sleep would obliterate what his conscious mind could not, but for once in his life he stayed awake. There was too much to think about. Rose would need watching. He wouldn't be able to let her out of his sight if she was liable to come out with drivel like that. Why had she gone off on that tack? What had the Orams said or done? They were her friends, Alice was like a daughter. It didn't make sense. Perhaps he ought to let the doctor have a look at her, perhaps she needed a tonic to buck her up. It would be a terrible job getting her down to the surgery but even worse getting the doctor here without telling her and if he *did* tell her she would refuse to let him in. Perhaps that might be a good thing. Could the doctor after all be depended on to understand Rose? Might he not take it too seriously and have her taken away? It might be better just to let things ride, for the moment.

Stanley let them ride not just for the moment but for the next few weeks. The day after the scene in the garden he met Alice and knew at once, the way she asked how Rose was, that she'd heard. He said she'd been a bit under the weather but was fine now and when Alice said shouldn't she perhaps see a doctor, he laughed quite convincingly and said that would be a lot of fuss about nothing. But he held the doctor over Rose all the time. If she started crying or shouting or banging he told her straight that he was thinking of sending for the doctor and it worked a treat. She shut up straight away. During the power cuts he wasn't so hard on her – he let her snivel away because he felt like snivelling himself with no telly on. The house was so cold that he wasn't surprised she went to bed – he felt like doing it himself but hung on hoping to get at least the late TV shows. She was better off in bed with her hot water bottles anyway – it kept her out of mischief.

Everything went quite well until one morning, a week or so later, when he was filling in his football pools. There was no power cut and he was nice and cosy with the fire on full blast and a schools programme on telly and a cup of tea at his side when he heard Rose shout, 'Stanley – come quick – oh, this is too much!' He felt bitter that she had to interrupt him now and waited, hoping she'd come and tell him whatever it was, but the shouts continued and he reluctantly got up and put a saucer over his tea and trudged off to find her.

She was standing in the living-room, her hand flat against a pane of glass.

'What's wrong now?' he said. 'What's up? What's all the noise about?'

'Look,' she said dramatically, 'look what they've done now – I thought I heard a noise in the night, it was them, him, doing that.'

Stanley looked at the pane of glass. She had taken her hand away and was pointing at it. He felt, more than anything else, a deep embarrassment.

'Now then,' he said, 'there's nothing wrong with the window.'

'Nothing wrong? Is smashed nothing wrong? Look, I cut my hand feeling it.' He knew without looking that there was nothing wrong with her hand.

'Have a cup of tea,' he suggested, 'there's still some in the pot. You sit there at the table and I'll bring it in.'

He was pouring the boiling water into the teapot to freshen what was left of the tea when she screamed and half the water went over his hand, scalding it.

'What now?' he said.

Her hands were spread out on the top of the table. It was a round, mahogany table, highly polished.

'Look, look,' she said, 'it's all scratched, oh, how could they, how could they, they've taken a knife to it, such wickedness, such vandals, oh it's too much – look Stanley, feel it, feel it – it's ruined – fetch the polish, fetch the duster.' He brought them. She polished the polished table frantically.

'Do you think that's better? Do you think they've gone a bit?'

'They've gone completely.'

'No, no, they're still there, oh what will it be next, what next?'

Stanley felt sick. There was a great to-do for another hour afterwards but finally he got her to concentrate on the pie she was making for lunch and when he saw she was absorbed he left her and returned to his cold tea. He sat and supped it, regardless. Nausea had dried his throat out and he would have drunk anything. He hadn't bothered arguing with Rose – experience had by now shown him that was no good. Better to let her run on and agree with her and then direct her interests elsewhere. But he couldn't keep doing that, not all the time, and suppose he wasn't here when she had one of these fits, suppose he was at the Club or out for a newspaper or doing the shopping? That was another thing – doing the shopping. He'd always been a bad shopper. Even if she just sent him for a half a pound of butter he always managed to get the wrong sort, but now she insisted he did all the shopping, on his own. She wouldn't go out, absolutely refused. He had to toil backwards and forwards with heavy bags while she sat at home waiting to find fault.

The sickness in his stomach had gone. He sat there with a Biro in his hand, fully intending to think things out and decide once and for all what must be done, but the trouble was he couldn't keep his mind on the problem. It was always the same – his eye caught this or that and he became distracted and found, later, that he hadn't been thinking about Rose at all. He was always hopeful that nothing else would happen and amazed when it did. Listening to his wife singing away in the kitchen he felt again that everything would blow over, otherwise how could she sing like that? All she needed was patience and he had plenty of that. It suddenly struck him that Rose might not remember what she said when she had one of her funny turns, and acting on the spur of the moment he went through to the kitchen.

'That looks a good pie,' he said.

'Well it won't be if you get in the way.'

He smiled, relieved, and full of courage said, 'Do you want me to get some new glass?'

'Glass? What for?'

'That broken window pane you were worried about.'

'What broken window pane?'

There was no doubting her mystification.

'Never mind,' he said.

'Riddles this morning,' she said, sniffing. 'Keep them to yourself when I'm busy.'

Stanley was immensely reassured. All Rose was suffering from was a little brain-storm now and again. The thing to do was to keep her busy and yet calm and just deal with things as they came and she would get over them. It helped him tremendously to come to this conclusion – slow, steady, dependable, that was the technique and it suited his nature admirably. Whenever she shouted, whatever disaster she claimed to have uncovered, he went to her side and exclaimed with her and then by degrees, promising to mend or restore whatever it was, he led her on to doing some simple household task that would take her mind off things. It worked very well but it took its toll: he felt drained after each struggle and in desperate need of comfort himself.

It was to satisfy this need that Stanley kept going to the Club on Tuesday afternoons. He only stayed one hour instead of two but it bucked him up no end. He never talked about Rose, of course, never uttered a word. People made remarks about him looking off colour but he just let them. It was very important that nobody should know how worried he was just at the thought of leaving Rose unguarded for even an hour. Before he left he always tried to make sure she was busy, actually suggesting little jobs to her so that if she had been fully herself she would have bitten his head off. He liked her to be washing clothes or tidying drawers or ironing or something like that. What he didn't like was her just sitting and staring waiting for him to go. He couldn't leave when she was like that – it was quite impossible. He had to hang on till she took something up or else not go at all, however much he wanted to. The prospect of what he might come back to was too inhibiting.

He knew, one Tuesday afternoon in the middle of March, that he shouldn't go. Rose had done nothing all morning. There'd been a power cut from six a.m. to nine a.m. and another scheduled for noon to three p.m. So he hadn't bothered trying to get her up. It was sleeting as they lay in bed, last night's hot water bottles cold and clammy at their feet and their breath coming in frosty gasps. No point in getting up until the fire came on and the cooker and the kettle so they could make something to warm themselves up. They said on the wireless you shouldn't leave electric appliances on during a cut, especially at night time, but they ignored that. If the fire was burning half the night then well and good. They were entitled to any heat they could get.

About half past ten Stanley came out of a lovely sleep and got up and took Rose some tea. No thanks, of course. She just lay there staring at the sleet and he left her alone and went downstairs and got some bacon going, hoping the delicious smell would bring her down, but it didn't. He shouted up, at half past eleven, that if she didn't look sharp the next cut would be on and she'd miss the lovely warm, but his warning had no effect. She seemed to wait till the very minute the red bars faded to black before she appeared, white-faced, dressed in scruffy, egg-stained clothes and her hair unbrushed. Without speaking, she went to the sink and started washing up.

So by three o'clock, when Stanley was due at the Club, the writing was on the wall. There she was, immobile, hands clasped in her lap, staring at nothing.

'Heat'll be on in a minute,' he said, 'and that's us for today.'

No response.

'Why don't you bake a cake when the oven comes on?' he asked. 'I like to smell a cake when I come in. It's a long time since you made one. You've got all the stuff, haven't you?'

Not a flicker of interest.

'Come on now,' he said, 'it isn't that bad.'

At that, she turned and looked at him and began to laugh. He laughed with her at first, pleased to have made a joke even if he didn't understand what it was, but then her laughter turned peculiar as it so often did these days, turned shrill and nasty.

'Oh get out,' she said, 'get out of my sight, get to your precious club and stay there.'

'I don't know what you'd do if I did,' he said.

'Don't you? Don't you?'

'No I don't. Now come on, pull yourself together.'

In a sudden whirlwind of energy she was on her feet and rushing past him and had her hat and coat on before he was halfway down the hall after her.

'Here, where are you off to? You don't know how cold it is, you haven't been out for weeks.'

'I know I haven't.'

'Where are you going?'

'Mind your own business.'

She flung the door open and a cloud of rain and sleet blew in. Anxiously, he went after her but as he reached their gate he saw her turn into Alice's gate, saw her ring the bell, saw the door open, saw her go in. Relieved, he went back into the house, wrapped himself up more warmly, and in good heart went off to the Club.

Chapter Nineteen

Alice's reaction was one of fear – fear, and a sense of guilt – that distressed her. When she saw Mrs P. at her door she felt as though the police had come for her, as though she was about to be accused, charged, tried, condemned, executed – and all the time unable to get them to believe in her innocence. She tried to smile, to be welcoming but succeeded only in being ingratiating. Mrs P. did not heed her greeting anyway, but rushed past and into the kitchen as though she owned it.

'It's lovely to see you,' Alice said, 'after all this time.'

'You knew where I was,' Mrs P. said.

'I did come, once, but Mr Pendlebury said – '

'Once, just once. We've been starved to death in that place while you were warm here. Never thought of us with your gas central heating did you?'

'But we haven't any heat either – it needs electricity to work the pump – we haven't – '

'Got a gas cooker, haven't you?'

'Yes, but – '

'Nobody cares about old folk.'

'Mrs Pendlebury, I *do* care but you wouldn't let us help, you wouldn't even take candles and a lamp when Tony brought them round.'

'I've never asked anyone for anything, never.'

'I know you haven't – we wanted to give you them without you asking but you wouldn't take them.'

'You don't know what it's been like in there – terrible, terrible – and he doesn't care, he goes his own sweet way – oh, it's been murder, murder, I can't stand it any more, and I'm dying, rotting, my body is rotting, rotting . . .'

The tears came like an avalanche. She sat at the kitchen table and howled and cried with her mouth open, ugly tearing sobs that made her cough and splutter until it was impossible to tell whether it was phlegm or grief that racked her chest and forced her to thump it again and again. Alice turned away and put the kettle on, overwhelmed by the feeling that being a spectator to this kind of crisis could only bring upon her total disaster. Her hands shook as she poured milk out and she spilled the sugar everywhere. Silently, she handed the tea to Mrs P. who took it and cried into it and then sipped it in funny little spluttering sips.

'Mrs Pendlebury,' Alice said, coming to sit very close to her and putting an arm round her shoulders, 'listen carefully. You're not well, you need to see a doctor. Remember your eyes and how pleased you were when you got spectacles? Remember how silly you said you'd been and how nice the man was? Well, this is just the same, only it's your nerves not your eyes – '

'No I'm dying, my body's rotting, rotting.'

'What's the matter with it? Have you a pain? Where, tell me – or what is it? Is it your insides? Is it?'

'I'm not telling nobody, you'll never get it out of me, never.'

'Listen, I'll go with you to the doctor, I'll ring up now and make an appointment and we'll go together.'

'I don't want a doctor. No, nobody can do anything. I'd do away with myself, I would, but I'm not the type, I'd never do a thing like that, never.'

'I should think not – you've so much to live for, you're going to Australia soon and – '

'Oh, that was pie in the sky, I see it all now, clear as crystal.'

'But you're wrong, I know you are – look, you're depressed, we're all depressed with this horrible weather and those awful power cuts, it isn't surprising. When spring comes we'll all feel better and the strike will be over soon – but you need help now.'

'Nobody ever helped me, never.'

'But you won't let them, you're too independent and brave, you've got to take help when it's offered.'

'No, I'll soldier on, there's no other way.'

But she stopped crying. Her chest still heaved but her face was under control and she drew away from Alice's half-embrace.

'Well,' she said, with a semblance of normality, 'how've you all been keeping?'

'Fine, thank you. Amy's started nursery school.'

'You're getting rid of her quick.'

'She was longing to go – all her friends do.'

'Keeping up with the Joneses. Well, times change.'

'Come in and see her.'

'Yes, I will.'

'Come today, for tea. She's at Sam's now but she'll be back at half past four.'

'I might. I'll see. Well I'd best be going, hadn't I.'

'No – you stay as long as you like, I'm only doing odd jobs that I don't really want to do.'

'No, I'd best be going.'

She sat on for a while, watching Alice take cutlery out of a drawer, reline it with fresh sticky-backed plastic, and replace the cutlery. Her eyes, red-rimmed and still watering, seemed mesmerized by the knives and forks. Several times she reached out and helped pile spoons up, taking an obvious pleasure in fitting bowl to bowl and handle to handle. Alice made the job last as long as possible, measuring and remeasuring the plastic and fitting it most carefully. When the job was done, she put the drawer back in the unit and immediately took out another, full of dusters and tins of polish and pegs and other kitchen utensils. They hadn't said a word.

'They're so boring, these jobs,' Alice said, at last, feeling it was important to get on a casual footing before Mrs P. left, important to fill her mind with chatter of one sort or another so that she might forget what had gone before.

'I like tidying,' Mrs P. said, abstracted, 'always did. Here, give me them dusters. They need washing, I can see that.'

'Yes, they do. I'll fill the machine with that kind of thing and do a whole dirty load.'

'Hand washing's the best.'

'But dusters don't need the best, do they?'

'I've had some of my dusters twenty years and that's with hand washing.'

'But think of the time it's taken.'

'Time's cheap. I've plenty of time.'

'When you were young you can't have had – you must have wanted to save time then.'

'What for?'

'Well, to do other things with, things you enjoyed doing – playing with Frank, reading, going for walks, that kind of thing.'

'Time was never any problem.'

They stuck on that. Mrs P. had all the dusters soaking in a bucket before Alice could stop her and they even laughed together over the sight of Mrs P. still with her gloves on dropping the dusters into the soap and water. Yet Alice's unease deepened rather than lessened. Mrs P. was hanging on for something she couldn't work out. She felt this was her last chance – something must be said or done before it was finally too late. But what? What could she say? What could she do? There seemed an impasse she couldn't get over. Mrs P. was on the other side holding her hands out and she couldn't reach.

'I'd better be going,' Mrs P. said, sighing. 'Stanley will be back soon wanting his tea.'

'You won't stay till Amy comes then?'

'No. My miserable face is no sight for a child.'

'Your face isn't miserable.'

'That's a matter of opinion. I'm going anyway. Thank you for the tea. I'm sorry I bothered you.'

'You didn't bother me. I've worried and worried about you ever since – ever since Christmas, but I didn't want to interfere, you seemed so – '

'I hope I never bothered anyone.'

'No, you don't, but I worry about you, I wish all the time there was something I could do.'

'Nobody can do anything.'

She looked as though she might cry again but stopped herself in time and marched out. Alice followed her, trying to think of something to say and failing.

All Mrs P.'s jumble of words came back to her the rest of the day. She fed and bathed and read to Amy in a daze, incapable even of focusing properly. She had to stop herself over and over again from doing stupid things, and it wasn't till much later when Amy was safely in bed and Tony not yet home that she saw the significance of Mrs P.'s unexpected visit. Surely she wanted her, Alice, to take charge? Surely it was the only way she knew of saying she needed help and none was forthcoming? Within a few minutes of this thought Alice was convinced it was right. She must call a doctor. Without any doubt it was her absolute duty. But who was Mrs P.'s doctor? She couldn't remember. Only Stanley would divulge that. She must see Stanley, find out who their doctor was and call him, or better still get Stanley to call him.

She slept quite well once that had been resolved. Tony, bored as ever by the topic, had been surprisingly supportive, even offering to call the doctor himself, but she felt she could do it better. At ten the next morning she watched for Stanley going for his paper. He was late, but then he was probably waiting for the mist to clear. When at last she saw him shuffle out, she was ready to follow him, her shopping basket in her hand. It was easy to catch up with him, easy to say cheerfully, hello, Mr Pendlebury, easy to fall into step with him. Only what she meant to say was difficult.

'It was nice to see Mrs Pendlebury yesterday,' she said when they were almost at the corner.

'Yes. Does her good having a chat.'

'She's quite a stranger now.'

'Well, the weather's been bad and she's had a few off days.' Stanley was amiable, quite relaxed.

'Does she ever see your doctor about – about her off days?'

'No. She doesn't believe in doctors and she might be right.'

'Who is your doctor? Mine's Graham.'

'Thompson. Nice young chap. In partnership with Dr Hall. We've always had him.'

'Has Mrs Pendlebury ever seen him?'

'Oh yes – broke her leg once, years ago, and he came then though in the end she went to the Outpatients. That'd be 1962 – no, 1963.'

'And hasn't she seen him since?'

'No, I don't think she has, been no call for her to really.'

They were at the paper shop. Stanley was perfectly willing to stand and talk for ever but they were getting no nearer the problem.

'Mr Pendlebury,' Alice said, standing fully in front of him and lowering her voice though there was no one at all about, 'I think you should take Mrs Pendlebury to see Dr Thompson or get him to come to your house. She's not well, really – I'm so worried about her.'

'Oh no need to worry,' Stanley said, smiling. 'You let me do the worrying. There's nothing wrong with her that a spot of sunshine won't put right.'

His complacency and the sheer stupidity of his attitude gave Alice courage.

'I'm sorry to contradict you but I think she's very ill, physically and mentally.'

She saw at once she should never have used the word mentally. Stanley immediately straightened himself up, took his hands out of his pockets and said, 'Mentally? What's she been saying?'

'She said she felt she was dying.'

'Rubbish. When did she say that?'

'Yesterday. She was very upset.'

'Well, that's it, isn't it? We all say things we don't mean when we're upset. She *was* upset yesterday, I remember that. Yes, she was a bit off colour. You don't want to take any notice what she says when she's off colour, it doesn't mean a thing.'

'But it does – she meant it. She said her body was rotting away.'

'She's never been in better health – '

'Then she's – sick, sick in another way.'

'Sound as a bell.'

'She said she wanted to commit suicide.'

'Now that's enough!' Stanley was sharp. He glared at Alice. 'Enough's enough.'

'She *did* say that and I didn't know what to do. Please, Mr Pendlebury, don't be offended – I only want to help. She really must see a doctor or something awful will happen.'

'Not while I'm there. I'll look after her. It'll all pass over.'

'I don't think it will.'

'You're entitled to your thoughts. I'll see you're not bothered again.'

'It's not a question of being bothered – I want to help. I feel she came in to me for help.'

'She came in because I was going out, that's all. I won't go out again.'

'But that's silly – you need to go out. Mr Pendlebury, we heard her that night in the garden, and the banging and crying – it all adds up, she's really in need of medical attention.'

'It won't happen again.'

'That's not the point, I'm trying – '

'I'll have to get my paper. They'll be sold out.'

She waited, quite determined. Her feelings of affection and sympathy for Stanley were waning fast. He took an age and she knew if there had been another door to the shop he would have gone out by it. When eventually he emerged, his normal bland smile had been replaced by a look of hooded hostility.

'Are you going back now?' she asked him. One thing about Stanley, there was no suggestion of violence about him.

'Yes,' he said slowly.

'I'll walk with you,' she said. They both walked back down the street, Stanley pretending to be absorbed in the back page of his newspaper.

'Mr Pendlebury,' Alice said very quietly, 'if you don't promise to at least consult your doctor then I will.'

'I beg your pardon?' There was no mistaking the fact that slow though he was that had gone in straight away.

'I'm going to telephone Dr Thompson and explain and ask his advice.'

'Don't you dare.'

'I *do* dare. Mrs Pendlebury's health is more important than offending you.'

'Now look here, young lady,' said Stanley, brandishing his newspaper, 'I've said you mean well and no doubt you do, but there are some things I won't stand for and that's one of them. I don't want to be rude but you mind your own business, that's all. That's all – just leave my wife to me. I'll look after her. If a doctor's necessary, he'll be called. Now then.'

'But he's necessary now.'

'Not in my opinion and I should know. I've lived with my wife fifty years and I should know.'

'I'm sorry.'

'No harm done.'

They walked the rest of the way in silence, Alice trailing her empty bag against the railings. When they got to her gate she said again, 'I'm sorry. Mrs Pendlebury was going to come and see Amy. Could you ask her if today would be convenient, about four?'

'I don't think she can manage today.'

'Tomorrow then?'

'I think it would be better if we left it a while.'

So they did. Alice went inside more miserable than she'd gone out, and Stanley continued on his way. Nobody would guess how upset he was. It was lucky the army had taught him how to handle himself in a tough spot or he might have given himself away. The game was up. He ought to have realized that young couple would tumble to what was going on, he ought to have realized and forestalled them. He could have popped in and prepared the way with some story then they would have thought nothing of it. Now, they were suspicious. That talk of calling a doctor in had scared him stiff. A doctor only had to arrive when Rose was having one of her little turns and Bob's your uncle. Of course, if he came when she wasn't having a turn the laugh would be on them. She'd pass A1 then, no mistake. It was lucky the girl was soft when it came to the bit – he could see he'd impressed her. She wouldn't call any doctor. But nevertheless, now that the risk was so great, he must be prepared. Rose must be kept under observation night and day.

She was quiet enough the rest of March, and then the power cuts stopped and that helped and in April they had a week of lovely spring weather and he got her out as much as possible. She didn't want to go out but he insisted, practically dressed her himself and pushed her out. They didn't go far, just to the park and a couple of times to the Heath. He kept her away from crowds and noise. They sat and looked at the trees and flowers and she liked that. She was very white and seemed fatter than before which was funny because she hardly ate at all, just sat at meal times playing about with her food in the very way she had always hated other people doing. When he asked her if she felt all right, she said she had headaches and he advised aspirin and she took them quite obediently, two each morning, two after lunch, two at bedtime.

When the question of Australia came up at Easter he wasn't too worried when she wouldn't entertain the idea of going. Frank wrote and phoned and it was all very embarrassing. She wouldn't speak to him, just said she wasn't feeling up to it yet. Frank said perhaps in the autumn and, when Stanley asked her, she said perhaps, with no conviction at all. It would all have been a lot of bother anyhow, he had always said that, a lot of upheaval and fuss, when the thing to do was keep her quiet. There was no doubt in his mind that that was the best treatment. He realized with pleasure at the beginning of May that Rose hadn't had a turn for six weeks. He thought back to check that – perfectly correct. No turns, no tempers. She'd done one or two funny things but nothing too drastic, nothing that couldn't be justified if he tried hard enough. Burning all Frank's old letters, for example, was strange. She'd always treasured them, then one day she filled three carrier bags with them and took them into the garden and had a bonfire. When asked why, she said they were gathering a lot of dust. Well, that was reasonable enough. What good were old letters when you came to think about it? Then she called a rag and bone man into the house one morning – hauled him in off the street – and got him to take away several objects that were perfectly good. It was only afterwards that it dawned on him they were all the presents Alice had ever given her. When he tackled her on this she said she'd gone off useless ornaments. Odd, but not outrageous. She'd always had whims, it was just they were getting stronger.

In June, the Club had its annual outing, a day out by coach to Margate. Stanley had always gone, always enjoyed it and looked forward to it. There was nothing he wanted more than to go this year. He'd put his name down way back in January – no harm in that – and kept it there even when he knew he couldn't go. When it came to June 1st, and they all had to confirm, he dithered and dothered and finally left his name there.

Still no harm, still not committing himself. But he wouldn't go, not unless Rose would go with him. He genuinely thought she might, since she'd gone on small trips with him without objecting, but at the very mention of a Club outing she turned stubborn. No, she would not go, no use asking. He could go on his own, she was perfectly all right. With her saying that, he thought about it. She *was* all right. He'd left her for an hour the last few Tuesdays and she'd been quite all right. Gradually, he convinced himself a day out would be in order, but worry still niggled away – and then he had an inspiration. If he tipped Elsie a wink she'd drop in that day, all casual-like, he was sure she would. Rose need know nothing about it, she could just turn up and that would be him covered. No explanations beyond the most perfunctory would be necessary. All he need say was that, as they hadn't seen each other for ages, how about coming over to see Rose when he was away for the day. He could say she was a bit low and would like a surprise. Elsie was quick on the uptake, she would get the message.

June 8th was the day, a Wednesday. All the omens were good. It was a bright, clear day, not too hot, the sort Rose liked. She was up before him and when he woke and heard her singing an almighty sense of relief went right through him down to his toes. She was as cheerful as anything and the minute he saw her in the kitchen turning her cupboards out he knew he need have no worries. Cupboards took all day – she'd still be engrossed when Elsie came about two o'clock. She even snapped at him and told him to get his clumsy hands out of that drawer when he was looking for his plastic mac and that was the best sign there could be. She'd been very, very quiet for far too long, very amenable and placid, pleasant enough at first but ultimately disturbing. But now he could see all was truly well and he left for his outing in excellent spirits. He gave her a peck on the cheek and told her to be good and he might bring her a Duncan's Walnut Whirl back, and she laughed and pushed him away and off he went. He was going to have a marvellous day. It would be unforgettable.

*

Rose listened. He'd gone. She went up the stairs and looked out of the window. He had gone. She waited. He didn't come back. He'd gone, she was quite alone. She laughed and had to stuff a handkerchief in her mouth to stop herself. Silly old man.

Nimbly she went back downstairs, two steps at a time, thudding all the way, not even holding on to the banister. She was excited, she knew that. Her hands were hot and a vein throbbed in her head. She remembered jumping downstairs at home and getting the belt for waking her dad. No belt now. She could do what she liked, nobody could stop her.

In the kitchen, she slammed the cupboard doors shut. That had taken him in. She'd no intention of doing the cupboards. No, today she had some scores to settle, while Stanley was away.

Alice intended to spend the whole day in the garden. Amy was at nursery school and then having lunch and spending the afternoon with a friend. She had nothing at all to do except sunbathe.

It was only eleven o'clock but the sun was already hot. She had one of those wickerwork sun-chairs, loaded with soft cushions, positioned under the apple tree so that her head was in the shade but her body in the sun. The sun on her face gave her a headache and her face came out in funny blotches. They said, at the ante-natal clinic, that this was quite normal in pregnancy but they bothered her and she didn't like to feel they were in any way her own fault. She was otherwise very happy to be pregnant again. Everything had gone as it should and she found herself un-worried about the last four months, somehow just knowing it would be all right this time. They'd said not to upset herself, to take things very easily in every way and she intended to. Now that contact with the Pendleburys seemed to have been severed there was nothing to upset her anyway.

She supposed she must have dozed off, for when she next looked up the sun was in quite a different position and she found she'd been lying fully in its glare. The skin on her stomach was stinging and there was a tight feeling across her eyes. Cross with herself, she moved the chair into the shade and went to get a drink. When she came out again, she sat upright and read a magazine. Perhaps, if it was going to be too hot for her to stay in the garden all day, she would go inside and sleep properly. Idly, she looked round the garden, admiring the semi-wilderness. There was a heat haze everywhere, wrapping the greenery in softness. She half closed her eyes and the leaves split into millions of fragments, each one spiked with sunshine.

In this dreamy, half-conscious state the small sounds in the garden next door did not at first make any impression on Alice. They were small, soft, regular noises – little clicks, very faint, and tappings and whirrings. She heard them but they did not disturb her, not till a louder, more regular thump began. Then she opened her eyes and listened. It was a metallic bang, as though a spade or some similar object was being knocked against a dustbin lid. She sat up even straighter and carefully put on a towelling robe she had beside her, tying the belt in an unnecessarily secure knot. She stayed quite still, thinking. It wasn't really a noise like the other noises all those weeks ago – there was nothing frantic about the tempo. Really, it was quite melodic, as though someone was amusing themselves like a child might. Then the area where the noise was coming from seemed to change – from being higher up the garden, near the house, it became lower down, near the garages, and then it changed again to the centre. Peeping out from underneath the tree. Alice saw Mrs Pendlebury looking over the wall. She was holding a rake in one hand and a trowel in the other and banging them together, end to end, like peculiar cymbals. And she was smiling. Relieved, Alice got up and went down the garden thinking she would invite her over and tell her about the baby.

'Hello, Mrs Pendlebury, isn't it a lovely day? Isn't it hot?' Alice called as she made her way through the overgrown raspberry canes.

'Yes, yes it is,' Mrs P. said.

'How nice to see you looking so well,' Alice said, still not really looking at her neighbour, still with her head down, untangling herself from the bushes in order to reach the wall.

'Yes,' Mrs P. said.

'Have you been gardening in this heat?' said Alice, reaching the wall at last, and putting one hand on the warm bricks. Almost before she felt the roughness below her hand there was another roughness on top – Mrs P. had dropped the rake and clamped her hand on top of Alice's, securing it by the wrist. Startled, Alice looked into her face and instinctively drew back, but with her hand so tightly held could not move more than a few inches from the wall. She was aware of her heart thudding and of the need to keep very, very calm.

'What a lovely day,' she said again, weakly, her voice cracking with fear.

'Yes, yes it is,' Mrs P. was still smiling, but she had put the other hand, the one holding the trowel, in front of her eyes, apparently shielding them. They both stood there without speaking, hands locked together, and then Alice said, 'I was wondering if you'd like to come round and have some tea?' As though she'd been struck, Mrs P. backed away, loosening Alice's hand. 'No!' she shouted, 'no I would not, not after what's been going on, no I would not.' Alice felt her freed hand. There were nail marks on the wrist but she nursed it with gratitude. She'd been afraid she'd faint if Mrs P. held on to her for just one more second. Now she felt more in command she dared to look over the wall and not shy away from what she saw. Mrs P. was standing with her legs apart, brandishing the trowel, as though astride a horse. She was so white-faced that there appeared no dividing line between her skin and her hair – both were horribly moulded together as though a sheet of plastic had been stretched over them, distorting the texture of both hair and skin, making both into a kind of colourless rubber. Her eyes stood out all the more clearly, each circle of blue rimmed by red, each wide open, propped open, quite unblinking. She seemed to be gritting her teeth or grinding them, her mouth moved but it was closed, the lips compressed and then thrust out and then compressed again. The knuckles holding the trowel were rocks in the flabbiness of her hand and held all the visible tension in her body. As she began to speak she kept taking steps backwards, all the time holding the trowel first up and then down, pushing it through the air like a piston.

'I'm not silly, you know,' she shouted, 'I'm not silly in the head, I know what's been going on and I won't have it, I won't put up with it a minute longer. What I want to know is what are you going to do with that husband of yours? Eh? What are you going to do about him?'

'Tony?'

'Yes, Tony, precious Tony and his friends. What's he got to frighten two old folk for, what've we ever done to him? Why has he got to break our windows and scratch our table, eh? Why?'

'But, Mrs Pendlebury, Tony's only been in your house once and you were there – '

'I'm not silly, you can't fool me with that, you've had our key, haven't you, you're the only ones ever had it.'

'But you gave it to me and I gave it straight back.'

'Not straight back, you had it a week and there are places you can get a copy made in a few hours.'

'But, Mrs Pendlebury, you've never left your house, you've always been there, how could anyone have done anything without you knowing it?'

'I don't know how, that's what I want the police for, that's their job, it's up to them to find out how and why and for what. I don't know why he hates us, why he has to do all this, and you, don't look at me like that as though butter wouldn't melt in your mouth, you're in it as well, after all I've done for you, the love I've given your child, the things I've showered on her, and all for what, for what, to have you turn on us for nothing, for not letting that nurse have our flat, don't you try to pretend that wasn't what did it, that was the beginning, that was the start, just because I wouldn't let her have our flat and why should I, why should I do anything else for you, eh, after all I've done, treating you like my daughter, like poor Ellen, and feeling so sorry for you when your baby died, all wasted, wasted.'

She had backed right down the garden, still stabbing the air with the trowel, shouting all the time. Alice hadn't moved or spoken since the tirade began. She concentrated on keeping very still and on trying to get into her expression nothing but a steadiness she did not feel. She waited until Mrs P. had gone inside, until the door had slammed shut, before she moved, and then she went back into her own house, dreadfully tired, and sat down. A calmness had come over her, succeeding the turmoil that had invaded her when Mrs P. took her hand. There was no point in going to see Stanley. Her way was quite clear. She must ring Dr Thompson at once.

Chapter Twenty

Elsie was very angry when she arrived at half past two to find nobody was in. She stood on the doorstep and rang and hammered and looked through the silly letter-box and even the keyhole and then she tried the side door and shouted, but all to no avail. She just knew that Rose was in, not because Stanley had told her she would be but because the house somehow breathed Rose was hiding. Determined not to be beaten, Elsie used all her cunning to gain entry. She found a call-box and rang Rose's number, but nobody answered: she couldn't be tricked. Remembering the garage and the little lane at the back she went right round the block and found the entrance to it and located Rose's garden and tried to find a way in, but the barbed wire on top of the fence frightened her. She banged on the garage door and tried to force it open, almost succeeding, but finally had to give up. Furious, she returned to the front of the house and kept her finger on the bell for fully five minutes.

Thinking how typical of her sister-in-law this was, Elsie then went off and found a café and had a cup of tea, just on the off-chance Rose might have popped out for a while. She went through the same performance an hour later and then she had to make a decision – to hang about till Stanley came back from his trip and really show Rose up when she got inside, or go home. She would dearly have loved to have camped on the doorstep, just to see Rose's eventual discomfiture, but common sense prevailed. She might wait a long time. Stanley had said six but you never knew with these trips. Better to go home and vent her spleen later, on Stanley. Reluctantly, Elsie went off down Rawlinson Road, turning the corner out of it just as Dr Thompson's car turned into it, thereby missing a scene she would have paid a thousand pounds to see.

Dr Thompson had no better luck. His heart was not exactly in his job as it was then presented to him, but he honestly spared as much time as he could to ring the bell and bang at the door. When there was no reply there wasn't really much he could do. The circumstances as reported to him by the young woman next door didn't exactly warrant breaking in, or even reporting it to the police. From the way it had been described to him – and the girl had been impressively flat and factual – he was by no means certain that Mrs Pendlebury was certifiable. The girl hadn't wanted to lodge a complaint with the police, she'd made that clear. All she wanted to do was help. Standing on the doorstep Dr Thompson decided that, for the moment, he would leave it, and return to his afternoon-off's swimming. He would call again after evening surgery, and if he got no reply then he'd think what to do. Thoughts of Mrs P.'s possible suicide did occur to him, but he thought it unlikely. He knew Stanley Pendlebury well enough and somehow felt that he was a reliable fellow, the sort of chap who would certainly call if his wife had reached that stage. He'd come back at half past seven and try again, that was much the best thing. His informant might think he had failed in his duty but that was too bad.

Stanley wandered into Rawlinson Road about half past six feeling very tired but quite drunk with happiness – also with two whiskies that he hadn't been able to escape having. He wasn't a drinking man, not these days, and he always left before the celebration that marked their return got going, but he hadn't been able to refuse those two drinks from his two best friends. As they rightly said, he was always refusing things these days, always dashing off. Knowing Elsie was with Rose had given him a nice sense of security and so he'd become his old affable self and stayed behind a little while. Nobody could grudge him that. It would be a long time before it happened again.

He put his key into the door and turned it but had some difficulty getting in. He examined the lock and was surprised to see all the screws were loose round the plate that held it to the door. Furthermore, there were scratches on the metal as though somebody had been trying to chip the whole thing off with something sharp. Fascinated, Stanley could not leave it alone. He stood looking at the damage and inwardly exclaiming. It was a wonder Rose had not called his attention to this before. Luckily, he'd seen it first so he needn't mention it until he'd made it good.

The house was quiet, not an unusual state of affairs but strange after the hubbub of the day. He felt a little light-headed coming in from the still bright light outside to the gloom of the hall. Rose and Elsie must be in the garden. He walked through into the back room and looked out of the window but he couldn't see them. Perhaps they were in the sitting-room and hadn't heard him going past. He turned round to go back and Rose's bright eyes looking at him from the corner of the living-room gave him a turn. 'There you are,' he said, 'where's Elsie got to?'

'I don't know about any Elsie,' she said.

'Didn't she come? She was going to come, she was going to drop in and surprise you.'

She didn't reply to that. He peered at her, to see what she was doing, why she was sitting in that corner.

'Did you get your cupboards done?' he asked. She started laughing then and the last pleasant lightness the whisky and the good time had given him disappeared. He knew at once she'd done something silly and before anything else, before anger or concern or fear, he felt bitter. It had to be today, the one day he'd enjoyed himself, she had to go and do whatever she'd gone and done today. That was going to take a lot of forgiving.

'What you doing in that corner?' he said.

'Sitting.'

'Well sit somewhere sensible.'

He went into the kitchen and put the kettle on, looking for signs of what had happened. Everything looked in apple-pie order. Maybe it would be better just to ignore her, to quietly read his newspaper, drink his tea, watch some television and go to bed. The idea of such tactics appealed to him strongly.

He gave Rose a side-long look as he went past her again. 'I'm taking my tea into the front,' he said. She just smiled and nodded. He didn't like the look of her at all. Hardly had he got himself settled in his chair before he heard the doorbell. It was an evening when he didn't feel like being bothered but with Rose in her present state he didn't want her going to the door and it was just the time when she would break with her normal habit and go. Taking his newspaper with him to show he was busy, Stanley went to answer the bell. He was taken aback to see Dr Thompson there.

'Evening, Mr Pendlebury,' the doctor said, and made to step inside. Instinctively Stanley took a step himself, closer to him, so that he had to recoil slightly and step back.

'There must be some mistake,' Stanley said, 'you've got the wrong house.'

'No,' Dr Thompson said, 'I haven't. I just thought it was a long time since I'd seen your wife and I thought as I was visiting in the street it might be a good time to pop in and see her.'

'She's out,' Stanley said. It was the first thing that came into his head. 'She's gone out.'

'Oh,' Dr Thompson was clearly amazed. 'Has she been out long?'

'No,' Stanley said, 'and she won't be back till late.'

'Well, there's not much point in me coming in. How is she these days?'

'Fine.'

'Good. I'd heard she wasn't so well, that's all.'

'Who did you hear that from?'

'Oh, around, you know. Well, I'd better get on. Give my regards to Mrs Pendlebury.'

He went on standing in the doorway a minute or two longer. 'You're all right yourself, are you?'

'Yes, thank you.'

'Good. Let me know if I can be any help, won't you?'

'Yes, I will.'

To be quite sure, Stanley stood at the door until the doctor had got in the car. Only when he'd moved off, with a slightly embarrassed wave, did he close the door, close and bolt it. Then he threw his newspaper down and went back to Rose, snapping the electric light on and closing the curtains as he went into the room.

'Now then,' he said, 'out with it. I don't want any nonsense, I want the truth. What have you been up to?'

'Nothing.'

'The doctor wasn't here for nothing was he? And that was the doctor, you heard it was the doctor didn't you? He's a busy man, I don't expect he came here for nothing – he came because somebody told him to come, that's why, because you must have been up to something and somebody heard you or saw you. What have you been doing? Out with it – I don't want nods and smiles, I want the truth.'

'I haven't been doing anything.'

'Who've you been talking to? You must have been talking to somebody, saying silly things. Who was it? Was it Alice? Have you been talking to her?'

'Yes.'

'I knew it. And what did you say? What rubbish did you tell her that she had to go sending for the doctor? Eh?'

'I told her straight.'

'Straight! What did you tell her straight?'

'About that husband of hers breaking in here and doing all that damage, scratching my table and breaking my windows. I told her I was sending for the police and you can't stop me.'

Stanley breathed very deeply. He should have seen this coming.

'It might teach you a lesson,' he said, 'if I let you send for the police. Do you know what they'd do with you, you with your cock-and-bull story? They'd lock you up. See how you'd like that – they'd lock you up and you'd never get out, not as you are.'

'I want the police.'

'I've a good mind to send for them and let you *see*. It's not done you any good me putting up with you all these months, humouring you, it's just made you think you can get away with anything, that's all, and it's time you learnt you can't, not in this life. That doctor would have tumbled to your little game straight off and then what would you have done? If I hadn't been smart enough to get rid of him, if I hadn't seen which way the wind was blowing. I don't know what I'm going to do with you and that's a fact.'

Stanley paused, struck by the truth of what he had just said. He *didn't* know what he was going to do with her, not now she'd spilled the beans all over the place. It was dreadful to think what might have happened if that doctor had got in – it made his mouth dry just thinking of it. They'd cart her away straight off, not realizing she was just going through a bad spell, same as everyone did at some time or other. He sat down at the table, suddenly weak at the knees. Everything had changed. There was Elsie to reckon with, sharp as a needle, she'd be on to him in no time wanting to know what was up, smelling a rat. What would he say to her? He wasn't a good liar, he didn't like lying, but nothing except lies would do in this situation. And Alice, what about her? She'd sent for the doctor, he couldn't blame her. Or could he? Rubbing his forehead with the flat of his hand Stanley thought about that one and gradually a new emotion chased all the others out – humiliated, that's what he'd been. Treated like dirt, made to look small, passed over. He went hot and cold at the thought. He hadn't been consulted about his own wife, she'd gone over his head, treated him like a lodger in his own house, and after he'd warned her. Well, that was something he could do something about. He got to his feet and pulled his cardigan straight.

'I'm going next door,' he announced. 'You say there and don't do anything silly.' She went on smiling, crouching there on that stool in the corner. 'You sit there and don't move till I come back. There's some sorting out I have to do. I won't be more than five minutes, have you got that?'

'I've got it. It was her sent for the doctor.'

'Yes, it was and I want to know why.'

'I don't want a doctor.'

'I know you don't. Now don't you move.'

'I've the supper to think of.'

'You can make the supper and that's all.'

This seemed to please her. She got up and started towards the kitchen, wiping her hands on her apron. The smile had gone and she was frowning. 'I expect you've been eating rubbish all day on that trip of yours. It's time you had a decent meal to settle your stomach.'

'Yes it is.'

'I'll get on with it then. Are you going in like that?'

'What's wrong with me? Yes I am. What I have to say won't take five minutes.'

'I should think so too,' she said, and seemed even more pleased.

Stanley rang the Orams' bell with absolute authority and never took his eye off the glass panel at one side. The minute he saw a shadow appearing he would be ready to rush in whatever they said. It wasn't his usual behaviour but then this was an emergency. They had some shocks coming to them in this house. Just because he seemed meek and mild they thought he wouldn't say boo to a goose. Well, they would be surprised. He could be angry just like anyone else and he knew his rights better than most.

Alice answered the door. She'd been resting, still feeling upset about the day's events, still trying to work out what Dr Thompson had meant. She felt confused and uncertain and wished Tony would come home. Her first reaction when she saw Stanley was one of relief, but the way in which he brushed past her and said, 'There are a few things I'd like to say to you,' alarmed her. He stood in her kitchen, swaying slightly, rocking on his heels, and his expression was sullen. It was frightening to have this violent change of personality in anyone – they might have been total strangers who had never had anything to do with each other the way he glared at her.

'Have a seat,' she said.

'No. What I have to say won't take five minutes.'

'Then sit down for five minutes.'

'No. I'd rather not in the circumstances.'

He refused to smile at her. Trying hard to remind herself they were two mature adults Alice controlled the flutters of fear that rippled through her stomach.

'What circumstances?'

'Did you send for Dr Thompson?'

'I rang him, yes. I'd no alternative.'

'You admit it then. Right. You mind your own business, that's all I have to say to you. Keep your nose out of our lives, thank you very much. Is that understood?'

Alice felt the colour rise in her face and when she started to cry she did so out of choice, out of a desire to escape the whole situation.

'It's no good you crying,' Stanley said, 'you did what you did and we don't want anything more to do with you and now I'll say good night.'

He turned to go, but Alice was quicker and running across the room slammed the kitchen door and stood with her back to it.

'No,' she said, 'I won't let you, I won't have it, it's stupid and ridiculous two adults behaving like this. I won't be treated like some disgusting peeping-tom, some sneaky horrible person. We've been friends for more than two years, we've helped each other and had good times together and I won't have it all smashed and trampled on because you choose to do so. And I won't talk to somebody who hasn't the manners to sit down in my house when I invite him to. I'm quite prepared to stand here all night unless you sit down so we can discuss this in a civilized way.'

She was violent and loud and Stanley saw at once she was working herself into a state. For that reason alone, he assured himself, he was obliged to sit down.

'You won't change my mind,' he said, 'not however much you shout. I'll give you five minutes and then I must go.' He sat down on the edge of a kitchen chair and continued to stare at her without blinking.

'Why do you think I sent for the doctor?' she asked him.

'I don't want to know about whys and wherefores. You sent for him as though it was your business and that's enough for me.'

'Mr Pendlebury, if I'd looked over the garden wall when your wife attracted my attention and I'd seen her lying on the grass with her leg bleeding you would have expected me to send for the doctor wouldn't you? You wouldn't have wanted me to let her bleed to death and mind my own business would you? It's just because it's her mind not her leg that you're upset – I sent for him because she needs immediate medical attention, psychiatric help. She's sick in her mind and you can't go on ignoring it.'

'There's nothing wrong with her mind. She has her off days – '

'Off days! Mr Pendlebury, your wife was stark raving mad this afternoon.'

'Don't talk ridiculous.'

'I'm not – you obviously don't know what she said, she accused my husband of entering her house and breaking furniture and windows, she talked of sending for the police – '

'There's no question of the police. She gets these ideas, that's all.'

'She gets them because she's deluded, because she's going through some kind of breakdown. I've asked you and asked you to take her to a doctor and you won't. What does she have to do to convince you – kill herself, kill you? Do you want murder before you'll take her seriously?'

'I can look after her perfectly well.'

'But you can't, nobody could. She needs skilled attention.'

'We'll see about that.'

'But you don't! That's precisely the point – you never see about anything, you just let it go on and on.'

'That's my business.'

'And mine – oh yes, and mine, my business.'

'She's nothing to you.'

'She is – she's another human being, she's my friend and neighbour, I'm sick of all this pushing people into slots as though they had nothing to do with each other – why won't you believe I care for her, why isn't she my business?'

'You're no relation, there's – '

'Why do I have to be a relation? What have her own brothers and sisters ever done for her, how close have they ever been? She doesn't even know where they all are, she doesn't know if they're alive or dead, I've meant more to her than any relation. Why do you keep pushing me away? What terrible motives do you think I have? Why should I do as I've done except through love?'

Stanley was more embarrassed than he had ever been in his entire life. This young woman had got carried away, there was no mistake about that – he wished to God he'd brushed past her after he'd said his say and not got trapped like this. She was scarlet in the face, half crying, and talking all this stuff about loving Rose – he didn't know which way to look. It suddenly dawned on him that it was Rose all over again, all this fuss and carry on, and he wished there was a man about to handle her. In his anxiety just to get away he forgot what he had come about. The important thing now was to calm her down and make his escape.

'I expect you meant well,' he said, hoping to mollify her.

'Anyway, what's done is done. There's no need to upset yourself.'

'Why are you laughing? I suppose I am funny. I suppose I look silly to you and sound melodramatic but I feel so upset, I don't know what to do to show you how I feel.'

'I wasn't laughing,' Stanley said, though in truth he had been, his lips had started smiling of their own accord and he couldn't stop them. He was glad when she seemed to believe him and came and sat down too.

'I was frightened,' she said, 'she terrified me.'

'I won't leave her again. I wouldn't have left her in the first place but it was the Club outing and she seemed quite well.'

'Why didn't you ask me to come and see her? Or I would have invited her for the day, if you'd told me.' He shifted uncomfortably in his chair. 'She's turned against us, hasn't she? She really does think Tony comes in and smashes her things.'

'I've told her to see sense – it's only now and again.'

'Mr Pendlebury, they wouldn't take her away you know – they'd treat her at home, with drugs.'

'No. I'm her only salvation.'

It was Alice's turn to stare at him. It seemed impossible that he should believe what he'd just said, but he did, he said it so confidently, smiling, sure he was right. Anything she might say in reply would be inadequate, and then the more she thought about it the more she thought he might, in some kind of crazy, twisted way, have spoken no more than the truth. He'd been married to Rose over fifty years, she reminded herself – didn't that entitle him to some confidence? She thought of all the sick people filling the wards of mental hospitals, of all the drugs poured into them and the machines used on them – were they worth more than Stanley's belief that he was her salvation? Her own conviction that Rose needed expert help began to wane. She tried to see it from Stanley's point of view, shut up in that house with her, day after day. It was hard to know whether he was wicked or wise to keep her to himself.

'Will you have some tea?' she said.

They had tea, but nothing could quite wipe out the things they had said to each other. Stanley was polite and even managed to make a small joke, but he was constrained all the same by Alice's clearly revealed opinion of him, and she, in turn, smiled and was friendly but couldn't forget how he had intended to treat her. When he finally stood up and said he must get back she had no idea how she stood.

'I hope everything will be all right,' she said.

'Oh, don't you worry – it'll all blow over.'

'What if – what if she – Mrs Pendlebury – has another attack – another turn?'

'I'll just have to take things as they come, that's all.'

'Well, if you need any help, if there's anything I can do – '

'I'll remember.'

But he knew he would never call on Alice's services again. Rose had been right all along – best keep yourself to yourself. It saved so much trouble. She was a nice girl, very kind, but too highly strung for his liking, too liable to get het up over nothing. Her husband was more his cup of tea, a steady fellow who knew the score, could take a hint, or that Charlotte along the road, she was a solid type. It was pity she hadn't been the one to befriend Rose instead of Alice. Rose needed stability, that was it. That was all he had to do – keep calm, go along with her, the same old formula that had worked before.

Stanley ignored the part of him that said it hadn't worked. To start thinking that would be fatal.

Chapter Twenty-one

It was like being shelled, like enduring a twenty-four-hour bombardment and no relief in sight, with the enemy coming up over the hill in never-ending waves. Stanley feinted this way and that, made the best use of his ammunition, lay doggo as long as he could, but after a month he knew he could not go on much longer. Complete surrender was near, and with it would come total anarchy. Rose would run amok. His tired body – tired with tearing about after her, tired with getting up at all hours with her – and his reeling brain would both give out. He would just lie down and accept defeat, not caring what she did to herself or to him.

There had been no possibility of keeping calm and steady. From the minute he came back that day from Alice's, Rose had become obsessed with the one idea calculated to create the maximum amount of havoc: they must sell the house. He reasoned with her, he argued till he was hoarse, he pretended to agree hoping the scheme could be dropped after a decent interval, but it was no use. She wanted to sell the house. It was, she said, the solution to everything. It was the only thing that would save her sanity – yes, he had heard her say that – 'It will save my sanity,' she'd said and, though the fact that she could say that told him her sanity couldn't really be threatened, he felt the warning was too plain to ignore. If she wanted to move so badly, they must move. Her reasons were silly – she said she was the laughing stock of the neighbourhood – but that didn't matter.

They had never sold a house before. Quitting their rooms had been straightforward, merely a matter of giving notice and handing in the rent book, but Stanley quickly discovered selling a house was hideously complicated. Rose was adamant that they didn't need an agent – all they had to do, or all Stanley had to do, was put an advert in the local paper. That would fetch them. Unfortunately, it did, in hordes. Their bell never stopped ringing, from nine in the morning on the day the advert appeared, and there were couples queueing outside. Rose was furious, livid with rage. She told him to go and tell them all to go away – but how could he when he'd put an advert in? They were all crazy too – offering £20,000 and more without even coming in. Some of them waved cheques at him and some had bundles of notes. It was all horrible and confusing and Stanley was quite overcome. All he could think of to say was that it was a mistake, but some of them wouldn't take no for an answer. They pushed pieces of paper with their addresses on through the letter-box asking him to contact them if he changed his mind. There was no peace for a week afterwards.

Stanley hoped it would put Rose off, but not a bit of it – she was more determined than ever. The only difference was that she conceded they might need an agent and sent Stanley round the area writing down names and addresses from boards. When he brought them back – terrified at leaving her even for a few minutes – she took one look at the list and picked one at random. Stanley had to phone straight away. They were very keen and sent a young man round immediately to take particulars. He put Rose into a high old state of excitement by telling her they would get £25,000 with no trouble. She was triumphant when he'd gone, flushed and happy, chanting, 'We're sitting on a gold mine', and, 'The sky's the limit', over and over again.

When people came to view the house, he had to show them round. Rose wouldn't have anything to do with it. She stayed in the garden until they'd seen round the house and then she slipped in by the side door and upstairs while they inspected the garden. On no account would she speak to any of them, though afterwards she wanted to discuss what the prospective buyers looked like and even what they wore, until Stanley was bored to death. It seemed to give her such pleasure that all the people who came were such 'quality'. She didn't want to sell the house to riff-raff but to somebody who would appreciate it. Stanley didn't dare tell her the nature of the disparaging remarks generally made.

Within a short time they had a firm offer of £27,000, subject to contract. Rose was ecstatic. She mouthed, 'say yes', at him while he was on the phone and did a little dance when he told her the contract would be ready in two days and that a deposit had been paid as a demonstration of good faith. He felt the time had come to explain to her the legal implications of what they were about to do and tried to speak solemnly to her, but she pooh-poohed his approach and said she understood everything perfectly well, thank you very much: she knew all about it taking six weeks to exchange contracts and about the deal being final after that. She said she could tell him quite a lot he didn't know she knew. What Stanley most wanted to know was what next? What were they going to do after the house was sold? Where would they go?

Rose was scathing at his lack of foresight. Where would they go? Where had they always wanted to go? Stanley couldn't for the life of him think. He wondered if she was thinking of Australia and his relief was enormous when she announced Bournemouth. Well, it was new to him. He didn't know they'd always wanted to go to Bournemouth. All right, they'd had two holidays there and several outings for a long day but that was the beginning and end of any connection with Bournemouth. Trust Rose to develop an attachment to a place she hardly knew. He asked her what was so attractive about the place and she said the sea air. He replied Margate, where they went for their Club trips, had sea – but she wouldn't even let him finish. Margate was a common-as-muck place she declared, a place she wouldn't be taken to in a box. So he gave in, and merely pressed her to tell him where exactly they were going to go in Bournemouth. She said anywhere, she didn't care, they'd find somewhere when they got there. He asked her what they would do about the furniture and all their belongings with no address to send them to, and she turned on him and accused him of spoiling everything.

As far as Stanley was concerned, there was nothing to spoil. The even tenor of his life had been utterly ruined. But Rose would go on as though they had been incredibly lucky and was literally transported by the thought of their good fortune. She talked a lot of rubbish about silver linings and everything turning out for the best. Her shrill singing and all the noise she seemed to make these days got on his nerves. The only time she stopped was when they went out and then she behaved with a modicum of decorum. She came with him on several occasions to the estate agent's office, rather to his surprise, and was absolutely charming to everyone, laughing and smiling fit to burst. Though he was pleased at her going out and taking such an interest, he was upset by one thing. On the way to the agent's they had twice met Alice, and Rose had neither returned her greeting nor looked in her direction, just ignored her and walked straight on. It upset Stanley. He himself said hello and nodded and wanted to stop, but he had to rush on to keep up with Rose. He tried to challenge her on this but it was no good – she refused to discuss her attitude, merely saying she had an elephant's memory. What that was supposed to mean, Stanley couldn't for the life of him fathom.

Harried and hurried, Stanley was glad to get to bed at night, but he was allowed no proper rest. Around one in the morning

Rose would get up and wander around the house weeping and wailing and clutching her nightdress in both hands. He couldn't leave her to roam about so he had to get up too and accompany her on her tour. He couldn't decide whether she was sleep-walking or not. Certainly, she didn't reply when he talked to her but then that was nothing new. On the other hand he saw in her face, creased and red with crying though it was, a look of the old Rose that made him think it was only at night time that she was really herself. The smirking, staring, blank look of the day gave way to a pitiful, worried, distressed look that he recognized from other days. She was terribly upset but not hysterical. She would finally end up on the bed sobbing in his arms as though her heart would break and shaking her head pathetically when he tried to comfort her. Once she said, 'I don't know what got into me,' and another time, 'What will she think, what will she think,' but he didn't try to open up either remark, just patted her on the back and concentrated on getting her back to sleep.

Elsie, when she came over a few weeks after all this had been going on, was shocked by his appearance. She came un-announced, on Sunday afternoon, and when he opened the door she said, 'Good God, whatever's happened to you?' He just said he'd had a slight cold but she wouldn't let the subject alone, going on and on about how he looked at death's door. She naturally went on to ask, with a sniff, how Rose was, and he was aware that she had no intention of believing him when he said Rose was fine.

'I suppose you heard about me coming as I said I would?' she accused him.

'No, no I didn't, but I guessed you would, I knew I could rely on you. I was sorry you were put to all that trouble for nothing.'

'She was in, of course, I knew that.'

'No, she wasn't, she went out, that was what upset the apple-cart. My fault really, always risky trying to plan surprises.'

'Where is she then? Don't I rate a hello?' – and Elsie looked suspiciously about the room.

'She's busy. There's a lot to be done. I dare say she'll be down later – I don't suppose she heard the bell.' Then the whole story of them selling up had to come out and luckily Elsie was so dumbfounded that the emphasis was shifted away from Rose's health. By the time Rose did appear Elsie was too busy concentrating on the details of the house sale to notice her.

'I would never have thought it,' she said, 'never – your house has always been your pride and joy – to sell up, to go so sudden – I can't work it out.'

'Yes, well,' Stanley said, keeping a careful eye on Rose, 'they say change is good for you.'

'Change! I'll say – but what made you do it, what made you think of it? That's what puzzles me – you must have a reason.'

'We have reasons,' Rose said, smiling that smile Stanley had come to hate, that teeth-showing, wide, stretched-tight smile, nothing like her real, quirky, up-at-the-corners smile.

'Well what are they?' Elsie said, not at all put off by the looks the two of them were exchanging.

'That would be telling,' Rose said. 'We're not at liberty to say.'

'Why not? What's happened?'

'Nothing.'

'Then why can't you say?'

'It's difficult to explain,' Stanley said, 'just a feeling we wanted to see a bit more of the world.'

'Oh well,' Elsie said, deeply offended, 'it may never happen.' She started pulling her gloves on, even though she hadn't yet had the tea she'd been offered. 'I expect it will all fizzle out in the end.'

'What do you mean?' Rose asked. Stanley thought she looked blue round the mouth and moved his chair closer to her.

'Oh, nothing, just a feeling it may never happen,' Elsie said, as usual a little frightened when she saw she had scored. 'After all, you didn't get to Australia and you were set enough on that. You might never sell the house – it wouldn't surprise me one little bit.'

'Bitch,' Rose said.

'I *beg* your pardon?'

'Bitch,' Rose said again, and began to cry.

There was a moment, standing on the doorstep, when Stanley felt very tempted to ask Elsie back in and unburden himself. After he'd smoothed everything over and Rose had gone to bed, or at least to her bedroom, Elsie had been most understanding. She'd actually said she was sorry for stirring things up and you couldn't get handsomer than that. But in the end, he let her go. Once you started roping in other people you were done for. It made him realize that what he most looked forward to about Bournemouth was not knowing a soul. He became quite inspired at the thought of some bungalow, all on its own, where they wouldn't be bothered. He would find a club to go to – bound to be one a bus-ride away – and Rose would have peace.

It was just as he was at last getting enthusiastic that Rose called the whole thing off. She just said one morning she didn't like the people the house had been sold to and she wasn't going to do anything to oblige them. There was a terrible fuss, really terrible – Stanley's head ached with the arguments that went on – but Rose was adamant. They withdrew from the sale just in the nick of time, the very day contracts should have been exchanged. He was angry with her, said she'd made a monkey out of him, but she didn't care. She was her old snappy, bad-tempered self and wasn't the least bit sorry. Stanley felt dizzy with it all, and afraid of possible repercussions. It came as no shock when, after two weeks of moping about day and night, Rose suddenly bounced up and said she'd changed her mind again and wanted to sell. He could find a different agent, different people.

That was when Stanley took matters into his own hands, at last. He wasn't going through all that rigmarole again for nothing. She was having him on, playing with him, and it wasn't right, he'd had enough of all that. The time had come to lay down the law. He'd decided what to do – the house would have to be sold – but he would do it and tell Rose afterwards. That was the way.

Tony said life would go on as usual and of course it did. She did all the things she usually did – housework, shopping, sewing, playing with Amy. The day-to-day routine went on effortlessly and she had no objection to it. But it was no good pretending that she was happy. The presence of Rose Pendlebury next door introduced Alice to a kind of mental torment completely new to her.

She had often read, in the newspapers, of neighbours harassing each other. There was one case in particular that had always stuck in her mind, in which a quiet, peace-loving man had suddenly murdered his next-door neighbour who had been subjecting him over a period of years to excessive noise and intrusion of every sort. There was no question of Mrs P. doing anything like that but the strain of enduring her hate gave Alice the same feelings of persecution. She simply couldn't bear not just the fact of Mrs P.'s antagonism but also the unfairness of it. She found herself all the time rehearsing what she wanted to say to Mrs P. and had fantasies in which her former friend confessed how wrong she had been and asked forgiveness. She wrote endless letters, sometimes getting as far as the letter-box with them, and then snatched them back.

Tony was no help. Relieved that Alice had not brought a miscarriage on herself, he then went so far as to congratulate her on getting rid of the Pendleburys. They now used either Charlotte's or the Stewarts' *au pair* for babysitting – it was all beautifully easy and conscience-free and Tony never missed an opportunity to point this out. They had lost nothing, he insisted. It was all just as well, it had all worked out perfectly. In time, he was sure the old couple would come round sufficiently to exchange greetings and smile, and that was all they wanted. He advised Alice to go on saying hello to Mrs P. – he quite agreed it would be childish to behave as she did – but not to bother herself if there was no reply. One day there would be and until there was she remained above reproach.

Alice didn't know if she could wait that long. Every time she saw the Pendleburys coming down the street she wanted to hide. Walking, instead, directly towards them required courage. Her heart would thud, her limbs sing with peculiar pins and needles, and her face flamed. She hated these physical manifestations of apparent guilt. She knew Mrs P. would notice, even when seeming not to look, and she couldn't bear the conclusions she felt were reached. Every day she saw them, long before they saw her, she struggled with common sense – and lost. Soon she was crossing the road to avoid them, yanking Amy after her. It was stupid and silly but she couldn't face the alternative.

When Alice first heard the Pendleburys were selling their house, astonishment was quickly followed by immense relief. It was the only possible solution, one she had never dared hope for. She even managed to convince herself that it was in their best interests – the house was too big for them, they couldn't cope with it. Together with the rest of the road she followed what details they could glean about the sale and waited with them for the removal van to appear. When the weeks went by and there was no sign of the Pendleburys evacuating the premises, she found to her surprise that she was oddly glad. That would have been no fitting end. What cowardice on her part to hope for such an end! Her own defeatism, the negative way she saw she had looked at the problem, disgusted her. There would never have been any hope of rebuilding the relationship if Mrs P. had gone. She was deeply ashamed that, though she had publicly said the woman was sick, she had not really treated her as sick. She had had no real compassion in her heart at all, she had been far too interested in the wrongs she had suffered, the injuries she had sustained to her own ego, truly to care about Mrs P. She must have another chance.

Rose felt as if she had been very, very ill, as though she had been through the valley of the shadow of death. The only way she knew she was better was when she realized she had been ill – like waking and finding the light was coming through the window and it was day, so there must have been a night. She was dreadfully tired and weak, but one morning in September she got out of bed and breathed a great sigh of contentment.

She didn't know what she was going to do. Like Peter, she had denied that girl next door three times. What she had done to her this last time she was not yet ready to think about – small steps first. A weight had been lifted off her but movement was slow to come. Stanley, of course, knew at once what had happened. His face relaxed for the first time in months but he made no reference to her recovery. Sometimes he asked her questions about matters that were a complete mystery to her and they both knew then the extent of the disease that had attacked her, and were overawed in retrospect.

One day in late September Stanley said he would like to take her to the seaside before the days started to get short. He had been on two trips lately himself, with Elsie and George, in the car. They had asked her to go but she had refused, politely, not yet feeling strong enough, still wallowing in the sweet melancholy that had replaced the sharp, painful anger of the spring and summer. But that day she felt better, and she said yes. They went by train, of course. Stanley called it a mystery tour and wouldn't tell her their destination – which added to the novelty. When they arrived she saw they had come to Eastbourne and was amused at Stanley's originality. They had never been to Eastbourne.

She liked the town very much and enjoyed walking about the centre. The air was lovely and she breathed it easily. After lunch, Stanley said they'd take a ride to the outskirts and, though amazed at his daring, she was happy to agree. They came to a pleasant estate about a mile outside the town, bungalows and suchlike set in pretty gardens with views over the sea. They got out of the taxi and paid it off and walked around a bit and then Stanley stopped at an ordinary enough bungalow. It had a bit of garden in front, with hydrangeas in it, and a bit more to each side, just grass. Behind, there were some big trees and a road and more bungalows.

'Nice place, isn't it?' Stanley said, standing at the gate.

'It's all right,' Rose said, 'easy to run. A little like Elsie and George's place.'

The minute she said it, she had that strange feeling that sometimes afflicted her of knowing with absolute certainty what was going to be said next.

'Yes,' Stanley said, 'I suppose so, but it's a lovely situation, lovely views. You can see the sea from the front rooms.'

Rose didn't bother asking him how he knew.

'Quite a way from shops,' she said. It was important for Stanley's sake that she should be truthful.

'There's a bus every ten minutes straight to that town centre you liked.'

'Nice and quiet, a bit lonely.'

'Plenty of houses about, just nicely spaced that's all.'

'It's high, steep.'

'Good air up here, no dirt.'

'Anyway, what of it?'

He pushed the gate open. 'I've bought it,' he said, 'for our retirement, took a chance and bought it on spec. What do you think?'

'I never thought you had it in you,' she said, because that was what would please him most.

They moved in October without a word to anyone. They both took a great delight in hoodwinking the street, Rose entering into the spirit of the thing as much as Stanley. Because Elsie and George knew someone in the business, the removal van was quite prepared to come in the evening when it was dark, and the whole operation went without a hitch. Hardly anybody saw them go. No stares, no comments – they just slipped away almost unobserved. Except by Alice.

As she pulled the door to behind her, Rose knew she was being watched. It couldn't be helped, she hadn't expected to quite get away with it in that quarter. At least it was dark and the girl couldn't see her face, thank God. She was entitled to think they were running away out of shame – that was part of her cross. She knew she ought to go and see Alice and say sorry – she didn't know for what – and goodbye, but she couldn't do it. The cruelty of leaving was like cutting a tumour out of herself. All her life, she would live with the loss of the only person ever to like her better than she liked herself, the only person willing and able to make her see her fellow humans as friendly and giving. The girl, Alice, had been a blessing, but she was not a saint. It was only natural that she never wanted to see her again. She had hoped, given time, that they might at least salute each other and smile, and who knew what would have grown from that? But Stanley had cut time off and it was just as well. There would be no reprieve. The justice of it pleased her – she pleaded guilty and there was no reprieve.

As she got into Elsie and George's car, a sound stopped her – the sound of a very young baby crying. Rose looked up and saw the curtain move at the first-floor window and Alice in a dressing-gown appear in front of it holding a bundle. The room behind her was brilliantly lit. She knew, from long practice, how little the person standing there could see. Hesitantly, she raised a hand to her lips and blew a kiss to the child she had not even realized existed. For a moment she waited, but there was no answering salutation. Humbly, she got in the car. It was no more than she deserved.

'I'm sure,' Alice said, turning away from the window with her ten-day-old son, 'I'm sure I saw Mrs Pendlebury getting into a car. Do you think the baby will make any difference? Do you know what I'm going to do? Tomorrow I'm going to go round and knock on the door and act as though nothing had happened and show him to her. That's what I'm going to do.'

FOR THE BEST IN PAPERBACKS, LOOK FOR THE

In every corner of the world, on every subject under the sun, Penguin represents quality and variety – the very best in publishing today.

For complete information about books available from Penguin – including Puffins, Penguin Classics and Arkana – and how to order them, write to us at the appropriate address below. Please note that for copyright reasons the selection of books varies from country to country.

In the United Kingdom: Please write to *Dept E.P., Penguin Books Ltd, Harmondsworth, Middlesex, UB7 0DA.*

If you have any difficulty in obtaining a title, please send your order with the correct money, plus ten per cent for postage and packaging, to *PO Box No 11, West Drayton, Middlesex*

In the United States: Please write to *Dept BA, Penguin, 299 Murray Hill Parkway, East Rutherford, New Jersey 07073*

In Canada: Please write to *Penguin Books Canada Ltd, 2801 John Street, Markham, Ontario L3R 1B4*

In Australia: Please write to the *Marketing Department, Penguin Books Australia Ltd, P.O. Box 257, Ringwood, Victoria 3134*

In New Zealand: Please write to the *Marketing Department, Penguin Books (NZ) Ltd, Private Bag, Takapuna, Auckland 9*

In India: Please write to *Penguin Overseas Ltd, 706 Eros Apartments, 56 Nehru Place, New Delhi, 110019*

In the Netherlands: Please write to *Penguin Books Netherlands B.V., Postbus 195, NL–1380AD Weesp*

In West Germany: Please write to *Penguin Books Ltd, Friedrichstrasse 10–12, D–6000 Frankfurt/Main 1*

In Spain: Please write to *Alhambra Longman S.A., Fernandez de la Hoz 9, E–28010 Madrid*

In Italy: Please write to *Penguin Italia s.r.l., Via Como 4, I-20096 Pioltello (Milano)*

In France: Please write to *Penguin Books Ltd, 39 Rue de Montmorency, F-75003 Paris*

In Japan: Please write to *Longman Penguin Japan Co Ltd, Yamaguchi Building, 2–12–9 Kanda Jimbocho, Chiyoda-Ku, Tokyo 101*

BY THE SAME AUTHOR

Lady's Maid

'Compulsively readable ... at each climax of the story, from the Brownings' runaway romance to her own equally compromised and complicated marriage, the lady's maid speaks directly and at the last most movingly' – *Guardian*.

'Fact and fiction are skilfully interwoven ... beautifully done' – *Evening Standard*

Have the Men Had Enough?

'Mercilessly exact and unsentimental about the desolation of old age and the barnacles of family life ... It is a moving love story, a condemnation of the way we treat our old friends and loves, a rage against the dying of the light' – Philip Howard in *The Times*

'It's compulsive reading, and ends as it begins, with questions ... that spill out of the covers' – Lorna Sag in the *Observer*

Significant Sisters
The Grassroots of Active Feminism 1839–1939

Significant Sisters traces the lives and careers of eight women, each of whom pioneered vital changes in the spheres of law, education, the professions, morals or politics. Each forged her own particular brand of feminism, yet all engaged with courage and determination in the battle against the injustices and limitations imposed upon women's freedom.

'A serious book but immensely readable because it is so well-written' – Susan Hill

also published:

Georgy Girl
Mother Can You Hear Me
Private Papers